Dear Reader,

If you know me through my thrillers, *Red* may surprise you. *Red* is a reissue of the 1995 novel that launched my career. Although this novel doesn't contain my trademark mystery and high body count, it does offer readers other hallmarks of a Spindler novel: lots of drama and a fast-paced plot, characters you love— and love to hate—complex relationships and an emotional edge. I hope you find *Red* the novel I intended it to be: a big, fun, juicy read.

As always, I love to hear from my readers. You may contact me at P.O. Box 8556, Mandeville, LA 70470 or through my Web site, www.ericaspindler.com. In addition, visit my Web site to read my blog, learn about special promotions, freebies and to enter my monthly contest.

Thanks again and best wishes,

ERICA SPINDLER

RED

MIRA®

MIRA

ISBN-13: 978-0-7783-2716-5
ISBN-10:   0-7783-2716-7

RED

Copyright © 1995 by Erica Spindler.

www.MIRABooks.com

Printed in U.S.A.

To Nathan, my husband, my friend and my love.
For always being there,
for weathering every emotional storm with calm,
reason and love.
I couldn't do it without you.

Book One

Becky Lynn

1

Bend, Mississippi
1984

No place in the world smelled quite like the Mississippi Delta in July. Overripe, like fruit left too long in the sun. Pungent, like a drunk's breath at the edge of a whiskey binge. Like sweat.

And it smelled of dirt. Sometimes so dry it coated the mouth and throat, but most times so wet it permeated everything, even the skin. Becky Lynn Lee lifted her hair off the back of her neck, sticky with a combination of perspiration and dust from the unpaved road. Most folks around Bend didn't think much about the smell of things, but she did. She fantasized about a place scented of exotic flowers and rare perfumes, a beautiful world populated by people wearing fine, silky fabrics and welcoming smiles.

She knew that place existed; she'd seen it in the magazines she poured over whenever she could, the ones the women at Opal's snickered at her interest in, the ones her father raged at her about.

None of that mattered. She had promised herself that someday, somehow, she would live in that world.

Becky Lynn picked her way across the railroad tracks used not only to ship rice, cotton and soybeans out of

Bend, but to divide the good side of town from the bad, the respectable folk from the poor white trash.

She was poor white trash. The label had hurt, way back the first time she'd heard herself referred to by those words; it still hurt, when she thought about it. And she thought about it a lot. That's the kind of town Bend was.

Becky Lynn lifted her face to the flat blue sky, squinting against the harsh light, wishing for cloud cover to temper the heat. *Poor white trash.* Becky Lynn had been three the first time she'd realized she was different, that she and her family were *less than*; she still remembered the moment vividly. It had been a day like this one, hot and blue. She'd been standing in line at the market with her mother and her brother, Randy. Becky Lynn remembered clinging to her brother's hand and looking down at her feet, bare and dirty from their walk into town, then lifting her gaze to find the other mothers' eyes upon them, their stares filled with a combination of pity and loathing. In that moment, she'd realized that there were others in the world and that they judged. She had felt strange, self-conscious. For the first time in her young life, she'd felt vulnerable. She had wanted to hide behind her mother's legs, had wanted her mother to tell the other women to stop looking at them that way.

Becky Lynn supposed that had been back before her daddy had turned really mean, back when she still thought her mother to be an angel with magical, protective powers.

But maybe she had already realized that her mother wasn't an angel, that her mother didn't have the ability— or the strength—to make everything all right, because she hadn't said anything. And the women had kept staring, and Becky Lynn had kept on feeling as if she had done something wrong, something ugly and bad.

Most times now, the respectable folks, even the customers she shampooed down at Opal's Cut 'n Curl, looked right through her. Oh, while she shampooed them they talked to her, but mostly because they liked to hear the sound of themselves and because they knew she was paid to listen and agree with them—something their husbands almost never did. But when they came face-to-face with her on the street, they looked right through her. She wasn't sure if they pretended they didn't see her because she was one of Randall Lee's brood or if they truly didn't recognize her 'cause they'd never really looked at her in the first place.

But whichever, she'd decided being invisible suited her just fine. In fact, she preferred it that way. She felt less different when she was invisible. She felt…safer.

Becky Lynn took a deep breath as she cleared the railroad tracks. The air always seemed a bit sweeter this side of the tracks, the breeze a degree or two cooler. She stepped up her pace, hoping to get to the shop early enough to spend a few minutes looking over the *Bazaar* that had come the day before.

Up ahead, Becky Lynn caught sight of a fire-engine red pickup truck barreling past the square, coming in her direction, a cloud of dust in its wake. Tommy Fischer and his jock gang, she thought, her heart beginning to rap against the wall of her chest. Probably on their way to pick up her brother. She darted a glance to either side of the road, to the fields thick with cotton, knowing there was no place to hide but searching for one, anyway. Sighing, she folded her arms across her middle, jerked her chin up and kept on walking.

The group of boys began to howl the moment they saw

her. "Hey, Becky Lynn," one of the teenagers called, "how about a date?" In response, the other three boys began to hoot in amusement. "Yeah, looking good, Becky Lynn. My dad's Labrador retriever's been lonely lately."

That brought a fresh burst of amusement from the boys, and she tightened her fingers into fists, but kept walking, never glancing their way. Even if it killed her, she wouldn't give them the satisfaction of knowing how much their comments hurt.

Tommy slowed the truck more, swerving to the road's dusty shoulder. "Hey, baby…check it out." From the corner of her eyes she saw the two boys in the back of the pickup unzip their flies and pull out their penises. "If you weren't so ugly," taunted Ricky, the meanest of the group, "I'd even let you touch it. You'd like that, wouldn't you, baby?"

The urge to run, as fast and far as she could, screamed through her. She fought the urge back, compressing her lips to keep from making a sound of revulsion and fear.

Ricky leaned over the side of the truck and made a lewd grab for her, forcing her to step off the shoulder and into the muddy field. Tommy gunned the engine and tore off, spitting up gravel and dirt, the boys' laughter ringing in her ears.

Becky Lynn ran then, the gravel road biting the bottoms of her feet through her tattered sneakers, the bile of panic nearly choking her. She ran until she reached the safety of Bend's town square.

Drawing in deep, shuddering breaths, Becky Lynn leaned against the outside wall of the Five and Dime, the corner building on the railroad side of the square. She pressed the flat of her hand to her pitching stomach and squeezed her eyes shut. Sweat beaded her upper lip and underarms; it trickled between her shoulder blades. The image of the boys, holding their penises and taunting her, filled her head, and her stomach rolled again. They'd never done anything like that before. She was used to their taunts, their obscene suggestions, but not...this.

Today they'd scared her.

Becky Lynn hugged herself hard. She was safe, she told herself. It was getting toward the end of summer, the boys were bored and got off on seeing her squirm. In a month they would start football practice and wouldn't have the time or energy to seek her out.

Then she would have to face their jeers at school.

She fought against the tears that flooded her eyes, fought against the despair that filled every other part of her. She had nobody. Not one person in Bend she could turn to for help or support. Alone. She was alone.

Even as fatigue and hopelessness clutched at her, Becky Lynn curled her fingers into fists. She wouldn't give up like her mother had. She wouldn't. And someday, she promised herself, she would show Tommy and Ricky and everybody else in this two-bit town. She didn't know how, but someday they would wish they'd been nice to her.

2

Becky Lynn managed to avoid Tommy Fischer and his gang for an entire week. It hadn't been easy, they had seemed to be everywhere, just cruising, looking for trouble. Looking for something to ease their boredom, she supposed. She had made up her mind it wouldn't be her.

Darting a quick, uneasy glance behind her, she stepped onto the square and started for the Cut 'n Curl, moving as fast as she could without running. Bend, named for its location at a bend in the Tallahatchie River between Greenwood and Greenville, had been built around a town square. The civic and commercial center of town, the courthouse, police station and mayor's office were all located here, as well as the two best dress shops in town—the nearest mall being in either Greenwood or Greenville, the nearest real city Memphis. Shaded by magnolia and mimosa trees, sprinkled with azalea and oleander bushes, the square was the closest Bend, Mississippi, got to the places Becky Lynn saw in her magazines.

But not close enough, she thought, hearing familiar laughter and the gun of an engine behind her. She glanced over her shoulder and her heart flew to her throat. Tommy Fischer had decided to take a swing around the square.

The Cut 'n Curl in sight now, she started to run, reaching the shop in moments. She pushed through the door with such force that the brass bell hanging above it snapped against the glass.

Miss Opal stood at the first hair station, adding another coat of spray to her platinum blond beehive. She set down the can of spray and turned to Becky Lynn. "What's the rush, child? You look like you've seen the devil himself."

Driving a bright red pickup. Becky Lynn sucked in a deep breath and forced a smile. "No, ma'am. I just didn't want to be late."

Miss Opal smiled. "You're never late, Becky Lynn. And I want you to know, I do appreciate it."

Heat stung Becky Lynn's cheeks, and she folded her arms self-consciously across her chest. "You want me to start straightening up?"

Miss Opal tilted her head and drew her eyebrows together in concern. "You okay today, Becky Lynn? You look a little pale."

"Yes, ma'am. Fine."

As if unconvinced, Miss Opal slid her gaze over her, eyes narrowed behind her rhinestone-studded cat glasses. She stopped on Becky Lynn's feet. "Did you eat this morning?"

Certain the woman could see her toes poking against the too-tight canvas sneakers, Becky Lynn shifted, propping one foot self-consciously on top of the other. "Well…no. But I wasn't hungry."

Miss Opal shook her head, which was as close to critical as she ever got. Becky Lynn had long ago decided that the hairdresser had about the biggest heart in Bend. Rumor around town held that Miss Opal came from trash herself, from over in Yazoo City. Rumor also told that she had managed to escape by cracking her daddy over the head with an iron skillet and emptying his pockets of his pay. Becky Lynn didn't believe any of it, Miss Opal seemed way too nice to have done any of those things. And if she had, Becky Lynn figured her daddy had deserved it.

"You'd better run right over to the Tastee Creme. Marianne Abernathy is our first appointment and if the doughnuts aren't here, I'll never hear the end of it." Miss Opal made a clucking sound with her tongue. "Ever since Doc Tyson put her on a diet, Ed counts each bite she puts in her mouth. I reckon she's been looking forward to getting her hair done all week."

She opened the cash drawer, took out a five and handed it to Becky Lynn. "Go on now and get those doughnuts. And don't forget the ones with the strawberry jam."

"Yes, ma'am." Becky Lynn hesitated at the door, thinking of Tommy and his pickup full of boys. *What if they were out there waiting for her?* She caught her bottom lip between her teeth and looked hopefully at her boss. "You sure you don't want me to straighten up first? It would only take a few minutes. I'd be happy to do it."

The woman frowned and shifted her gaze from Becky Lynn to the bright day beyond. She returned her gaze to Becky Lynn, looking her straight in the eye. "You're sure nothing's wrong, child? Because if there is, I want you to feel you can come to me."

Becky Lynn stared at the older woman a moment, a lump in her throat. Could she go to Miss Opal? If she told her what the boys had done, what would she say? Would she believe her? Becky Lynn gazed into the woman's kind eyes and thought that maybe she would.

She wanted to tell, so badly the words trembled on the tip of her tongue, begging to jump off. She wanted to be assured that everything was going to be all right, that Tommy and his jock gang wouldn't bother her again. That they would be punished for what they'd done to her.

Right. And purple pigs flew around the town square. Becky Lynn squeezed her fingers into fists, crumpling the bill. Even if Miss Opal believed her, nothing would change. Boys like Tommy and Ricky, from families like theirs, would never be held accountable. Not when the offense had been committed against the likes of her. That wasn't the way things worked in Bend, Mississippi.

She swallowed past the lump and shook her head. "No, ma'am. Everything's fine. I was just wondering…has the mail come yet?"

Miss Opal made a sound of amusement, looking relieved. "Becky Lynn Lee, you know as well as I do, the postman doesn't come till almost noon. Now go on and get those pastries."

Becky Lynn made it to and from the Tastee Creme in record time.

And without a sign of Tommy Fischer's truck. Fayrene and Dixie, the other two hairdressers—stylists, they liked to be called—arrived just as Becky Lynn got back with the box of doughnuts.

Fayrene breezed by in a suffocating cloud of the Chanel No. 5 her boyfriend had given her for her birthday the week before, and Dixie stomped in complaining of her husband's latest get-rich-quick scheme, something about raising catfish in their back pond.

As the morning passed, their conversations buzzed around Becky Lynn—that tacky Janelle Peters was cheating on her husband again; Lulie Carter had gotten herself engaged to a professor from the college over in

Cleveland and those bad Birch boys (poor white trash) had been caught smoking marijuana.

She let them talk, keeping half an ear trained on the door, waiting for the postman's cheery greeting and praying today would be the day the new *Vogue* came. She liked all the glossy magazines, *Bazaar* and *Cosmopolitan* and *Elle,* but *Vogue* was her favorite.

Becky Lynn didn't know if everyone could see that *Vogue* was the best, but to her it practically shouted its superiority. (After all, didn't cream always rise to the top?) And from her reading, she knew that only the best photographers shot for *Vogue,* that the top models fought for the covers. Production quality was, to her admittedly untrained eyes, flawless.

She didn't just look at the photographs—she studied them, their angles and locations, the way colors, values and textures were combined, and the mood created by using the various elements together. And she studied the models, their positioning and expressions, their hair and makeup and clothes.

Although she would never have the courage to admit it out loud, she figured she'd gotten pretty good at recognizing which pictures were the best. They were all good, but some…just seemed to have something special. A magic. Or sparkle. Just the way some of the models had something that made them stand out from all the others.

She wished, just once, she could find out if she was right. It would be fun to—

"Ouch! Becky Lynn Lee, that water is too hot."

"Sorry, Mrs. Baxter," she murmured, adjusting the temperature. "How's that?"

"Better." The woman shifted her considerable weight

and glared up at her. "You need to get your head out of the clouds and pay better attention to your job. You're lucky to have it."

After all, you are poor white trash. "Yes, ma'am."

"I swear, you people just don't take anything seriously. Why, just last night, I was saying to my Bubba…"

And so the morning went. Finally, just after twelve, the postman arrived. And her prayers were answered. The August *Vogue*. She held the magazine almost reverently. Isabella Rossellini graced the cover. Again. She'd held that top spot in June, too. July had been Kim Alexis. They were two of fashion's best.

Opal gave Becky Lynn permission to take her lunch break, and hugging the magazine to her chest, she grabbed a leftover doughnut and headed back to the storeroom. Although she could have taken a seat in the waiting area out front, or at one of the unoccupied stations, she preferred to be alone.

Sitting cross-legged on the floor, she gazed at the cover with a mixture of admiration and envy. Isabella's eyes, dark, velvety and inviting, practically jumped off the page; the model's lips, curved into a provocative half smile, were full and tinted a deep rose. The photographer had closed in on the model's face, focusing on the eyes and lips, creating an image that was at once fresh and sophisticated.

What must it feel like to be so beautiful? she wondered, taking a bite of the doughnut. Powdered sugar from the pastry sprinkled onto the glossy photo, and she brushed it carefully away. What must it be like to be so admired, so sought after? To be so beautiful?

What must it be like to be loved?

Longing, so sharp it stung, curled through her. It must be wonderful, she thought, taking another bite. It must be like living a dream.

"What do you see in those things, anyway?"

Startled, Becky Lynn looked up. Fayrene stood in the doorway, studying her over the tip of her lit cigarette. Rarely did anyone inquire after her thoughts, and never had Fayrene, the self-appointed queen of the Cut 'n Curl. She swallowed. "Pardon?"

"Those magazines." The blonde gestured with the cigarette and her bracelets jangled. "The way you study them." She shook her head and exhaled a long stream of smoke. "If you ask me, it's weird."

"Leave the girl alone," Opal called from around the corner in the mixing room. "She's on break, and she's not hurting anybody."

Fayrene pouted. "I wasn't trying to be a smartass or anything. I really want to know. I mean, I like to look at the pictures, too. But not like *that*." She turned back to Becky Lynn, arching a neatly penciled eyebrow in question.

Cheeks on fire, Becky Lynn lowered her gaze to the glossy image before her. How did she explain something she felt so deeply? How did she voice dreams that were so close to her heart yet so far from reality? And if she found a way, would the other woman understand—or laugh?

Her hands began to shake, her palms to sweat. She cleared her throat, then met Fayrene's gaze once more. "I don't know," she said softly. "It's just that the models are all so…beautiful…so sophisticated, and all. I just look at them and think—"

"Becky Lynn," Fayrene interrupted, waving the cigarette again. "Wake up! I mean, I like to look at those gals and dream once and a while, too. But you can't dream your life away." She shook her head and her bleached-blond mane tumbled across her right shoulder. "As I always say, no sense reaching for a star, you're never going to catch one. Besides, even if you did manage to, it'd only burn your fingers."

With this obvious attempt at cleverness, Fayrene paused, waiting for a response. When Becky Lynn didn't give her one, she made a sound of irritation. "Work with what you have. You're tall as most men and have a face that…well, let's be honest, girl, you're never going to be prom queen. I mean, your features alone are all nice, but put together, they…"

Fayrene hesitated as if really looking at her for the first time. A strange expression crossed her face, then she shook her head. "But you do have good eyes and teeth, and if you would just give me a couple hours with your hair and a bottle of bleach, we could change that carrot top of yours to a sensational-looking blon—"

"Fayrene," Dixie interrupted, "Bitsy's timer went off a couple minutes ago. If you frizz her hair again, she's going to pitch a fit."

Fayrene swore and started back out into the shop. She stopped and looked back at Becky Lynn. "Think about what I said, girl. Not everybody can be somebody special."

Becky Lynn slumped back against the wall, the other woman's words having sucked the pleasure out of the moment. She looked down at the photo of Isabella Rossellini, the image blurring with her tears. Fayrene had missed the point. Sure, she dreamed of being as beautiful and self-confident as the women in the magazines, but she wasn't an idiot. And she didn't want to be prom queen.

Her love of the glossies wasn't about being beautiful. It was about dreaming of a wonderful place nothing like Bend, a place where boys didn't expose themselves to girls who hadn't done anything more than be born poor and ugly. It was about being accepted, about being loved.

"Fayrene gets a bit caught up in herself sometimes," Miss Opal said from the doorway. "She wasn't trying to be mean."

But she was, anyway. Becky Lynn swiped at a tear, horrified at the show of emotion. After a moment, she looked up at the other woman. "Isn't it all right to dream, Miss Opal? Is it so wrong to wish for something you know you can't possibly—" Her throat closed over the words, and she shook her head.

Opal crossed the room, stopping before her. She laid a hand on Becky Lynn's shoulder and gave it a gentle squeeze. "No, child. It's not wrong. Now, come on. I need you to do a shampoo."

Becky Lynn stopped at the end of the dirt driveway and gazed at the small, square house before her. *Home.* She hugged the magazines Opal had given her tightly to her chest. In the fading light, its once-white exterior, now chipped and gray, looked even more dismal, more beaten— as if even the house had given up hope of something better. The picket fence that circled the property, once, she supposed, white and jaunty, was now dingy and broken.

She started up the driveway, dragging her feet. Funny how fast the hours at Miss Opal's passed, and how slow the ones here did. Time had a way of doing that, she thought. Of standing still for misery.

Becky Lynn smelled the whiskey the moment she stepped onto the sagging front porch. She hated the sweetly sour smell. Sometimes she would wake in the night and feel as if she were being suffocated by it. It permeated everything, her clothes, the furniture and bedding, her father's skin.

Her life.

Becky Lynn couldn't remember a time before the reek of whiskey.

Until that moment, she'd managed to forget today was Friday. The day her father got his pay. The day he drank the best, Jim Beam sour mash. He bought a fifth on the way home from the foundry, and he drank until the bottle was empty or he passed out, whichever came first. The rest of the week he settled for the best he could afford. Most times on Thursdays he couldn't afford anything, so he slept. Becky Lynn looked forward to Thursdays almost as much as she did the arrival of the new glossies. Almost.

Through the tattered screen door she heard "The Family Feud's" closing music. Why her father loved that show so much, she couldn't fathom. He never laughed. He never tried to predict the highest scoring answers. Other than an occasional grunt, he just stared at the television screen. And drank. And drank.

Considering the time, her father had no doubt been at that very thing for a couple of hours now, just long enough to have gotten stinking mean, just long enough to be spoiling for a fight. If she had been just a few minutes earlier, if she had arrived in the middle of the lightning round, she would have had a much better chance getting inside without her father noticing.

Cursing her own timing, she slipped quietly through the

door. She knew exactly where to place her hands so the door wouldn't squeak, knew precisely how far to push it in before it scraped the floor.

She held her breath. Her father's back was to her as he stared at the TV, and pressing herself against the wall, she inched toward the kitchen. If she was lucky, she would avoid his ire tonight. If she was lucky, she would be able to ease by him and—

"Where do you think you're goin', girl?"

Becky Lynn stopped, recognizing his tone, the slurring of his words, from a hundred times before. Her stomach turned over; the breath shuddered past her lips. So much for luck.

She swung toward him, forcing a tiny, stiff smile. "Nowhere, Daddy. I just thought I'd see if Mama needed a hand in the kitchen."

He grunted, and raked his bloodshot gaze over her. A shiver rippled through her as he stared at the apex of her thighs. When he met her eyes again, his were narrowed with suspicion. "You been out whoring around?"

"No, sir." She shook her head. "I had to stay late at Opal's. We were busy today, even for a Friday."

"What d'you got there?"

She tightened her arms on the magazines. "Nothing, Daddy."

"Don't tell me 'nothing,' girl!" He lurched to his feet and crossing to her, ripped the magazines from her folded arms. She bit back a sound of dismay, knowing the best way to avoid the full brunt of Randall Lee's fury was to be as quiet, as agreeable, as possible.

He stared at the magazines a moment, spittle collecting at the corners of his slightly open mouth. Then he swore.

Wheeling back, almost losing his balance, he threw the magazines. Becky Lynn jerked as they slammed against the wall. "How many times I told you I don't want you readin' this shit. How many times I told you not to spend money on—"

"I didn't!" she said quickly, breathlessly. "These are the old issues. Miss Opal gave them to me. If you'd check the mailing labels, you'd see—"

"You tellin' me what to do, girl? You sayin' I'm dumb?" He took a menacing step toward her, his fists clenched.

"No, sir." Becky Lynn shook her head vigorously, knowing that she had somehow, once again, crossed the invisible line. But then, it had always been like this with her father. She'd never had to do anything in particular to set him off.

Her mother appeared at the kitchen door, her face pinched and pale, her eyes anxious. "Becky Lynn, baby, why don't you come in here and help me with the supper."

A ripple of relief moved over Becky Lynn, and she sent her mother a look of gratitude. Randall Lee didn't like interference and he wasn't averse to turning his rage onto his wife. And it was an awesome rage. But then, her father, at six foot four inches tall and as big as a tree trunk, was an awesome man.

"I'd better help Mama," she whispered, taking a step toward the kitchen.

Her father grabbed her arm, his big hand a vise on her flesh. She winced in pain but didn't try to jerk away.

"How much you make today?"

"Twelve dollars." *Seventeen, counting the five she'd tucked into her shoe.*

He narrowed his eyes. "You'd better not be lying to me."

She straightened and looked him right in the eye. "No, sir."

"Empty your pockets." He dropped his hand and stepped away from her, weaving slightly.

She did as he asked, handing him the money. He looked suspiciously at her, counted it, then handed her two dollars back. She stared at the crumpled bills, thinking of the heads she'd washed that day, of the hair she'd swept off the floor. And of the fact that there would probably be enough money for her father to drink Thursday night.

Bitterness welled inside her, souring in her mouth. She supposed she should be happy, she thought. Most times, he took it all.

Her brother, Randy, came in then, the screen door slapping shut behind him, and her father's attention momentarily shifted. He swung toward his oldest child. At eighteen, Randy, who had been held back in the third grade, was already as big as his father. And almost as mean. His disposition on—and off—the field had moved his fellow football players to nickname him Madman Lee. "Where've you been, boy?"

Randy shrugged. "Out with the guys."

Randall Lee opened his mouth as if to comment, then just snorted with disgust and turned back to her.

Randy shot her a cocky glance and ambled toward the kitchen. Frustration welled up inside her. Her father rarely attacked Randy. Not Randy, star tackle on the Bend High School football team. Because he was a jock, and because he had the right friends, boys like Tommy Fischer.

No, he saved all his hatred and bitterness for her. He always had. And she didn't know why.

Suddenly furious at the unfairness of it, she jerked her

chin up. She looked at her father, not bothering to hide her contempt. "May I go now?"

"You'll go when I say so."

"Why do you think I'm asking?" *Idiot. Asshole.*

At her tone, a mottled red started at the base of his thick neck and crept upward. He grabbed her arm again, but this time he twisted it until she cried out in pain. "Where'd you get the right to put on airs?" he snapped. "Just like your mother, thinkin' you're some kinda queen." He dragged her to the room's single window, twisting her arm again, forcing her to face her reflection. Tears stung her eyes and she fought to keep them from spilling over. "Take a look, girl. What man's ever goin' to marry you? Tell me that." He shook her so hard her teeth rattled. "I'll probably be stuck looking at your ugly mug for the rest of my life. Now get outta here, it makes me sick to look at you."

He flung her aside, so violently she hit the wall, much the same as her magazines had only moments before. Her head snapped back, cracking against the wallboard. Pain shot through her shoulder. She sank to the dirt floor, thinking, oddly, of the pretty pink and white linoleum at Miss Opal's. Flecked with silver, it was always so clean it shone.

Shaking her head to clear it, she sucked in a deep breath and using the wall for support, eased to her feet. Her father had returned to his place in front of the television, and she saw him bring the bottle to his lips. She stared at him a moment, hatred roiling inside her, the urge to lunge at him, to claw and hit and scratch, thundering through her. Its beat matched that of the blood pounding in her brain, and she pictured herself doing it. Just walking up to him and smashing her fist into his face.

Becky Lynn squeezed her eyes shut, fighting back the urge. She wouldn't lower herself to his level. For even worse than living the nightmare that was her life, was living his. Becoming like him.

Besides, he'd probably beat the hell out of her before she could get in the first punch.

She limped to the kitchen. Her mama and Randy were there. Her mother chattered softly about the things that needed to be done that weekend, and Randy stood by, his stance uncomfortable and stiff. Neither of them met her eyes, but Becky Lynn could see it in their faces, in their downcast gazes: *If it wasn't you, it might be me.*

She couldn't say they were wrong. She knew they weren't. And she knew that was why Randy never interceded for her, why her mother never openly tried to comfort her. They didn't want to incur Randall Lee's wrath.

Becky Lynn squeezed her fingers into fists. She'd interceded for Randy before; she had stepped into the line of fire on his behalf. She had done the same for her mother; she still did.

They didn't even have the guts to look at her.

She drew in a shuddering breath, pain spearing through her shoulder once more. She was so weary of living alone with her fear. With her despair. Wasn't Randy? Wasn't her mother? It hurt to hold it in, day in and day out. Didn't they long, as she did, to share their pain? Didn't they long to have someone to whisper with in the dark, to hold on to and love?

Tears stinging her eyes, Becky Lynn shifted her gaze to the other room, to the magazines scattered obscenely across the floor. Her gaze landed on an old *Vogue,* on model Renée Simonsen's beautiful, smiling face.

Someone to whisper with in the dark, she thought, hopelessness clutching at her. Someone to lean on, someone who would give her one perfect moment without fear. Her eyes swam; the model's face blurred. Turning her back to the glossy image, she crossed the kitchen and began to help her mother with the peas.

3

"Becky Lynn, baby, come here."

Becky Lynn stopped at the front door. Feeling like a prisoner who had gotten caught a moment before she'd made her escape, she turned to her mother. The other woman stood just outside the kitchen; she wore the floral print housecoat Becky Lynn had bought her two Christmases ago. The rose pattern which had been so vibrant and pretty when she'd purchased it, looked tired and gray. Like her mother. And everything else in this house.

Becky Lynn gazed at her mother's gaunt face and shadowed eyes, pity moving over her. And fear. Fear that by age thirty-six she, too, would look beaten and without hope.

She pushed the thought away, and forced a smile. "What is it, Mama?"

Her mother's lips curved into a wispy smile. "I thought I might brush your hair."

Becky Lynn hesitated. She'd planned to hike to the river before it got too hot, and spend her day off from Opal's sunning and reading. She had several magazines, a soft drink and a sandwich packed in her knapsack. It would be her last opportunity before school started; she'd been on her way out the door.

She darted a glance over her shoulder, to the bright day,

and bit back a sigh. Her mother derived too much pleasure from it to deny her this ritual. The river would wait.

"That sounds nice, Mama," she said, smiling again. She set down her knapsack and crossed to one of the chairs around the kitchen table, choosing one that faced the window.

Her mother positioned herself behind Becky Lynn and began, with long, smooth strokes, to pull the brush through her daughter's hair. Familiar with the ritual, Becky Lynn wasn't surprised when her mother began to tell a story about her own childhood. The only talks they'd ever had, the only moments of mother-daughter comradeship, had been while her mother ran the brush through her hair.

Becky Lynn had often suspected that she was her mother's favorite, although she never understood why. Perhaps because her father hated her, perhaps because she looked so much like her mother's father or because she reminded Glenna Lee of someone else she'd once known, someone who had been kind to her. Whatever the reason, she held that suspicion to her as if it were the most prized possession on earth.

"It's the color of strawberry soda pop," her mother murmured after a moment. "You get it from your Granddaddy Perkins. You never met him, he died just after you were born."

About the time Daddy lost the farm, Becky Lynn thought. Because of his drinking. And laziness. But she didn't say that. "What was he like?" she asked instead, even though she already knew. Her mother had talked about Granddaddy Perkins many times before. He had adored his only child. And Randall Lee had despised him.

She sensed her mother's smile. "He was a nice man. A good husband, a good daddy." She laughed lightly, the sound faraway and youthful. "He called me his little princess."

A lump formed in Becky Lynn's throat. How, after being someone's princess, had she ended up with a man as base and cruel as Randall Lee? Why had she married him?

And why did she allow him to treat her and her children so badly?

Becky Lynn wanted to ask her mother, the questions teased the tip of her tongue. She swallowed it. She couldn't ask; her mother had been hurt enough. "He sounds nice, Mama."

"Mmm. He was nice." Her mother continued brushing, but Becky Lynn knew her thoughts were far away.

After a moment, the older woman murmured, "Did I ever tell you about the dress I wore to the prom? It was white and dotted with these pretty little pink flowers. The most delicate pink you ever saw. I felt like a princess in it." She laughed softly. "And my date looked like a prince. He wore a tuxedo and brought me a rose corsage. It was pink, too."

A rose corsage. Becky Lynn imagined her mother, a blushing teenager, wearing that frilly white dress, the cluster of roses pinned to her chest, and tears flooded her eyes. She fought the tears back, fought the emotion from clogging her throat. "Your date, who was he, Mama?"

Her mother hesitated, then shook her head. "Nobody, baby. I forget."

She'd asked the question before; she'd gotten the same answer. But her mother hadn't forgotten, Becky Lynn knew. The boy had been someone special. So special, her mother feared saying his name.

Becky Lynn fisted her fingers in her lap. Her father wasn't even in the house and her mother was afraid. "I thought you and Daddy were high school sweethearts?"

The brush stilled for a moment, then Glenna Lee began stroking again. "After your Granddaddy Lee's heart attack, your daddy had to quit school to work on the farm. He didn't go to the prom."

And he never forgave you for going, did he? Becky Lynn drew her eyebrows together. What else did he not forgive her mother for? "But where did you meet him?" she asked. "The boy you went to the prom with, I mean."

Glenna hesitated again, then murmured, "He was from the high school over in Greenwood. My daddy knew his. He arranged it."

"Granddaddy Perkins didn't like Daddy much, did he?"

Her mother tugged the brush through her hair, and Becky Lynn winced. "No, not much."

"But you married him, anyway." She heard the accusation in her own voice and for once, didn't try to hide it. "Why did you, Mama?"

Her mother paused, then dropped her hand to her side. The brush slipped from her fingers and clattered onto the table. "Your daddy wasn't always…the way he is now. Having to quit school changed him. He got bitter. He started to drink. Try to understand, baby, he was the star of the football team his junior year and had dreams of playing ball for a college, of being a professional player someday. He dreamed of getting away from Bend."

Try to understand? Becky Lynn froze, disbelief and fury warring inside her. Did her mother want her to feel bad about what Randall Lee had given up? Two weeks had passed since he'd knocked her around and the bruises he'd given her had finally faded to faint green blurs. It had been a full seven days before she'd been able to shampoo a customer without wincing. Everyone at Opal's had noticed and whispered about her behind their hands.

She laced her fingers in her lap, trying to control the anger surging through her. She didn't care what Randall Lee had given up; she would never forgive or excuse him his cruelty. Never.

"What about your dreams?" Becky Lynn asked, her voice shaking. "You had dreams, too, Mama." She twisted to look up at her mother. "And what about mine?"

The other woman met her gaze; in that instant, her mother's eyes were clear, full of life and hope. "You're smart, Becky Lynn," Glenna said, a tremor of urgency in her voice. "You could go to college, make something of yourself. You're special, baby. I've always known it."

Dry-mouthed and stunned, Becky Lynn gazed at her mother. "You really…think so? You think I'm…" She couldn't say the words; they felt wrong, foreign, on her tongue. They felt impossible.

"I do, baby. That's why your daddy…why he… You're special. You're strong." Glenna cupped Becky Lynn's face in her hands. She shook her lightly. "Listen to me. You can make something of yourself. Have a career. A life away from Bend. You could go to Jackson or Memphis."

Becky Lynn covered her mother's hands with her own. "You could come with me, Mama. He wouldn't come after us, I know he wouldn't."

The light faded from her mother's eyes, and she extricated her hands from Becky Lynn's. "Your scalp'll be raw if I brush anymore. Go on now, I know you had plans."

Becky Lynn shook her head. "But, Mama, I don't understand. Why won't you come? Why—"

"Go on, baby," she said again, turning her back to Becky Lynn. "Your mama has things to do."

Glenna Lee started for the doorway, stopping when she reached it. She looked over her shoulder at her daughter. Becky Lynn saw resignation in her eyes. "I'll be here when you get back, Becky Lynn. I'll always be here."

Her mother's words stuck with Becky Lynn during her hike to the river. She held them close to her heart; she replayed them like a mantra in her head. *You're smart, Becky Lynn... You could make something of yourself... I've always known you were special.*

Her mother believed in her. She'd never voiced that belief before, nobody had. Not ever. Until today. Becky Lynn tipped her face up to the cloudless blue sky and smiled. It felt wonderful. Magical, even. She never would have guessed how something so small could make her feel so big.

The river in sight now, she cut across Miller's Lane, heading for the shade on the other side. In the short time she'd been with her mother, the sun had crawled considerably higher in the sky, the temperature seeming to have doubled with it. Even the birds had quieted, as if saving their energy for later in the afternoon, when the sun dipped once more.

Becky Lynn stopped and wiped her forehead, longing for the Coke tucked inside her knapsack. It seemed impossible that September was only a matter of a few weeks away; it felt as if the heat would never break. But that's the way summers were in the delta, hot, humid and as long as forever.

By the time she reached the river, her T-shirt was soaked and her hair clung uncomfortably to the back of her neck. She selected a shady spot under a big, old oak tree, sank to the ground and dug her soft drink out of her bag.

She popped the top and took a long swallow. The sweet, fizzy drink tickled her throat and nose, and she took another long swallow before easing her head against the tree and closing her eyes. Becky Lynn held the cool can to her forehead, smiling to herself, thinking again of her mother's words…and of the day she would leave Bend behind forever.

Her smile faded. But leaving Bend meant leaving her mother. Glenna Lee wouldn't go. She'd made it clear that she felt some sort of responsibility to stay. Some sort of responsibility to her husband.

Why? Becky Lynn drew her eyebrows together. Did she love him? Is that why she stayed? If so, how could she? How could she feel anything but fury and hatred when she looked at him?

What was between her mother and father that she didn't know about?

Maybe nothing. Becky Lynn frowned and took another swallow of her drink. She didn't like to think that, didn't like to think that her mother stayed with her husband because she didn't have the guts to leave him, or because she was resigned to her fate.

A twig snapped behind her, and Becky Lynn twisted to look over her shoulder. Her heart stopped, then started again with a vengeance. Coming from the direction of the road was her brother and his gang.

"Well, looky, looky, Randy," Tommy called out. "It's your little sister."

At the boy's mocking words, she scrambled up, collecting her knapsack and soft drink. She'd hiked forty minutes to get to this spot; she'd claimed it first. And now, right or wrong, fair or not, none of that mattered. All she cared about was getting as far away from these boys as fast as possible.

"Where ya going, Becky Lynn?" Ricky drawled, planting himself in front of her. "You're going to make us think you don't like us."

"Yeah," said Tommy, moving to Ricky's right. "You'll hurt our feelings."

"I'm going home now," she said as calmly as she could around her thundering heart. "Excuse me." She made a move to step past Tommy; he blocked it.

"Excuse you?" Ricky taunted. "I don't think so." He angled a glance at Tommy. "What do you think, Tommy?"

"Nah." The boy grinned, and a shudder moved up Becky Lynn's spine. "I don't think so, either."

She tried again, this time moving to her left. Ricky blocked her. Tears pricked her eyes, and she fought against them. It wouldn't do for them to know how helpless and vulnerable she felt. Taking a deep breath, she inched her chin up. "Let me pass."

"Where are our manners? You didn't say the 'P' word, Becky Lynn." That brought fresh snickers from the boys.

Fear soured on her tongue. She swallowed. "Let me pass…please."

"Well…since you asked so nice." Ricky smiled thinly and stepped aside.

Relief, dizzying in its sweetness, spiraled through her. She started past him, but didn't get three steps before he grabbed her arm, stopping her. Relief evaporated, replaced

by a fluttering panic. She should have known they
wouldn't let her go before they'd had a chance to really humiliate her.

"Don't you touch me, Ricky Jones," she said, jerking
her arm from his grasp.

The boys made a collective sound of amusement. Ricky
took another step closer. Behind her, Tommy blocked a
retreat. "She said that just like a queen, didn't she, boys?"

"Yeah," Tommy chirped in. "A queen bitch."

Becky Lynn dared a glance at Randy. He slid his gaze
away, his expression twisted into a resigned grimace. He
wasn't going to help her, she realized, the panic clutching
at her. She was on her own. Always on her own.

Screwing up her courage, she forced herself to take
one step, then another. When she took the third, Ricky
grabbed her bottom and squeezed, digging his fingers into
the soft flesh of her right cheek. Her control snapped. She
took physical abuse from her father; she had all her life.
She wasn't about to take it from this spoiled boy. She
swung around and slapped his hand as hard as she could.
"I told you not to touch me, Ricky Jones!"

For one moment, electric with tension, the boys were
quiet. A cloud moved over the sun; the breeze stilled.
Somewhere above them a bird screamed. Then fury lit
Ricky's eyes. And hatred. She recognized both from years
of seeing them in her father's.

She'd made a mistake. A big one. Her breath caught as
real fear moved through her. The kind of fear that stole
one's breath and free will. She ordered herself to run; her
feet wouldn't move. Instead, she stared at Ricky Jones in
dawning horror. He meant to hurt her.

A cry in her throat, she ran. She didn't get ten feet

before Ricky caught her and dragged her back. Her Coke slipped from her fingers and hit the ground, the carbonated beverage foaming from the can's small mouth. She squeaked in fear as she fought to free herself.

He shoved her up against the tree, which only minutes ago had offered her such sweet shelter from the sun. The bark bit into her back, and she smelled beer on his breath. Her stomach rolled, and she made a sound of revulsion and fear.

"Come on, guys," Buddy Wills said suddenly, nervously. "Leave her alone. Let's go have some fun."

"We're having fun right here," Ricky said softly, not taking his gaze from hers. "Aren't we, Randy?"

Becky Lynn glanced pleadingly at her brother; he looked physically ill. "Randy," she begged, twisting against Ricky's grasp. "Please, make him stop. Plea—"

Ricky planted his open mouth on hers. He tasted of beer and tobacco; his breath was foul. He stuck his tongue deep into her mouth, and she gagged, straining against his grasp.

He kissed her again and again, his mouth open, sloppy wet with spit. He plastered his body to hers, and his erection pressed against her abdomen. She whimpered low in her throat, and squirmed, a shard of bark digging into her shoulder blade, piercing the thin fabric of her T-shirt.

Ricky dragged his mouth from hers, and looked over his shoulder at his buddies. She saw the laughter in his eyes, the triumph, and fury exploded inside her. Enraged, she wrenched an arm free and swung at him, catching him off guard, nailing him in the side of his head. "You bastard! Get off of me!"

"Sonofabitch!" Ricky stumbled backward, then lunged

for her again. "Cunt! Bitch!" He slammed her back against the tree, so hard she saw stars. "Tommy, Christ, give me a hand here!"

Tommy jumped forward and pinned her arms. She fought him as best she could, twisting, arching, trying to kick.

Ricky put his hands on her breasts, squeezing them, pinching at the nipples. "Hey, Tommy, these are some nice little titties. Have yourself a squeeze."

"No!" She freed a foot and managed to jam it onto one of theirs, but without enough force to do anything but amuse them.

Tommy laughed and pulled at her breasts. "Ricky's right. How'd we miss these, guys? All we'd need now is a paper bag. Come on and have a feel, Buddy."

The other boy took a step back, shaking his head. "No way. This isn't right." He looked at Randy. "It's not right."

Tears streaming down her cheeks, Becky Lynn flailed her head back and forth as the two boys continued to paw at her. "Please," she whispered, horrified beyond words by what they were doing to her, humiliated and ashamed. "Please… Randy…don't…let them…"

She looked at her brother, begging him, and saw the fear and horror in his eyes. In that moment, she realized he cared more about being one of these boys' friends than he did about her, his own flesh and blood.

"If her tits are good," Ricky said, spittle collecting at the corners of his mouth, "maybe her pussy'll be okay, too. What do you think, Tommy?"

"No!" She arched her back, straining against Tommy's hands. "Leave me alone… Randy…don't let them—"

Ricky shoved his hand between her legs, and she screamed, vaguely wondering why she hadn't before.

Tommy slammed his hand over her mouth, catching the sound. She bit down, heard Tommy's oath and tasted blood. His blood.

"You wet yet, Becky Lynn?" Ricky asked, grinding his fingers against her. "Huh, baby?" He poked at her through the denim of her shorts, and she cried out in pain, the sound muffled by Tommy's hand.

"Shit, guys," Buddy said, stepping forward, looking as if he was going to puke. "This isn't right. It's Randy's sister, for Christ's sake." He grabbed Ricky's arm. "Come on, man. Leave her alone."

Ricky jerked from the other boy's grasp, fury tightening his features. "Get your own piece, asshole."

Buddy looked at Randy. Becky Lynn could see that if Randy didn't put up a fight, Buddy was going to back down, as well. And she would be lost.

Randy moved to stand beside Buddy. "Leave her alone," he said, his voice shaking.

"What's a matter, Madman? Afraid?"

Randy, bigger than all of them, curled fingers into fists. "Fuck you, Fischer. I'm not afraid of anything. You want to take me on? Just say the word."

For long moments, the boys faced one another. Then Ricky and Tommy dropped their hands and stepped away from Becky Lynn. "Hey, man, we didn't mean any harm. We were just havin' a little fun. That's all."

Becky Lynn ran. Leaving her precious magazines, not bothering to straighten her T-shirt. She ran until sweat poured from her and each breath tore at her chest and side.

Fun. They were just having a little fun.

A sob wrenched from deep inside her. *Dear Jesus, she'd wanted to die, and they'd just been having a little fun.*

Becky Lynn didn't slow even when she caught sight of her house. Limping, gasping for breath, she reached it. Her mother stood on the front porch, still wearing the floral housecoat. She stared blankly out at nothing, and her gaze flickered to her daughter as Becky Lynn climbed onto the porch. But she didn't speak, didn't comment. Becky Lynn knew that she didn't even see her. Not really.

Becky Lynn pushed through the screen door. Her daddy sat in a stupor on the couch. She moved past him; he didn't acknowledge her in any way. Thank God. She didn't know what she would have done if he'd chosen that moment to lay into her. She only wanted to be alone. To be in her own bed. To never be touched again.

Becky Lynn slipped into her bedroom, crawled onto the mattress and pulled the blanket over her. She curled into a tight ball, trembling so violently her teeth chattered. So cold, she thought, curling herself tighter. She was so cold.

She squeezed her eyes shut, and her head filled with the suffocating smell of Ricky's breath, hot against her skin, filled with the feel of Ricky's tongue poking in her mouth, with the sensation of being trapped, overpowered.

She shoved a fist into her mouth to keep from crying out. Why had Ricky and Tommy done that to her? What had she done to deserve such cruelty? Such loathing?

Why her? Why always her?

Tears, hot against her cold flesh, slipped from the corners of her eyes and rolled down her cheeks, pooling at the corners of her mouth. She'd been trapped. Like an animal. Unable to free herself, unable to escape.

A sob caught in her throat. She'd fought them. But they'd been stronger; they'd held her down. The sob forced its way past her lips, ripping through the quiet room.

They'd put their hands on her; she hadn't been able to make them stop, hadn't been able to escape.

She'd wanted to, more than anything in the world. She still did. Escape Tommy and Ricky. Her father.

Escape her life.

Hopelessness overwhelmed her, and she pressed her face into the sagging mattress, tears of shame and despair choking her. As she cried, the nightmare of the last hours began to dim, being replaced by those magic moments with her mother earlier. *You're special, Becky Lynn... You could make something of yourself... You could move away from here.*

Becky Lynn curled her fingers into the rough, frayed blanket, holding on to those words, their warmth licking at the cold. Somebody thought she was special. One person in this world believed in her. That meant something. It was important.

If nothing else, it would get her through another day.

4

Fear became Becky Lynn's constant companion. At school and Miss Opal's. At the bus stop in the mornings, walking home from work in the evenings.

Razor sharp, the fear left her every sense heightened, her every nerve twitching. Waiting. For the worst to happen. Waiting for the moment when she would come face-to-face with Ricky and Tommy, for the moment when they would find her alone and completely vulnerable.

Oddly, the same fear that heightened her senses also numbed them, creating a wall between her and the world, a barrier that kept her from experiencing anything but her fear.

So she lived with it. She ate it and slept with it, it accompanied her to school and work. She awoke in the night, breathing hard, bathed in sweat, feeling suffocated by the emotion. Sometimes she awakened to the smell of Ricky's foul breath, to the sensation of his hands on her breasts, between her legs, and she would hold the pillow to her face to muffle her cry of terror. Of revulsion. Those nights she would be unable to sleep again. She huddled under the blanket, watching light touch the sky, praying for sleep yet praying more that it wouldn't come.

She had lost weight. Her eyes had become shadowed.

Already quiet, she had stopped talking at all. No one had noticed. Not her mother or a sibling, not a teacher or Miss Opal.

But then, she hadn't expected that anyone would. Just as she hadn't considered telling anyone what had happened. She knew, in her heart and gut, that telling would only make her situation worse.

Becky Lynn retrieved the broom and dustpan from the back of the beauty shop and began cleaning up. Miss Opal had just finished her last appointment of the day and Fayrene and Dixie had left more than an hour ago. It had been slow, even for a Wednesday.

She tucked a hank of her hair behind her ear, moving the broom over the shiny floor, making sure she found every corner and cranny, wanting to do a good job for Miss Opal. The woman had gone to the high school principle and convinced him to give Becky Lynn special dispensation to miss last period study hall so she could work afternoons at the Cut 'n Curl.

Becky Lynn bent to maneuver the broom under Fayrene's workstation. She had needed the money, and she was only too happy to get away from school early. She drew her eyebrows together in thought. She had feared the first day of school, feared seeing Ricky and Tommy, so much she'd been physically ill. Yet that day and the ones following had slipped by until a month had passed without incident. The boys hadn't approached her again. They hadn't touched her, hadn't exposed themselves or teased her much at school. In fact, they had been distant. Almost polite.

She had told herself that she was safe. She had told herself they had forgotten her, that they were busy now with football, their girlfriends and school functions.

Yet, no matter how often she reassured herself, something about their distance unsettled her. And her sense of being threatened grew with every day.

She frowned and swept the last of Mrs. Peachtree's gunmetal gray hair into the dustpan. In the delta, the quieter, the more still and heavy the air, the worse the coming storm was going to be. That's the way the air had felt to her every day since the river. Heavy, ripe with waiting and so still she could hear her own heart pump.

Maybe they had scared themselves, she thought, shuddering. Maybe Buddy Wills's words had sunk into their thick skulls.

Or maybe Randy had demanded they leave her alone.

She tightened her lips into a grim line and emptied the dustpan of hair into the trash. Her brother was no hero—especially hers. The last thing he would ever do was stick up for her. He had made that clear the day by the river and every day since. The bastard wouldn't even look at her.

The bell jangled against the shop's glass door. Becky Lynn glanced over her shoulder, expecting to see Miss Opal's husband, Talbot. He usually stopped by around this time to see how his wife was doing and to find out what she had planned for dinner.

Instead, Ricky and Tommy sauntered through the beauty-shop door, their lips twisted into self-satisfied smirks. She froze, a chill racing up her spine. *Had they come looking for her?*

Of course not. Becky Lynn drew in a deep breath, working to calm herself, to slow her runaway pulse. She wasn't alone. They couldn't touch her now, they couldn't hurt her.

"Hello, boys." Opal snapped the cash drawer shut and smiled. "What can I do for you?"

"Hello, Miss Opal, ma'am."

Tommy stopped at the counter, Ricky a step or two behind him. Becky Lynn tightened her fingers on the broom handle, praying neither of them looked her way.

"Mama sent me by to pick up a bottle of that strawberry shampoo she likes so much. She said to tell you she'd pay you when she came in on Saturday."

"That'll be fine." Opal took the receipt book out of the drawer and began writing up the transaction. "We goin' to win that big game Friday night?"

"Yes, ma'am," Ricky said proudly. "We're goin' to kick some Wolverine butt."

"You bet," Tommy added. "Those boys'll be sorry they ever came to Bend."

"That's what I like to hear." Miss Opal rummaged under the counter, then made a sound of annoyance. "I had a bottle of that shampoo set aside to take home myself. I bet Fayrene up and sold it. Lord knows, I shouldn't expect her to walk ten feet."

"Becky Lynn," she called over her shoulder, "fetch me one of those strawberry shampoos from the display in back. You know which one I mean."

Becky Lynn watched in horror as Tommy and Ricky turned and looked at her. The broom slipped from her nerveless fingers, clattering against the linoleum floor. She stared stupidly at them, unable to breathe, to move.

Ricky's mouth curved into a cold smile. Her heart began to thrum, her palms to sweat. *She'd wanted to die, and they'd just been having a little fun.*

Miss Opal frowned. "Becky Lynn? The shampoo."

"Yes, ma'am," she whispered, turning and crossing to the Redkin display. She took a bottle from the shelf, her hands trembling so badly she almost dropped it.

A little fun. They'd just been having a little fun.

She carried the bottle to Miss Opal, her eyes downcast, her feet leaden.

"Hiya, Becky Lynn."

She lifted her gaze to Ricky's, terror choking her. He looked her straight in the eye, arrogantly, without apology or fear. His gaze, as flat and emotionless as a shark's, mocked her. She had a sense that he knew everything she felt, and that she amused him.

She curled her fingers into fists. Because of who he was, he thought he could get away with anything. "Hello," she said, digging her nails into her palms, her voice high.

He smiled again, this time broadly for Miss Opal's benefit. "I haven't seen you much around school. Where have you been hiding yourself?"

Aware of Miss Opal's gaze, she shook her head, her mouth dry. "Nowhere. I've been…nowhere."

Ricky picked up the bottle of shampoo and tossed it to Tommy. "We'll catch up with you later, Becky Lynn. Right, Tommy?"

The bottle slapped against Tommy's palm, and he wrapped his fingers around it. "Yeah. One of these days."

A sound of fear escaped her, small and breathless. It slipped unbidden past her lips, and Miss Opal looked at her sharply. "Becky Lynn, that delivery of products still needs to be unloaded and checked in. It's in the storeroom. See to it now, please."

Becky Lynn nodded, relief stealing her breath. She turned and fled to the storeroom. Once there, she brought her trembling hands to her face. *"We'll catch up with you later,"* Ricky had said. *"One of these days."* Tommy had agreed.

She had been right to feel threatened; she hadn't been paranoid. Ricky and Tommy hadn't forgotten her; they had just put her on hold.

From out front, Becky Lynn heard Miss Opal tell the boys goodbye and to say hello to their mamas, then heard the bell jangle against the door.

Bitterness rose like a bile in her throat; tears burned the back of her eyes. No one would ever believe Tommy and Ricky were anything but model young gentlemen, no one would believe they could do any wrong. Not them, not two of Bend's favorite sons.

Becky Lynn crossed to the product shipment and knelt on the floor beside the box. She took out the packing list, the printed words and numbers swimming in front of her eyes, her tears making reading it an impossibility.

Where could she hide? How could she protect herself? She lowered her head to the box and rested her forehead against it. The tears slipped down her cheeks and off the tip of her nose, splashing onto the packing list clenched in her hands. She had no one to turn to, no one who would believe her.

"We need to talk." Miss Opal came into the room, shutting the door behind her.

Becky Lynn wiped away the tears on her cheeks, then darted a look over her shoulder. Miss Opal stood just inside the room, hands on her hips, her expression stern. "Ma'am?"

"Becky Lynn Lee, I want you to tell me what's going on with those boys."

Becky Lynn gazed at the other woman, a glimmer of hope blooming inside her, pushing at her fear and despair, at her loneliness. She could tell Miss Opal. Miss Opal would believe her.

She drew in a shuddering breath. "You mean Ricky and Tommy?"

"Yes." The hairdresser took a step toward her, shaking her head in disappointment. "Just because some folks around Bend think you're trash doesn't mean you have to act like it."

Becky Lynn frowned, her heart beginning to pound. "Wh-what do you mean?"

"You've been sleeping around with those boys, haven't you?"

"No!" The word ripped from her as she jumped to her feet. She faced her boss, hurt and betrayal swelling inside her, souring in her mouth. The only person who had ever been supportive and kind, the only person she had ever thought she could, just maybe, turn to, believed she was no better than a tramp.

"I would never…those boys…they—"

"Becky Lynn Lee," Miss Opal interrupted, her expression and tone righteous, "you listen to me. Your reputation is yours alone. Nobody can take it from you, and likewise, only you can throw it away. And once it's gone, it can never be retrieved."

Becky Lynn thought of that day by the river, her head filling with the memory, her stomach turning with it. Ricky and Tommy had touched her when she hadn't wanted to be touched, they had taken without asking, without consent. She would never feel clean again.

She faced Miss Opal, all her hurt, all her anger and fear,

her humiliation, rushing to her lips. "You'd never think those boys would do something wrong…something awful! Oh, no, not fine upstanding boys like Tommy Fischer and Ricky Jones. You could never imagine that they might… that they might hurt me."

Becky Lynn fisted her fingers. "I thought you…cared about me. I thought you believed I was something better than everyone else did. I see now that I was—"

She choked back the words, and swung away from Miss Opal once more, curving her arms around her middle, holding and comforting herself because no one else would.

"What are you saying, Becky Lynn? Did those boys—" The older woman cleared her throat. "Did they touch you?"

"Yes," she whispered, not turning, not wanting to see Miss Opal's expression.

Miss Opal's silence deafened. Becky Lynn turned and faced her, spine ramrod straight. "What are you going to do now? Fire me? Call me a liar?"

For a long moment, Miss Opal said nothing. Then she sighed, the sound old and defeated. "I'm sorry, child. So…sorry. I do believe you." She folded her hands in front of her. "Though I wish I didn't."

Miss Opal sighed again. "You were behaving so strangely…and those boys, there was something about the way they looked at you. I jumped to the conclusion that you…had…that you were…"

Sleeping with them. Just the way poor white trash would. Becky Lynn lifted her chin defensively and drew in a ragged breath. "Don't worry about it," she whispered, her voice thick. "If I'm not fired, I'll finish unpacking that order now."

Miss Opal touched her shoulder lightly. "I'm so sorry," she said again. "Please forgive me."

Becky Lynn shuddered. Miss Opal's touch was gentle, reassuring.

She would love to be held, would love to lean against the older woman and sob out her fears. She would love to forget what Miss Opal had accused her of. But she knew better than to do any of those things. When she forgot her place and who she was, she got hurt.

She shrugged off Miss Opal's hand. "Don't worry about it."

"But I will worry about it. I'm fond of you and…and I feel terrible about what I just suggested. You're a good girl, and I knew you wouldn't do that, but I… Look at me, Becky Lynn. Please."

Becky Lynn turned and met her boss's eyes. Miss Opal looked genuinely distressed. Her already hawkish features were pinched, her eyes soft with regret. As she gazed at the other woman, some of her anger, her indignation, slipped away. Even as she softened, she inched her chin up.

"You're right to be angry with me. I was wrong, and I'm terribly sorry." Miss Opal caught her hands. "Now, Becky Lynn," she said quietly but in a tone that brooked no argument, "I want you to tell me what those boys did to you."

Becky Lynn shook her head and tugged against the other woman's grasp. "I'm fine."

"That's not what I asked you, Becky Lynn Lee." She tightened her fingers. "What did those boys do to you?"

Becky Lynn gazed at Miss Opal, the truth pressing at her, begging to be told. She sucked in a deep breath. She wanted to tell; she wanted someone to believe her. She wanted Ricky and Tommy to be punished.

But she was afraid.

As if reading her thoughts, Miss Opal reached out and tipped her chin gently up. "You can trust me, child," she said softly, as if reading her thoughts. "I promise I'll help you if I can."

Becky Lynn lowered her eyes to her toes. Her heart began to thunder; the blood rushed to her head until she was dizzy with it. "They…touched me. Ricky and Tommy…they shoved me up against a tree and they—" Tears flooded her eyes, hot and urgent. "They touched my breasts and my…"

She lifted her eyes to Miss Opal's, tears blurring her vision. "They wouldn't stop. I begged them to, but they…wouldn't."

The hairdresser made a sound of distress and drew Becky Lynn into her arms and against her bony chest. "Poor, baby. Poor, sweet child." She stroked Becky Lynn's hair, murmuring words, sounds, of comfort.

"They wouldn't stop," Becky Lynn repeated, reliving the horror of those minutes. "Buddy tried to talk them into leaving me alone, but Randy just stood there. My own brother—" She buried her face in Miss Opal's shoulder.

The hairdresser's hand stilled for a moment, then she resumed her rhythmic stroking. "Becky Lynn," she asked quietly, "did those boys…did they rape you?"

She shook her head, sniffling, tears soaking the other woman's blouse.

"Thank God for that." Miss Opal took in a deep, thoughtful breath. "Did you tell your parents?"

Becky Lynn eased away from Miss Opal and met her

eyes, her own still swimming. "Daddy wouldn't have… believed me, and even if he did, he wouldn't have done anything about it. And Mama, well…she's got enough troubles of her own."

Miss Opal's lips tightened with disapproval, but she didn't comment.

"Did you tell one of your teachers, a school counselor, or—"

She shook her head again. "I didn't tell anybody."

"Then we must decide what we're going to do."

"Do?" Becky Lynn repeated, stunned. "What do you mean?"

"Well, we can either go to Ricky's and Tommy's parents or to the police—"

"No!" Becky shook her head again, this time with growing alarm. She could imagine what Tommy's and Ricky's parents would think of her accounting of events, could imagine how the police would react. Within hours, Bend would be buzzing with the story about how that trashy Becky Lynn Lee lied about the stars of the Bend High School football team. She couldn't bear the thought of people talking about her that way. She couldn't bear the speculation.

Panicked, she clasped her hands together. "Don't you see? Nobody will believe me. They'll think I was the one…that I wanted attention. It would be awful, I couldn't stand it."

"You can't let them get away with this," Miss Opal said, her voice tight. "It isn't right."

"You didn't believe me at first, why would anyone else?"

The older woman sighed heavily. Becky Lynn could see her boss struggle to decide the best thing to do.

"Please, Miss Opal. Please don't tell." Becky Lynn caught the older woman's hands, fear coiling around her, squeezing at her chest until she could hardly breathe. "I'm afraid of what will happen if you do. They might—"

"What could they do, child? It's keeping something like this secret that will hurt you. We must go to their parents or the authorities."

"No, please…" Becky Lynn clutched Miss Opal's hands. "Just promise me you won't tell. Please."

The hairdresser made a soft sound, part affection, part reticence. "All right, Becky Lynn. I won't tell. For now. But I don't like it."

"Thank you, Miss Opal. Thank you so much."

"But you must promise me that if those boys do anything to you, anything at all, you'll come to me at once."

Becky Lynn smiled. "I will. I promise."

The woman touched Becky Lynn's cheek lightly. "I don't want you to think you have no one to turn to. Never again."

5

Becky Lynn promised, and as the days slipped into weeks, she was filled with a sense of well-being and security. Partly because Ricky, Tommy and their gang never bothered her and partly because Miss Opal had taken to watching over her like a mother hen.

The older woman insisted on driving Becky Lynn home from work, insisted that when she did walk, she take the most traveled routes, and had even taken to sending Fayrene or Dixie for the pastries on Saturday morning. Fayrene had herself in a snit over it, but Miss Opal didn't seem concerned in the least over the other hairdresser's pique. She always found a more pressing job for Becky Lynn, one from which she couldn't be spared, even for a few minutes.

Becky Lynn smiled to herself as she scrubbed the first shampoo bowl. For the first time in her life, she had a sense of what it must be like to have a mother, a mother in the real sense of the word, even if only part-time. It was nice to have someone who worried about her, someone who cared about what happened to her. It made her feel special. It made her feel cocooned and safe.

"Becky Lynn, you sure you can make it home without a ride?"

She lifted her gaze to Dixie. The other woman stood at

the shop's front door, buttoning her coat. Becky Lynn nodded. "I'll be fine. It's not even dark yet."

The hairdresser looked longingly over her shoulder. Her last two appointments had canceled, and she wanted to go home. Becky Lynn couldn't blame her—it had been a busy day, and she had a family to take care of.

She returned her gaze to Becky Lynn. "You're sure? Miss Opal was pretty insistent that I drive you. She made me promise." Dixie pursed her lips in thought. "I could ask Fayrene."

Becky Lynn had no doubt how that request would be met. The other hairdresser was in back now, sulking because Dixie was going home and she would have to stay and close the shop. "I'll be fine. Really."

"Okay." Dixie fastened a scarf around her cap of curls. "Miss Opal sure was tickled about going to see her granddaughter cheer at that pep rally. You going?"

Becky Lynn shook her head. "I don't think so."

"Well, okay then. See you tomorrow afternoon."

As Dixie stepped out into the gathering dusk, Becky Lynn had the sudden urge to call her back and beg her to wait. The words, the plea, sprang to her tongue. She took an involuntary step toward the door, starting to call out, then stopped, shaking her head at her foolishness. If ever there was a night she didn't need to worry about walking home, it was tonight. As key players on the Bend High football team, Tommy and Ricky, and just about everybody else in this football-crazy town, would be busy at the pep rally.

She shook her head again, and went back to scrubbing the shampoo bowls. No, tonight she had nothing to fear.

Forty-five minutes later, she and Fayrene parted company at the square. Although just past five, shadows already swallowed the peripheral edges of the square and pressed inward, gobbling up the last of the light.

Becky Lynn looked straight ahead, toward the main road and the brightly lit homes and neighborhoods that lined it, then to her right and the road that led across the railroad tracks and through the worst part of Bend but straight to her house. She could save twenty minutes. Her stomach rumbled, and the shadows eased closer.

She tilted her face to the darkening sky and thought of her promise to Miss Opal, thought of the hour and of Tommy and Ricky and the pep rally.

Even as a chill crawled up her arms, she shook her head and angled to her right, cutting across the square, moving as fast as she could without running. Tonight she had nothing to fear.

In minutes, she had left the lights of the square behind and was crossing the railroad tracks. As she cleared them, she noticed the quiet. No slamming doors reverberated through the night, no mothers called their children to dinner, no cars roared past. Not even a breeze stirred the trees.

She had passed into the part of Bend called Sunset. Due west of the square, the sun always seemed to set, bloody red, right on top of Sunset. Considered the worst part of town, worse even than her own shabby neighborhood, it housed the dirt poor.

The people who lived here were the ones her father felt superior to. These were the ones he put down and called names and hurt whenever he had the chance. She'd always thought that a sick, human failing, that need to find and denigrate someone less fortunate than yourself.

She shuddered and lifted her face to the dark sky.

She should have taken the long way.

Becky Lynn stepped up her pace, hiking up her collar higher on her neck. She glanced nervously to her sides. The sparsely populated area had homes that were nothing better than shanties, some of which were former slave cabins, left over from when this land had been part of a prosperous plantation; cotton fields and dilapidated out-buildings. She'd walked this way hundreds of times before; she had never felt threatened, had never been afraid.

Had Miss Opal taken such care of her that now, without the woman's guardian gaze, she felt afraid? Silly, she thought, hugging herself. She was being silly.

From her left, she heard a sound, something soft and thick, like a muffled laugh. From her right, the scurry of something through the grass, some small frightened animal, then the sound of a twig snapping.

Becky Lynn stopped in the middle of the road, her heart hammering against the wall of her chest. She looked around her, peering into the shadows. "Is anyone there?"

Silence answered her, louder than any voiced reply. She sucked in a sharp breath and started walking again, stopping at the sound of her own name. It floated on the night air, called in a ghostly voice, the kind of voice used on Halloween by kids trying to scare one another, laced with both cunning and amusement.

Ricky and Tommy weren't at the pep rally.
They were here.

Her heart in her throat, she started to run.

From her right came the sound of someone running through the overgrown fields. A moment later, Ricky darted out of the shadows ahead of her, his smile eerily white in the darkness. "Hello, Becky Lynn."

She stopped in her tracks, fear rising like bile inside her. It turned on her tongue, threatening to choke her. She swallowed, fighting to find a shred of calm. "Wha-what are you doing here?"

"Waiting for you, Becky baby. We've been waiting weeks for you." He grinned and her blood went cold. "Just like we promised. Right, Tommy?"

"Right," the other boy answered, stepping out from the shadows to her left. "How'ya doing tonight, baby?" With a jerk, Tommy yanked another person forward. Buddy stumbled into view.

Buddy looked sick. He had something she couldn't make out clutched in his hand. She searched the shadows for her brother, but they'd obviously left him behind.

She took a step backward, glancing frantically around her, looking for a way to escape. Why had she done this? Why hadn't she listened to Miss Opal? She breathed deeply through her nose, working to keep her wits—what was left of them—about her.

"Lost your guard dog tonight." Ricky made a clucking sound with his tongue. "What a pity. For you."

Tommy laughed and Buddy hung his head.

"Bet she's going to enjoy seeing her granddaughter cheer. Right, Tommy?"

"I'd enjoy it, too, Ricky. She's one fine little piece."

They closed ranks and took a step toward her. Her fingers and toes went numb, the inside of her mouth turned to ash. A light burned from the house just behind her to her left. If she could just make it to that door, maybe someone there would help her.

She took another step backward, frantically searching for a way to distract them, for something that would give her the moments she needed to make it to that doorway. "Leave me alone," she whispered. "Please."

Ricky laughed and took another step toward her. "Now, why should we go and do that?"

"I haven't done anything to you. I just want to be left alone."

"Seems I remember you slapping me." Ricky turned to Tommy. "Do you remember that?"

"Sure do." Tommy grinned. "Slapped the shit out of you, right in front of us."

"Look," she said, panic clawing at her. "I'm sorry. I didn't mean to. I just—"

"What did you think you were going to accomplish by telling Miss Opal?" Ricky asked, his upper lip curling. "What did you think our parents were going to do? Spank us?"

Miss Opal had gone to their parents? Becky Lynn struggled for an even breath. *She hadn't kept her promise?* "Wh-what do you mean?"

"Did you really think anyone was going to believe we would touch you?" Ricky sneered. "Our parents laughed. They were offended at the suggestion."

"C'mon, guys," Buddy piped up suddenly, his voice high with nerves. "Let her go. If we're late for the rally, coach will have our heads."

"What do you think he's gonna do?" Tommy snapped, swinging toward the other boy. "Bench us for the big game? No way. Can't win without us."

"Buddy, you fuckin' pussy." Ricky practically spat the words. "We talked about this, we can all get a crack at her and still be suited up in time."

They meant to rape her.

With a sound of fear, Becky Lynn turned and ran. Her fear made it hard to breathe, it clutched at her chest even as she pushed herself to run faster. Her feet pounded on the dirt road, rocks bit into the bottoms of her feet, she angled off the road and toward the lit doorway.

Safety within reach, she opened her mouth to scream for help; one of them tackled her from behind, knocking her to the ground, knocking the wind out of her. She tasted dirt and her own blood, pinpoints of light flashed behind her eyes.

In the next moment, a hand was forced over her mouth and she was being dragged, Ricky at her head and Tommy at her feet, from the side of road and behind a dilapidated shed. She struggled, dimly aware of Buddy following behind, dragging his feet.

If she had any hope, she realized, it was Buddy. If only Ricky would take his hand off her mouth, she could beg Buddy to help her; she could scream. But he didn't, and his grip partially covered her nose, as well, and she felt light-headed from the lack of oxygen.

Dear God, she thought, struggling for air, this couldn't be happening to her! The words played through her head like a continuous tape.

"You got the paper bag, Buddy?"

"This has gone far enough." Buddy cleared his throat nervously. "I mean, joking about it was one thing, but—"

Ricky tightened his grip on her and glared at the other boy. "You going to be a pussy all your life, Wills? Or are you a faggot? Give me the goddamned bag!"

The boy hung back, his face white with fear. "What if we get caught? What if—"

"We're not going to get caught."

"What if she tells? Jesus, Ricky, we could go to jail!"

"You are such a fucking girl, Buddy." Ricky laughed, the sound twisted and evil. "Who's going to believe her? Nobody, that's who. Our folks didn't believe Miss Opal, they laughed at the thought that we would touch her. You think I would do this if I didn't know I could get away with it?"

They were raping her because they knew they could get away with it.

And because they thought she was nothing.

"Now bring me the goddamned bag so I can put it over her head. Then help hold her down." Ricky's hand slackened as he faced the other boy.

They were going to put a paper bag over her head so they wouldn't have to look at her. Sons of bitches! Bastards! Fury ate her fear, and with Ricky's attention diverted, she propelled herself up, knocking him sideways. Enraged, she flew at Tommy, raking his face with her nails. He howled with pain. He pried her off him, then wheeling back with his fist, punched her.

His fist connected with her jaw, and her head snapped back, pain shooting with blinding intensity through her skull. She reeled backward and hit the ground, her head cracking against a rock. Pain shot through her head, then light. Brilliant white and blinding.

Everything went black.

When Becky Lynn came to, she saw only black, could only draw a shallow breath, closed as she was in the damp, tight box. Disoriented, she tried to move her hands but found them anchored, found her legs nailed down, stretched at a painful angle.

It took a moment to realize where she was and what was

happening, a moment for reality to rudely reassert itself. The weight of a body pressed her into the damp, fecund earth, hands held her immobile. Her clothes had been pushed or torn aside, the night air chilled her skin, although she knew the iciness she felt had little to do with the temperature.

It was Ricky on top of her. She knew him by his stench.

Sounds and sensations flashed crazily through her head. The ooze of the earth against her skin, the smell of sweat and mud, the pain of an object being forced into her, sawing and tearing. The paper bag crackled as she flung her head from side to side in an agony of pain and shame.

A dog began to bark, a high excited sound that ripped through her head, drowning out the sound of Ricky's labored breathing. Of Buddy's fear and Tommy's anticipation. Of her own mewls of despair.

Ricky grunted with release, like an animal, and fell against her. The sound turned her stomach, and she knew that guttural noise would feed her nightmares forever.

"Come on, Ricky." Tommy's voice shook, and she heard him frantically unbuckling his belt, yanking down his zipper. "You've had your shot, give somebody else a cha—"

The dog started its high-pitched barking again, and a light came on, spilling into the black, followed by the screech of a screen door being opened. "Who's out there?" a woman called.

Becky Lynn opened her mouth to cry out, to scream for help, but nothing came out but a ragged whisper, so weak even the boys didn't hear her.

"Oh, shit." Buddy whimpered and released her legs. "Oh, shit, Ricky—"

"Shut the fuck—"

"I know somebody's out there, and y'all better git. I'm callin' the police. You hear me?"

The three boys froze. Becky Lynn could feel their sudden tension, could almost hear their thoughts— Buddy's relief, Tommy's disappointment, Ricky's hatred.

"I'm callin' the police," the woman repeated, louder this time. "I'm callin' 'em now." The door slapped shut.

Buddy didn't wait. He jumped up and ran, stumbling out of the brush and into the road, puking when he reached it.

"Come on, man." Tommy sounded panicked, even though he didn't release her hands. "We gotta go!"

"Thanks, baby," Ricky whispered. "And don't you fret none, I'll make sure Tommy and Buddy get their turn."

He bent his head and took her right nipple into his mouth, sucking it, swirling his tongue over it. She gagged, the tenderness of the gesture grotesque, obscene. He lifted himself from her, and she kicked out blindly and as hard as she could. She caught him in the groin. She knew by the feel and by the sound he made—a high whine of pain—and she wished she could see his face contort.

"Bitch! Cunt! I'll—"

Tommy tugged on Ricky's arm. "She called the cops, man! We've got to get out of here."

Ricky must have agreed, for in the next moment, Tommy released her hands, and she heard the two boys run off.

Becky Lynn clawed at the paper bag, wrenching it off. She ripped at the stiff brown paper, tearing it into smaller and smaller pieces, whimpering and grunting like a wounded animal. The paper cut her fingers; they burned and bled, but she kept tearing at the bag until nothing was left but pieces too small and broken to hold on to.

Shuddering uncontrollably, she slumped to her side and curled into a tight ball.

6

Light leaked from the edges of the small, haphazardly covered windows, spilling weakly into the darkness. With a strangled cry of relief, Becky Lynn crawled up onto the sagging front porch.

Home. She'd made it home at last.

She rested her forehead against the porch floor, struggling to even her shallow, ragged breathing. She hurt. Her belly, her head and jaw, between her legs. But the physical pain didn't compare to the ache inside her, the ache that couldn't be measured in physical terms, the damage that couldn't be repaired or healed with bandage or salve. Inside, she'd been ripped to pieces.

She would never be whole again.

Shaking, Becky Lynn grasped the porch railing and pulled herself to her feet, trembling so badly she feared she would fall. She had no idea of the time, no idea how long she'd lain behind the outbuilding, bleeding and raw, waiting for the wail of the police siren that had never come.

Images, horrific and unwanted, flashed lightning-like through her head. She squeezed her eyes shut, her stomach pitching. She held the vomit back through sheer force of will. She wouldn't be sick, she wouldn't allow Ricky and Tommy to take anything more from her—they'd already taken the only things that had been truly hers, the only things that had been worth having. Her body. The last vestige of her girlish idealism. Her hope.

She crossed the porch to the door, thinking for the first time of her family. She had never been late before, had never failed to show up by dinnertime. She pictured herself, how she must look—dirty, bruised and bloody, her clothes ripped. She curved her shaking fingers around the doorknob. Had anyone worried at her absence? When they saw her, what would they think?

She opened the door and stepped inside. And smelled the whiskey. Its stench hung in the air like a cloud, and she realized dimly that her father had somehow scraped together enough money for a fifth.

She shifted her gaze. He sat slumped in front of the television, Randy beside him, pale and tense. Her father didn't move, but as the door screeched, her brother turned his head. He met her eyes and for one electric moment stared at her, then slid his gaze guiltily away.

Her brother had known what his friends had planned to do to her.

She sucked in a sharp breath, the realization spinning through her, bringing her to a point past anger or disbelief, past hysteria. Had her brother encouraged them? Had he laughed with them when they talked about how they would put a bag over her head so they wouldn't have to look at her while they raped her?

The sickness threatened to overwhelm her again, and she brought a hand to her mouth, fighting it back. Tears stung her eyes. "How?" she managed to say, her voice thick with tears and grief. "How…could you? You're my brother."

Randy lifted his gaze to hers. She had the brief impression of a deer, frozen in the shocking glare of headlights. His expression, pinched and frightened, took on an ashen pallor.

"When we were small, remember how we played together? None of the other children would come…near us. Remember?"

Randy shifted uncomfortably and lowered his eyes once more. She shook her head, her pain nearly unbearable. "I would have done anything to protect you. I did protect you. So many ti—" She curved her arms around herself. "And now you…you let them…do…this to—"

She choked this last back, unable to take her brother's guilty silence, the damning truth of that silence, a moment longer. Turning toward the kitchen, she went in search of her mother.

Glenna Lee sat at the kitchen table, still as a stone, gazing at nothing, her eyes vacant, her hands working at a fold of her robe. Becky Lynn stared at her, at the way her fingers moved back and forth over the worn terry-cloth.

"Mama?" she whispered, clutching her hands together in a silent prayer. "Mama, please."

Her mother blinked, focusing on her daughter for the first time. Shock moved across her mother's expression, a dawning horror, then her features cleared, relaxing into an almost childlike mask. "Hello, baby."

Becky Lynn swallowed. "Mama, look at me. Please." She crossed to her mother and stopped directly before her. "I need you to see me, Mama."

"Of course I see you, baby." She tipped her head back, curving her lips into a small, simple smile. "Did Miss Opal keep you late?"

Becky Lynn shifted her gaze to the stove clock, its face cracked and coated with a film of grease but still readable. Nearly eleven. Five hours had passed since she'd left the Cut 'n Curl. Five hours spent in hell.

"No, Mama." Her chin began to quiver, and her eyes filled. "Mama, some boys…they… Mama, they hurt—"

Her mother shook her head and clucked her tongue. "She shouldn't keep you so late on a school night."

Becky Lynn drew in a ragged breath, her vision blurring. "Don't do this, Mama. I…need you. Please. I need you so much."

Her mother clutched her robe so tightly her knuckles poked out, stark and white even against the faded terry. "Go on to bed, baby. Everything will be better in the morning."

Becky Lynn took a step backward, a cry slipping past her lips. Her mother couldn't deal with this. She wouldn't deal with it. Turning, Becky Lynn returned to the living room. She crossed to her father, stopping directly in front of him, blocking the TV.

"Daddy," she whispered, twisting her fingers together, "please help me."

He lifted his eyes to hers. His were dull and red from drink. He grunted.

"Some boys hurt me, Daddy. They—" Her throat closed over the words and she struggled to clear it. "They forced me…they—"

As if suddenly seeing her, her father moved his gaze over her. "Where've you been, girl?"

"I'm trying to tell you. Tommy Fischer and Ricky Jones—" She darted a glance at her brother. His head was lowered, his shoulders hunched. "They…they raped me. They knocked me down…and held my hands and feet—"

Her father lurched to his feet, forcing her backward. "Don't you make up stories to cover your whoring!"

"No!" Becky Lynn shook her head violently. "No…they put a bag over my head and—"

"Randy?" Her father swung toward his son, weaving slightly. "Those boys your friends? The ones on the team?"

Randy glanced up, then away, looking like he wanted to puke. "Yes, sir."

"They at the rally t'night?"

"Yes, sir."

Becky Lynn fought for a breath. "It happened before the pep rally! They talked about how they were going to explain to the coach, they—"

"Lying whore," her father snapped. "Get out of my sight, before I beat the hell out of you."

Becky Lynn stumbled backward. Her mother stood in the kitchen doorway, white as a new sheet, visibly trembling. Becky Lynn met her eyes, pleading silently. *Stand up for me. Mama, I need you.*

But her mother didn't stand up for her. For long moments, she stood gazing at her daughter, unmoving save for the way she clutched and released the vee of her robe.

Becky Lynn's vision blurred. She had no one here. Not in this house. Not in Bend. No one who believed in her, no one who cared enough to stand up for her. Ricky and Tommy could rape her as often as they liked, and no one would care.

She blinked, clearing her vision, looking at her mother once more, a strange feeling of relief moving over her. Her mother had set her free. Now, truly, there was nothing for her in Bend.

Turning, Becky Lynn limped toward the bathroom.

"Don't come cryin' to me if you get knocked up!" her father shouted from behind her. "You hear me? I won't have none of your ugly bastard brats in this house. You hear me?"

Becky Lynn closed the bathroom door behind her, muffling the sound of her father's rage, and latched it. She crossed to the old claw-footed tub and turned on the faucets. Kneeling, she pushed the rubber stopper into the drain, then stood and stripped off her soiled clothing, avoiding her reflection in the small mirror above the sink.

They had put a bag over her head so the wouldn't have to look at her while they raped her.

She stepped into the tepid water, then sank into it. It flowed sweetly over her, like a baptism, cleansing her of Ricky's touch, his smell. His hate.

She rested her head against the cool porcelain and closed her eyes.

As if from outside her body, hovering above, she saw herself. Her body folded into the tub, scrunched down so she would be submerged, her skin so white it blended with the tub, the shock of red hair around her face, floating around her shoulders. The bruises. The blood that leaked from her and into the water, muddying it.

They would be back.

She wanted to cry, to howl with rage and pain, yet she had no tears, couldn't muster emotion enough for rage. She felt…a numbness. A nothingness. A weird kind of void that was at once a sweet relief and completely terrifying.

As the water became almost too cool to bear, she opened her eyes and sat up. Carefully, she soaped her thighs, her bruised womanhood, washing away dirt and blood. She winced as she moved her hands over herself, knowing from experience that physical bruises healed. And that invisible ones did not.

There was blood underneath her fingernails, Tommy's from when she'd scratched him, and she dug her nails into the soap, moving them back and forth on the slippery bar, not stopping until they were clear. Clean and free of him. She soaped her hair next, scrubbing it, rinsing it. Scrubbing again.

The water turned dark and ugly. Her stomach heaved, but she choked the sickness back. She drained the tub, then sat naked in the empty bath, her arms closed around herself, teeth chattering.

Thoughts raced dizzily, crazily through her head, like the twisted path of a roller coaster.

I won't tell, Becky Lynn... You must promise me that if those boys do anything to you, you will come to me...

What did you hope to accomplish by telling Miss Opal... Who did you think was going to believe that we'd touch you... Our parents laughed...

Lying whore... Get out of my sight...

Don't do this, Mama...I need you... Mama, please help me...

I'll make sure Tommy and Buddy get their turn...

Tears choked her, and Becky Lynn gasped to breathe. She brought her hands to her face and sobbed, pressing her hands against her mouth to muffle the sound, wishing that, somehow, holding back the sounds of her pain would erase it.

After a time, the violence of her sobs lessened, then ceased altogether, until the only sound she had energy enough to make was a broken mewl of despair. Soon, even that became impossible and she rocked, her arms curved tightly around herself.

Reaching up, she turned the faucets on full blast, half expecting her father to burst into the bathroom and rage at her for wasting water. Even as she waited, clean water slipped over her again, inch by comforting inch. The water warmed her, bringing her senses back to life. She rested her cheek against her drawn-up knees, her mother's words from what seemed like a lifetime ago, nudging into her consciousness.

You're special, Becky Lynn. You could move away from Bend, make something of yourself.

She squeezed her eyes shut, pain ripping through her. Nothing could be special here. Not in this house. Not in Bend.

Tonight her mother had set her free.

She had to take care of herself, no one else would. And as much as she loved her mother, she couldn't help her, couldn't save her from the fate she had resigned herself to.

Becky Lynn leaned her head against the tub-back and pictured the places in her magazines, clean and lovely, populated by beautiful smiling people. She pictured the brilliant sun and the warm breeze, imagining both against her skin. It never rained in those places. There wasn't any dirt, nor the lingering smell of sweat and rotting fields. In the places of her magazines, boys didn't hurt girls just because they were ugly and poor.

She would go there, to California; she would start a new life.

Becky Lynn pulled the stopper from the drain and stood. Shivering, she dried herself, then wrapped the threadbare towel around her. She went to the bathroom door and cracked it open. The house slept. In the next room, her father snored.

Even though he was impossible to wake out of his drunken slumber, Becky Lynn tiptoed across the hallway and into her room. She dressed quickly and quietly, then threw her remaining clothes into a duffel bag, her few knickknacks and toiletries, she retrieved her toothbrush, the shampoo and toothpaste. She'd saved everything she'd made at the Cut 'n Curl over the past couple of years, everything left over after her father had taken his share, and hidden it under a loose floorboard. Careful not to make a sound, she retrieved and counted it, then stuffed it into her jeans pocket.

Nearly two hundred dollars. It wasn't much, but it would have to do.

She hesitated outside her parents' door, then crept into their room. Her father's slacks lay in a heap on the floor. She picked them up and searched one pocket, then the other. Her fingers closed over a couple crumpled bills. Hands shaking, she pulled them out. Twenties? Where had he gotten this money? she wondered. She didn't care, he would only waste it on drink.

She took the money, keeping one twenty and putting the other into her mother's secret grocery stash on her way out of the house.

At the front door, she stopped and turned back, taking one last look at the place she had called home for nearly seventeen years. She had called it home, but it had never been one. She had never been safe here, had never been loved.

She would never be trapped again.

As she slipped through the door, she thought she heard the sound of weeping—her mother's weeping. Becky Lynn paused, her chest tightening. "Mama," she whispered, taking an involuntary step back inside.

The smell of whiskey filled her head, a sense of smothering gray with it. She shook her head and her senses cleared, a familiar picture filling her head. Of blue skies and palm trees, of brilliant sun and smiling faces. Becky Lynn squared her shoulders. She couldn't help her mother, couldn't save her, no matter how much she wanted to.

The time had come to save herself.

Hiking her duffel bag higher on her shoulder, Becky Lynn turned her back on the house and life she had always known, and stepped out into the cold, black night.

Book Two

Jack

7

Los Angeles, California
1972

The way eight-year-old Jack Gallagher figured it, women were about the best things in the whole world. He loved the way they smelled, sweet like flowers, fresh like sunshine. He loved the way they felt, soft and warm and smooth; he loved their curves, their pillows of perfumed flesh, loved the way they spoke to him, in voices that were gentle and mostly lilting.

Jack's earliest remembrances were not of his mother, his crib or toys, but of the changing parade of girl-models who had cuddled and stroked him, the girls who had given him kisses and candy, who had wiped his baby tears and brought him gifts.

Many a time as an infant and toddler he had nestled his face into a pair of smooth, soft breasts, and basked in the pure joy of it. His mother, the most wonderful of all the wonderful women in the world, said he had the ability to turn even the most ill-tempered and demanding model into a candidate for Miss Congeniality with nothing more than an adoring look or smile.

Men, on the other hand, he had learned, were not so easy to please. They had no time or use for a boy's questions or curiosity. They made it plain that having him on the set was a nuisance they put up with only because of Sallie Gallagher's abilities as a makeup artist, and only for as long as it suited their purposes.

From the beginning, he understood the importance of staying out of the way, of staying quiet while the others worked. The Great Ones, the photographers who moved like kings through the studios, making demands and accepting total obedience and deference as their due, did not like being interrupted or disturbed, especially by a small, inconsequential boy. And their displeasure, when evoked, was both swift and fierce.

So Jack had found places to hide and play, had created imaginary worlds where he was always the hero—the inside of a circular rack of clothes would become a castle or cave, a group of chairs shoved into a corner a magnificent sailing ship, the prop room an enchanted kingdom.

From his secret places, he had seen and learned many things. The first time he'd seen what men and women did together, how they touched each other, he'd almost peed in his pants. He remembered staring in shock and thinking it gross, impossible. He remembered looking down at himself and wondering if his would ever get so big.

He had also learned the rules of grown-up life: that the truth was negotiable, as was just about everything else in the world with the exception of artistic integrity; that life operated on the barter system—you gave someone something they wanted, you got something you wanted in return; and finally, he had learned that beautiful things were special. The most special. To have beauty in your possession was to have a prize, a measurable commodity worth as much—or more—than any other.

Jack slumped onto the battered leather couch, shoved against the far wall of the busy studio. At eight, he was too old to play such games, too old to hide and pretend. Instead, he stayed in the background while The Great Ones worked. He watched. And made his plans.

Made his plans because the last and most important thing he had learned from his secret hiding places was who he really was.

Giovanni's bastard brat.

He hadn't known what those words meant, not the time he'd first heard them, but they had stuck with him. They sounded important, although something about the way they'd been uttered had made him feel dirty, as though he'd done something he should be ashamed of.

He had kept the words to himself, guarding them, turning them over in his head. When he had finally found the courage to ask his mother, she'd looked unhappy and upset, but had gently explained. He had nodded in understanding, and had never brought it up again. Neither had she.

Jack drew his knees to his chest and studied The Great One. Giovanni was the greatest of all The Great Ones, considered the king of all the kings, the reigning monarch of fashion photography.

His father. Giovanni was his father.

Jack sucked in a deep breath, willing away his nerves, the tight fist of hope burning in his chest. Sissies and babies were nervous. And Jack Gallagher was neither baby nor sissy. He was the great Giovanni's son, an important thing to be—he couldn't be weak, or nervous, or too hopeful. It was time he started becoming a man, like Giovanni. *His father.*

Jack cocked his chin proudly and pictured himself walking through the studio, his father's arm thrown casually but possessively across his shoulders. He pictured the others' looks, could almost hear their whispers—*Did you know, Jack is Giovanni's son...*

Jack had it all figured out; his mother had never told Giovanni that he was Jack's father, she couldn't have told. If she had, Giovanni wouldn't brush by him as if Jack were nothing, he wouldn't look through him as if Jack didn't exist.

She hadn't told because he was already married, and she didn't want to cause trouble with his wife. Jack drew his eyebrows together. He'd also considered that his mother hadn't wanted to share him with his father, but he didn't like to think that was true. He was sure she'd had her reasons, and even though he loved his mother, he wanted Giovanni to know. He wanted a father. He wanted *his* father.

He would tell him. Today.

Jack smiled to himself and imagined Giovanni's face when he told him. Imagined his initial surprise, then his pleasure. He would clasp Jack to his chest, then announce to all that he had found his son.

They would do things together. His father would show him how to do things, guy things. He would clap him on the shoulder in encouragement and approval, the way Jack had seen other fathers do to their sons.

Giovanni probably didn't like baseball or fishing or camping out, but that was okay. It didn't matter what the two of them did together, it was only important that they be together. That finally, he have his father.

A violent stream of Italian broke his reverie. Jack opened his eyes.

"I do not work with amateurs!" Giovanni shouted, in English now, handing his camera to his assistant. He strode forward to face the object of his displeasure, a young model just off the foreign circuit. She cringed.

"If you cannot give me what I want," he demanded, gesturing broadly as was his way, "what good are you? If I have to ask you twice, you cost too much. There are many pretty faces, *bella.* If you want to be the face who works with Giovanni, then you give me what I ask for. *Capisce?*"

"I'm sorry," she whispered, wetting her lips. "I'll try harder. I can do it. I know I can."

Giovanni lowered his voice and gently tipped her face up to his. He trailed his thumb across her damp lower lip. "That's what I want, *bella,* vulnerable. Your eyes now, they tell me everything. Yes!"

His assistant was beside him in a flash, handing him the camera. Giovanni began shooting immediately, alternating between shouting approval and insults.

The model would be in tears later, Jack knew. She would be exhausted, wrung out. He had seen this scenario played out a hundred times before. She would cry and curse and swear she was getting out of the business. She would curse Giovanni, call him a son of a bitch who deserved to die. But the chromes would be good. Very good. A successful session with Giovanni could make a career.

And later, she would trail adoringly after The Great One. And maybe, if The Great One was so inclined, she would do *it* with him.

Jack cocked his head to the side, studying the photographer as he worked. Giovanni was handsome, with the look of the Italian aristocracy he was reputed to be descended from. He had high cheekbones and a broad forehead, a chiseled mouth that could be either giving or forbidding, a slash of dark eyebrows over piercing eyes, eyes so dark they were almost black. He wore his hair brushed straight back from his face, and while he worked, it would sometimes fall across his forehead. The photographer would sweep it back with an impatience, a leashed power, that Jack watched with awe. Indeed, everything about Giovanni seemed powerful; he emanated it in waves that both exhilarated and cowed everyone around him.

Jack practiced being like Giovanni. At home he would stand in front of the mirror for hours, mimicking the older man's gestures, his looks, the way he spoke. He would gaze at his own reflection, searching for the resemblances between them and despairing at the few he found: the shape of his face was wrong, more narrow and angular; his eyes weren't dark and stormy, but the vivid blue of his mother's; his hair, chestnut instead of black, wavy instead of straight. So he stared at his reflection and willed himself to grow as strong as his father, as powerful.

He would make his father proud. He didn't know how or when, but he would.

Jack looked back at Giovanni. The photographer had wrapped for lunch; he was talking with the client and the ad agency's art director. Everyone else was either eating or socializing. Giovanni never ate. He never socialized. He prowled and smoked cigarettes, he checked his equipment, he conferred with his assistants and drank the espresso he insisted on having whenever and wherever he was shooting.

This would be his only opportunity to approach his

father, Jack knew. If he missed it, it could be weeks, or longer, before he got another.

As the art director and client walked away, leaving Giovanni alone, Jack jumped to his feet, excitement and stark terror clawing at his gut. He'd been waiting all his life for this day. He wasn't going to blow it just because he was scared.

He started across the studio toward the photographer, palms sweating, legs unsteady. He reached him and squared his shoulders. "Excuse me."

Giovanni turned slowly. He glared down at Jack, arching his eyebrows ever so slightly as if considering a pesky insect.

Jack shifted under the man's stare, panic turning his mouth to vinegar. "I…um…I—"

Those dark eyebrows arched a fraction higher, and the man made a soft sound of impatience. "Well?"

Jack shifted from one foot to the other, searching for the best way to start. He must have taken a fraction too long, because with a snort, Giovanni started to turn away.

Jack's heart stopped. He'd lost his chance! After all this time, all his waiting, he couldn't just let him walk away! He grabbed the photographer's arm. "Wait!"

Giovanni stopped and looked back. Beneath his hand, Jack felt the photographer stiffen.

"I just—" His throat closed over the words, and he cleared it. "I just wanted you to know that…you're my… dad."

Giovanni said nothing. He simply continued to stare at Jack, his expression unchanging. To his horror, Jack felt tears prick his eyes. They gathered in his throat and chest, threatening to choke him.

He fought them off, barely. "Did you…did you know that?"

"Of course." Giovanni frowned, his dark eyebrows lowering ominously. "Your mother and I have an arrangement."

An arrangement? His mother and Giovanni had…an arrangement? What did that mean? "I don't…understand. You're my father."

"I have a son. Carlo is my son." Giovanni shook off Jack's hand, turned and walked away.

Jack stared after him, frozen to the spot, his world crashing in around his ears. *Giovanni had already known about him. He had known all along.*

His father didn't want him. He had never wanted him.

Tears choked him. He thought of his dreams, his plans, thought of the hours he'd spent imagining them together as father and son, and a howl of pain and rage flew to his throat. He battled it back, fingers squeezed into tight fists.

His father had another son—Carlo. A son he called his own, a son he wanted. Hatred and jealousy built inside Jack, stealing his hurt, his urge to cry. Carlo, Jack thought again, despising the sound of the name.

Jack lifted his gaze. It landed on Giovanni, standing across the room, talking with a model. He set his jaw in determination. Giovanni would want him for his son. Someday, Jack promised himself. Someday, Giovanni would want him.

8

Someday, Giovanni would want him for his son.

Jack's promise to himself was never far from his mind. It burned bright and hot inside him, coloring each year that passed, years that transformed him from a trusting boy into a cocky, worldly-wise sixteen-year-old.

That day, those words, shaped his life. They gave him direction, focus. He vowed he would prove himself worthy of his father's love. He vowed he would show Giovanni what a great mistake he had made when he rejected him.

At first, he hadn't known how he would do it; he had only known the desire twisted in his gut so tightly, there were days he thought of nothing else. Then it had come to him. He would meet his father, and beat him, in his own arena.

So while the other boys in his class at high school had involved themselves with sports and girls and parties, he had planned his future. He read everything he could about photography, talked to every assistant who would give him the time of day, studied every photographer's technique, equipment preference and work habits.

He had needed a camera, so he had worked anywhere he could for anyone who would pay him. After school, he'd grocery shopped and run errands for the old ladies in the apartments around his and his mother's. At night, he'd bussed tables and done dishes at the Italian restaurant on the corner. At shoots, he'd done the gofer work everyone else hated. He now owned a used Nikon F2 with a motor drive and two lenses.

Jack ran his fingers lovingly over the camera's black metal body, over its levers and buttons. His camera. His first piece of professional equipment, the first of many. He would need a medium-format camera soon, more lenses, tripods, lights, umbrellas and darkroom supplies; he would need a place to work.

But the 35mm was a good place to start, it gave him flexibility and mobility. It was the single piece of equipment that Giovanni used more than any other.

Jack frowned and set the camera back on the shelf above his desk. Since that day eight years before, he'd only seen The Great One a handful of times. His mother had stopped bringing him to Giovanni's shoots. She'd claimed it was her own choice and had nothing to do with the photographer, but Jack thought otherwise. He believed Giovanni had asked her to keep him away. As if by keeping him out of sight, he could deny his existence.

Whenever Jack thought about it, his determination, and his anger, grew.

As did his curiosity about his half brother. He wondered about him: what he was doing, what he looked like, if they would like each other if they ever met. He never allowed himself the foolishness of imagining them as friends, as real brothers; facing his father had taught him a powerful lesson about caring too much and about opening himself for rejection. He had promised himself he would never be so naive again.

But he wondered about Carlo, anyway. He looked for him. For some mention of him, for a picture. His mother, an avid face-watcher, took all the fashion magazines, took glossies like *Vanity Fair* and *Lears,* took commercial pulp like *People.* He scoured them all.

Finally, he had found a mention in *People*'s Passages section. Carlo's mother, a former model, after having been involved in a tragic, disfiguring car crash, had committed suicide. The blurb mentioned her husband, fashion photographer great Giovanni, and their son Carlo.

Jack slid open the magazine and stared at the blurb and accompanying photograph, eyebrows drawn together in thought. She'd been beautiful, Carlo's mother. Now she was dead. Did that mean Carlo would come to live with Giovanni? Had he already? The magazine was many months old, the news could have been dated already by the time the magazine had gone to press.

From the other room, Jack heard the sounds of his mother moving around, getting ready for work. It was early, not quite six, but she had a shoot with Giovanni today, a big editorial spread for *Vogue,* and support staff had to be on location and working hours before the shoot actually began.

She would know about Carlo.

He stood, tucked the magazine under his arm and sauntered to the other room. His mother stood in front of her bathroom mirror, putting the finishing touches on her makeup. He cocked his head, considering his mother. Tall and curvaceous with flyaway sandy-colored hair, a scattering of freckles and a fondness for offbeat clothes, his mother looked part tomboy and part bohemian bombshell.

He stopped in the doorway and smiled at her. "Hey, Mom."

"Hey to you." She looked at him, and her eyes crinkled at the corners. "You're up and dressed early."

"You know how excited I get about school."

She made a face at his sarcasm. "If you put a little effort into it, you might enjoy it."

"I don't have anything in common with all those kids. They're like babies." He tucked his hands into the front pockets of his blue jeans. "Big job today?"

"Mmm. Giovanni has eight models booked. It's going to be tough wrapping the shoot in one day."

"I'd like to come. I could help out."

She frowned and dropped her lipstick into the small zipper bag she took everywhere. She met his gaze in the glass, then looked away. "You have school."

"So? I've missed before."

"You're in high school now. It's different. The stakes are higher."

"I get okay grades. I hold my own."

"You're very bright, Jack. And I'm proud of what you've done." She zipped the bag. "My answer is still no."

"I can't go because Giovanni doesn't want me around." He folded his arms across his chest. "That's it, isn't it?"

She sucked in a sharp breath. "We've been through this before, Jack. Your not coming has had nothing to do with Giovanni. It's been my decision."

"Is his precious *Carlo* going to be there? Is that why he doesn't want me around?"

She made a sound of surprise. "What do you know about Carlo?"

He handed her the magazine, opened to the blurb. She read it and met his eyes. "I see you know the basics."

Jack cocked his chin. "Is he living with his dear,

devoted daddy? Is that why I've been shut out of all the great man's shoots? Giovanni doesn't want his legitimate son dirtied by contact with his illegitimate one, right?"

He said the last with a sneer, and his mother's features tightened with anger. "You know better than that, Jack. *I* don't want you there because I don't think it's good for you. And yes, Carlo is living with his father. He's been on location with us."

"I want to get a look at him. That's all." Jack made a sound of frustration. "He's my half brother, I don't see why wanting that is so wrong."

She crossed to him. Even though she was tall and he was only sixteen, she had to tip her head back to meet his eyes. "I don't think it's good for you to be around Giovanni or Carlo."

"Why?"

She touched his cheek lightly then sighing, dropped her hand. "Isn't it obvious? Giovanni hurt you. The situation is hurtful. I love you, Jack. I don't want you hurt more than you already have been."

"I can handle it," he said, curving his fingers into fists. "I'm not a baby, after all. I'm not eight anymore. I won't cry, for Pete's sake."

She said nothing. He saw sympathy in her eyes, and he hated it. He turned away from her and crossed to the window. He stared out at the street for a moment before turning back to her, frustrated. "I want to go. I love going on location. Those people are my friends. I belong there."

She shook her head. "Not this time. I'm sorry. Maybe another."

"Mom, I—" He bit the words back, angry with her, furious that Carlo would be there, and he was being excluded. "You say you're doing this to protect me, it feels like you're punishing me."

"Oh, Jack. That's the last thing I want you to feel." She went to stand beside him, and laid a hand on his arm. "I don't think it's healthy for you to be around Giovanni or Carlo. Try to understand, I'm your mother and I have to do what I think is best for you."

"Well, you're wrong. It's not what's best." He shook off her hand, knowing it would hurt her. "It's unfair. And it stinks."

"I'm sorry, Jack, but I've made my decision."

"Thanks, Mom." He swung away from her. "Thanks a lot."

Jack went to school, but he didn't stay. He wanted to get a look at his brother. He wanted to meet him. He decided, despite what his mother wanted or thought, that was exactly what he was going to do.

The shoot was being held at Giovanni's studio; Jack had been there at least a hundred times before. Giovanni preferred studio work, he preferred sharp, controlled lighting and minimal backgrounds. Using both with figure and fashion created an almost surrealist fashion scenario, one that had been the hallmark of his style. Critics lauded his work as portraying the existentialism of modern life with a cool, sexual chic. It stirred the viewer. It created controversy. It had made him a star.

Giovanni's studio was located in an old warehouse district in Los Angeles. Not the most trendy or safest part of the city, it afforded the huge, reasonably priced spaces required by fashion photographers. Giovanni's space encompassed two floors of an old furniture warehouse. On those two floors there were changing and wardrobe rooms, several prop rooms, a room for makeup, one for hair, two bathrooms, an office and two large spaces for shooting, one with an abundance of natural light, one with none. The second-floor studio had an eight foot by eight foot section of floor that could be removed to provide dramatic, bird's-eye angle shooting from above.

Jack made it onto the set without problem. Tank, as everyone called Giovanni's doorman/driver/bouncer, let him in, commenting on how little they'd seen of him lately. Jack shrugged, told him he'd been busy and swaggered inside.

Jack saw that he'd come at a good time—things were not going well. Giovanni was shouting at everyone in English and Italian—the lighting wasn't right, the models were incompetent, his assistants slow. The entire staff was under fire, and everyone was rushing to make corrections and adjustments.

No one had time to notice him, and he made it to the second floor without being spotted by his mother. Jack found an unobtrusive spot behind the action and looked for *him*. He didn't have to look far. Carlo stood beside Giovanni, so close their shoulders almost brushed, hanging, Jack could tell, on his father's every word. As Giovanni talked, he put his hand on his son's shoulder. Possessively. Proudly. The way a father did a son.

Jack swallowed hard, not able to take his eyes from the two, even though watching them made him ache. Giovanni explained the lighting to Carlo, explained what he was looking for and why he wasn't satisfied. The father teaching the son, sharing his knowledge, his experience. The way a father was supposed to, the way Jack had once fantasized Giovanni would show and teach him.

"Hey, Jack."

He dragged his eyes from Giovanni and Carlo to look at the model who had come up to stand beside him. Gina was seventeen, but had started modeling on the circuit at twelve. Dressed now in a low-cut satin sheath, with her hair swept up on top of her head and diamonds dripping from her ears, she looked twenty-five. And sexy as hell. Many of his adolescent daydreams had centered around her.

Jack smiled. "Hey to you."

"That's Giovanni's son," the model whispered, following his gaze. "Carlo."

Giovanni's son. Hearing the words spoken affected him like a fist to his chest. His breath caught and he struggled to speak and breathe normally. "Yeah? How come I've never seen him before?"

"He's been around the last couple of months." She reached up to brush a curl off her forehead, then dropped her hand. One of the first rules of modeling was never touch your hair or face—doing so could ruin what the hair and makeup people had spent hours creating, and earn a major chewing out.

She leaned closer. "His mother killed herself. Slit her wrists. Rumor mill has it that he found her. Gross, huh?"

Jack's chest tightened. He couldn't imagine his mother doing such a thing, let alone finding her that way. "Tough break," he muttered, not wanting to feel sympathy even as the emotion welled up inside him.

Gina laid a hand on his arm. "He's cute, don't you think? He looks like his dad."

Sympathy evaporated, replaced by something harder and colder. Something that squeezed him so tightly, it hurt to breathe. Carlo did look like Giovanni. He had the man's dark hair and eyes, the same build and skin tone—all the things Jack had so longed to see in himself all those years ago.

He scowled at the model. "If you like that swarthy European type."

She giggled. "Sara does."

He arched his eyebrows, not in the mood for games. "What's that supposed to mean?"

She leaned even closer. "I hear he and Sara did *it*."

Jack caught a whiff of cosmetics and hair spray, her satin bodice brushed against his arm. His body stirred; his mouth turned to ash.

"Like father like son, I guess." She moved her fingers in a rhythmic sweeping motion on his forearm. "I hear Carlo gets around. A real party animal."

Jack swallowed, his eyes dropping to the plunging neckline of Gina's dress. He caught a glimpse of one small, round breast. "No way," he murmured, his jeans growing tight. He shifted uncomfortably, not thinking about Carlo doing it, but about himself doing it. With Gina. "He's just bragging."

"Uh-uh. I heard it from Sara herself." She giggled again and darted a glance over her shoulder. "I've got to go." She squeezed his arm and met his eyes. "Catch me later. Okay?"

Jack watched her walk away, his heart thundering, his mouth dry. He had kissed Gina. Once. He remembered that wet, desperate exchange in the dark wardrobe room and arousal tightened in his gut.

He had wanted to kiss her again, but they'd been interrupted. In truth, he had wanted to do more than kiss her. Much more.

He still did. So bad he ached.

Tugging, inconspicuously, he hoped, at the crotch of his jeans, he turned his gaze back to Carlo and Giovanni. Was it true? he wondered. Had Carlo and Sara done it?

He scowled, jealousy clawing at him. He didn't want to believe it, but Gina and Sara were friends, good friends. They were the same age and had gotten into the business about the same time. He couldn't imagine either of them lying about this.

That meant his brother had had sex. Something he had only fantasized about. *"Like father like son,"* Gina had said. Photography wasn't the only arena where his father was a legend. For years, Jack had listened to the models whisper behind their hands about what a great lover Giovanni was. Carlo, it appeared, was following in his father's footsteps.

An hour passed. While Giovanni worked in earnest, Carlo milled around the studio, talking and laughing with people on the set. Jack never took his eyes off the other boy, anger and resentment building inside him. These were his friends, people he had grown up with. He hated that Carlo seemed to have fitted in so quickly, he hated that everyone seemed to like his half brother. He told himself he had no reason to feel betrayed, but he did, anyway.

Carlo stopped beside Gina and bent close to whisper in her ear. The model tipped her head back and laughed, and Carlo placed his hand on the small of her back. He leaned close again, and as Jack watched, he moved his fingers a fraction lower.

Jack saw red. Gina was his, and he wasn't about to let this come-lately son of a bitch make a move on the girl he wanted. He thundered across the studio, not bothering with stealth, forgetting about Giovanni, about his mother and the fact he wasn't even supposed to be here.

Jack reached the two in moments and stopped beside them. "Take your hand off her," he said, fisting his fingers.

Carlo turned slowly and met Jack's eyes. "Excuse me?"

"You heard me." Jack glared at Carlo. "Take your hand off her. Now."

Carlo's mouth tipped up in a lazy, amused smile. "Fuck you. I don't hear her complaining."

Jack took a step closer, his blood boiling. "She doesn't have to, I'm complaining for her."

"Jack," Gina whispered, paling.

Carlo narrowed his eyes. He swept his gaze over Jack, recognition dawning in his eyes. "So you're the bastard."

Anger charged through Jack, but he held on to it. "And you're the dickhead."

"I wondered when we would meet." Carlo arched his eyebrows arrogantly. His English was perfect, but he spoke with a slight accent. The accent made him seem more mature, more sophisticated than Jack. Jack felt ten years younger instead of only one. He hated that.

While Jack struggled for a comeback, Carlo laughed softly. "Dad told me about you. He said you were…an embarrassment."

Jack wanted to lunge at him. He fought to control the urge. He took a step closer to the other boy. A full head shorter than his half brother, Carlo was forced to tip his head back to keep Jack's gaze. "That may be, but I could kick your ass."

"You Americans, always such cowboys. I've never understood it."

"You Italians, always such pussies. I've never understood it." They'd attracted attention, and a growing group gathered around them. Jack ignored them and curled his hands into fists. "Come on, I'll take you on right now."

"Dannazione!" Giovanni shouted, striding across the set, his face red with rage. "What the hell is going on?" A nervous titter moved through the crowd, even as it parted for him. He stopped in front of Carlo. "What are you doing?" he demanded again, turning his furious gaze on his son. "Explain yourself, Carlo. *Immediatamente!*"

Carlo paled, his cool arrogance disappearing. "Nothing. I wasn't doing anything." He cleared his throat. "I was just talking, and this…this boy started a fight."

Giovanni turned to Jack, his expression thunderous. "What are you doing here? You don't belong here."

Those words hurt more than any others could have. Jack slipped his fingers into the back pockets of his blue jeans and shrugged as if he didn't have a care in the world. "Hanging out. What are you doing here?"

Giovanni swore. "How dare you two disrupt this shoot."

"You're right," Carlo said quickly. "I'm sorry. My behavior was unforgivable."

Jack angled up his chin. "Seems to me, you're the one who's disrupting this shoot. We were just…talking."

"You impertinent little shit." The photographer swept back the hair that fell across his forehead. "Get out! I don't want to see you again. Not ever. You understand?"

"No problem, *Dad.* But you get this. One day, I'll be kicking you off my set. One day, you're going to see what a big mistake you made."

Giovanni hesitated, surprise flickering across his expression. Then he swore. "Tank! Escort this…*bastardo* out."

"Jack!"

Jack turned to see his mother pushing through the crowd, her expression stricken. He swore silently.

"What's going on?" She stopped beside him and looked from him to Giovanni to Carlo and back. "What are you doing here?"

Jack opened his mouth to explain; Giovanni spoke first. "I should fire you right now, Sallie. If I ever see your boy on my set again, I will. And if I fire you, nobody else will hire you. Got that?"

"You leave my mother out of this, you son of a bitch!" Jack faced the older man, his fists clenched. "I came on my own, and this has nothing to do with her."

"It has everything to do with her, because you're her son. Think of that the next time you decide to tangle with me." Giovanni clapped his hands. "Show's over. Everybody back to work."

Tank grabbed Jack's arm. He shook off the beefy man's hand. "I don't need any help," he said tightly. "I'm going."

He turned and walked away, aware of his mother's distress and his half brother's amusement. Emotions churned in his gut, and he muttered an oath. He hadn't meant to lose his cool. He hated that Carlo had gotten the best of him, hated that—

"Jack, wait!"

Jack stopped at the front door and turned. Gina hurried to catch up with him, her progress slowed by her gown's narrow skirt.

When she reached him, she glanced over her shoulder, then returned her gaze to him. "Outside."

They stepped through the door and sunshine spilled over them, almost blinding after the artificial light of the studio. She smiled. "I just wanted to, you know, tell you that I liked what you did in there." She lifted her shoulders. "I'm…flattered that you got into a fight over me. It was cool."

One corner of Jack's mouth lifted. "Yeah?"

"Yeah." She moved closer and laid her hands on his chest. She tipped her head back to gaze provocatively up at him. "I'm sorry you have to go, though."

He placed his hands on her hips, instantly aroused. "Come with me."

She made a sound of disappointment. "I can't. You know that."

He inched her closer. He wanted to kiss her, and he knew in his gut that she would let him. But he also knew it would ruin her mouth and get her in trouble. Instead, he trailed a finger over her collarbone and down to the place slippery satin ended and warm flesh began. She shuddered.

"Meet me later," he murmured.

"Where?"

"You tell me."

She thought a moment. "My house. Bring your books. I'll tell my mother you're helping me with my French."

"I don't know dip about French."

She smiled, slow and sexy, and his pulse went crazy. "Don't worry, Jack. I'll teach you."

She turned and walked to the door. When she reached it, she turned back to him. "Eight-thirty. I'm in the book." Without another word, she turned and walked inside.

9

By the time Jack got home, the rush of adrenaline and anger that had enabled him to boldly face down Giovanni had evaporated, leaving in its wake shaking hands, a runaway heart and legs that felt like rubber.

Jack fell onto his bed and struggled to draw in a deep, even breath. He couldn't put his mother's face, her stricken expression, out of his mind. Giovanni had blamed her for her son's actions. He had threatened to fire her, had warned that if he did, no one else in the industry would hire her.

The last hadn't been an idle threat. He had seen the cold determination in the photographer's eyes. Giovanni didn't care about Sallie Gallagher or her livelihood; he wouldn't think twice about ruining her professional reputation.

And, Jack knew, it wouldn't take much. *Getting fired once could do it.* The fashion industry was a small one, one in which everyone knew everybody else's business. He'd seen people from every area of the business have to fight their way back after having screwed up once. Time was money, the client's money. And clients paid astronomical day rates for models and photographers and support personnel. One major shoot could cost upward of a hundred thousand dollars. Everyone had to do their job, do it well and quickly.

Jack glared at his ceiling, at the long, thin crack that ran diagonally across it. Dammit. He'd really messed things up for her. He hadn't thought further than himself, hadn't considered the consequences of his actions or that they might affect anyone else. It had never even occurred to him. It did now.

Gina. He squeezed his eyes shut, arousal charging through him. She had told him to "catch her later" and had promised to teach him French.

French. Did that mean what he thought it did?

Tonight could be the night. It could happen, he could lose his virginity.

He sat up and dragged his hands through his hair, his head filled with images of Gina: Gina smiling at him; Gina, her body outlined by clinging satin; Gina, her lips moist and parted. He sucked in a sharp breath. He'd been waiting his whole life for this opportunity. He wasn't about to miss it.

Four hours later, Jack glanced at the stove, at the pot of Ragú spaghetti sauce that bubbled there. He had made a salad, Italian bread was buttered and ready for the oven.

Where was she? He looked at the clock and frowned. Almost six-thirty. At five, everyone connected with a shoot either went home or on overtime. And overtime was avoided at all costs.

So, where was she?

Even as the question moved through his head for the dozenth time, he heard the front door open. *Show time.* He took a deep breath, suddenly feeling six instead of sixteen. "Hey, Mom," he called. "I'm in here."

She came into the kitchen. Without looking at him, she dropped her purse on the counter and reached for the mail.

He cleared his throat. "Hi, Mom."

She lifted her gaze from the mail and fixed it on him. She didn't smile. "Hello, son."

He swallowed hard. She was still angry. And she was hurt. He felt like a complete jerk. "I made dinner."

"I see that." She returned her attention to the mail. "It looks good."

She said nothing more, and he shifted from his right foot to his left, her silence damning and uncomfortable. Unable to take it another moment, he cleared his throat again. "I'm sorry, Mom. I really am."

She met his eyes. "Are you?"

He hung his head and stubbed the toe of his Nike against the tile floor.

"I can't tell you how upset I am by this." She made a sound of frustration. "What were you thinking of? Disobeying me that way, behaving like that at a shoot? You know better."

"I'm sorry," he said again, folding his arms across his chest but hiking his chin up stubbornly. "I didn't think. I just…reacted."

"Do you see now why I didn't want you there? Do you understand?" She crossed to the stove and stared at the pot of sauce for long moments, then turned to face him once more, her expression troubled. "Did you get it out of your system, Jack? Do you think you can leave it alone now?"

"What do you mean?" He drew his eyebrows together. "Get what out of my system?"

"Carlo, Giovanni, the whole thing. This obsession you have isn't healthy. I sympathize, I do. But—"

"Obsession?" he interrupted. "You think I'm *obsessed* with them? Great, Mom. Just great."

"What do you expect me to think?" She crossed to

stand before him and looked him directly in the eye. "Why do you want to be a fashion photographer?"

"It has nothing to do with *him*." He glared at her, so angry he could hardly speak. "I…I just like it. It's cool."

"Oh, Jack."

"I hate when you say my name like that, as if you pity me." He spun away from her, crossed to the refrigerator, then faced her once more, fists clenched. "What do you expect me to feel? Shouldn't I be curious about my half brother? Shouldn't I wonder about him? Is that so weird? Maybe you'd understand if your mother had put you in the same position. But she didn't, did she?"

Sallie flinched at the blow. "You have to let your anger and your hurt go, Jack. You say I can't understand them, but I think I can. You have to let them go."

She crossed the room and stopped in front of him. She reached out to touch his cheek, but he jerked his head away. "Don't let your anger at Giovanni, or me, control your life. If you do, it'll ruin it."

She didn't understand, Jack thought. He wasn't hurt, he wasn't even angry. He hated Giovanni. And he was going to show him what a big mistake he had made.

"You know about that. Right, Mom? About ruining lives."

She took a step back from him, looking as if he had slapped her.

Remorse barreled through him, but he knew it was too late to take back his words.

"How have I ruined your life?" she asked softly. "By having you? By loving you?"

"I'm sorry," he said softly, stuffing his hands into his front jeans pockets. "I didn't mean that."

"But I think you did. And that's why I'm worried."

"Mom—"

"No." She held up a hand. "No more. Not now." She glanced at her watch and sighed. "There are some things I need to discuss with you, but I can't now. I'm going out tonight."

"Out?" Jack repeated, surprised. His mother rarely went out at night. She spent so much time on location out of town that when in town, she enjoyed being home.

"I'm meeting an old friend." She slipped out of her vest and hung it on the back of one of the chairs set up around the small oak table. "You've never met her. She got out of the business right around the time you were born."

"She was a makeup artist, too?"

"She did hair. She opened her own salon fifteen years ago and has done quite well."

Jack frowned. Something about his mother's tone bothered him. "Why are you meeting her?"

She met his gaze, drawing her eyebrows together. "I told you, she's an old friend. Besides, it's not your place to question me. I'm the parent here, and you're in big trouble."

"But Mom—"

"No buts." She crossed to the phone. "I'm calling Mrs. Green next door to let her know I'm going out and to ask her to check up on you."

"Check up on me?" Jack squared his shoulders, outraged. "I'm sixteen, not twelve."

"Then act it." She picked up the phone. "You're not to leave the house. No television tonight, no phone, no stereo."

No Gina. He took a step toward her, hand out in entreaty. "But, Mom, I wanted to ask if I could go—"

"No way." She punched out the neighbor's number, then propped the phone to her ear with her shoulder. "You're grounded."

Grounded? He bristled. She had never done that to him before, and he didn't like it. Not one bit.

When she got off the phone, they ate dinner. Quickly and without conversation. They straightened up the kitchen together, then she went to freshen up. While she did, Jack thought about Gina, about her invitation and about the evening's possibilities.

The evening had no possibilities, he reminded himself glumly. He was *grounded*. Swearing under his breath, he dragged out the phone book and looked up Gina's number.

He found it, picked up the phone, then returned the receiver to its cradle without dialing. He wasn't going to cancel his date.

Mrs. Green never heard a thing. He called the woman early, told her he wasn't feeling well and was going to turn in. Although only eight, it sounded as if he had awakened her. *Some watchdog.* He slipped out of the apartment and headed down the street to Tony's, the Italian restaurant where he worked. Danny, one of the other busboys, had offered to lend Jack his wheels before. Tonight, Jack was going to take him up on his offer.

With a promise to have the car back by midnight, he started off. Gina lived in the Hollywood Hills, located in the foothills of the Santa Monica Mountains. He found her house without a problem, though it took longer than he had expected.

Grabbing the stack of textbooks—none of them

French—he started up her walkway. He prayed she was here and wasn't too mad that he was late.

Gina opened the door before he had a chance to knock. She wore a pair of tight-fitting jeans and a chambray shirt, tucked into her denims and unbuttoned at her throat. He moved his gaze over her, his chest tight. "You look… great."

"Thanks." She smiled. "I thought you weren't coming."

"Sorry. It was tough getting out tonight."

"Your mom's really pissed, huh?"

"You could say that." Gina stepped aside so he could enter. He looked around. The house was modest in size but very nice; the wall across from the door was covered with framed copies of Gina's ads and magazine covers.

"My mother's wall of glory," she murmured, following his gaze.

He returned his gaze to her. "Where is she?"

"Out with her boyfriend." Gina made a face. "The guy's a sleaze ball."

Her mother was out? Jack's pulse began to thud. "She didn't mind that I was coming over?"

"She didn't know, and she won't be home till late. She never is." Gina grinned and motioned with her head. "Come on."

She led him to the back of the house, to a large, comfortable room outfitted with leather furniture, light oak paneling and wall-to-wall bookshelves. "This was my dad's room before he left. I spend a lot of time in here."

"Your dad left?"

"A couple years ago. He's living in Laguna now with his girlfriend." She wrinkled her nose in distaste. "Mom says it's a case of arrested development. Sharla isn't much older than I am." Gina shuddered. "I have friends older than she is."

"I'm sorry."

Gina shrugged and plopped down onto a big couch. She patted the seat next to her. "Sit by me."

He swallowed, his throat dry, and realized he was nervous. He berated himself silently. He would bet Carlo was never nervous. He would bet that by now, Carlo would have already gotten his hand in her pants.

Disgusted with himself, Jack crossed and sat on the couch. He turned to face her, and threaded his fingers through her silky blond hair. "You're so beautiful," he murmured.

She flushed, pleased. Cupping the back of her head, he drew her toward him and kissed her, slowly and deeply. She sighed and wound her fingers in his hair.

He ended the kiss, but didn't release her or move away. "I've been fantasizing about doing that since the last time."

Her lips curved up. "Then why don't you do it again?"

Jack didn't have to be asked twice. He caught her mouth, then her tongue. Gina didn't waste any time. Their lips pressed together, she unbuttoned his shirt. When she'd pushed it off his shoulders, she started unbuttoning her own.

He pushed her hands away, and with shaking fingers did it for her. Within moments, she was nude from the waist up. Jack gazed at her perfect breasts, at their soft fullness, at her nipples, standing straight out, begging for his mouth, and he struggled to get his breath. He thought he might explode just looking at her.

"You can touch them," she whispered, straddling his lap. With a groan, he cupped her breasts, then buried his face in them. She smelled like flowers and felt like heaven. He breathed deeply, his heart thundering in his chest, the pulse in his head.

She rocked against him, her soft pelvis to his hard one, his arousal painfully evident. He sucked in a ragged breath and shifted his hips. "Oh, God, Gina…" He groaned and moved against her again.

She wrapped her arms around his neck and nipped his earlobe. "Did you bring a rubber?"

His heart stopped, then started again with a vengeance. *He'd blown it! Shit, shit… How could he have been such an idiot?*

Groaning, he dropped his head against the couch back. "I didn't…uh…think that we were—"

"Going to do it?"

"Yeah."

She rested her hands on his shoulders. "You're a virgin, aren't you?"

Jack flushed, thought about lying, but figured he wouldn't get away with it. He nodded. "Are you?"

"Nope. Lost it at fourteen. To my uncle."

"Your uncle?" Jack repeated, swallowing hard. "Did he, you know?"

"Rape me?" She shook her head. "Nothing like that. And it's not as bad as it sounds. He's my father's brother by his father's second marriage. He was only twenty-four."

She leaned into him and her breasts pressed against his chest. It felt so incredible, he thought he was going to die. "Does that bother you?" she asked.

"That you did it with your uncle?"

"No." She rocked her pelvis against his once more. "That I'm not a virgin."

Jack couldn't see why it would bother a guy. After all, the two of them fumbling their way through the act couldn't be nearly as pleasurable as her guiding him would be. He shook his head. "Does it bother you that I am?"

"I think it's sweet. I've never been anybody's first before." She walked her fingers up his chest. "I liked the way you stood up to The Great One today."

He smiled. "Yeah?"

"It was a real turn-on. I never saw anybody stand up to him before."

"Maybe more people should." He slipped his arms around her and stroked her back. "He's an arrogant asshole."

"So, do you want to do it?"

He wanted to do it so bad, he felt as if he were going to explode. He forced back the frenzy building inside him. "What about…protection?"

She thought for a moment, then grinned. "We're safe. No way am I getting pregnant tonight."

Thank God. He had waited so long for this.

They came together in a frenzy of mutual excitement. Jack moved his hands, then his mouth, over her. Her skin was soft and warm and white. And so smooth. He cupped and kneaded and stroked her breasts. He nipped and licked her nipples, liking the way they drew into tight buds, not able to get enough.

She fell onto her back, dragging him with her. He ran his fingers over her curves and valleys, he slipped his hand under the waistband of her jeans, not stopping until he reached the crisp curls at the apex of her thighs. He dipped his hand in, touching a woman for the first time. She was unbelievably hot there, and wet. He slipped his fingers into her and she cried out, throbbing against his hand.

He almost came in his pants. He took his hands away from her long enough to strip out of his clothes, his jeans almost impossible to get off because of his erection. She wiggled out of her jeans, too, and after she kicked them aside, she drew him on top of her, then inside her.

She was hot and wet and tight. The breath hissed from his lungs. *So this is what it's all about,* he thought, amazed, stunned. *No wonder…no wonder…*

He would never be the same, he knew. In the space of a heartbeat, his life was changed forever. This thing, this act, was more powerful than anything he had ever experienced or felt, with the exception of his hatred for Giovanni. And where his hatred for Giovanni ate at him, this released him. He suddenly understood things he hadn't before— why his mother had done what she'd done, why she had gotten involved with a man who didn't love her, why men and women hurt each other, why they clung to each other.

With understanding, some of his anger slipped away. His mother hadn't had a choice, this pull was too strong to deny.

He didn't know how he had lived so long without this. He knew he would never be able to live without it again.

Her body caressed his, stroked his. He moved instinctively, racing toward release, too involved in his own pleasure, and wonder, to think about hers. And then it was over, quicker than he would have liked. Much quicker.

He ran his fingers over her face, already thinking about doing it again, wondering if she would. Wondering now, too late, if she had been satisfied, worrying that she hadn't.

He had read things, had heard the models talk about which guys were the best lovers, which ones took the time to make them happy. He wanted Gina to be happy. He wanted to be one of the photographers they whispered about and called a fantastic lover. The way they whispered about Giovanni.

Her eyes were closed. He cleared his throat, and she looked at him. "Was it…okay for you? I…hope it was."

She smiled, her eyes filling with tears. "Yeah. Thanks for asking. Nobody has before."

He frowned and threaded his fingers through her hair. "Nobody?"

"Uh-uh. We were always more rushed." She slipped her hands behind his neck, her expression somehow sad. "Except for the first time, it was always on location. So we had to hurry. And be careful not to muss my face and hair."

He wanted to ask who she had made it with. The question pushed at him, but he fought it back. He rolled onto his side so they faced each other. He wasn't surprised, not really. He knew what went on between models, photographers and about everyone else associated with the business.

It was just that Gina was so young and that until this year—as was industry practice—her mother had accompanied her to every go-see, every shoot. He asked her about it.

She nuzzled her face into his shoulder. "Mother and I have been doing this so long, she doesn't notice much anymore. Besides, she's so caught up in the whole thing, I don't think she would have minded if she had known I was doing it with Giovanni."

Jack stiffened, and she smiled. "I know what you're thinking, that he's so old. But he's still sexy. He makes it with everybody. Besides, it was kind of a thank-you for using me that first time."

"You've only done it with him once?"

"Uh-huh." She lifted her chin. "Did you know, I was the youngest one there today. Of all the girls, I had the least experience."

He didn't reply and after a moment, she drew her eyebrows together, studying him silently. "Does that… gross you out or anything?"

He thought of her doing it with Giovanni and wanted to retch. But he supposed he could understand. Giovanni was a powerful force in the fashion community; he could do a model many favors. So he lied. "Why should it?"

"Well, I heard something today. Can I ask you about it?" Jack had an idea what she had heard but told her to ask anyway. "I heard that you're his son. Giovanni's."

"His bastard son. Yeah, it's true."

"Wow. I've never known one of those before. A bastard," she said as if testing the sound on her tongue. "What's it like?"

He shrugged nonchalantly as if he had never thought about it before. "I don't know. It's just the way it is."

"It's pretty cool." She sat up and stretched, her breasts lifting with the movement. He became instantly erect. "Did you know that Kim got a nose job free for doing it with a plastic surgeon she met at an agency party? Sara's decided she's going to get some tits. I might get a boob job, too. What do you think?"

He thought he was going to pop off just looking at her. He reached up and cupped her breasts. "I think they're perfect."

"They're too small." She arched her back as he moved his hands. "Shooters are always saying so."

Jack sat up and brought his mouth to them. She whimpered with pleasure. "They're crazy," he muttered, taking a nipple into his mouth and sucking it. "I think they're terrific."

For long minutes, they didn't speak. Jack continued to kiss and stroke and cup her breasts. He found loving her that way unbelievably satisfying, exciting. He couldn't get enough of her.

He brought his mouth to hers. "I want to taste you everywhere. I want to touch you, to stroke you." He caught her bottom lip and drew it into his mouth. "I want to make you come."

She shuddered, and he pushed her backward gently, until she lay sprawled on the couch. He splayed his hands across her abdomen and lowered his head. Her belly quivered as he trailed his lips and tongue across her soft, warm flesh. "You taste so good, Gina. You're so beautiful, so soft…"

She tangled her fingers in his hair. He touched her everywhere. He explored and learned, about a woman's body and about what pleased this woman. She arched and moaned and squirmed. She tried to pull him to her, again and again, but each time he stopped her. He wanted to please her, but he also wanted to know, finally, how to please a woman.

He slid his hands between her thighs, moving them up until he found her center. Wet and almost unbearably hot, he sank into her.

"Can I taste you here?" Jack didn't wait for her answer, but placed his mouth exactly where he longed for it to be. She gasped and lifted her hips off the couch in response; he tasted and tested again.

He grew bolder, his body tautened, as she whimpered

and moaned, as she squirmed under his hands, to his kisses, his caresses. He couldn't get enough of her, couldn't taste enough. He found every part of her body to be perfect, enchanting. He loved her every texture and scent, every taste, every sound she made.

She cried out and bucked up against his mouth, her hands twisted in his hair. He felt her throb and quiver, and he knew a sense of such overwhelming power. In that moment, she was his. He was the center of her universe. He had made her cry out with pleasure, only him.

His control slipped, and while she still shook with her release, he thrust into her. She wrapped her arms and legs around him, and they rocked together until he exploded inside her.

Afterward, she stared at him in adoration and shock. "That's never...I never..." She let the words trail off, looking embarrassed and near tears.

Jack threaded his fingers through her damp hair. "Didn't you like it?"

She flushed. "I loved it."

He leaned his forehead against hers and grinned. "So did I."

For a long time after that, they didn't speak. They lay on their sides, facing each other, Jack's sweater pulled partially over them. The mantel clock ticked loudly in the otherwise quiet room.

Gina's eyes were closed, her breathing soft and even. "Are you asleep?" he asked.

She opened her eyes. "No. Just thinking."

"What about?"

She caught her bottom lip between her teeth. "I was wondering, where did you learn to do, you know, all that?"

"I've seen and heard a lot of stuff. Mostly on location."
He grinned. "You'd be surprised what a kid can learn by
keeping his eyes and ears open."

She giggled. "I like surprises."

She fell silent again, and Jack propped himself up on an
elbow to gaze down at her. She arched her eyebrows.
"What?"

"Just looking."

"Oh."

"Gina?" She met his eyes again. "Are you going to
keep modeling?"

"For sure. After this semester, I'm quitting school. I'm
already a year behind, and I can't keep up."

"School's not my favorite thing, but my mother would
have a fit if I even thought about dropping out."

"Mine doesn't care. This is my career, and I can only
do it while I'm young." She tilted her head, studying him.
"What are you going to do when you get out of school?
Go to college?"

He shook his head. "I'm going to be a fashion photographer."

"Like your dad."

"I don't think of him that way," Jack corrected grimly.
"The only thing we have in common is blood. You've got to
give a shit to be a father. Or a son. Besides," he said, his voice
tight with determination, "I'm going to be better than him."

"Carlo's going to be a fashion photographer, too. He
told Sara."

Jack narrowed his eyes. "I'm going to be better than
both of them. You can bet on it."

She looked up at him, her cheeks and eyes glowing. "I
believe you will be."

"Do you, Gina?" He smiled at her, pleased, feeling suddenly like the experienced one, the one in control.

"Yes," she whispered, her voice thick. "I think you're going to be able to do anything you put your mind to."

He pressed his mouth to hers in a quick, hard kiss. "When did you say your mother was going to be home?"

Together they glanced at the wall clock. "Not for a while."

"Great." He curved his lips into a slow, satisfied smile. "As long as we're here, what would you say about—"

He leaned close to her and whispered what he would like to do in her ear. Laughing, she drew him to her again.

Much later, Jack and Gina dressed in silence. He felt spent, energized, taut, and relaxed all at the same time. Gina walked him to the door, facing him when they reached it. "I wish you didn't have to go," she said softly, her cheeks bright with color.

He cupped her face, leaned down and kissed her. "Can I call you?"

She sighed. "Oh, yes."

He opened the door and started through it. She caught his hand, stopping him. "Jack?"

"Hmm?"

"Tonight, I did it with you just because I…wanted to. It didn't have anything to do with…anything else." She clung to his hand. "And it's never…been that way for me before. It's never felt so…good."

Satisfaction and pride swelled inside him. He brought their joined hands to his mouth. "Gina, can I ask you something? It's important."

She nodded, searching his serious expression. "Anything."

"Don't have sex with him. With Carlo. Okay?"

"Because he's your brother?"

"Because I don't like him. I don't like him a lot." He tightened his fingers on hers. "It's really important to me, Gina. Can you promise?"

"I promise, Jack." She smiled up at him. "I'd do anything for you."

10

"Jack. It's time to get up."

Jack cracked open his eyes. His mother stood in his bedroom doorway, her expression troubled. His pulse began to thud in his head. She had found out about last night. But how? He had returned his friend's car by the stroke of midnight, and had beaten his mother home by thirty minutes. He had heard her come in, had pretended to be deeply asleep when she had looked in on him.

But still, he could see that something was wrong.

"Morning," he managed to say, his voice a rasp. He struggled into a sitting position. "What's up?"

She crossed the room to his bed, then sat gingerly on its edge. "We need to talk about what went on yesterday."

Images of him and Gina flew to his head, and his manhood stirred.

He swore silently and quickly shifted his gaze, afraid that if he looked her in the eye, she would read every one of his thoughts, that she would know.

"How are you feeling?" She laid her hand on his forehead. "You're a little flushed."

He jerked his head back, embarrassed. "I'm fine, Mom."

"Mrs. Green told me you called. Early." She drew her eyebrows together in concern. "You're sure you're okay? You feel a little warm."

If his mother knew why he felt warm, if she could read his mind, she would have a heart attack.

He sat up straighter and looked her in the eye. "I wasn't sick, Mom."

"You weren't?" She shook her head, confused. "Then why did you call Mrs. Gre—"

"I sneaked out."

She drew a sharp, surprised breath. "You what?"

"I sneaked out. I had a date with Gina."

"Gina, the model?" his mother asked faintly.

"I went to her house." *And fucked my brains out. It was the greatest night of my life.* "To study with her," he added, lacing his fingers together in his lap. Surely he could live with the small lie? After all, there were things a son could never tell his mother, even in an effort to be honest. "She invited me over when I was at the shoot yesterday."

His mother stared at him a moment, obviously thrown off balance by his admission. "Why didn't you ask me if you could go?"

"I started to, but you grounded me."

"But you went, anyway."

He hiked his chin up a fraction at the hint of both hurt and puzzlement in her voice. "Yes."

She searched his expression. "And you're not sorry?"

He thought of the night before and shook his head. How could he be sorry? Last night had been the most wonderful experience of his life. "I'm sorry I tricked you."

"You're grounded again. For a month."

"I know. I understood the consequences last night."

She stood and crossed to his bedroom window. For several moments, she stared out at the day, the bright sky marred by smog. "You could have gotten away with it. I didn't know," she said as she swiveled to look at him.

"Yeah." He lowered his gaze to his hands, then lifted it to hers once more. "But a man stands up for his actions."

"A man? Oh, Lord." She brought a hand to her head, making a sound of dismay. "What am I going to do with you? I'm way out of my depth here."

"It's okay, Mom. Every kid grows up."

She laughed and turned back to the window, the choked sound anything but amused. He saw that her fingers shook as she ran them along the window ledge.

"What's wrong?"

She turned and met his eyes. "You're only sixteen, that's what's wrong. Practically a baby, still. You're my…" She shook her head and looked out the window again.

For a long time, she said nothing. Then she suddenly faced him once more. "For a long time, I've been thinking about making a change. And I… Last night, I came to a decision. I'm getting out of the business."

Jack stared at her, confused. "What do you mean, getting out of the business?"

"Just what it sounds like. I'm not going to do fashion work anymore." She crossed to the bed, and gazed solemnly down at him. "This is no life for you, Jack. Lord knows, I should have seen it a long time ago."

"No life for me?" He shook his head, struggling to digest her words. "I love what we do."

"*We* don't do it, Jack." She pressed a hand to her chest. "I do. I'm a makeup artist, it's how I make a living. You're supposed to live like a kid. Like a regular teenager. You're supposed to go to football games and dances. You're supposed to have a steady girlfriend and go to the movies with your friends. You're not supposed to be surrounded by adults all the time."

"That's such bullshit!"

"Jack!"

He threw back the covers and sprang out of bed. "Well, it is!" He flexed his fingers, his heart thundering. "Who says I'm supposed to live differently? Just because your childhood was different than mine, just because the kids at school's lives are different than mine, doesn't mean mine's been wrong. Maybe they're the ones whose lives are weird."

She shook her head. "You don't understand. You don't see because you're—"

"This has something to do with *him,* doesn't it? After yesterday, he said something to you, didn't he?" Jack glared at her, furious. "What say does he have in my life? You have an *arrangement,* remember? I'm yours and he doesn't give a shit."

"This has nothing to do with Giovanni. And don't swear at me."

"Then don't do this, Mom."

Wearily, Sallie brought a hand to her forehead. "I see I've made the right decision, only too late. I don't know how I could have let this go on so long. Taking you out of school so often, away from your friends, from any semblance of a normal—"

"I don't have any friends at school."

"Because you're not there enough."

"No, because they bore me. I've been all over the world, a lot of those kids haven't been farther than their grandmother's house."

"Jack, try to understand. I want what's best for you. And

this isn't it. This anger you have isn't it." She took a deep breath. "I've been thinking about making this change for a long time. Since you were eight and Giovanni…" She shook her head again. "But I didn't know what I could do. How I would support us. Now I know."

She paused, as if giving him a chance to question her. He folded his arms across his chest and refused to look at her.

She made a sound of frustration and crossed once more to the window. "I'm going to open my own shop. Hair, makeup and make-overs. The kind of shop—"

"A beauty parlor?" he said, disbelieving. "Great, Mom. You're going to go from working on the most beautiful women in the world to doing little old ladies with blue hair."

She stiffened. "My shop is not going to cater to 'little old ladies with blue hair.' It's going to cater to people of fashion. People from the industry, and people with the money to follow, and make, trends. The work we do is going to be trendsetting, it's going to be fashion." She crossed her arms and narrowed her eyes. "Besides, as you very well know, I don't do hair."

He didn't reply, just glared stonily at her, and she went on. "The money will be better. Steadier. Won't that be nice? After all, you might want to go to college someday. How would I afford that?"

"I don't care about college. I'm going to be a fashion photographer. You know that."

"Oh, Jack."

"It's not what you think." He hiked up his chin. "It's not because of Giovanni."

"No?"

"No." He squared his shoulders, determined. "I don't want to be like him. I'm going to be better than him."

She clasped her hands together and met his gaze evenly. "He's financing the shop for me."

"What?" Jack fisted his fingers, rage and impotence roiling inside him. Unable to stay still, he strode across the room, then back, stopping in front of his mother, shaking with fury. "I can't believe that after everything, you would do this. I can't believe you would get in bed with him again."

She stared at him a moment, shocked silent. When she spoke, her voice quivered with both hurt and anger. "This is a good thing for me. For us. I'm getting too old to travel the circuit, and whether you realize it or not, you need a normal life. I'm grateful to Giovanni for this. He's not doing it because he slept with me years ago... Lord knows, he's slept with everybody. He's doing it because he believes it will be a successful business venture. And because he believes in my abilities, as a makeup artist and a businesswoman. Something you obviously don't."

She stalked to the door, turning to face him once more when she reached it. "If you don't see that, well, it's too damn bad. Because it's my life and my career, and I'm the one who makes the decisions around here."

"I do believe in you," Jack retorted, flexing his fingers. "More than he does."

"It's not a competition, Jack."

"No? Then why does it feel like one?"

Her expression softened. "That's a good question, son. It's one I suggest you think about."

His eyes burned, and he lifted his chin again, stubbornly, defiantly. He cleared his throat. "When's this...this thing going to happen?"

"I'm going to start working on it right away. The first thing I've got to do is find the right space. Will you help me?"

He let out his breath in an angry snort. "No way."

"Fine. I would have liked to have you with me on this, but I can do it without you."

"Go for it." He refused to look at her. "Have a ball."

"Do you want to know what I'm going to call it?"

"Not particularly."

She didn't take no for an answer but then, he hadn't really expected her to. "The Image Shop. What do you think?"

"The Image Shop," he repeated softly, liking the sound of it, hating that he did.

"Well?"

He swung toward her, and met her gaze evenly. A dozen different emotions barreled through him, not the least of which was frustration. "I think it sucks, Mom. I think this whole thing sucks."

Book Three

The Image Shop

11

Los Angeles, California
1984

Becky Lynn stood in the center of the biggest, busiest bus terminal she had ever seen, frozen to the spot in terror. She didn't know which way to go or what to do next. People, strange-looking people of all colors and in all kinds of dress, wove their way around her. All with purpose, all seeming to have someone to meet or someplace to go. Many shot her angry glances for blocking the way, a few bumped into her as they passed, then continued on their way without a murmur of apology or regret.

She clutched her duffel bag to her chest, afraid someone might try to snatch it. A woman on the last bus had warned her of that possibility and to be careful.

Becky Lynn drew in a deep, fortifying breath. This wasn't what she had expected but then, so far, nothing about her journey had been—from the one hundred and forty-five dollars the one-way ticket had cost her to the alternating fear and relief she had felt during the course of the two-day trip. With a shudder of apprehension, she wondered what other surprises awaited her.

Taking another deep breath, she started blindly forward,

moving with the crowd. She couldn't stand in one spot forever, no matter how reassuring it felt.

She caught sight of an information counter and angled toward it. She stopped in front of the counter and waited. The woman on the other side didn't look up from her magazine. Becky Lynn cleared her throat. "Excuse me."

The woman lifted her gaze. Her eyes widened a bit, as if in horror, then her expression melted back into one of jaded disinterest. "Yeah? Can I help you?"

"Could you please tell me how I get to…" Becky Lynn's voice trailed off. Where did she want to go? She couldn't point at the woman's magazine, opened to a sunny ad and say, *"How do I get there?"*

"Can I help you?" the woman said again, impatiently.

"Hollywood," Becky Lynn said. "How do I get to Hollywood?"

The woman narrowed her eyes, fringed with thick, dark lashes, and moved them over Becky Lynn. "Honey, you're a long way from home, aren't you?"

"Yes, ma'am."

The woman shook her head, as if in resignation. "Your best bet is a city bus." She reached under the counter and produced a map and schedule. She slid it across to Becky Lynn, circling a place on the map with a red pencil. "Catch it here. It's a dollar-ten, exact fare."

"Thank you." Becky Lynn scooped up the map. "Oh, and which way is the ladies' room?"

Attention already shifted back to her magazine, the woman indicated the general direction without looking up. Becky Lynn followed and within moments stood before the bathroom mirror.

She gazed at her reflection, her stomach turning. No

wonder the woman behind the counter had looked at her that way, no wonder people on the bus had averted their gaze from her. She looked awful. She looked like what she was, a runaway, a victim of violence.

She moved her gaze over her reflected image. After forty-eight hours on or between buses, her hair was snarled and ready for a scrubbing. Her jaw, swollen and a bluish green, stood out in stark contrast to her unnaturally pale skin. Her eyes were hollow and dark from sleeplessness, her clothes dirty and rumpled.

Her vision blurred, and she grabbed the edge of the sink, light-headed. Except for the half of a bologna sandwich and Oreo cookie that the woman riding beside her between Dallas and Los Angeles had given her, and the few things she'd gotten from vending machines along the route before that, she'd had nothing to eat since leaving Bend.

She sucked in a deep breath, pain mixing with hunger. She hurt so bad, the bruises on her face, the ones on her body, inside her body. She hadn't wanted to eat, but had known if she didn't, she would collapse.

Becky Lynn fished in her pocket for the small bottle of aspirin the same woman who had shared her food had given her. The woman had seen her grimace and shudder in pain, and had given her all that she had. Becky Lynn had been touched by her kindness.

Becky Lynn uncapped the bottle and spilled the contents onto her palm. Only two left. She would have to buy more, and soon. Even though they only cut the pain, she didn't know what she would have done without them. The pain would have been unbearable.

She popped the tablets into her mouth, turned on the

water and bent to catch some in her cupped palms. Her hands shook so badly it took three tries to get the water to her mouth, and the aspirins partially melted on her tongue. She gagged, her empty stomach clenching at the bitter taste.

A woman herded her two small children into the bathroom. She caught sight of Becky Lynn, grabbed her children by their collars and steered them away from her. As if Becky Lynn had some sort of disease, she thought. As if being near her would contaminate them. The older of the two children whispered something Becky Lynn couldn't catch, and the mother hushed her.

Becky Lynn watched them hurry toward the row of stalls, tears stinging her eyes. It hurt, though she couldn't blame the mother for protecting her children. Lord knew, she wished her own mother had tried to protect her.

She thought of her mother, of the weeping she had heard when she left the house. The tears welled up and she blinked against them. Her mother hadn't been asleep. Her mother had known she was running away, and had let her daughter go.

Her tears dried. Leaving had been the right decision; she hadn't had any other choice. Her mother had seen that as clearly as Becky Lynn had. That's why she hadn't stopped her.

Becky Lynn turned back to the sink and the running water. She washed her face. That done, she dug her comb, toothbrush and toothpaste out of her duffel. She brushed, combed, then fashioned her hair into a tidy braid, using a rubber band she found on the floor.

After using the facilities and making sure she had all her belongings, she headed back out into the busy terminal, then out to the street.

Her first glimpse of Los Angeles took her breath away. Everywhere she looked, she saw buildings, huge, taller than she had ever seen before, ones made of concrete and steel and mirrors.

She'd never been farther than Greenwood and had never seen a skyscraper. She tipped her head back and stared up at their tops and the perfect Easter-egg blue sky. The height of these buildings dizzied her, the reflection off their mirrored sides caught the bright sun and shone, blindingly white.

She swiveled her head from left to right, taking in everything she could, stunned and astounded and exhilarated. Cars, there were hundreds of them. She had never seen so many in one place, had never seen so many kinds before. Most of them looked expensive, real expensive. They had fancy hood ornaments and gleamed like the one-carat diamond ring Lurline Gentry had flashed around down at the Cut 'n Curl until everyone had been sick to death of it.

Becky Lynn gawked as a limousine rolled past, brilliant white and as long as two pickup trucks. What would it be like to ride in one of those? she wondered, catching sight of another expensive-looking car, the driver talking on the phone while driving.

She shook her head and turned her attention to the people rushing by her. They looked so different from the people of Bend. In Bend, people were either black or white, rich or poor. Not here. Here, she saw people of all colors, from all walks of life. Many dressed strangely and wore their hair in bizarre colors and styles. Becky Lynn gaped as a man and woman strolled past, both dressed in leather and chains, their hair shaved on the sides and spiked high in front and on top.

Nobody else paid the pair any undue attention.

She wouldn't be a freak here. Becky Lynn smiled, optimism and excitement moving through her. Here, she wouldn't stand out as different. Everybody was different. Here, no one would know she was Becky Lynn Lee, poor white trash and outcast of Bend, Mississippi. She could start over, forge a fresh identity, a new life. Just as she had hoped.

She found the bus stop, just as the bus pulled up to the stop. She paid her fare and climbed aboard, smiling to herself. *No doubt about it, her luck had begun to change.*

12

When the sun set, the streets of Hollywood changed. The tourists went in, businesses closed. The bars and clubs opened and the night people came out. During the afternoon, Becky Lynn had enjoyed the warm, exhaust-scented breeze, the gleam of uninterrupted sun on the sidewalks and buildings, the rush of humanity. She hadn't felt alone or threatened.

Now, the gleam of sunlight had been replaced by the unnatural glare of neon and by dense, black shadows. Now she felt absolutely alone, and every dark corner, every recessed doorway, threatened.

She had to find a place to stay.

Becky Lynn curved her arms around herself, clutching her duffel bag to her chest. She had wasted precious time this afternoon strolling, seeing the sights, breathing in her freedom. She had stopped at Denny's and splurged on a real meal, ordering more than she had any business buying, stuffing herself until her stomach hurt. Only then, as the sun had begun to set, had she thought about finding shelter for the night.

How could she have been so careless? she wondered, turning onto Sunset. How could she have been so stupid? She had tried several motels, but none had been cheap enough. At several, one night would have cost more than she even had left.

Forty-five dollars.

She took a deep breath. Not enough, not nearly. If she blew everything she had on one night, what would she do for every other night? She had to be smart; she had to keep her head. If she acted out of fear or desperation, she would be lost.

"Hey, sweet thing." A frightening-looking man sauntered toward her. He had long, stringy hair and wore tight black jeans and a black leather jacket, open to the waist to reveal his bare chest. "Wanna score some dust?"

She shook her head and scurried around him, her heart pounding.

He swung around and fell into step beside her. "I can fix you up. Just tell Johnny what you need."

"I don't need anything," she said, voice shaking. "Just leave me alone!"

She started to run, remembering the last time she had run like this, remembering being knocked flat, being dragged off the road. Fear choked her, and even as she told herself not to look back, she did.

The sidewalk was empty behind her.

Becky Lynn whimpered with relief. He hadn't followed her. *She was safe. For the moment, safe.* She slowed to a brisk walk, even though each breath hurt, even though her legs ached and her head throbbed.

She couldn't stop. She wouldn't. Becky Lynn forced away thoughts of her pain and fatigue and concentrated instead on putting one foot in front of the other, block after block.

Up ahead, a motel's pink neon sign flashed. *unset otel.* Both the *S* and the *M* were burned out, the sign flashed at irregular intervals, as if each time about to flash its last.

As she neared the motel, she saw that it was small and seedy, but infinitely better than the street. And maybe, she thought, daring to hope, just maybe, affordable.

Becky Lynn reached the motel and stepped inside. The lobby stank. Of day-old sausage, sweat and cigar smoke. The latter came from behind the registration counter. Clamped between the clerk's teeth was the stub of a fat, green cigar.

Becky Lynn wrinkled her nose and crossed to the desk. The man dragged his gaze from the small TV on the floor behind the counter. "Yeah?" He didn't try to hide his irritation at being disturbed.

"Could you tell me your rates, please?"

"Twenty-two a night, fifty a week." He spoke around the cigar. "In advance."

She could afford that, even though it would make a frightening dent in her meager funds—but not nearly as frightening as the idea of sleeping on the street. She dropped her duffel to the floor, weak with relief. "I'll take a room. Just for tonight."

"Can't you read?" The desk clerk jerked his thumb in the direction of the glass doors and the flashing neon sign beyond. "No vacancies."

"No vacancies?" she repeated hollowly, looking over her shoulder at the sign. She turned back to him, pleading. "But...don't you have...anything? Please. I have no place to sleep."

"Sorry, kid. Come back in the morning." He took the cigar out of his mouth. Ashes floated down to join others on the front of his once-white T-shirt. "By this time of night, we're full up with hookers, dealers and folks just too messed up to make it home. Come back tomorrow."

He returned his attention to the television, and she stared at him. "Please," she whispered. "Anything."

The man didn't look up, and gaze swimming, Becky Lynn bent for her duffel. She lifted it to her shoulder and crossed the room, dragging her feet, loath to leave the light and safety of the shabby lobby behind.

She let herself out, but stopped in the lit doorway. Where should she go now? she wondered, shivering. What should she do?

Immobilized by fear and indecision, she did nothing. Minutes passed. A car full of young men honked and shouted an obscenity, another slowed down as if to take a look at her, then drove on.

The clerk opened the door. He'd exchanged the stub for a fresh cigar. He scowled at her. "Listen, kid, you've got to move it. You look like you're hustling, and you're going to bring the cops down on my ass."

She looked at him, her eyes swimming. "But I don't have anywhere to go."

"That's not my problem, kid." He made a sound of frustration. "There's a police station up the street. They'll take care of you. Clear outta here."

He shut the door in her face, then stood on the other side of the glass door, glaring at her. He jerked his thumb, and she picked up her duffel and headed back out onto the street.

The police station. Right. They would call her parents, first thing. Becky Lynn set her mouth in determination. She wasn't going back to Bend, not ever.

She walked. Minutes became hours; her duffel bag grew heavier, her legs more leaden. Fatigue and desperation became a quiet hysteria. She couldn't go on. She had to stop, to rest. She came upon a narrow side street, lined with deeply recessed doorways.

Becky Lynn stared at the street, at the doorways, trembling with exhaustion. In one of those doorways, she wouldn't be visible from the street. She could sleep there. The thought of sleep, of stopping and closing her eyes, pulled at her. If she could rest for just a little while, she would be able to figure out what to do. She would be able to go on.

Even as she crossed to the first doorway, her every instinct warned her from it. She stopped before it, searching the darkness, fearing that someone, or something, hid in its depths. Carefully, slowly, she inched her foot into the shadows, heart thundering, certain that at any moment a hand would circle her ankle and drag her to the ground.

Nothing happened. No clawlike hand grabbed at her; the doorway was empty. Looking quickly to her sides and behind her, she ducked into the shadowed doorway, and sank to the concrete. She pressed herself into the corner, drawing her knees tightly to her chest.

For long moments, she sat that way, heart pounding, waiting for some sort of alarm to go off, afraid to relax or shut her eyes.

If she made it to morning, she thought, fatigue overcoming her, everything would be all right.

In her dream, Ricky stood over her, yelling at her. He had trapped her, and terrified, she pressed herself deeper into the corner of the steel cage. As Ricky yelled, he poked at her with his penis, which was long and hard and hurt her.

"Get up! You hear me? Get up! I've got a business to run."

Becky Lynn moaned and stirred. Ricky swore, and nudged her viciously with his penis.

"You can't sleep in my doorway. Come on, get up." He swore again, loudly and with disgust. "You kids, every night it's another one of you."

"Stop," Becky Lynn muttered. "Stop…please." She lifted her head, her arms with it, ready to ward off a blow. She blinked as light stung her eyes. A man stood above her. Not Ricky, but a stranger. Dressed in a long white apron, he held a broom, handle down, pointed at her. With his thick white hair and beard, he looked like Santa Claus. She stared at him, confused, disoriented.

The man's expression changed, pity replacing the disgust and annoyance of a second ago. He cleared his throat. "Sorry, kid, but you've got to go. I've gotta open up."

She blinked again and looked around her, her dream evaporating. She remembered: the street, dark and frightening, populated by strange people, her exhaustion, this doorway.

Sunlight. Morning. She had made it.

"Look, kid, do I have to call the cops?"

She shook her head mutely and pulled herself to her feet. Her back and shoulders screamed in protest at having been contorted so long; her legs and head ached.

She winced as she picked up her duffel, and fought to get it to her shoulder. "I'm sorry," she whispered, darting a glance at the man, then shifting her gaze to her feet. "I had nowhere to go."

He said nothing—she hadn't expected him to reply—and she started for the street.

The man let out a long breath, then muttered an oath. "Here, kid."

Becky Lynn stopped and looked back at him. He held out a twenty-dollar bill. She stared at it, heart thundering. *Twenty dollars. A fortune. A miracle.*

She crossed to him and reached for the money, hand shaking. Instead of letting it go when her fingers closed around it, he drew back a fraction. She met his eyes, startled.

"If I find out you used this for drugs, I swear I'll…" He glared ferociously at her, but she saw the kindness in his eyes, anyway. "I'll kick your butt. Got that?"

"I won't," she murmured. "And I'll repay you someday. I promise."

"Sure, kid." He let go of the bill, and she drew her arm away and stuffed it into her pocket. He opened his mouth as if he wanted to say something else, then shook his head, turned and went into his store.

Becky Lynn returned to the Sunset Motel. She almost cried with relief when she saw the *no vacancies* light had been turned off. By the light of day, it looked even shabbier than the night before. The place could be teeming with rats and roaches, for all she cared; the creatures on the street frightened her much more.

She paid for a week in advance. That left her less than twenty dollars for food. How long would that last her? she wondered, staring bleakly at the assortment of bills and coins she piled in the middle of the faded bedspread. Not long.

She had to find a job, and quickly. But who would hire her, looking the way she did? Everyone she had come into contact with had either looked at her in horror, disgust or pity. Just the kind of freak an employer wanted to hire.

Stop it, she told herself, squeezing her eyes shut. If she

started thinking that way, she would never find a job. And she would find one. She had to. Tomorrow.

She gathered together the money, folded the bills neatly and tucked them into her shoe, dropped the coins into her change purse. She pulled back the covers and crawled under them, curling into a tight ball.

She closed her eyes and the image of her mother's face filled her head. She heard her voice, those times when it had been just the two of them, when her mother had run the big brush rhythmically, lovingly, through her hair.

You're special, Becky Lynn. You're smart. You could make something of yourself.

Becky Lynn pressed her face into the pillow, holding on to that thought, those words, her chest tight with tears. She missed her mother so much. She wished she could touch her, wished she could hold her for a moment.

Even though her mother had been unable to be a real mother, the way one should be, she was the only one Becky Lynn had ever known. And in her own way, as best she could, she had loved her daughter.

Tears squeezed from the corners of Becky Lynn's closed eyes. Her mother had wanted her to go, to escape. Her decision to run away had been the right one, the only one she could have made.

If only it didn't feel so wrong.

Becky Lynn slept for twenty-four hours. When she awakened, she ventured cautiously out. The new day looked exactly like the old one, nothing had changed but the faces on the street. Famished, she went in search of a grocery and found one a couple blocks down, on the corner.

She bought a carton of milk, a jar of peanut butter and a loaf of bread. That small purchase used almost half her money. She paid the cashier, struggling to keep her distress from showing. As he bagged her items, she asked if he had any job openings. He said no without even looking at her.

At least she had asked, she thought, fighting discouragement. At least she had tried. All it had cost her was a sliver of her confidence.

Becky Lynn reached the motel and let herself into her room, then bolted the door behind her. She made herself a sandwich and gobbled the first half down. She ate like a pig, stuffing the food into her mouth, licking her fingers and the knife, picking crumbs off the bedspread. She consumed the last half more slowly, trying to pace herself. She wanted another, her stomach screamed for it, but she held off, her mouth watering. She had to ration her food.

Somewhat sated, she sat cross-legged on the bed and assessed her situation. She had a roof over her head and food in her belly. Two days ago, she'd had neither. She thought of Ricky and Tommy, of her father and brother. Three days ago, she had been at their mercy. Now they couldn't touch her, they couldn't take what wasn't theirs, couldn't belittle and demean her. And although people looked at her with disgust and pity, they didn't hate her. They didn't want to hurt her for being nothing more than herself.

She leaned her head back against the headrest and gazed up at the cracked and peeling ceiling. In a way, she fit in here, in Hollywood. The street was populated with other outcasts; she blended in. She had never blended in before, had never known what it was like to be one of many rather than singled out and different.

She liked it. It made her feel invisible, made her feel, somehow, stronger.

Smiling to herself, she lifted a hand to her jaw and trailed her fingers across it. The swelling had gone down, the vivid bruise had faded to a yellow-green shadow. The bruises on her body, too, had begun to fade; the ache between her legs had subsided. Now it only hurt when she remembered, when her defenses slipped, allowing the nightmare to seep into her head.

She would take one more day to sleep and heal, then she would clean herself up and hit the streets in search of a job. If she had to, she would knock on every door, talk to every business owner or shop manager in Hollywood. Someone would hire her.

The next day was a bust, and the next two after that. No one was hiring. They took one look at her and said no. Most times, they hadn't even given her an opportunity to beg.

Every evening, exhausted and discouraged, she locked herself in her motel room and spent the night thinking of the minutes and hours ticking past, eating up her paid-up week at the motel, worrying about what would become of her if she didn't find a job.

Becky Lynn closed her eyes and pictured some of the girls she saw on the street, many of them obviously younger than she, their eyes outlined in black, their skirts short and tight, their hair teased high. Their expressions desperate, lost.

It was laughable, but she longed to help them. She had caught herself wanting to offer them advice, money, a way out. She, who in some ways was worse off than they; she, who would face a similar decision, a similar fate *if she couldn't find a job.*

Becky Lynn curved her fingers into fists. No way. She wouldn't end up like them. She would eat garbage and sleep in the street before she would sell her body. She would rather die than be touched the way Ricky and Tommy had touched her.

She returned her attention to the phone book's Yellow Pages, open on the bed in front of her. Until now, she had tried every business she had come upon, from coffee shops to boutiques, banks to souvenir shops. She had never worked anywhere but the Cut 'n Curl. It made sense to use her previous experience to try to find a job. It would give her an edge. She didn't know why she hadn't thought of that before.

A piece of the motel's stationery and a pen in her lap, she ran her index finger down the list of nearby beauty parlors. A few she had already tried, the rest she listed on the paper with their addresses. To save time, she located them on the phone book map, then made her own map, closest shop to farthest, relisting them in the most efficient way to visit them.

The next morning, she set off for the first shop on the list. She had passed it several times, she realized, as she reached the address, but hadn't known what it was.

The exterior of the shop was faced with pink and green marble. The street number and shop's name was done in shiny brass, and a green-and-white-striped awning stretched from the double glass doors almost to the street.

Becky Lynn frowned. She had learned quickly that there were two kinds of establishments in Hollywood— ones for the rich, and ones for those who were not. She had also learned that the ones for the rich hadn't wanted her to cross the threshold. Most had doormen or valets who stood guard outside to ensure that someone like her, who either didn't know the rules or chose to ignore them, wouldn't happen across.

This shop was no exception. Only today, this moment, the guardian of good taste was not at his post.

She darted a quick glance over her shoulder. What the heck. It was a long shot, but what did she have to lose by trying? She ducked under the awning and strode to the heavy double glass doors. The worst they could do was ask her to leave. It wouldn't be the first time.

She stepped through the door, and the throbbing beat of Tina Turner's "What's Love Got To Do With It?" hit her like a hammer. As did the smell of freshly brewed coffee.

She moved her gaze over the room before her, and she caught her breath. This shop was nothing like the Cut 'n Curl back home. It was huge. And fancy. Overstuffed white leather couches graced the sitting area, balanced by delicate chairs made of striped chintz. The tables were made of the same green and pink marble pieces as the shop's facade, their bases of brass. On a marble buffet sat a silver coffee service and tray of delicious-looking pastries, the likes of which Becky Lynn had never seen before, and certainly not at the Tastee Creme back home.

She stared at them a moment, her mouth watering, then dragged her gaze back to the room. The walls were hung with black-and-white glossy photographs of women celebrities. Becky Lynn crossed to them. *Brooke Shields. Isabella Rossellini.* She looked closer. *Renée Simonsen. Daryl Hannah.*

The photographs were signed. Heart pounding, she swung to another wall, this one covered only with writing. She crossed to it, then stopped, her mouth dropping. *Sig-*

natures. She blinked, not believing her eyes. *Farrah Fawcett. Nancy Reagan. Kathleen Turner.*

Becky Lynn took a step backward, away from the wall. She didn't belong here. Dear Lord, she had been turned out of dumps the last few days; a place like this would never hire her.

"My God, is that your natural color?"

Startled, Becky Lynn whirled, hand to her throat. The woman who stood across the room from her wore black, silk trousers, an equally soft white blouse and a thin, black tie. She looked classy, sophisticated. Like a woman of means and style.

Becky Lynn pictured herself, her faded jeans and T-shirt, her threadbare sneakers and plain face. She didn't belong here, Becky Lynn thought again, curving her arms across her chest. "Pardon, ma'am?"

"Your hair color." The woman took several more steps into the room. "Is it your own?"

Becky Lynn brought a hand self-consciously to her hair and swallowed hard. "Yes, ma'am. Mama always said it reminded her of strawberry soda pop."

"Strawberry soda pop?" the woman repeated, her eyes crinkling at the corners with amusement. "How delightful. And how descriptive."

The woman closed the distance between them. She met Becky Lynn's gaze evenly. She had the bluest eyes Becky Lynn had ever seen—and the kindest. "I'm sorry if I startled you. If it's any consolation, you startled me, too. Did Mac let you in?"

Becky Lynn shook her head. "No, I...the...the door was open."

The woman shifted her gaze to the glass door, then

brought them back to Becky Lynn. She moved her gaze over her, as if suddenly realizing that the girl standing before her wasn't expected and didn't belong. Her smile faded. "Can I help you?" she asked.

"I'm…s-sorry," Becky Lynn stammered, taking a step backward. "I'll leave now."

The woman drew her eyebrows together and cocked her head, and Becky Lynn could see that she was both confused and suspicious. Her gaze slid to the silver service, then to Becky Lynn. "Did you want something?"

Becky Lynn caught her bottom lip between her teeth. *Ask her. You have nothing to lose.* "Yes, I—" Her voice quivered, and she struggled to control it. "May I speak to the owner or manager, please?"

"I'm Sallie Gallagher," she said. "I own this shop. Can I help you?"

Becky Lynn clasped her hands together. "I'm, um, looking for a…a job." Emotion choked her, and she cleared her throat. "I was hoping you might have something."

The woman opened her mouth, an automatic "no openings" forming on her lips. Becky Lynn recognized it from the dozens of others she'd heard in the past few days.

Her heart sank and tears rushed to her eyes. But even as they did, they warred with desperation. She wouldn't give up without a fight. She couldn't.

"Please," she said quickly, before the woman could speak. "I'll sweep, scrub sinks, run errands. Anything you ask. I have experience. And I…I really need a job."

The woman drew her eyebrows together again, studying Becky Lynn. She looked her in the eye once more. "You have experience?" she asked in a soft, thick voice. A voice that reminded Becky Lynn of the Mississippi River in August.

Becky Lynn nodded, her pulse beginning to pound. "Yes, ma'am."

"Where?"

Becky Lynn hesitated, then pushed aside her worries of being tracked down or found out. "At the Cut 'n Curl back home. I shampooed customers, and swept, ran errands, took care of inventory and even mixed colors…sometimes." The last she fudged on, but figured if she had to, she could fake it.

"Back home," the woman repeated. "Where is that?"

Becky Lynn wrapped her arms around her middle. "Mississippi, ma'am."

"I see."

She was going to turn her away! Becky Lynn saw it in her eyes, heard it in her voice. Desperate, she said, "I'm a hard worker. I learn real fast. And I'll…I'll…" Once more tears swamped her, and again she struggled to hold them off.

The woman pursed her lips, as if deep in thought. "You really need this job, don't you?"

Becky Lynn nodded and hung her head.

"Are you in some sort of trouble?" Becky Lynn looked up and away, and the woman frowned. "With the law?"

Becky Lynn jerked her gaze up. "Oh, no, ma'am. Nothing like that. I wouldn't ever do anything…like that."

"You're not into drugs, are you?"

Again Becky Lynn shook her head vehemently.

The woman lowered her eyes for a moment, then met Becky Lynn's again. "Okay, I'll give you a chance. One chance. I can only pay minimum wage to start, and I'll expect you to work your tail off for it. But if you prove yourself, if you manage to fill some cracks around here, I'll give you a raise."

Becky Lynn brought her hands to her chest. *A job! She had a job!* The words raced through her head, making her dizzy with relief and gratitude.

"Thank you, ma'am! Thank you!" She burst into a broad smile, the first since Ricky and Tommy had cornered her. "I won't let you down. You'll see."

The woman smiled back. "I hope not. Now, let's get some things straight right off the bat. Call me Sallie, please. 'Ma'am' makes me feel ancient."

"Yes, ma—Sallie."

"Next, I need to know what I should call you?"

"Becky Lynn," she answered, flushing.

Sallie smiled again, warmly. "I'll need you to fill out an application and a W-2. If you would like to start today, we could use you. We're booked solid."

"Oh, yes, ma'am…I mean, yes, Sallie."

"Good." Sallie Gallagher held out her hand. "Welcome to The Image Shop, Becky Lynn."

13

In the four years that passed since his life-altering experience on Gina's couch, Jack saw Gina as often as possible. He didn't call it love, and neither did she. Neither of them thought of their relationship as an exclusive one: Jack knew Gina saw other people, slept with other people; she knew the same about him. Sometimes they would lie together and laugh about their experiences, or share intimate details of their other relationships.

Jack checked his watch, noted that Gina was now, officially and characteristically, thirty minutes late. Unperturbed, he continued studying the proof sheets from a job he had wrapped yesterday. He and Gina understood each other, had similar likes, dislikes and experiences; they enjoyed each other's company. And their sexual chemistry together was good. Very good.

So if what they had wasn't deep or emotional, it was honest. And in a town and an industry that thrived on illusion, hype and ego, that was a rare and special thing, more dependable, more trustworthy than love could ever be.

Over the years, he had closely guarded what they had. So had she.

Jack thumbed through the proofs, his lips lifting with satisfaction. The job, for a small but exclusive clothier on Melrose, had paid well and the shots were good. He paused on the most powerful, most effective shot of the group and studied it, pleased. Shots like this one in his portfolio, his book, would take him a long way.

Too bad the client's opinion differed from his on which shots were the best.

The client's loss. Jack had told him so, and the man had thanked him and gone with his own choice, anyway.

Jack made a sound of disgust, tossed the proofs on the light table and stood. It never ceased to amaze him that someone would pay him good money for his expertise, then totally disregard it. Sometimes human nature was so ridiculously fucked.

He stretched, then checked his watch again, wondering what time Gina would actually arrive. He couldn't complain, even if he were the type; Gina modeled for him for free, a gift of her time and talent, a gift of her well-known face. Her face in his book gave him added professional stature; it opened doors that would otherwise be closed to him. A pecking order existed in the industry, the top girls worked with only the top shooters, star power with equal star power.

And Gina's star shone considerably brighter than his.

For the moment.

Jack stretched again, itching to get to work, his nerve endings humming with the need to do *something*. He loathed inactivity. His time in his studio, his time spent on his photography, was limited. Every day that passed had to bring him closer to his goal; every day that didn't, ate at him. He burned to be further along than he was. He yearned for the day he could toss his success in Giovanni's face.

Impatience surged through him. He fought it, but still it

churned inside him, burning in his gut. He crossed to his studio's back wall. To it he had pinned his best photographs, copies of his ad work—the Rolex watch ad for a Rodeo Drive jeweler, the beach piece he'd done for the tourist commission, the album cover for a hot local rock band.

Jack moved his gaze critically over each shot, understanding the folly of loving them just because they were his own. Satisfied, he shifted his gaze to the center of the wall, to the two-page spread from *Los Angeles* magazine he had pinned there, a constant reminder of who he was and where he was going.

Carlo's spread. Carlo's work.

He gazed critically at his brother's work, determination and dislike eating at him, fueling him. Carlo had rocketed from a nobody-beginner like himself, grubbing for jobs, to a photographer with budding name recognition, a photographer who had his choice of jobs and models.

Not because of talent or hard work, but because he was Giovanni's son. His acknowledged son. Jack flexed his fingers. In the past two years, he had watched door after door open to Carlo, he had watched Carlo grow in professional stature. He knew from his sources on the grapevine, that Carlo supported himself with his photography, supported himself in nice style, and that he had for a long time.

Being Giovanni's bastard didn't open any doors. But that was okay. He would show them both, he would make it without favors or entrées.

He and his half brother had run into each other on the street. Carlo had seen a piece of Jack's work, and had laughingly mentioned it. *"Small jobs become you, Jack,"* he had said. *"Keep it up."*

Jack had wanted to lunge at him, had longed to knock him to the ground and bloody his nose. Instead, he had smiled coolly and asked his brother if he would be able to do anything at all without *Daddy's* help.

When Carlo's mouth had tightened at the barb, Jack had experienced a glimmer of satisfaction.

But only a glimmer. Because as much as he hated to admit it, Carlo had talent. Jack narrowed his eyes, studying his brother's work. Carlo had developed a style similar to his father's, striking, simple, highly sexed.

Jack had discovered that, for himself, he preferred movement, he preferred daylight and shooting outdoors because of the opportunities both afforded him. He had also discovered that he preferred complexity of composition and light, the baroque instead of the minimal.

He had talent, he knew he did. And not a moderate talent. He had something special, call it an eye, or vision, or skill. He knew it with his gut, with that place inside him that responded with an *ahh* when the shot was right. And it responded that way a lot.

Jack turned away from the photo-wall and faced his small studio, a mere six hundred square feet. Compared to Giovanni's twelve thousand, his space was laughable. But it was his. He worked hard to maintain it. He waited tables at night, at a trendy bistro in Beverly Hills; during the day, he called on ad agencies, combed the fashion mart with his book, shot up-and-coming models.

The door burst open, Gina with it. "Sorry I'm late!"

She raced into the studio, portfolio tucked under her arm and tote bag slung over her shoulder, her long blond hair wild from the wind. She drove a bright red Alfa-Romeo convertible; he had never seen it with the top up.

He grinned and cocked his head to the side. "Bad morning?"

She crossed to him, dropped the tote, stood on tiptoe and planted a friendly kiss on his lips. "I had four go-sees. I'm getting pretty sick of this shit. I mean, when are they going to start booking me on the strength of the work I've done? Why do I have to come in for a face-to-face?"

Jack shook his head, his lips lifting. "Because, my beauty, the client wants a chance to gawk at you." He wiggled his eyebrows. "Maybe even get a chance to see you in your skivvies."

She snorted. "More like a chance to feel me up in my skivvies. The old fart patted me on the ass. Can you believe it? I should be beyond this crap."

He laughed. "Ah, the burden of being an object of beauty."

She slipped her T-shirt over her head and tossed it at him. "Eat me, Gallagher."

"Later. We have work to do." He caught the bundle and sent it back to her. "Clothes are behind the screen."

She muttered something about all work and no play, but took her bag and shirt to the changing area. Today, they were going to work inside. He was going to work with his medium-format camera and tripod, both of which he found confining but necessary. He needed variety in his book.

"How'd it go with the Klein people?" she called from behind the screen.

"It didn't." His rep had gotten him and his book an audience with the Calvin Klein people. They'd been looking for a new shooter for the designer's spring collection catalog. It would have been a financial boon for his career, but more, it would have elevated his professional stature by light-years. "They liked my work but said I didn't have enough experience." Jack snapped a Polaroid back onto his Hasselblad. "They said to come back in a few years."

She peeked around the screen at him. "I'm really sorry, Jack."

He met her eyes, in them he saw genuine regret. He shrugged. "There'll be other opportunities."

"At least you got in the front door. Your name's in front of them now."

"Right," he muttered, frustration and impatience eating away the ability to be satisfied with such a small step. The only thing that meant anything, that counted for anything, was landing the job.

While she finished changing, he busied himself with setting the lights, loading film backs and arranging the other equipment he might need for the shoot. He couldn't afford an assistant, and he wouldn't want to stop the momentum of the shoot by having to scramble for more film or something else he might have forgotten.

"At least Carlo didn't get it, either."

Jack's hands stilled on the film back, and he turned toward the screen. "What did you say?"

She hesitated. "I heard through the grapevine that he got a call, too. And that he didn't get the job. If it's any consolation, I'm sure it kills him that you got a call."

Jack frowned. "Word's out on the street that I got a call?"

She hesitated again. "Well, it's not a secret, is it? I mean, this is a small industry."

"Who else went in besides me and Carlo?"

"I'm not sure."

Jack drew his eyebrows together, a funny feeling in the pit of his stomach—a feeling that she knew something she wasn't telling him. He shrugged off the sensation, his wild thoughts. What did she know? And why wouldn't she tell him? They told each other everything.

"You almost ready?" He passed the light meter over the set, testing the reflected light, even though he would have to reread it after she sat down. "I'd like to do this while were both still young."

"Testy bastard," she said cheerfully, coming out from behind the screen. She wore tight, ragged blue jeans, a black leather jacket with a plain white T-shirt underneath and black biker boots. "What do you want me to do with my hair?"

"Leave it for now. I want it wild." He moved his gaze assessingly over her. He wanted a tough, almost butch look. Her all-American blond, blue-eyed beauty contrasted with the toughness, creating a kind of visual shock. "Take off the T-shirt. Nude under the jacket is going to be great. And let's darken your eyes."

Minutes later, Jack was positioned behind the camera, Gina in front of it. At the camera, time stood still for him. The world around him ceased to exist. Reality became the rectangular image he saw through his camera's eye.

He and Gina worked together easily, at times seeming to read each other's minds. "Great, good. Cock your head…that's right." She responded without hesitation or question to each of his demands.

It was a pleasure working with her, as it was with any experienced model. She'd lost all self-consciousness years ago, she understood how to give a shooter exactly what he needed, understood how to improvise when the shooter didn't know what he wanted, filling in the blanks. When he worked with Gina, he didn't have to think of anything but the shot.

When he felt he had enough good shots to choose from, he straightened, his focus shifting back to the world of the living and breathing. He grinned. "You were great, love. As always." He crossed to her and kissed her. "We've got some really good stuff here." He kissed her again, this time more deeply.

She curled her fingers into his shirt and angled a provocative glance up at him. "No wonder I feel like celebrating." She shrugged the jacket from her shoulders, leaving her torso bare, then slid her hand up around his neck and drew him down. "Come here and let me show you my appreciation."

Never a man to argue, he did just that.

Later, Jack prepared the film for processing while Gina changed into her street clothes and removed her makeup. He smiled to himself as he sealed and marked each roll of film, already thinking ahead to the test shoot he had scheduled for three-thirty. He had seen the girl at the mall and had approached her about modeling. Only fourteen, she would be accompanied by her mother.

"Want to go eat?" Gina ducked her head out from behind the screen. "My schedule's clear and I'm starving."

"Sounds good. Mexican?"

"Too heavy. How about Thai?"

"Fine with me." He slipped the Hasselblad into its case, then packed the lenses.

Gina had laid her portfolio on the equipment table, next to his camera bag. Curious, he picked it up and began leafing through it, stopping on two images of her he had never seen before.

The images were about sex. Both head shots, in them she looked directly into the camera, her lips parted and curved slightly up, her eyes sleepy and satisfied. The ad might be hawking a new fragrance, but the sense of smell had little to do with what was happening here between photographer and model.

He recognized the photographer's style. And even if he didn't, in this business, everybody knew which photographers had which clients.

This was Carlo's work. *Wildflower* was Carlo's client.

She came out of the bathroom. "You wouldn't believe what I heard about Patti Han…" Gina's words trailed off as she saw what he was looking at. "What are you doing?"

"Looking at your book." He met her gaze. "Any reason I shouldn't be?"

"Of course not." She cleared her throat and shifted her gaze. "Why don't we go eat now? I'm starving."

"So you said." He returned his gaze to Carlo's image of her. "You didn't tell me you'd done a shoot with Carlo."

"Didn't I?" She smiled stiffly. "It must have slipped my mind. I did it a couple months ago."

"These are good."

"Thank you."

"Very good."

She crossed to him and held out her hand for the portfolio. She looked guilty as sin. "Thank you. Again."

He ignored her hand, suddenly angry. "You practically ooze sex."

"What's that supposed to mean?"

He met her gaze evenly. "You fucked him, didn't you?"

She caught her breath. "You son of a bitch. How dare you—"

"You did, didn't you?" He pulled in a slow, steadying breath. "I can't believe you did this."

She curved her outstretched hand into a fist. "Don't moralize, Jack. Just give me the goddamned book."

"How many times, Gina?" He tossed the portfolio onto the table, disgusted. "Are you still seeing him? Is that how you knew about Calvin Klein?"

Her expression told him everything, and he swore. Swinging away from her, he crossed to the window. The day was perfect, just as every day in L.A. was, the sky almost too blue to be true.

He turned to face her once more. "I thought we were friends. I trusted you."

"Oh, please, stop with the wounded act." She placed her fists on her hips. "How many models have you taken to bed? Or should I ask, which models haven't you?"

"That's not the point."

"No?" She flung her head back. "Then what is?"

"Carlo is." He closed the distance between them. He looked her straight in the eye. "Why, Gina? Why him?"

She didn't hold his gaze. Turning, she went to her purse and fumbled inside for her cigarettes. She found the pack, pulled one out and with fingers that shook, lit it.

She breathed in deeply, then exhaled and turned to him. "We don't have something exclusive here, Jack. I see other people, so do you. I don't appreciate this guilt trip."

"I don't care if you screw the whole goddamned universe, but not him. Never him."

Her eyes filled. "Well maybe that's why I fucked him. Because you don't give a shit."

"Now who's packing a guilt trip? Do you want what we have to be exclusive?" Although she said nothing, he could see that she didn't. He crossed to her once more. "Besides, I do care for you. We go back a long way, we've shared a lot of secrets. You know all of my secrets. I trusted you with them, Gina. That's the point. That's what this is about."

"Me and Carlo, it was just sex. And business." She drew on the cigarette. "You're making way too big a deal out of this."

He wasn't. And she knew it. Because she understood him, and that's what stung.

He touched her cheek lightly, then dropped his hand. "If you had asked me to stay away from a certain woman, a certain model, if it was important to you, I would have. I would have respected your wishes. Because we're friends. Because we do things for each other."

"That's not fair!" She stubbed out the cigarette. "We're in totally different positions. You, as the photographer, have all the power. You give the jobs, you decide who works. The only power I have, I have to make. And there are only two ways I can do that, and both are with my body. You know that."

She took a step closer to him, and laid her hands on his chest.

"You're special to me, Jack. More special than anyone else. And the things you do for me in bed, well…nobody comes close. Nobody ever has." She curled her fingers into his chambray shirt. "But he can do things for me, for my career, that you can't."

"I'll be able to someday," Jack said, frustration building inside him. And with it, hatred so intense it burned. "Just wait and see."

"I believe you," she said softly. "I believe in you. But I can't wait. My career is *now*, a few years from now, I'll be too old. If I'm going to get anywhere near the top, I have to do it now and any way I can. We both know it."

He did know it. He also knew it could never be the same between them again.

"You're better in bed, Jack." He met her eyes, and she slid her hands up to his shoulders. "A lot better. It's true." She stood on tiptoe and pressed herself against him. "He asks about you. He knows we're friends. But I've told him nothing." She laughed. "It drives him crazy. You drive him crazy."

He set her away from him. "We're through, Gina. I won't see you again."

She stared at him, shocked. "I can't…I can't believe you're doing this."

"The only thing I've ever asked of you, in all these years, is that you not sleep with Carlo. You said you wouldn't." He narrowed his eyes. "You didn't just sleep with him, Gina. You kept it from me. You lied."

"I was seventeen when I made that promise! That was so long ago, surely you didn't expect me to—"

"But I did, Gina."

He turned away from her; she caught his arm. "Jack, our friendship means so much to me. I know it means as much to you." She tightened her fingers. "Do you hate him so much?"

He met her gaze evenly, without hesitation or doubt. "Yes, Gina. I hate him…so much."

14

Becky Lynn's first few weeks at The Image Shop flew by, at once exhilarating and exhausting, frightening and fun. The staff greeted her with a few raised eyebrows and a questioning glance or two sent Sallie's way, then resumed work.

Becky Lynn learned quickly that The Image Shop differed from Miss Opal's in many more ways than just size and decor. Nobody visited The Shop—as Becky Lynn had come to call it—for the kind of old-fashioned cuts and styles the Cut 'n Curl had specialized in. Here, customers asked for the styles, the looks, featured in the fashion magazines. Styles and cuts like the long spiky, the mushroom and half moon, the DA. Becky Lynn had yet to see a teasing comb, curlers or a can of the sticky hair spray Fayrene and Dixie had used with abandon; instead, the hairdressers here styled with mousse and gel, blow dryers and their fingers.

At the Cut 'n Curl, Fayrene, Dixie and Opal did everything, from nails to color to cuts. The artists at The Image Shop specialized. Bruce called himself the King of Curl. He was the shop's permanent-wave specialist, and heads from all over California (and the world, he claimed) came to him for their curls. A color analyst, Ali did nothing but color. Marty, Foster and Brianna were cutters. When women came into The Shop for makeup, a make-over or facial, they saw Sallie or Greg. If they wanted a manicure or pedicure, they saw Joy or Linda.

It boggled her mind, just as the variety of processes did, ones like foiling and cellophaning and spiking. Becky Lynn had realized in her first hour at the shop that telling Sallie she had experience had been a joke. At least she hadn't been asked to make good on her claimed ability to mix color—Ali would cut off Becky Lynn's hand before she would let her touch her precious formulas.

But Becky Lynn had decided that more different than The Shop itself or the techniques performed here, were the people who came through the front doors. The Shop's clients were the wealthy and the beautiful. They were all slim and tan; physically, visually, they looked…perfect.

She had never seen women who looked like this. Even the women who were no longer young had smooth, taut skin and bodies. Marty told her that out here, everybody who was anybody had their own plastic surgeon, and that growing old gracefully meant having tucks and lifts at regular intervals.

Becky Lynn supposed she wasn't surprised, considering the kind of wealth these women obviously possessed. They drove up in Mercedeses and Porsches, or were delivered to The Shop in chauffeured limousines or Rolls-Royces. Their jewels astounded her: diamonds bigger than black-eyed peas set into earrings and bracelets, emeralds and rubies that twinkled as brightly as Christmas lights. Their clothes were designer originals—that Becky Lynn recognized from the pages of *Vogue*.

In only one way did these manicured women resemble the Mrs. Abernathys and Mrs. Peachtrees of back home— their ability to look right through her. She was a nonentity to them, one of an army of invisible servants who waited on them day in and day out.

Becky Lynn thanked God every day for her invisibility. If one of these important women ever really looked at her, they would know the truth about her. They would know she didn't belong. And she would be fired.

She didn't doubt that because these women, with their jewels and designer originals and their meticulous cultured speech, wielded power.

In a way that the Mrs. Abernathys of the world only dreamed of.

In the way the Becky Lynn Lees of the world couldn't even dare to dream of.

Becky Lynn shook her head and returned her attention to her job, which at the moment was restocking the product displays. Around her, the artists worked. The artists gave The Shop its life, they made it special. Of both sexes, the artists laughed often and never seemed to stop moving.

She loved listening to them talk, listening to their stories, although she never joined in or offered an opinion. Their lives were all so different from anything she had ever known, and most of the time she found herself either enthralled or shocked.

They talked about the most current fashions, the opposite sex, the club scene. But the most frequent topic of conversation was sex. They were all frighteningly open about the things they had done and who they had been with. And so blasé about it all. They discussed sexual partners and techniques as openly and often as most people discussed the weather.

Two of the stylists were homosexual—and lovers. They

told her they preferred to be called gay, and hung on to each other and kissed right out in the open.

Becky Lynn had never met a gay person before. In Bend, the only gay person she had ever heard of had been run out of town on a rail. And at first, Bruce and Foster's affection for each other had made her feel uncomfortable. Threatened, even. But the more time she spent around them, the more she realized that their being gay didn't have anything to do with her. Besides, they didn't judge her; they accepted her the way she was. So who was she to judge? Who was she to point fingers and proclaim herself superior?

That was the way people in Bend thought, that was the way they treated anyone different than themselves. And she had vowed to leave Bend behind forever.

"Becky Lynn, hon, could you give me a hand over here?"

"Sure, Bruce." She tucked the small pad she used to take stock inventory into her back pocket and went to help.

"Hold these." The hairdresser handed her a basket filled with permanent-wave rods and tissues.

She watched him work, alternately handing him rods and tissues, listening as he bantered with the beautiful woman in his chair. She had an English accent and glorious green eyes; Becky Lynn recognized her from several magazine covers. Awed, she kept her gaze fixed on the basket of rods.

"I don't know what to do," the model whispered. "Tell me if I should take the booking. I'll have to sleep with him, I won't be able to resist. You know how weak I am."

"You must take the job. You said yourself, it's a fabulous career move. Goodbye *Cosmo,* hello *Vogue.*"

Vogue? Becky Lynn's heart began to thunder. She peeked at the woman from beneath lowered lashes. How could she even think of not doing it? If she herself ever had such an opportunity, which, of course, she wouldn't, there was no way she would even think of—

"But he's such a son of a bitch, Bruce."

"A son of a bitch who's great in bed." Bruce expertly rolled the model's hair onto the rod, not even looking at his hands. "Besides, my love, it's a cover."

Becky Lynn gasped.

The model's eyes snapped open; Bruce looked sharply at Becky Lynn. "Is there a problem, Becky Lynn?"

Heat burned her cheeks, and she shook her head. "No, it's just that…*Vogue*'s the best. I can't imagine…I mean, the cover of *Vogue* is…everything."

The woman's eyes widened. Bruce's angry gaze made it clear that she had made a mistake. A big mistake. As a nonentity, she was expected to be both deaf and dumb. To offer her opinion was tantamount to treason.

Fear stole her breath. What if Bruce fired her? What would she do? How would she survive? "I'm sorry," she said quickly, her voice shaking. "Forgive me. I shouldn't have said anything. I didn't mean to—"

"No," the model interrupted, waving a perfectly manicured hand. "You're right. Only the best make it to the cover of American *Vogue.* And I'm the best."

"Of course you are," Bruce murmured, taking the basket from Becky Lynn's hands in dismissal, sending her one last angry glance before returning his attention to the model. "You must take the booking."

Becky Lynn backed away, heart thundering, cheeks on fire. How could she have been so stupid? How could she have forgotten herself and her place that way? The only thing between her and the street was keeping Sallie and the other people here from realizing just how out of place she was at The Shop.

Fear clutched at her. She recognized the emotion from having lived with it every day, every moment, since running away from home. The fear that she would be forced to return to Bend, that a man would trap and brutalize her the way Ricky and Tommy had. The fear that she would be found not to belong and fired, that she would be ostracized.

It was that last she feared most. At night, she lay in the motel bed and listened to the sounds from outside, the gun of an engine, the sounds of a fight, the wail of a police siren, and she prayed she wouldn't do anything to draw attention to herself. That she wouldn't make a mistake that would clue them into who—and what—she really was.

Poor white trash.

She couldn't bear for it to start all over again.

She fought the fear and walked slowly and calmly from the room. She reached the stockroom, stepped inside and shut the door behind her.

She brought her trembling hands to her cheeks. When would she stop being afraid? She breathed deeply through her nose, her chest tight, her heartbeat fast. Would she ever know what it felt like to belong? To feel safe? Each time she felt a glimmer of safety, of belonging, she was wrenched back to reality. Back to fear.

Tears stung her eyes. She fought them as hard as she had fought her fear of moments before. Feeling sorry for herself was a ridiculous waste of time.

She had changed her life, she was much better off than she had been a mere few weeks ago.

Here, she was at no one's mercy but her own.

Her tears dried, and a sense of calm moved over her. She had made a mistake just now. But it hadn't been fatal. Bruce hadn't fired her; he hadn't verbally reprimanded her or called for Sallie.

Becky Lynn took a deep breath. She would work hard, keep her mouth shut and not make any more mistakes. She would make them believe she did belong. Everything would be all right.

15

True to her promise to herself, in the days that passed, Becky Lynn kept her nose to the grindstone and her mouth shut. At first, she had waited, heart in her throat, for Sallie to call her into her office for a reprimand, or worse, to fire her.

It never happened. Sallie remained as open and friendly as she had ever been. Even Bruce had seemed to have forgotten the incident. Finally, Becky Lynn began to relax.

"Becky Lynn, my darling here needs a chardonnay." Foster brought his hand to his chest and drew in his breath melodramatically. "She's recounting the most awful story, and she needs to brace herself. It's truly...tragic."

Becky Lynn bit back a smile and nodded. Foster's "darling" of the moment was the woman in his chair, a senior studio executive's wife and Hollywood power-luncher. She came in several times a week, Joy did her nails, Sallie her makeup and facials, Foster her hair. Today she was having her sleek blond bob trimmed.

Becky Lynn poured a glass of the wine, careful not to leave fingerprints on the glass, then selected a few tidbits and arranged them on a gold-rimmed dessert plate. Her job had developed into that of fetch-it girl or gofer. (She had only done a half-dozen shampoos, and then only because of a flu bug that had swept through The Shop; Sallie employed professional hairdressers to man the shampoo bowls.) She made herself available to the artists, for whatever they might need, restocked shelves, made sure the coffee was always fresh-brewed, the wine cold. In addition, she made certain The Shop always looked picture perfect, a job that included everything from straightening The Shop's multitude of magazines to wiping water spots from all the bathroom and shampoo room fixtures. People of wealth, privilege and beauty expected perfection. At The Image Shop, they got it.

Becky Lynn carried the wine and plate to Foster's station and set them carefully in front of the woman. "Here you are, Mrs. Cole," she murmured. "I brought you a small arrangement of fruits, biscuits and Brie, just in case you missed lunch."

Foster beamed at her for remembering that the last time Madeline Cole had been in, she had requested just such an assortment because she had, indeed, missed lunch.

"Thank you, dear. That's lovely."

"You're welcome, ma'am."

The woman looked at her, her lips tipping up in amusement. "Where in the world are you from?"

Becky Lynn's cheeks heated, but she met the woman's gaze evenly. "Mississippi, ma'am."

"Mississippi?" she repeated. *"Ma'am?"* Madeline Cole turned her gaze to Foster. "My God, Foster, where did Sallie find her?"

"Why, she's our own little Blossom," Foster mocked in the way Becky Lynn had come to recognize was without personal malice. "We believe she's actually a princess on the run. Her father is determined to marry her to a fat old king."

"With bad breath," Brianna chirped up from the next station. "And no hair."

Madeline Cole tilted her head. "Maybe she's in the federal witness protection program, hiding out from the mob. Next thing we know, my husband will be making a movie about her life."

"So, which is it, Blossom?" Foster grinned at her. "The fat old king or the mob?"

Becky Lynn swallowed past the lump in her throat, wishing she could think up a snappy comeback, something that would satisfy them so they would leave her alone.

"Come on, Blossom," Foster teased. "You can tell us. We'll only tell everyone else."

"Stop it, you two," Marty called from two chairs down. "You're embarrassing her. Besides, I need her to get me a fresh towel. Could you, Becky Lynn? This one is beyond sticky."

Grateful for Marty's kindness, Becky Lynn hurried to the shampoo room. The artists teased her sometimes, calling her Blossom because of her accent and making up fantastic scenarios about her. Not to be mean—at least not in the way people in Bend had been—but because they were curious. And because they were all so open, they couldn't understand her being so reserved.

But this was the first time they had ever teased her in front of a client. She took one of the fluffy, white towels from the shelf, and drew her eyebrows together in thought. Did that mean anything? Were they becoming more comfortable with her? Or was she seeming even stranger to them?

She returned to the main salon and handed Marty the towel, grateful to see Foster and Madeline Cole deeply into another conversation. "Thanks," she said softly.

"No problem." Marty smiled. "Why don't you take a

break? There's a bit of a lull right now and it won't last forever. Besides, it's already past two and you haven't sat down once."

That was true. Her feet ached and she did long to just sit, even if only for a minute or two. Still, she hesitated. "Sallie might need—"

"She just left for a lunch date." Marty shook her head. "Go on. You deserve it."

"Well…okay. But if you or anybody else needs me, I'll be in the break room."

"You got it."

Becky Lynn made her way to the staff's break room. Sallie insisted her employees use it, as she thought eating, smoking and talking around the clients both unprofessional and sloppy.

The room was empty and mercifully quiet. No throbbing rock and roll, no chatter, no hum and whine of blow dryers. Becky Lynn sighed, grateful to be alone, relieved to be able to let down her guard for a few minutes, minutes free of worrying about how she was acting or what someone might be thinking about her.

Rolling her tired shoulders, she went to the refrigerator, got herself a Coke and the apple she had brought with her to work. She took a giant bite of the fruit and crossed to the vinyl couch set up along the far wall. She sank onto it, making a sound of relief as she did. It felt good to get off her feet. She slipped off her sneakers and rubbed her arches. With her next paycheck she had to get herself a new pair of shoes, a pair with arch support.

On the floor beside the couch lay the new *Vogue,* the January issue. Someone had left it behind. Becky Lynn hesitated a moment, then picked it up. Sallie ordered every magazine imaginable for The Shop, but Becky Lynn had only glanced at them so far. She feared if she showed how interested in them she really was, she would be singled out and made fun of, the way she had been back home.

She took another bite of the apple and leafed eagerly through the magazine. She studied the photographs, the makeup and hairstyles. She noted which models and photographers were being used, what the most current style statement was. She stopped on an ad for Bloomingdale's. The model sported a long spiky haircut, similar to the one made a household name by Tina Turner's latest video. Marty had given a client the same style only days ago.

Becky Lynn tilted her head, studying the picture. Something about it didn't work. What was it? She narrowed her eyes. *The lighting. Of course.* She smiled. If the photographer had used a softer, less direct light, the shadows would have been less harsh, less jarring. And, in her unschooled opinion, more in keeping with the romantic style of the dress.

She flipped through several more pages, stopping on a dramatic shot for Armani. She drew her eyebrows together. *This shot was perfect, without flaw.* This photographer had used—

Marty bopped in, humming the newest Cindy Lauper tune. "Hey, Becky Lynn."

Becky Lynn lifted her gaze. Marty sported the androgynous look made popular by rockers like Annie Lennox of the Eurythmics, down to her super-short, bleached-blond hair. On her, it worked. "Hi, Marty."

The other woman crossed to the refrigerator, peered inside, then shut the door without selecting anything. She arched her eyebrows. "What are you looking at?"

"Nothing much." Becky Lynn folded her hands over the

magazine, hoping the other woman wouldn't pursue her question. "Everything okay out there?"

"Yeah. Fine." Marty lit a cigarette and crossed to the sofa. She sat on its arm, tipped her head and looked at the magazine. "That's David Bailey's work, isn't it?" she said, referring to the photographer.

"Uh-huh."

"He's been around forever." Marty pulled on the cigarette, then blew out a long stream of smoke. "I think he's the greatest."

"Who's the greatest?"

Brianna strolled in, followed closely by Foster. Becky Lynn sank lower in her seat. Brianna was an aspiring actress, and very full of herself. She had a lover, a sugar daddy, who kept her in high style. Of all the artists at The Shop, Brianna had the most beautiful clothes and jewelry, the fanciest car, the finest life-style. She made Becky Lynn uncomfortable, not because she had ever been unduly ugly toward her, but because she put on airs like the women back home who had been.

Becky Lynn shifted her gaze to Foster. As for him, she just didn't know how to take him. He was funny and smart, but she had learned quickly that his sharp tongue cut the unwary to shreds.

"David Bailey." Marty tapped the magazine page. "He captures a look better than anyone else."

"No way." Brianna dug a Coke from the back of the fridge. "No one's better than Giovanni. That whole sex thing he does, it's so potent."

Foster poured himself a mineral water. "Have you seen his son Carlo's work? He uses the same elements. He's a real comer."

"What about Avedon?" Becky Lynn asked before she thought to stop herself. "I think his work is really special. What he does with light and shadow, nobody else does that."

Conversation ceased. Everybody looked at her. Becky Lynn blushed and squirmed and cursed herself for opening her mouth.

Foster brought a hand to his heart. "My God, she speaks. Our little Blossom not only has a voice, she has an opinion."

"Fuck off, Foster." Marty put her arm around Becky Lynn's shoulders. "Don't mind him, he's just a prick."

He sniffed. "Could it be that you're just a bit homophobic?"

"Give me a break!" Marty glared at him. "Maybe it's more like I can't stand you and your snotty little asides."

Brianna stepped in quickly, obviously wanting to avert a full-scale argument. "Becky Lynn's right. Nobody has ever done with light and shadow what Avedon has. But mark my words, Jack's better than them all. Just wait and see."

Becky Lynn glanced from one to the other. "Jack who?"

"Jack Gallagher," Brianna supplied. "Sallie's son."

"He's gorgeous, too." Marty sighed. "And available in a you'll-never-catch-him sort of way."

"You should know, you've tried hard enough." Foster grinned. "But I have to agree. He does have a rather spectacular ass. Just beautiful."

"Like you'd ever get your hand on it," Marty retorted, standing and crossing to the mirror above the sink. "Jack is all man. One hundred percent U.S. heterosexual male."

Foster grinned again. "Such a pity."

Becky Lynn frowned, struggling, as always, to follow their lightning-fast conversation. "This Jack's a fashion photographer?" she asked, standing and crossing to the trash can. She tossed her apple core in, then wiped her fingers on the seat of her jeans.

"Uh-huh." Marty leaned toward the mirror and applied a glossy coat of bright pink to her lips. "You won't know his work yet. He's just starting out. But he's really good." She shot an antagonistic glance at Foster. "I think it's because he likes women so much."

Brianna made a sound of frustration. "Can't you two bury the hatchet? Don't you think you've fought over Kathleen Turner's head long enough? This is getting boring." Brianna turned to Becky Lynn. "Kathleen Turner was Marty's client. One day when Marty was booked solid, she needed her hair done. It was an emergency, she said. Foster did it."

"And did it supremely well," he added. "She's asked for me ever since."

Marty narrowed her eyes. "But Kim Alexis switched to me, and he can't stand it."

"You stole her out of pure peevishness." He glared at the other hairdresser. "You set out to do it. You—"

"Kim Alexis?" Becky Lynn interrupted at the same moment Brianna threw up her hands in disgust. "She's wonderful. Do you know how many *Vogue* covers she's had this year? I think she's just…the…"

Her words trailed off as silence fell over the room once more. Every gaze turned to her, and heat burned Becky Lynn's cheeks.

Foster arched an eyebrow. "You seem awfully interested in this stuff, Blossom. You harbor secret dreams of a modeling career, or something?"

Becky Lynn swallowed hard, feeling like a complete fool. She wanted to die. She wished she could crawl into a hole and hide forever.

Instead, she folded her arms across her chest and met his gaze, though it was hard to do so without cringing. "I'm not blind," she said softly. "Or stupid."

Marty glared at Foster again and squeezed Becky Lynn's shoulder. "He didn't mean anything by that. Really. Out here, everybody's trying to be something. Or somebody. That's all."

Becky Lynn shifted her gaze. How could she tell them she only wanted to be who she was? How could she tell them she was out here because she wanted to go through a day without being judged according to rules that had nothing to do with her, with the person she was?

She couldn't tell them. They wouldn't understand or care. And she wouldn't make herself vulnerable to them— or anyone else.

"I knew if I looked long enough," a man said from the doorway, "I'd find a sign of intelligent life. What is this? Some sort of hairdressers' convention?"

"Jack!" Marty sprang to her feet, her cheeks bright with color. She smoothed a hand over her short, black skirt. "What are you doing here?"

Becky Lynn turned. She had never seen this man— Jack—before. He stood in the doorway, hands thrust into the pockets of his faded, ripped Levi's, head tilted to one side, his expression amused.

"I had an appointment down the street," he said. "At Tyler Creative. I thought I'd stop in and see what's happening with my favorite girls."

"Absolutely nothing's happening." Brianna pouted.

"Where have you been keeping yourself, Jack Gallagher? It's been dull as death around here without you."

Sallie's son, Becky Lynn realized. She moved her gaze over him, surprised. He didn't look like his mother. Sallie was quietly attractive with soft features and nondescript coloring.

Not her son. Nothing about him could be called quiet. Or nondescript. He was big, at least six foot four, and possessed a strong, distinctive face. He filled the doorway, the room, with a kind of ferocious energy, a vitality that made her feel small and threatened.

He strode into the room as if he owned the moment and everyone in it. Not arrogantly, not possessively. But as if he understood he had everyone's undivided attention.

And he did.

He tossed his portfolio on the table and bent over Brianna's hand, his eyes crinkling at the corners. "I haven't been able to bear being around you since you hooked up with old what's-his-name." He brought her hand to his mouth. "You broke my heart."

"You bastard," Marty said cheerfully, lighting a cigarette. "I thought I broke your heart."

"I wouldn't break your heart, Jack." Foster blew him a kiss. "I promise."

"Just say the word—" Brianna lifted her face to his, her voice husky "—and old what's-his-name is history."

"He can't afford you," Marty snapped, sounding jealous. "Now me, I don't need so much to be happy. A little wine, a lot of sex, a few empty promises, more sex."

These women weren't kidding, Becky Lynn realized, stunned. Not Marty or Brianna. Both women, although completely different types, acted as if they adored Jack

Gallagher, as if they would do anything for him—or with him. They were practically fighting over the man.

Joy burst into the break room, Linda right behind her. "Jack! We heard you were in here."

First Joy kissed him, then Linda. Then Joy again.

"Our clients are soaking, so we can't stay."

"But we just had to say hi."

"Don't stay away so long next time."

"Promise?"

Jack laughed, promised and soundly kissed each woman again. Brianna and Marty looked on, obviously annoyed. Foster watched, his expression amused.

Becky Lynn curved her arms around herself, uncomfortable. What would she do if he tried to touch or kiss her? The memory of the night Ricky and Tommy had brutalized her, filled her head. Her palms began to sweat, her pulse to thrum. Fear choked her.

Jack Gallagher wasn't a boy. He was a man, a big man. He could overpower her. He could hurt her.

Becky Lynn told herself she had nothing to fear; she told herself she was overreacting. She took a step backward, anyway, intent on escaping before he noticed her.

No such luck. He turned his gaze to her; dimples cut his cheeks as he flashed his quick, beautiful smile her way. "Hi."

Her heart began to pound; the inside of her mouth turned to ash. She took another step backward, using everything she had to keep her fear from showing. "Hello."

"I'm Jack." He crossed to her, still smiling. "Sallie's son."

He had eyes like his mother's, an almost startling blue, framed by dark lashes. But where his mother's eyes were kind, his were keen, his gaze sharp with intelligence. This man could see right inside her, she thought. He could see everything she was—and wasn't.

"Yes, I know." She clasped her hands together. They shook. "The photographer."

"That's me." He smiled and swept his gaze over her. "Who are you?"

"That's our very own Blossom," Foster drawled. "Visiting us from way down yonder in Mississippi."

Jack arched his eyebrows. "Your name's Blossom?"

"No," she corrected stiffly, tired of Foster's sarcasm. "My name's Becky Lynn. Excuse me, I have work to do."

She angled past him. He caught her hand, stopping her. She lowered her eyes to his hand, large and strong as it curled around her own. He was too big, too strong, to fight off. He could overpower her without even trying.

"Don't run off on account of me, Becky Lynn. I'll be good, I promise." He looked at her, into her eyes, and smiled. "Besides, I have some influence with the boss."

Suddenly light-headed, she tugged her hand free of his. Acutely aware of all eyes on her, she squared her shoulders. "It was nice meeting you. Goodbye."

Jack watched the girl—Becky Lynn—hurry off, one corner of his mouth lifting with wry amusement. He couldn't remember the last time he'd gotten such a cold shoulder from a woman, if he ever had. This girl had looked at him as if he were the devil himself.

Behind him, the hairdressers hooted with amusement. He turned to face them, grinning. "I think she likes me."

"It's not you." Marty sauntered across to the table and opened Jack's portfolio. "That's just her way."

"You'll have to take your charm elsewhere, Jack." Foster laughed. "Our Blossom doesn't open up to anybody."

Jack shifted his gaze to the doorway through which Becky Lynn had disappeared. He drew his eyebrows together in thought, then swung his gaze back to Foster. "I wonder why?"

Foster shrugged and tossed his disposable coffee cup into the trash. "Don't know, don't care." He checked his watch. "I'd better get back at it. Nice seeing you, Jack."

Brianna checked her own watch, groaned and stood. "That's it for me, too." She stood on tiptoe and fitted her mouth to his. Her breasts pillowed seductively against his chest. "Call me, Jack. I'd love to get together."

Jack returned her kiss, murmured that he would, then watched her go. Marty was right, he couldn't afford Brianna, but what she wanted to do wouldn't cost a cent. And it just might be a once-in-a-lifetime experience.

"These are wonderful. They're new, aren't they?"

"Mmm." Jack crossed to stand behind Marty. He looked over her shoulder, studying the photos in question. "Good enough to get me a gig. Tyler Creative's art director went nuts over those shots."

"That's great, Jack. Just…great." She turned to face him. Tipping her head back to meet his gaze, she laid her hands on his chest. "They're incredible shots. Very sexy in a macho kind of way."

"You think so?"

"Uh-huh." She wet her lips and slid her hands to his shoulders. "I like that, you know that sexy…macho… thing."

His pulse stirred, his manhood with it. It wouldn't take

much, just a nudge, and she would be his. He could have her here, now. She would find a place where they wouldn't be disturbed.

She had a pretty body, boyish but still soft. A pretty face. Her breasts would just fill his palms, her mouth would open greedily under his.

His body hardened, and he swore silently. Marty wanted sex. But she wanted more, too.

And the "more" he couldn't give her.

He caught her hands and squeezed them. "This isn't a good idea, Marty. In fact, it's an extremely bad idea."

"What?" She leaned seductively into him. Her nipples were erect and poked against her thin spandex top. She would like to have them stroked and teased, he thought. She would like to have them kissed, would like to have him draw the peaks into his mouth. Her breasts, although small, were extremely sensitive. He could tell by the way she rubbed herself against him, could tell by the way her breathing changed as she did, could tell by the heat that came into her eyes.

He drew a ragged breath, completely aroused. "Sex, you and me."

"Why?" She moved her torso against his again. "Don't you think I'm attractive?"

He lowered his hands to her hips and drew her pelvis to his. He was rock-hard and ready. "Oh, yeah, I think you're attractive, Marty. Sexy as hell. But I also know that unlike Brianna, sex isn't all you want. Twenty minutes from now, you'd hate my guts because it would be over." He looked her straight in the eye. "And it would be over, Marty."

He shifted his hands so they cupped her backside.

Arousal shot through him, and he wondered where the hell this streak of chivalry had come from. "If I'm wrong, don't move a muscle because I'm right here and I'm ready. But if I'm right…"

He let the thought trail off and Marty hesitated a moment, then pushed against his chest. He released her and she spun away from him, but not before he saw that her eyes were bright with tears.

"Thanks a lot," she said softly. "For nothing, you shit."

Jack watched her stalk out, then made a sound of disgust. Great. He'd tried, for maybe the first time in his life, to be nice, to be a gentleman, and got called a shit. If he had acted like what she had accused him of being, he would be in the storage closet right now, screwing his brains out. Damn.

He swore again and closed his book, then zipped it shut. Nice guys did finish last. He had the ache in his groin to prove it.

"Oh…I thought you'd left."

Becky Lynn stood just inside the door, frozen like a deer caught in the sudden glare of headlights.

"Just leaving now."

"I need—" she pointed to the storage closet "—supplies."

A picture of him and Marty going at it in the closet filled his head, and he lifted his lips. Becky Lynn here would have had a heart attack.

He picked up his portfolio. "I'm not stopping you."

"I…I know." She angled her chin up, as if preparing for a battle, and skirted past him, putting as much physical distance between them as possible.

He drew his eyebrows together, suddenly annoyed. "I don't bite, you know."

She looked back at him, startled. "Excuse me?"

He tossed his book back on the table and crossed to where she stood. "I don't bite. I don't have some contagious disease. As far as I know, I don't smell. So what's the deal?"

She stared blankly at him a moment, then shook her head. "Nothing. No deal. I'm busy, that's all."

She turned her back to him, opened the storage-closet door and stepped inside. He watched her, mystified. "Have I done something to offend you?"

She shook her head but didn't look at him. He could see her counting and selecting bottles and jars. She wanted him to go away, to leave her alone, and she wasn't even being subtle about it.

He would be damned if he was going to give in so quickly. He leaned against the doorjamb. "How long have you been at The Image Shop?"

For a moment, she said nothing, and he wondered if she would even reply. Then she cleared her throat. "Two months."

He frowned, waiting for her to say something else, to give him a bit of background or an explanation for having come all the way to California from Mississippi. None came.

"Do you like it here? At The Image Shop?"

"Yes." She turned, her arms loaded with products. "Excuse me. I need to pass."

He stepped forward to help her, and she took a step backward, her expression panicked. He stopped, confused. "I was just going to offer to help." He gestured to her loaded arms. "You look like you need it."

"I don't. Thank you."

"You're being silly." He made a sound of impatience and reached a hand toward her. "You have more than you can carry."

"Don't!" She jerked backward, bumping into the metal shelves. With a sound of surprise, she swung sideways and the bottles tumbled from her arms, spilling across the tile floor. One of them broke open and gooey pink lotion oozed onto the white tile. The smell of watermelon filled the air.

"Oh, no." She grabbed some paper towels from the shelves behind her, bent down and began to mop up the mess.

He helped himself to some towels and squatted beside her to help. "Hell, I'm really sorry. I didn't mean to startle you."

She didn't reply or look up, and he wadded the sweet-smelling towels into a ball, feeling, ridiculously, like an ogre. "Sometimes I'm a little too pushy. I didn't mean any harm. Really."

"A *little* too pushy?" his mother said from behind them. "In that case, given to understatements, as well."

Jack glanced over his shoulder at his mother. She stood just inside the walk-in closet, her eyes on him, her expression both amused and exasperated.

"Hi, Mom." He grinned, stood and crossed to her. "Becky Lynn and I were just getting acquainted." He tossed the wet towels into the trash barrel just outside the door.

"I see that." She shifted her gaze to Becky Lynn. "I hope he wasn't bothering you too much. I used to look forward to his visits—" she met her son's gaze again "—until I realized how less productive the staff was when he was around. He walks in and immediately there's a commotion."

"Gee, Mom, I love you, too."

"He wasn't bothering me, Sallie." Becky Lynn stood, the bottles of products once more in her arms. "I better go put these out."

She scurried past him and his mother, and Jack watched her go. He drew his eyebrows together, and met his mother's gaze once more. "She's a bit skittish."

"A bit."

Jack arched an eyebrow. "What's her story?"

"I don't know." Sallie tucked her hair behind her ear. "A runaway, I suspect. In some sort of trouble."

He looked at his mother affectionately. "Another stray, Mom?"

"She works hard," Sallie said as they exited the storage closet, closing the door behind them. "The Shop's doing well, I can afford to pay an extra pair of hands."

Jack looked in the direction Becky Lynn had gone, wondering about her again. "She has an…odd face, doesn't she?"

"You're getting that look in your eyes, Jack." Sallie shook an index finger at him. "Stop it right now. You need to leave her alone."

He lifted his eyebrows in feigned innocence. "What look?"

"That challenged look. The one you get every time you're presented with something you can't have. You've been getting it since you were a toddler." She slipped her arm through his and laughed. "Sometimes I wonder if you weren't gifted with a bit too much charm."

He grinned. "Didn't you know? There's no such thing as too much charm."

"Except when you turn it on inexperienced and unsuspecting waifs." She looked at him sternly. "I mean it, Jack."

"You make me sound like I'm a Bluebeard, or something. I don't mean any harm."

"I know." Sallie faced him and touched his cheek lightly, lovingly. "But Becky Lynn's not a toy to be won, and she's not like the rest of the women around here. She's young. She's less experienced. I have a feeling she's been hurt badly."

"In other words, take my overabundance of charm to the beauty salon down the street."

Sallie wrinkled her forehead. "I'm serious about this, Jack. She's had a bad time, I think. And from what I've seen, she's very uncomfortable around men."

"I wonder why?"

Sallie lifted her shoulders. "I don't know, but she had…bruises when she first came in. They were faded, but not enough so she could hide them. And the expression in her eyes, it…"

Her words trailed off, and she drew her eyebrows together in thought. "When I looked into her eyes, I couldn't not give her a job. She looked so beaten, so sad. And yet I sensed such strength in her, such determination." Sallie shook her head and met Jack's gaze once more. "I had this feeling that I was her last chance."

"You've got a big heart, Mom. Too big sometimes."

"Not this time. She works hard, she's easy to have around. She doesn't complain or—"

"Even speak," he teased.

Sallie made a face. "Jack, do you take anything seriously?"

"My photography." Her smile faded a bit, and he made a sound of irritation. "I hate it when you look at me that way. I'm going to make it, Mom. Just wait and see."

"I believe you are, Jack." She sighed. "But I…worry about at what cost."

He fought back frustration. He and his mother had never agreed on his choice of profession, although she claimed to have confidence in his abilities. "You worry too much," he said softly. "You always have."

"I'm your mother. It's my job."

He lifted his lips. "I'm twenty. I think you're due for a vacation."

"That's not the way it works. You could be eighty, I'd still be worrying."

"I look forward to that." He gave her a quick hug, kissed her cheek and changed the subject. "I hear you had a date for lunch."

"Uh-huh."

Jack picked up his portfolio, and they walked to the door. "Victor again?"

"Uh-huh."

He made a sound of disgust. "You're not going to tell me a thing, are you?"

"Afraid not," she said cheerfully. "So, to what did I owe the pleasure of your visit?"

"I had planned to take my beautiful mother to lunch. Since *Victor* beat me to it, I guess I'll just have to come back tomorrow."

16

Becky Lynn turned off The Image Shop's sound system. Silence replaced the pulsing rock, and Becky Lynn sighed and let the quiet fill and soothe her. The day had been wild. Several celebrities had been in, one of them a rock star called Madonna, complete with her own entourage, including a member of the media. The clients who valued their privacy—though in Hollywood there seemed to be few of those—had been outraged; others, the ones who lived to bask in the light of notoriety, had been delighted. Whichever the scenario, the clients had been demanding and inordinately particular, the artists on edge and temperamental.

In the middle of it all, Jack had made an appearance. As always when he was around, all hell had broken loose. Brianna had shifted her attention from her wealthy customer to Jack, Joy had smudged a client's freshly applied lacquer in her hurry to say hello and Foster and Marty had begun to argue.

As for herself, his presence had so unnerved her, she'd spilled a glass of red wine across a client's lap—thank God the woman had been wearing a smock—and had completely forgotten several things Sallie had asked her to do.

Today, for the first time, Becky Lynn had seen Sallie not

only flustered, but angry. At closing, she had called a staff meeting and had given everyone a regular chewing out.

Rolling her tight shoulders, Becky Lynn moved through the silent salon, straightening as she went. Sallie had retreated to her office with a stout glass of wine and the books, everyone else had gone home.

Becky Lynn stepped into the waiting room. Everyone, it seemed, but Marty. She lounged on one of the leather couches, head back as she blew smoke rings toward the ceiling.

"I thought you'd left."

The hairdresser watched a perfect ring float to the ceiling. "I haven't decided where I'm going yet."

"How about home?" Becky Lynn straightened the magazines on the coffee table, arranging them into two large fans. She moved to a side table and did the same thing.

"Home's boring." Marty sighed and stubbed out her cigarette. "What are you going to do?"

Becky Lynn grinned. "Go home."

"But it's Saturday afternoon, soon to be Saturday night." Marty sighed again, and dragged her hands through her close-cropped hair. "I hate this time of day. There's nothing to do."

"Nothing sounds good to me."

Marty made a sound of disgust. "That's so unCalifornia. With an attitude like that, you don't deserve to live anywhere on the West Coast."

Becky Lynn laughed lightly and crossed to the buffet. It looked as if it had been hit by a bomb. Becky Lynn shook her head in disgust and began cleaning up the mess. She had seen barnyard animals with better manners than those of the rock star's friends. One of them had stuck a finger in each kind of pastry to see what it tasted like.

"Pretty gross," Marty said, coming up behind her. "I thought they'd never leave."

"Me, too." Becky Lynn stacked the mangled pastries onto a tray, shaking her head. "They have so much money, you'd think they would have a little class."

"But the two don't necessarily go together," Marty murmured. "Live in this town long enough, and you'll see that."

Becky Lynn thought of home, of Mrs. Abernathy, the Fischers and Joneses. Neither did money and kindness go together.

"Becky Lynn, can I ask you a question?"

She looked over her shoulder at Marty and nodded. "I guess."

"Now, don't get mad, but do you have any clothes besides—" she gestured broadly "—those?"

Becky lowered her eyes, taking in her faded plaid shirt, ancient, ill-fitting blue jeans and too-small canvas sneakers. Heat stung her cheeks, but she lifted her gaze unashamedly to Marty's. "Not many. Just what I've worn to work."

"That's what I thought." Marty narrowed her eyes, then smiled as if struck by an amazing thought. "I know these great secondhand shops on Melrose. They have all sorts of fabulous retro clothes and—"

"I can't afford clothes right now. Thanks, though." Becky Lynn returned her attention to the buffet, acknowledging disappointment. It would have been nice to go shopping with the other woman, nice to have new clothes.

Marty moved to the center of the room and lit another cigarette. For several moments, the soft hiss of Marty drawing on the cigarette was the only sound in the room.

"You're really lucky, you know."

Becky Lynn looked at her in surprise. Now, there was something she had never been called—lucky.

At her disbelieving expression, Marty laughed. "It's true. You're so tall and thin. There are tons of styles you could wear that the majority of women can't. Designers create styles for living hangers."

"Like me? And that makes me lucky?"

"Damn right."

Becky Lynn shook her head, hoisted the loaded tray and started for the kitchen.

Marty followed. "I bet you've never even thought about what style would be best for you."

Style? Her? Wouldn't Fayrene, Dixie and the rest of Bend have a good laugh at that one? She tossed the pastries into the trash. "I've never had the opportunity."

"Well, you have it today." Marty stubbed out her cigarette. "Come on, let's go take a look. You'll adore these shops, I know you will."

Becky Lynn loaded and started the dishwasher, then rinsed out the sink. She shut off the water and faced the hairdresser, exasperated. "Look, I know my clothes are… awful. But I don't have any money, Marty."

The other woman arched an eyebrow in disbelief. "Any money? Not a penny?"

"Well, hardly any."

"That's all you'll need. I promise."

Becky Lynn caught her bottom lip between her teeth, torn. She wanted to go, had looked at other women's clothes—the elegant fabrics, the brilliant colors and soft tones—and had longed for the same things for herself. Every morning she looked at the few ragged and ugly outfits she had and wished for something else, anything else.

Marty grinned up at Becky Lynn. "If nothing else, it'll be fun. I bet you haven't been out with a girlfriend since you moved here."

A girlfriend, Becky Lynn marveled several hours later. For the first time in her life, she had a friend. It felt weird and wrong, but also wonderful and right. She wasn't sure how to act, what to say or how to respond to Marty's sometimes ribald comments about the men they passed on the street. So she simply stopped thinking about how to respond, and just did, laughing and giggling and saying whatever came to her mind.

She couldn't remember ever having had so much fun.

Marty hadn't exaggerated about what they might find at the secondhand shops. In Hollywood, Becky Lynn learned, things were only desirable when they were new.

Nor had Marty been kidding about the prices. All the shop owners knew Marty, and they were happy to help. She told them she wanted the inexpensive stuff, and they had pulled out things that they'd thought they would never sell, taking even a bit more off their already giveaway prices.

Becky Lynn had no idea what to try on, which pieces to put together, and in some cases, how the garments were supposed to be worn. Overwhelmed, Becky Lynn turned to Marty for help.

The other woman chose ornate patterns and brilliant colors for her, chose soft gauzy fabrics and pencil-slim silhouettes. With each piece she tried on, Marty exclaimed over the difference in Becky Lynn's appearance.

Becky Lynn hung back, uncertain. The colors and

styles felt too bold for her, and yet when she looked at herself in them, she felt...different from herself. Like someone other than Becky Lynn Lee, poor white trash from Bend, Mississippi.

Not that the clothes made her beautiful—or even pretty—she had no illusions about that. But they did take her away from herself and her past, and that was the best a girl like her could hope for.

In the end, she bought several things, as much as she could afford, vowing to come back for another piece with each paycheck.

"Now, aren't you glad you listened to me?" Marty said as they took seats at a sidewalk café. "Wasn't I right about the prices?"

"I am and you were." Becky Lynn laughed and slid her bags under the table. "These are the first reasonably priced things I've found since coming to Hollywood. Everything's so expensive here."

"That's California. All this sunshine's not free, you know."

The waiter arrived. Marty ordered a margarita, Becky Lynn a Coke.

As he walked away, Marty wiggled her eyebrows. "Nice ass. Do you think he'd mind if I grabbed a handful?"

"Marty!"

The hairdresser laughed and lit a cigarette. "I shock you, don't I? I guess good little girls from the South don't talk that way." She blew out a long stream of smoke. "Tell me about yourself, Becky Lynn. All I know is that you're from Mississippi and haven't spent much time around plain-speaking women."

Becky Lynn lowered her eyes, at a loss. She should have

expected this question, should have prepared herself for it. But she hadn't.

Now, she only knew she didn't want to tell Marty about her past, didn't want to admit that she was trash, that her daddy was a no-good drunk. She couldn't bear to see Marty's expression change, couldn't bear the thought of seeing pity or revulsion in her gaze.

She drew in a deep, steadying breath. She had started over, started fresh. And she would never go back to being the old Becky Lynn Lee, the one who had been pitied and hated. Never.

The waiter returned with their drinks, and set them on the table in front of them. Becky Lynn took a swallow of the sweet, icy beverage, then returned her gaze to Marty's. The other woman sipped her margarita, her expression openly curious.

"I'm from Jackson," she began, clearing her throat. "My daddy was a farmer." She cleared her throat again and looked away. "He was…killed in a…farming accident."

"Oh, Becky Lynn, I'm sorry." Marty leaned across the table and touched her hand lightly. "What happened?"

"He was in the field, and he…he got run over by the tractor." She glanced at Marty, the other woman looked horrified. "My brother, Randy, was driving it. It was really bad."

"Sounds gruesome."

Becky Lynn ran her finger along the side of her damp glass, a feeling of freedom moving through her, a feeling of liberation. Marty believed her, so would everyone else.

"My mother took it real hard," she continued softly, working to hide her elation. "She was devastated. Then we lost the farm and well, money was really tight so I decided to…come out here."

Marty shook her head and sipped her drink. "What a story."

"I send Mama money every week, trying to help out. I worry, especially about the little ones."

Becky Lynn's eyes filled. That much was true. With her first paycheck, she'd sent a few dollars to her mother, through Miss Opal. She hadn't given a return address and had included only a brief note to assure Glenna she was okay. She trusted Miss Opal to make certain her mother got the money—and that her father didn't.

"Out of what you make?" Marty made a sound of astonishment. "You send money?"

"It's not much. A few dollars. But with Mama's situation every penny helps."

For long moments, Marty said nothing. Then she leaned back in her chair. "You must really miss her. My mom's just over in Pasadena, and sometimes I miss her like crazy. And when something's got me down, nobody is able to help me like my mom." Marty met her gaze. "You know what I mean?"

Becky Lynn's eyes filled with tears. She didn't know what Marty meant; she wished for all the world that she did. She blinked furiously against the tears, battling them. She lost the battle.

Marty made a soft sound of regret. "Hey, I'm sorry. I shouldn't have said that."

"It's okay." With the back of her hand, Becky Lynn wiped the tears from her cheeks. "I'm being silly."

"No, you're not. I know it's got to be tough." She hesitated a moment, then returned her gaze to Becky Lynn's.

"Why out here?" she asked. "Why southern California? It's such a long way from your home."

Becky Lynn folded her hands in her lap. "I chose here because in every picture I'd ever seen of California, it looked so beautiful. And the people always looked so happy. I thought it would be a good place to start a new life."

"You and a million other folks." Marty drained her drink. "Any regrets? Now that you're here?"

"No." Becky Lynn met the hairdresser's gaze evenly for the first time since they had sat down. "No regrets at all."

Marty had asked more questions—about Becky Lynn's supposed brothers and sisters, whether she would ever go home and what Mississippi was like. Some questions she had answered honestly, others she had improvised. She had experienced twinges of guilt at lying to someone who had been so nice to her, but she had pushed them aside.

That night, sitting alone in her motel room, she thought about her future, about what she wanted to do. Marty had wondered if she had regrets. How could she? she wondered, hugging a pillow to her chest. She had started her new life, and today she had begun to forge a new past. And now, at long last, she had a friend.

One of her dreams had already come true.

17

"Morning, Red."

Jack. Again. Becky Lynn's fingers froze on the coffee scoop, then they began to shake. Her first two months at The Shop, he had never come in, the last two months he had stopped in almost every day. And every time he did, he made a point of seeking her out. Of flirting with her.

Of calling her that name. *Red.*

She'd been called that before; with her hair, she had been born to the name. But the way he said the word, it didn't seem like a slur. It seemed almost…affectionate. Or as if he was paying her a compliment.

She frowned, feeling foolish at the thought. No male had ever flirted with her or paid her compliments. No male had ever shown any kind of interest in her.

Except Ricky and Tommy.

She shuddered and put the thought of them out of her mind. No doubt Jack Gallagher thought it funny to flirt with her, thought it a big joke. She had no idea what he hoped to gain from making her feel ugly and uncomfortable, but she had vowed she would never let him see her squirm.

Taking a deep breath, she looked over her shoulder. He stood alone in the doorway to the break room, head cocked, his amused gaze on her.

"Hello," she said curtly, then turned back to her work.

"Coffee ready yet?" She heard him move into the room, heard the sound of something being tossed on the table.

"I'm just making it now."

He came up beside her, leaned against the counter and yawned. "Make it strong, I need a jump start this morning."

Her pulse began to pound. Since the day he had cornered her in the storage closet, she had made a point of never being alone with him. Not that he had made any threatening moves toward her or tried to maneuver her into a position of vulnerability. She didn't think he meant her any physical harm, but she was still afraid of him.

He could overpower her so easily. She set the filter cup on top of the pot, then slid it into the machine. "Sorry. I make it the way Sallie asks me to."

For a moment he said nothing. She dared a glance at him from the corner of her eyes. He looked angry.

"Then make it hot," he said, his words measured, "because it's damn cold in here. I think I just got frostbite."

"Becky Lynn, my God. Is that you?"

Relieved to hear the sound of Brianna's voice, Becky Lynn swung around. Brianna stood just inside the room, staring at her in surprise. Becky looked down at herself, at her new outfit, then back up at the other woman. "Yes."

"You look much better." The hairdresser swept the rest of the way into the room. "I approve."

Becky Lynn ran her hand over the hip of the brightly patterned, midi-length skirt. "Oh...thanks."

"I guess," added Jack, rolling his eyes.

"Don't give me a hard time, Jack Gallagher." Brianna tossed her hair over her shoulder. "Come, I want you to see my new publicity photos."

The two sat at the table, and Becky Lynn turned back to

the coffeepot. She watched the dark liquid drip from the filter to the pot, shamelessly eavesdropping on their conversation.

"Bob had them done for me. Aren't they wonderful?"

"Very nice, Brianna. Who was the photographer?"

"Clark Kent." When Jack laughed, Brianna made a sound of indignation. "That's his professional name. I think it's a good idea, it's catchy, memorable. Do you know his work?"

"Can't say that I do."

Becky Lynn transferred the fresh-brewed coffee into the sterling pot for out front. She poured herself half a cup, then filled the cup the rest of the way with milk and added two hefty teaspoons of sugar.

"Would you mind getting me a cup?" Jack asked. She looked at him, and he smiled. "If it's no trouble. I take it black."

"Of course it's no trouble for her. Bring me a cup, too, Becky Lynn. Light and sweet." Brianna didn't take her gaze from the images of herself. "You don't mind, do you?"

She did mind, especially considering that she was the only one of the three who was actually performing Shop duties, but she poured the coffee, anyway, and carried it to them.

"Would you like to see, Becky Lynn?" Brianna asked, taking the cup from her hand.

"See what?" she asked, sliding her gaze to Jack. As her eyes met his, he arched an eyebrow as if in challenge. She stiffened her spine, and jerked her attention back to Brianna.

"These." The hairdresser motioned to the photographs

spread across the table in front of her. "Big Bob had them done for me."

Brianna had taken to calling her sugar daddy Big Bob. It had gotten to be a joke around The Shop because Bob was only five foot four—in his boots. In fact, the artists speculated the only big thing about Bob was his bank account.

Becky Lynn leaned forward, studying the photos. "You want to know what I think?"

"Sure." Brianna tilted her head back and smiled indulgently. "Why not?"

Becky Lynn cocked her head. The photographs were all of Brianna in different poses and outfits. "What are they for?"

"They're publicity photos," Brianna said importantly. "Head shots. For when I go to auditions and casting calls."

"Oh." Becky Lynn gazed at the photos, searching for something to say. Something complimentary. "They're real pretty, Brianna."

"Real pretty," the other woman repeated, frowning. "Is that all you have to say about them?"

Becky Lynn flushed, aware of Jack's gaze intently upon her. She shifted her weight from her right foot to her left. "They're really…nice."

"Nice?" Brianna huffed. "You're acting like you don't like them."

Becky Lynn folded her arms across her chest. "Why do you care what I think?"

"I don't." The woman drew a deep breath. "Of course I don't. It's just that, well…I can't imagine why you wouldn't like them. They're fantastic."

"Look at them, Becky Lynn." Jack smiled, and again

she had the sense that he was challenging her. "What do you really think? Be honest."

She glared at him, suddenly angry. He knew what she thought. He was baiting her. She stiffened her spine, and returned her gaze to the photographs. "Okay, I think...I think they look a little, I don't know...muddy."

"Muddy?" Brianna squeaked. "I don't think so."

"It's only my opinion. Sorry." Becky Lynn took a step back from the table. "I'd better get back to work."

Jack stopped her. "Which shot do you think is the best?"

She didn't hesitate. "This one. Because of the contrast between light and dark, and because she looks so...alive."

"Like I look dead in the others?" Brianna let her breath out in a huff and began to gather together the pictures. "Really, I—"

Jack covered the hairdresser's hand, stopping her movement and tirade. His eyes never left Becky Lynn's. "Which one is the worst?"

She studied them for a moment. "That's hard." She cocked her head. "This one, I guess. It's exceptionally flat."

"Don't encourage her, Jack!" Her cheeks scarlet, Brianna scooped up the photos. "Honestly, she's just a little hick from Mississippi. What does she know? I never should have—"

"She's right."

Brianna swung to face him, her expression stunned. "What?"

"She's right. These shots suck." He plucked the photographs from her hand and tossed them one by one onto the table. "No contrast, no life, uninteresting, flat. Where's the texture? How about an interesting angle or expression, for

Pete's sake? You look like a pretty girl in these, but there are a million pretty girls out there. Nothing about any of these tells me why Brianna James is special."

"But you said… A moment ago you—"

"A moment ago, I lied. I figured it wasn't any of my business, and if you were going to let some photographer who calls himself Clark Kent super-shooter take your photos, well, you deserved whatever you got. But since Becky Lynn here's been so honest, I might as well be, too."

"But…but—" Brianna looked near tears, and Becky Lynn experienced a stab of pity for the other woman. She didn't think Jack had needed to be so specific about the photographs' flaws. It seemed unnecessarily cruel to her. He could have made his point without hurting Brianna.

Jack covered Brianna's hand and leaned toward her. "They don't do you justice, Brianna." He lowered his voice to a silky-soft murmur. "You're too beautiful a woman to settle for these."

Becky Lynn watched in amazement as Brianna's tears evaporated and she turned to Jack, the expression in her eyes adoring. "But what am I going to do? Big Bob arranged to have these taken. If I—"

"Has he seen these yet?" Jack asked. She shook her head. "Hold off. I'll retake them."

"You, Jack?" Brianna curved her hands around his. "You'd do that for me? Really?"

He flashed the hairdresser a breath-stealing smile. Becky Lynn stared, dumbfounded as Brianna practically melted.

"Sure I would." He brought her hands to his mouth and placed a gentle kiss on her knuckles. Then he stood, stretched and tossed his disposable coffee cup in the trash. "My studio, say, Sunday morning at eleven."

Brianna rushed to her feet and planted a quick kiss on his mouth. "I'll be there. And...thanks."

Jack started for the door, then stopped and looked over his shoulder at Becky Lynn. His gaze was so intense, she took an involuntary step backward. "You come, too, Red. I think you'd enjoy it."

Without waiting for a reply, he walked out. Becky Lynn watched him go, feeling as if he had reached inside her and rearranged several of her vital organs.

That sensation stayed with her for the rest of the day. She couldn't shake it, no matter how hard she tried. Nor could she stop wondering why Jack had asked her to the shoot. The invitation had been both unexpected and unwanted. It had left her feeling at once enervated and on edge. And it had left her feeling torn between curiosity and fear.

As the days passed, bringing her closer to Sunday, her feeling of being torn grew. She vacillated between wanting to go and knowing that she wouldn't. She had tried to broach the subject with Marty, thinking the other, more experienced woman might have an idea why Jack had issued her the invitation, but Marty refused to talk about Jack. She had called him a son of a bitch and walked away. Which had left her even more confused—only a few weeks ago, Marty hadn't had enough words of praise to describe Jack.

Saturday, right before closing, Brianna had asked casually if Becky Lynn intended to come to the shoot. She had replied that she didn't know. Brianna had shrugged and given her Jack's address, just in case.

Sunday morning dawned bright and California blue. Becky Lynn climbed out of bed, thinking of the photo shoot. She wasn't going, of course. She ate her breakfast, then showered, wondering how far Jack's studio was from the motel. Even though she assured herself that she was only curious, she dragged out the phone book's map and checked it out.

Jack's studio was in Van Nuys, fairly close, especially by California standards. She shut the phone book. Not that it mattered, of course. She wasn't going.

At eleven-fifteen, Becky Lynn reached Jack's studio. She had purposely arrived fifteen minutes late to ensure that Brianna would have already arrived. Surely there wasn't any risk involved in coming here? What could happen with Brianna present?

She rang the bell and waited. Several minutes later, she heard a door slam, somewhere in the house. She frowned and checked her watch, her heart beginning to thrum. Something wasn't right.

Jack came to the door, a towel slung around his neck, his hair wet from a shower. His chest and feet were bare, his jeans were unsnapped and rode low on his hips.

He grinned and pushed open the screen door. "Hey, Becky Lynn."

A squeak of surprise and dismay slipped past her lips, and she took a step back from the door. "I…I'm sorry. I thought you said…eleven."

"I did. Brianna called early. She's running late, so I took my time." He moved his gaze over her. "She said you weren't coming."

Becky Lynn crossed her arms over her chest. "I changed my mind."

"I see that." He smiled again. "Come on in. I'll throw on a shirt."

She hung in the doorway. *Why had she done this? What in the world had she been thinking of?*

"Becky Lynn?"

She shook her head. "I don't think so. I'll just…wait out here."

He shrugged. "Suit yourself. I'll be inside setting up."

He turned and walked back inside, leaving the door open. She watched him go, her heart beating so heavily, she thought he must be able to hear it.

She let out a long breath and rubbed her arms to warm them, to dissipate the chill of fear. He hadn't tried to lure her in, he hadn't taunted her or made fun of her timidity. In fact, nothing about his manner had threatened. But still…

She caught her bottom lip between her teeth and peeked through the doorway. Immediately inside was a small foyer, and beyond that what looked to be his studio. To the right was a bedroom—she could see that his bed was unmade, to the left a kitchen and eating area. An open box of Frosted Flakes stood in the center of the small, round table, a coffee mug beside it. The *Los Angeles Times* was stacked on the floor by the table.

She shifted her attention once more to the studio. She heard him moving around, whistling aimlessly as he did. She saw equipment set up—stands of lights, a tripod, a roll-around cart covered with all manner of things she couldn't make out.

He crossed her line of vision, and she saw with great relief that he'd put on a shirt and a pair of loafers. He turned toward her, and she ducked out of his view, her heart in her throat. She folded her arms across her chest, fighting the curiosity that tugged at her, fighting the urge to throw caution to the winds and go inside.

The last time she had been so foolhardy, she had paid a horrific price.

She drew a deep, steadying breath and peeked past the doorjamb again. She couldn't see Jack, but she could hear him. Minutes ticked past. She stood in the doorway, feeling uncertain and foolish. Feeling torn.

She pressed her hand to her fluttering stomach. Not every man meant her harm. Not every man was an animal like Ricky and Tommy.

Finally, she took another deep breath and stepped inside. She left the door wide open behind her. If he made a move toward her, she would scream her head off; if he tried to close the door, she would run for it.

She crossed the foyer, realizing when she reached the studio doorway, that she had been tiptoeing. Jack looked up. Their gazes met, and he smiled, his blue eyes crinkling at the corners with the movement. "I knew you couldn't resist."

She folded her arms over her chest, immediately defensive. "Yeah? Why's that?"

He motioned to the studio around them. "Because this interests you, that's why. Because photography interests you."

She angled up her chin. "How do you know that?"

He opened a camera, dropped in a roll of film, then snapped it shut.

He grinned at her as he wound it. "You're here, aren't you? Against your better judgment, too."

He had her there. One corner of her mouth lifted involuntarily in acknowledgment of that fact. Jack saw it and smiled.

"Besides," he continued, setting the camera down,

"anybody else would have told Brianna those shots were good. Anybody else would have thought they were. You have a good eye. Where did you get your training?"

"I don't have any training."

"Your dad a photographer or something?"

Or something was right. She shook her head. "I've never been in a studio before. In fact, I..." She inched her chin up a fraction. "I've never even taken a photograph. I never had the opportunity."

"No way. Not even with an Instamatic?" At her expression, he shook his head in disbelief. "What kind of place is Mississippi? They do have indoor plumbing, don't they?"

Her cheeks heated. With embarrassment. And annoyance. "Yes, we have indoor plumbing. Mississippi doesn't have anything to do with the fact that I've never taken a picture. My family didn't...we didn't have much." She inched her chin up another notch. "Certainly not enough for luxuries like cameras and film."

But we had enough for whiskey, she thought bitterly. There was always money for that. But she would never reveal that to Jack Gallagher.

"Sorry." He picked up the camera and weighed it in his hand. "I shouldn't have said that."

"It's okay."

"Here." He held out the camera.

She looked from him to the camera, and back. "What?"

"Today you take your first photograph."

"I couldn't." She shook her head and took a step backward. "Thank you, but—"

"I insist." He grinned. "I don't think I could live with the thought that you'd never even held a camera in your hands. How could I sleep at night?"

She laughed, surprising herself, but still she eyed the camera warily. "What do I do?"

"Hold it up to your eye, focus and push the button. It's easy. Come here, I'll show you."

She did. He showed her how to focus and which button to push to take the shot, then handed her the camera. A funny little catch in her chest, she weighed it in her palm. It was much heavier than she had imagined it would be, the metal cool against her hands. Cool and solid. Substantial.

She returned her gaze to his. "But…what should I take a picture of?"

"How about me?"

She nodded and he stepped back. She lifted the camera to her eye, focused and snapped. At that moment, Brianna swept into the room, a garment bag slung over her shoulder.

"I'm here!" She stopped dead when she caught sight of them. She shifted her gaze from Becky Lynn to Jack and back. "I thought you weren't coming."

"I had a change of heart." Reluctantly, she handed the camera over to Jack. "I hope you don't mind."

"Of course not." Brianna sounded as if she minded quite a lot. She frowned and turned to Jack. "Sorry I'm late. Big Bob was being difficult."

Jack ambled toward her, and took the garment bag from her hands. "Couldn't bear to let you out of his sight, could he?"

Brianna sighed dramatically. "Being adored can be such a burden."

"I'm sure it is." A smile pulled at Jack's mouth, and Becky Lynn averted her gaze to keep from giggling out loud. She didn't think Brianna would appreciate her amusement.

"Let's take a look at what you brought to wear," he said, carrying the bag to the center of the room and laying it on the floor. "Come have a look, Becky Lynn. I'll be interested to see what you think."

She did, but he didn't ask her opinion. Jack became all business, totally focused as he began to work. He didn't look at her or Brianna, even as he spoke to them.

He took one outfit after another out of the bag, discarding each as unsuitable. Too fussy. Wrong value. Distracting. Boring. Brianna attempted to disagree once, he stopped her cold. "Do you want me to take these shots?" he asked. She did, obviously, as she made not even a sound of protest again.

He decided on a high-necked black catsuit, a nubby, natural-colored sweater, and a huge, softly patterned silk scarf, then directed Brianna to the screen to change.

While she changed and Jack finished setting up, Becky Lynn wandered around the studio. Everything about the place interested and awed her. She recalled the way the camera had felt in her hands, cool and weighty and somehow alive. Holding it, looking through the viewfinder had felt right. A little thrill, a shiver of excitement, had moved through her, and she had wanted to take another picture. Then another.

Would she ever see the photo? She would like to, she decided. She would like to have it—*the first photograph she had ever taken.* She smiled to herself and shook her head. She was being silly.

She crossed to the studio's back wall and stopped in front of it. She moved her gaze over the photographs pinned across its surface, studying them.

"Are these yours?" she asked as he came up to stand behind her.

"All but those." He indicated the ones at the center.

She wondered at their significance, but didn't ask.

"What do you think?"

She looked over her shoulder at him in surprise, drawing her eyebrows together. "You want my opinion?"

"Yeah, I do."

She searched his expression, looking for the joke, the taunt, the secret amusement at having made a fool of her. She didn't see anything but sincerity in his expression. She returned her gaze to the photographs.

"Give me the truth, I can take it."

"I think you're good. I think you're really good."

He laughed, but with pleasure not sarcasm or malice. "Nothing up here's too muddy, is it? Nothing's too—"

"I'm sorry, am I interrupting something?"

At Brianna's question, they both turned. Brianna had stepped out from behind the screen, obviously expecting them to be awaiting her with bated breath. She didn't mask her pique that they weren't. When Jack caught Becky Lynn's gaze, his filled with amusement. She responded involuntarily, smiling.

Then he went to work, retreating to the private place she had seen him go earlier. But this time, he retreated even further.

Becky Lynn hung back and watched, fascinated, knowing instinctively that she dare not get in his way. He tuned out everything but his camera and subject, and in a strange way it was as if they became one.

As he shot, he moved, never stopping. He coaxed and cajoled and complimented Brianna.

"You're an actress, Brianna, you have to act for the camera. That's right, emote a little bit. Good. Beautiful, love. These chromes are going to be great. Just wait. Give me a little more…come on…that's right."

Energy crackled in the room. An awesome energy, private and sexual. Becky Lynn rubbed her arms, rubbed the gooseflesh that rose on them. Jack was seducing Brianna, making love to her, without even touching her.

Engrossed, Becky Lynn responded to Jack's voice, his commands—tipping her head, softening her mouth, smiling.

She realized what she was doing and clasped her hands in front of her, feeling more than a bit foolish, but relieved to know that neither Brianna nor Jack had seen her. What would it be like to be on the receiving end of Jack's energy? Becky Lynn wondered. What would it be like to be Brianna, to be in front of Jack's camera, connected to it and him? What would it be like to feel like the most beautiful woman in the world, the only woman in Jack's world. For that, Becky Lynn guessed, was exactly what Brianna was feeling.

"That's my girl… Think sexy, the sexiest you've ever been in your life. Think about Big Bob."

Brianna burst out laughing; Jack caught the moment and wrapped the session.

"These are going to be fantastic," he said, rewinding the film. "You were incredible, Brianna. Very relaxed, a dream to work with."

"It's you, Jack. You just make me feel so…good." She stood and crossed to him. Stopping closer than appropriate for friends, she tilted her face provocatively up to his. "I don't know how to thank you."

Becky Lynn inched toward the door, uncomfortable. She could see that Brianna knew how she wanted to thank him, and if what Becky Lynn had felt during the last hour was any indication, Jack would be more than willing to accept the woman's gratitude.

She wasn't wanted here. She was out of place. Embarrassed and uncomfortable, she took another step toward the door.

"Don't worry about it, Brianna. It was my pleasure."

"But I want to thank you." Brianna slid her arms around his neck. "It would make me feel…so much better."

Becky Lynn cleared her throat. "Y'all, I've really got to go. Thank you, Jack. It was…interesting."

Jack disentangled himself from Brianna. "Do you have to go? We could all go out for a drink or a bite to eat."

She slid her gaze to Brianna. If she said yes to that, the other woman would claw her eyes out on the spot.

Becky Lynn smiled brightly and inched closer to the door. "No, I have to go. Thanks again. It was…great."

Jack smiled. "I'll bring the proofs by The Shop. So you can see them."

"I'd like that." She swallowed hard. "Bye, Brianna. See you Tuesday."

Turning, she escaped out the front door. It wasn't until she was a block away from Jack's studio that she realized she was trembling. And she wasn't sure why.

18

Jack couldn't get the funny-looking redhead with the soft drawl out of his head. *Funny-looking.* He frowned. He supposed that description wasn't fair to Becky Lynn. Odd-looking, awkward, even. She had a face composed of features that didn't quite fit together. Large, almond-shaped eyes in a color that, depending on her mood, shifted between brown and hazel. A mouth too full for her narrow face and a long but unbelievably straight nose. Strong and elegant on their own, together her features unsettled rather than pleased.

He looked Brianna's proofs over one last time. Brianna, on the other hand, was extremely attractive. Pretty features and coloring, nice proportions and shapes. Everything about Brianna's looks fit neatly together. And yet her face didn't interest him, it didn't call to his artist's eye.

Did Becky Lynn's? Jack shook his head, tucked the proofs into his portfolio and started for the front door. He supposed not. *She* interested him, the person. He had never met a woman so uncertain of herself. At times, her fear became almost palpable.

He drew his eyebrows together. His mother believed Becky Lynn was a runaway, believed she had run all the way from Mississippi to California. That took some guts. It took determination and confidence.

Or a lot of fear.

He suspected the latter to be more the case than the former. What had she been running from? What had been so bad, so frightening, that she had run almost all the way across the country to escape it?

Jack locked his apartment door behind him, jogged down the steps to the sidewalk, then to his car. He tossed his portfolio onto the front passenger seat, climbed behind the wheel and started the engine.

He pulled away from the curb, heading for The Image Shop. Brianna's shots had turned out good. Several of them were excellent. He thought she would be pleased, and if she wasn't, well…it wasn't his problem if she couldn't see quality.

He had no doubts about Becky Lynn's ability to see quality, however.

He swung onto the Interstate 5 going toward Hollywood. What would she think of the shots? Not that it mattered, but he was curious. She had a damn good eye. Not better than his had been at the same age, but good.

Even though she had never been exposed to photography.

He thought about that a moment. He had a hard time believing she was a complete novice, yet he did believe her. Not with his head, but with his gut. Becky Lynn didn't have the ability to lie, and she certainly didn't have the wiles to play games.

He liked her, he realized. Despite her lack of savvy, despite her timidity. There was something basic about her. Something real and down to earth. And she was smart, her intelligence showing through the evidences of hardship and poverty, through the thick drawl and lack of worldliness.

Traffic slowed to a crawl, then came to a standstill. He swore and eased back against the seat, resigning himself to the fact that there was nothing he could do about southern California's traffic problems in general or this traffic jam in particular.

So, instead, he inched the car forward as the cars ahead of him inched forward, his thoughts returning to Becky Lynn. What was her story? And why did he scare her? He didn't think of himself as particularly threatening, especially to women. So why did he make her all but jump out of her skin?

Before Sunday's shoot he hadn't realized he unsettled her. He had assumed she disliked him. Or that she disliked men in general. But when she had refused to come into his place, choosing instead to wait alone on the front porch, he had known.

He had looked into her eyes, really looked, and had seen fear. He frowned, remembering. The emotion had been raw and real; it had taken him totally by surprise.

What was she so afraid of? It would be interesting to uncover her secrets, he decided, traffic clearing as if by magic. He accelerated and swung around the car in front of him, anxious now to reach The Image Shop and start his day. He had several things scheduled, including combing the fashion mart for potential clients. One of these days, it would pay off; one of these days, a designer was going to give him a shot. When one did, Giovanni and Carlo had just better watch their backs.

Moments later, he pulled up in front of The Image Shop and greeted Mac, who rushed forward to open Jack's car door.

"Hey, Jack. What's up?"

"Just bringing by some proofs." Jack tossed the valet his keys. "I won't be long. Twenty minutes or so."

"I'll leave it right here."

Jack thanked him and let himself into the salon. Tuesdays weren't quiet, no day at The Shop was, but as days of the week went, it was less wild. He had come early, hoping to beat the majority of clients, and he saw that he had. Foster was at work, as was Marty. Brianna hadn't yet arrived, Foster told him when he asked, and Becky Lynn was in back.

Marty said nothing, giving him the same cold shoulder she had given him ever since he had turned down her offer of sex. He couldn't figure it, and supposed he never would, but it grated nonetheless.

He found Becky Lynn in the break room storage closet, unpacking a box of products. He dropped his portfolio on the table. "We've got to stop meeting like this."

Startled, she swung around, hand to her throat. Her eyes met his and the expression in hers was anything but happy to see him. "You scared me," she said stiffly.

"So I gathered. Sorry." He slipped his hands into his pockets and cocked his head. "How was your day off?"

"Fine."

She folded her arms across her chest, and he sensed that she wished she was anywhere but alone with him. "You know why I'm here?"

She shook her head.

"Brianna's proofs. Remember, I told you I'd bring them by?"

"You've got them already?"

Her expression softened, her stiff wariness replaced by an almost childlike eagerness. He grinned. "Yeah. Processing film takes no time at all." He turned, unzipped his portfolio and pulled out the two eight-by-ten proof sheets. He held them out. "I think they turned out pretty nice. What do you think?"

She dropped the packing slip back into the box she'd been unloading, and crossed to him, dusting her hands on the seat of her pants. She took the photos. He noticed that her hand trembled as she moved her gaze almost greedily over the shots.

"Here, look through this. It'll help." He reached into his pocket, took out a loupe and handed it to her. "Coffee ready?"

She didn't answer; he suspected she hadn't even heard him. He left her to the proofs, went to the coffeepot and found it half-full. He poured himself a cup, then took a sip, studying her as he did.

Without instruction, she held the loupe to her eye and the proof sheet, moving from one shot to the next, her expression rapt. *She really loves this,* he thought. It wasn't simply interest. It wasn't even fascination. She loved it. He drew his eyebrows together. Why? What made this woman tick?

She lowered the loupe; reluctantly, he thought. She set the proofs gingerly on the table, then clasped her hands in front of her. "Thank you. For letting me look at these and for letting me come to the shoot."

"You're welcome." He arched his eyebrows in question, waiting for a comment. When none came, he shook his head. "Are they that bad?"

"Pardon?"

"The shots. Are they so bad, you don't want to comment?"

"No!" She shook her head vehemently. "Not at all. I just didn't…I didn't feel it was my…place to comment."

"Not your place to comment?" He arched his eyebrows in disbelief. "You were a part of this shoot, in on it from the beginning. You have an excellent eye, and you were right about those other shots. Of course I'm interested in what you think."

She flushed, looking at once embarrassed and pleased. "I think they're great," she said softly. "I think they're wonderful." She twisted her fingers together. "Marty and Brianna were right about you. You're… you're as good as any of those guys in the glossies, Jack. Better, even."

He grinned and tossed his half-full disposable coffee cup into the trash. "Better than any of those guys, huh? You made my day, Becky Lynn." He closed the distance between them and touched the tip of her nose. "And here I thought you were going to pound me into the ground."

At his touch, she took a quick step back from him. "Why would you think that?"

Her voice sounded small suddenly, and afraid. She didn't like to be touched, he realized. She didn't want him to touch her. He had crossed an invisible line.

He took a step away from her, giving her space. "Well, it's obvious you don't like me. It's been obvious from the first."

"That's not true." She folded her arms across herself. "It's just that…just that I—"

"Jack!" Brianna sailed into the room. "Foster told me you were here. Are they ready? Do you have them?"

Becky Lynn used the other woman's entrance to make her escape. She murmured something about needing to see if anybody out front was looking for her, and hurried from the break room.

Cheeks stinging, she rushed into the main salon, glancing wildly around for something to do, for something that would occupy her thoughts.

Something that would put Jack Gallagher and the way he looked at her out of her mind.

She found nothing. None of the artists called out a request; the buffet was stocked, the waiting room neat. She passed by Sallie's office; her boss only nodded absently at her.

Becky Lynn drew in a shaky breath. Jack looked her in the eye when she talked. He listened to her. He acted as if what she had to say mattered and as if he thought her opinions had value.

Nobody had ever treated her like that before. Nobody.

She brought a shaky hand to her chest. Why did he do that? Why couldn't he treat her the way everybody else did? Then she would know how to act around him, then she wouldn't forget who she was.

Jack did make her forget herself. The way he treated her made her feel…special. The way he called her Red. He made her feel different than she was—less ugly, more like the girl she had always longed to be.

Stupid, she thought, glancing frantically around her again. She wasn't different; it was Jack who was different. And she had better not forget it.

She ducked into the bathroom and locked the door behind her. She crossed to the mirror above the sink and gazed at her reflection. She saw herself as she had been the night she'd dragged herself home after Ricky had raped her. As she had looked after she had learned of her brother's betrayal, the way she had looked as her mother had turned away from her.

Tears choked her. It hurt to look at herself. She was ugly. She was the same girl the boys at school had called names and barked at. She was the same girl whose father reviled as too ugly to ever be loved, the girl over whose head boys had shoved a paper bag so they wouldn't have to look at her face while they raped her.

The tears welled up and spilled over, but still she forced herself to gaze into the mirror. Jack made her forget she was that girl. He looked at her as if he didn't see how ugly she was.

But he had eyes. He did see.

She fisted her fingers on the edge of the sink, her knuckles popping out, whiter even than the porcelain. If she forgot that, she would be vulnerable to him. If she forgot that, he could hurt her. Not the way Ricky and Tommy had, but in a way that would leave its own brutal scar.

She squeezed her eyes shut. She wouldn't let him hurt her; she wouldn't let anyone hurt her, not ever again.

"Becky Lynn." Marty tapped on the door. "When you're done in there, Sallie needs to see you."

She opened her eyes and took a deep breath. "Okay," she called, turning on the cold water. "Be right out." She splashed the water on her face and wrists, then patted them dry. She wouldn't forget; she would be safe.

Moments later, she reached Sallie's office. Her heart sank. Jack was with his mother, saying goodbye.

He saw her and smiled. "I'm glad I ran into you before I left. I have something for you." He partially unzipped his book and thumbed through it. He found what he sought, and pulled out an eight-by-ten photo. He handed it to her, looking pleased with himself.

It was a shot of him, and she stared at the photograph, not comprehending.

"It's yours," he said. "Turn it over."

She did. Scrawled at the bottom in black marker, he'd written: *Red's first photograph. February, 1985*

Her hands started to shake. She gazed at the image, touched more than she should have been. The gesture meant nothing to him, but to her it meant…everything. No one had ever given her anything before. No one had ever been so thoughtful.

So this was how it felt to be treated with kindness, she thought, lifting her gaze to his. This was how it felt to be treated like a person whose feelings mattered.

"I don't know what to say, Jack. I…just, I—" She swallowed past the emotion choking her, and smiled weakly at him. "Thanks."

19

Becky Lynn propped the photograph of Jack on the nightstand by her bed and during the long hours of the evenings and nights that passed, she gazed at it, memorizing everything about the image—the fuzzy lighting, Jack's smile and the way his gaze boldly met the camera's, the slightly off-center composition.

And every time she did, a little thrill of excitement ran through her. It wasn't a good shot by any stretch of the imagination, but to her it was the most precious thing on earth. She had taken this photograph. It was hers. It represented something she felt but couldn't touch—the good things, the way her life had changed, the way she had begun to change inside.

Nobody could take that away from her.

She picked up the photo and touched its glossy surface with the tip of her forefinger. She hadn't seen Jack since that morning two weeks ago, and her mood had swung between relief and regret. Relief because when she faced him, she had to remind herself who and what she was. And regret because he made her forget.

She narrowed her eyes, gazing once more at the photograph she had taken of Jack, longing burning in the pit of her gut. She longed to know what he knew, longed to do what he did, to be a part of something so special and exciting.

What would it be like to be able to create beautiful images? What would it be like to be able to capture the essence of someone or something on film, immortalizing it for all time?

It would be wonderful, she thought. It would be perfect. If she could do that, she would have everything.

20

"**B**ecky Lynn!" Brianna raced into the break room. "Sallie just called. She needs you to bring her her color box. Right now."

Becky Lynn jumped up, gathering together the remnants of her lunch. "Where is she?"

"At Jack's studio. She's doing makeup for him—" Brianna sucked in a quick breath. "This is the most important job he's ever gotten, and I could tell from her voice that things aren't going well."

Jack's studio. A shoot. Becky Lynn's heart began to pound, her palms to sweat. She acknowledged anticipation. Tossing the rest of her Coke and bag of chips into the trash, she hurried to the doorway and Brianna. "But how will I get—"

"I already called a cab." The hairdresser stuffed two twenty-dollar bills into Becky Lynn's hand. "Come on, let's get Sallie's colors."

They did, and by the time Becky Lynn made it to the front door, the cab was waiting. Eighteen minutes later, the driver pulled up in front of Jack's building. She paid the man and stepped out of the vehicle.

Sallie appeared at the front door. "Becky Lynn, thank goodness. Come inside. Quickly."

Becky Lynn did as Sallie asked. From her position just inside the door, she saw Jack in his studio setting up. He looked shaken. Becky Lynn frowned. She had never seen Jack look anything but completely confident.

"Becky Lynn?" Sallie called from the kitchen. "My colors."

"Sorry." Becky Lynn dragged her gaze from Jack and followed Sallie into the kitchen. Two models, dressed in silky wraparound robes, sat at the table waiting, talking softly, their makeup half done. They spared her hardly a glance.

Sallie took the box of eye and cheek colors from Becky Lynn's hands. "I can't believe I forgot this. I never would have in the old days. It shows how little fashion work I do anymore."

Becky Lynn folded her arms across her chest. "Brianna said this was an important shoot for Jack."

"Uh-huh." Sallie tipped the first model's head back and began applying blush. "Tyler Creative agreed to give him a crack at Jon Noble Clothiers. They're a small, high-end chain with a store on Rodeo Drive."

"How come Jack doesn't look too happy about it?"

Sallie rifled through the box. "The photographer he hired to assist him today got another gig and stood him up. Jack's called everybody he knows, and no one's available."

Becky Lynn glanced toward the studio, then back at Sallie, butterflies in her stomach. "Can he do it alone?"

"Sure. Close your eyes, please." Sallie tested a color on the back of her hand, then applied it to the model's eyes with short, sure strokes. "It's a matter of appearances, really. He can do the shoot without an assistant, but it won't run as smoothly, or go as quickly. He assured the people at Tyler that he was a professional operation, and now it'll look like he's—" She smudged the shadow and made a sound of frustration. "I can't talk now, Becky Lynn. I have to concentrate."

Becky Lynn backed out of the kitchen and into the hallway. She gazed into the studio, at Jack adjusting the lights, his mouth set in a grim, determined line.

She could help him. Maybe.

She shook her head and called herself a fool. What did she know about being a photo assistant? She should make certain Sallie didn't need her, then catch a bus back to The Shop.

Becky Lynn didn't move. One minute became several, and her heart began to thrum. She inched toward the studio doorway, stopping when she reached it. Still, he didn't look up.

She cleared her throat. "Jack?"

He met her gaze. She could feel his frustration and aggravation as an almost palpable thing. "Not now, Becky Lynn."

She clasped her hands together. "Sallie told me what happened. Maybe I can…help." The words squeaked past her lips, sounding high and frightened even to her own ears, and she wondered if she had lost her mind. What if he took her up on her offer?

He met her gaze again, this time in question. "You could help?"

"Maybe." She drew in a deep breath. "You'd have to tell me what to do."

He narrowed his eyes in thought, as if weighing her willingness to help with her lack of knowledge, then nodded. "You're about to get a ten-minute crash course in being a photo assistant. You're sure you can handle this?"

She clasped her hands tighter and tipped up her chin, not sure at all. "Yes."

"Come on, then. We don't have a moment to waste."

He moved through the studio like a whirlwind, dragging her into the maelstrom with him. "You'll have to adjust the lights and the reflectors." He explained how each worked, how one reflector bounced light to fill in shadows, how another diffused and softened the light, eliminating any hard shadows.

"Make sure the seamless stays clean." He motioned toward the large roll of white paper hung from a high rack at the back of the set. The paper had been unrolled to form a smooth, unrelieved background that spilled across the wooden floor. "Watch that it doesn't buckle or crinkle under the model's feet. Remember, anything out of order, no matter how small, can ruin a shot."

"Watch for everything," she murmured to herself, following him, wondering what she had gotten herself into.

He crossed to a roll-around cart. On it sat twin 35mm cameras. He picked one up. "You'll have to load and unload for me during the shoot. Watch." He popped open the camera back, dropped in a roll of film, fitted the end of exposed film in place, closed the back and turned the crank on the top of the camera. "When I've finished one roll, I'll hand you the camera, you hand me the freshly loaded one. While I'm shooting, you unload and reload. If I have any special processing instructions, I'll have you mark it on the roll then. Got it?"

She nodded, so afraid, she could hardly breathe.

"Also, I'll need you to adjust the models and their clothes. Don't worry, I'll direct you, and I'll be specific. Tyler's art director will probably give direction, too. Whatever you do, don't get flustered. Even when you're uncertain what to do, act like you know exactly what you're doing." He looked her in the eye. "In this business, appearance and attitude is everything. It's all one big, beautiful illusion. If you look confident and self-assured, they won't question you."

"Confident," she repeated, drawing in a tight breath. "Self-assured. Anything else?"

"Yeah, no interruptions. If the phone rings, you get it. If someone comes to the door, get rid of them. I don't care if the president himself has come to call, I'm not to be disturbed." He grinned. "Got all that?"

She didn't have a choice, because no sooner had the words passed his lips than the clients arrived. The two men—Tyler Creative's art director and Jon Noble Clothier's ad manager—were friendly, to a point. Becky Lynn had the sense that they were reserving judgment on Jack and his ability to handle their account until after the shoot.

Unlike the way it affected her, their *we'll see* attitude didn't seem to faze Jack. In truth, he seemed more cocky, more confident than she had ever seen him. If she hadn't known for a fact that ten minutes ago he had been nervous and on edge, she never would have believed it. And if he felt any hesitation, had any second thoughts about passing her off as his photo assistant, he hid them completely.

She sucked in a deep, calming breath. Create the illusion of confidence, she told herself. The illusion of self-assurance. They would believe it.

Jack introduced her as his new assistant, and she waited a moment for one of them to jump up and shout, "Fraud!" But neither did and the shoot got under way.

As he had when he'd shot Brianna, Jack fixed one hundred percent of his energy on his work. Nothing escaped his eye; nothing intruded on his concentration. He was a marvel to watch, and several times Becky Lynn found herself holding her breath in awe.

After the first couple minutes of the shoot, she didn't have time for the luxury of awe. Jack's directions starting coming, and she had to react, and react fast.

"The model on the right's jacket is puckered...the one on the left's sleeve is slightly twisted...tilt the light on the right a quarter of an inch downward...tap the reflector in back...good, now get the light meter, it's on the trolley..."

When she shifted her attention momentarily from Jack to the models, she was awed all over again. They astounded Becky Lynn. They knew just what to do, just how to move. They never touched their hair, makeup or clothes, always waiting for her or Sallie to make the adjustment.

Becky Lynn watched them, envy balling in the pit of her stomach. Envy not of their beauty—although they were that—but of their self-confidence, of their ease with their own bodies. She couldn't imagine what it must be like to feel that way; she knew she never would.

Her biggest test came the first time she had to load film. Her hands shook so badly she almost dropped the camera. But finally, on her third try and just as Jack had to have the camera, she got it loaded. She handed it to him and he nodded, just tipped his head the littlest bit in acknowledgment of her accomplishment, and her heart took flight.

It was a giddy, heady sensation. That moment and every moment after. She forgot her nerves. She forgot she didn't know anything about photography and simply followed Jack's directions. She even found herself laughing at something Tyler's art director said, found herself reacting to details she saw needed adjustment a moment before Jack asked her to.

It was weird, almost as if she could read his mind. She caught his eye once and saw that he thought so, too. She saw that he was surprised. And pleased.

Time flew. Before it seemed the session had even started, Jack called it a wrap. With a sense of shock, she realized she had done it. She had made it through the shoot without embarrassing Jack or herself.

She swung toward Jack, so happy she felt like shouting it, wanting to share her happiness, wanting his approval. Her smile faded. He was with the models, thanking them with hugs and kisses, congratulating them.

She turned away quickly, feeling foolish. Uncertain what to do with herself, uncertain what a real photo assistant would do, she made herself busy. She turned off the spots, hung and straightened the garments the models had worn, rolled up the seamless, arranged the equipment on the trolley.

Sallie came up to her and touched her lightly on the shoulder. "You did a great job, Becky Lynn. For Jack, thanks."

Sallie's thanks warmed her, but Becky Lynn sensed the other woman was trying to make up for something her son had—or hadn't—done. "You're leaving?"

"I need to get back to The Shop. I've got a four o'clock appointment."

"I'll come with you."

"No." Sallie smiled. "Take the rest of the day off. You earned it. Tell Jack I said goodbye."

While the models changed into their street clothes, Jack huddled with the art director and ad manager. She couldn't hear what they were saying, but she could tell by the animated way they talked, that they were pleased. Very pleased.

After much laughing and backslapping, Jack walked the clients to the front door. One of them looked back at her and smiled. "Thanks, Becky Lynn. See you next time."

Next time, she thought wistfully, returning the man's smile and wave. She had fooled them; they had believed her to be a real photo assistant. But there would be no next time.

The models left next, leaving her and Jack alone. Suddenly self-conscious and uncomfortable, she clasped her hands together. "It was really fun, Jack. Thanks."

He smiled and shook his head. "Hey, I should be thanking you. You did great, Becky Lynn. You were fantastic."

She smiled, her cheeks warming. "I'm glad I could help."

"As soon as Tyler pays me for the job, I'll get a check to you."

"I didn't do it for money. You don't have to—"

"Yeah, I do. You did a job, Becky Lynn. And you did it well. I'll pay you the same thing I would have paid Troy."

A dozen more "buts" jumped to her lips; she swallowed them all. She could use the money. "Well...okay." She took a step backward toward the door. "I suppose I better go."

"Stay." She looked at him in question, and he dragged his hands through his hair as if needing something to do with them. "After a shoot, I have all this energy. If you leave now, I won't know what to do with it." He motioned in the direction of the front door. "We'll sit on the porch. I'll get us a beer."

"I don't know." She caught her bottom lip between her teeth. "I shouldn't, I—"

"Aw, come on, just one drink." He cocked his head and grinned at her. "What else do you have to do?"

She stuffed her hands into her pockets, not really wanting to go, anyway. "Okay. But I...I don't drink alcohol."

"That's cool." He went to the refrigerator and rummaged around inside, then looked back at her. "I have a Coke or an orange Nehi."

"Coke."

"Great. I'll be out in a minute."

Becky Lynn stepped out onto the front porch. The late-afternoon breeze was cool against her cheeks, and she pressed her hands to them, realizing that she was flushed. Realizing that the fluttery sensation in the pit of her stomach was excitement instead of fear. She smiled to herself, then laughed out loud.

"You have a nice laugh."

She swung around, startled and embarrassed. The heat in her cheeks became fire.

"You should do it more often." He pushed through the screen door and crossed to her. "I hope a can's okay. I forgot to fill my ice trays."

"That's fine." She took the soft drink from his hand, not surprised to see that her own shook. She sank onto a stair.

Jack followed her down. He took a long swallow of his beer, then turned to look at her. "How old are you, Becky Lynn?"

"Seventeen."

He tapped his finger against the side of his beer bottle. "Thanks for not taking that drink. I would have been contributing, although I can't say it would have been the first time."

She looked away, out at the street, her head suddenly filled with the reek of whiskey. "That's not why I turned it down."

"No?" He took another swallow of beer, his gaze still on her. "Then why?"

She looked at him, then away once more. "I knew some folks back home who drank. I'm not interested in becoming like them."

For a moment, he said nothing. She glanced at him only to find him studying her. "What?" she asked, her voice thick.

"I was wondering… What's it like where you come from?"

She thought of the house she grew up in, of her father, the smell of whiskey and the taste of fear; she thought of the way Ricky and Tommy had laughed as they shoved a bag over her head.

"It's ugly," she murmured, the memories choking her. "It's uglier than you could imagine."

"I don't understand."

She started to stand. "I should go. Thanks for the—"

He caught her hand and tipped his head back to meet her gaze. "I withdraw my question. Please don't go."

She hesitated, then sat back down. They both stared silently out at the street, although he fidgeted—drumming his fingers on the porch floor, tapping his bottle against his knee, alternating between gazing up at the sky and out at the street.

Finally, he stood and prowled the porch. She saw what he meant about pent-up energy. She felt it emanating from him in waves.

"Today went great," he said, stopping and looking at her. "The chromes are going to be fantastic. I feel it." He saluted her with his beer bottle. "I owe a lot of it to you."

She shook her head. "You could have done it without an assistant. Sallie said so."

His lips lifted. "True. But today was important. Today I went up a rung of the ladder. Jon Noble's a retail account, but it's closer to editorial. It's closer to fashion."

"What do you mean?"

He began to pace once more. "I don't want to be a retail photographer, Becky Lynn. I don't want to spend my life doing sale catalogs and department store circulars. I want to do designer work. I want to do editorial." He stopped moving and met her eyes. "I want to do *Vogue.*"

That she understood. Because in a strange way, she wanted to do *Vogue,* too. She had always wanted to. "You will, Jack," she said softly. "I know you will. You're so talented."

He looked at her, into her eyes, and smiled. Her breath caught, and she had the feeling that for that brief moment she was the only woman in the world.

"I always wanted to be a fashion photographer," he continued softly, his voice edged with steel. "It's the only thing I can ever remember wanting to be."

She curved her hands around the cold Coke can. This was a new Jack she was seeing: intense, almost frighteningly determined, a man who would let nothing or no one get in his way. "You're so good, Jack. I can't imagine you as anything but."

He laughed and shook his head, almost as if laughing at himself, and the intensity of the moment before evaporated. "Actually, I didn't have much of a choice. Sallie didn't open The Image Shop until six years ago. Before that, she did fashion work for all the greats. She took me with her."

He ran his index finger absently along the rim of his glass. "A lot of it was location work. I went to my first shoot when I was a month old. At six months, I did Valentino's spring collection in Paris. By ten, I'd been everywhere—Africa, India, London. Paris and Italy many times. So when it came time to pick what I wanted to do with my life, what choice did I have? Fashion's in my blood."

She stared at him, feeling awed and inadequate and totally out of her league.

He met her gaze, arching his eyebrows in question. "Why are you looking at me like that?"

"Your life…it's been so exciting. And it all sounds so wonderful." She leaned her head against the stair railing and sighed. "The Peachtrees back home went to Florida every year, to Walt Disney World. Once, they even went on a cruise." She shook her head. "I thought them the richest, most sophisticated people in the world. But compared to you, they're just country bumpkins."

He grinned. "Country bumpkins, huh?"

"Yeah." She flushed and looked away. "Like me."

"I don't think of you that way." He squatted beside her, forcing her to tip her head back and meet his eyes. "You're too smart for that, Red."

She gazed into his eyes, her heart in her throat. "I wish you wouldn't call me that. It makes me feel…" She swallowed hard and inched her chin up a fraction. "I just don't like it."

"I'm not making fun of you," he murmured. "And it's

more than your hair. The name just seems to fit you. I don't know why, it just does."

He touched her cheek, lightly, with just the tips of his fingers. She felt the touch clear to the pit of her stomach. She scurried to her feet, panicked, heart thundering. "I've got to go."

He followed her up. "I didn't mean anything by that." He made a sound of frustration. "It's just…the way I am. I wasn't trying, you know, to come on to you."

"I know." She cleared her throat, feeling both foolish and frightened. She descended one of the stairs, backward. "I've still got to go."

"I'll drive you."

She shook her head. "I'll take the bus."

He swore. "Becky Lynn—"

"Thanks for today." She took the last two stairs, her heart beating almost out of control. "I…enjoyed it. Goodbye, Jack."

Turning, she walked away as quickly as she could without running.

For a long time after Becky Lynn left, Jack sat on the porch, thinking about her. Wondering about her—her fears, her past, what made her tick. She was just a kid, but she had a lot of guts. She had really helped him out today. She had stepped into the role of his photo assistant so effortlessly, it had seemed as if they'd been working together for years.

And then she had all but run away, and because of nothing more than a simple brush of his fingers against her cheek.

He frowned. When he had told her he hadn't meant anything by that touch, he'd been honest. He'd never had

a relationship with a woman that hadn't involved sex. Or
the anticipation of sex. Until now. He didn't think that way
about Becky Lynn; he hadn't imagined, not once, what it
would be like to make love with her.

He took a long swallow of his beer, draining it. Why
had he forgotten her unspoken rules? How could he have?

Becky Lynn didn't like to be touched. It frightened her.

Jack stood and went inside for another drink. He dug one
out of the fridge, twisted off the cap and smiled. He felt
relaxed with Becky Lynn. There weren't any power strug-
gles between them, sexual or otherwise, no clashing egos.
Hell, she didn't even seem to have an ego of her own. And
she was good for his—she thought he was a wonderful photographer, she hung on his every word. Maybe it made him
a power-hungry, egotistical jerk, but he liked her praise.

He took a swallow of the cold beer. He didn't have to
prove himself to Becky Lynn, he didn't have to prove he
was as good as Giovanni, or Carlo, or anybody else.

With Becky Lynn, he didn't have any ghosts.

He could work with her, he realized. He would like to
work with her.

But could she work with him? Would she make a good
photo assistant? He narrowed his eyes in thought. Photo assistants had to be tough under pressure, unflappable and able
to deal with fourteen different crises at once, including temperamental models, clients, art directors and photographers.

It wasn't an easy job. The pay sucked.

But if you loved the work, he acknowledged, it made
all the negative aspects worthwhile.

Becky Lynn loved the work. He knew that without even
asking her. And she was a natural. She had a good eye, she
had the creative bent.

But she was young. She lacked the technical skills.

He wandered back out to the front porch and the clear early evening. He gazed up at the darkening sky. Technical skills could be learned. A good eye couldn't. And even though she was chronologically young, he had the feeling she had lived more than a lifetime already.

The question was, could she do it? Did she have what it would take to do the job, and do it great? He drew his eyebrows together in thought. She would have to get over her fear of being alone with him. Of being touched. She would have to learn to go toe-to-toe with him or any other man.

Could she do it? he wondered again, settling on the top step. How could he be sure?

Richard Avedon was in town this week, shooting an editorial spread for *Vogue*. Wednesday, Sallie had said. She had agreed to do the makeup as a favor to the photographer, an old friend.

Jack tapped his beer bottle thoughtfully against his knee. He had planned to go; he never missed an opportunity to see Avedon shoot. He could invite Becky Lynn to come with him. It would give him another opportunity to assess her potential, her interest in photography, her ability to tolerate him. It would also give her the opportunity to see the difference between a retail shoot and one for a fashion editorial spread. To take the job, she had to have a clear idea of where he intended to go.

He brought his beer to his lips, satisfied with his plan. He would clear her missing work with Sallie first. With that hindrance out of the way, Becky Lynn wouldn't turn down the chance to go to a *Vogue* shoot. He knew her well enough already to know that.

And if she did turn him down, he would have his answer.

21

Becky Lynn did not turn down Jack's invitation. She was surprised by it, suspicious of his motives, and more excited than she had ever been in her life. She was going to a *Vogue* shoot; she was going to see the great Avedon at work. Never in her wildest dreams would she have believed it. She wasn't certain she did now.

When she had asked him why, Jack had said he wanted to thank her for her help the other day. He had insisted he wanted to bring her to the shoot even though she assured him it wasn't necessary. Something in his voice had nagged at her, and she'd had the funny feeling he wasn't telling her everything, that he had a reason for inviting her along other than thanks.

In her eagerness to go, she pushed the feeling aside.

The shoot was being held at the L.A. Children's Museum, and by the time she and Jack arrived, the set already bustled with activity. The hair and makeup people were hard at work; Sallie managed only a curt nod of greeting in their direction. Richard Avedon was a slight, wiry man with a quick smile, huge eyes and boundless energy. He seemed to be everywhere at once, his photo assistants scurrying after him.

Becky Lynn hadn't imagined it would be so wild, so frenetic. The magazine pictures she poured over looked so controlled, so flawless. She hadn't imagined their creation would be so filled with life and human frailty—tempers flared, obscenities flew and laughter abounded.

"It's so different than your shoot," she murmured, lifting her gaze to Jack's.

"That was retail, even though high-end. This is editorial fashion. This is what I want to do."

Jack stayed right by her side, although he seemed to know just about everybody. To the people who stopped to say hello, he introduced her simply as Becky Lynn, and she saw more than a few eyebrows raise in question.

As they made their way around the set, Jack pointed out the various personnel—there were so many more than at his small shoot—and described their functions: the magazine's art director and fashion editor, the photographer's assistants, the hair and makeup artists, the fashion consultants. He expanded on what she had already learned about lighting and equipment. Fascinated, she hung on his every word.

When Avedon began to shoot, she looked at Jack in surprise. "His camera is different than yours."

"That's a medium-format camera, a Rolleiflex. It gives a larger, finer-grain image than a 35mm, and a lot of professionals prefer it."

"But you don't?"

"I have one, but I like the 35mm more. I like the way it feels in my hand, the way I can move with it." He shrugged. "Equipment choice is extremely personal. Every professional needs something different from his camera."

He fell silent a moment, then leaned toward her once more, indicating one of the models. "Every shooter has a different style. A different kind of energy they bring to a shoot. See the way Dick has her exaggerate her movements? See how dramatic and theatrical it is? That's pure Avedon."

She did see, and time slipped by as she watched, totally enthralled.

Every once in a while, Jack wandered from her side, only to return minutes later. When he did, he would continue his narration for her, explaining every aspect of the proceedings. Becky Lynn had a sense that he wasn't just being nice or solicitous, but that he was actually trying to teach her.

"A fashion shoot like this one is a costly affair," he murmured, close to her ear. "For one thing, photographers fly all over the world on location. They bring whatever models they've booked, as well as their entire shooting staff. The client, in this case *Vogue,* pays everybody's expenses."

Becky Lynn knew her eyes must be as big as saucers. "So Avedon doesn't live here?"

Jack shook his head. "Paris, Milan and New York are the three most important fashion centers in the world. Los Angeles is the next. A great many American models and photographers make their home base New York because it's so convenient. But it's not absolutely necessary to live there. A good number prefer the sun and fun of California, even though it's a smaller market."

The minutes ticked past. The models changed into one frothy spring concoction after another—gauzy print shirts and short flounced skirts, revealing halter tops and skimpy shorts, long lacy dresses in vibrant pastels. Avedon had them frolic in the waterworks machine, splashing each other and laughing; he had them make giant bubbles and pop them in one anothers' faces; he had them don motorcycle helmets and hike up their long skirts to straddle the police motorcycle in the City Streets exhibit.

Becky Lynn smiled to herself and turned to comment to Jack. As she did, a hum moved through the room, a collective murmur of excitement and surprise. Becky Lynn craned her head to see what the furor was all about.

A man strode across the set. He moved like a king and as if he were, the crowd parted in deference before him. Her mouth dropped in surprise, and she found herself taking a step back, making room for him to pass.

Avedon had become aware of the commotion and stopped shooting. He turned, his furious expression shifting to one of surprise and pleasure when he saw the man.

"Can it really be?" Avedon said, smiling, handing his camera to his assistant. He crossed the set to meet the other man, and the two embraced.

Jack grabbed her arm, startling her. She turned toward him, the naked animosity in his expression taking her breath. "Jack, what—"

"We're getting out of here."

"But—"

"I'm going. With or without you."

He let go of her arm and stalked off. She hesitated a moment, trembling with fear and surprise. *What had happened? What had she done?* She glanced around her, at the crowd of strangers. Some of them were staring at her, obviously having seen and heard Jack.

Her cheeks heated, and she felt suddenly the way she had at three, standing barefoot and dirty in the market line with her mother and brother, the other mothers staring at her.

She didn't belong here.

Heart thundering, Becky Lynn turned and hurried after Jack. By the time she pushed through the museum's front doors, he was halfway to his car. "Jack! Wait!"

He didn't hear her, and she started to run. By the time she caught up with him, he had reached the car. He saw her and yanked open the front passenger door. "Get in."

She hung back, heart pounding. "No."

He scowled. "Becky Lynn, get in the goddamned car."

She took a step backward. "No. I'm taking the bus."

He swore and dragged a hand through his hair, visibly working to get a hold of himself. After a moment, he took a deep breath and met her gaze. "You're not taking the bus," he said quietly. "I brought you to the shoot, I'm bringing you home." He motioned the open door. "I've got it together now, I'm perfectly capable of driving. Please, get in the car."

She hiked up her chin, fighting the tremor that moved through her. "Why did you act like that? Did we leave because of that man?"

"Yes." Jack shifted his gaze, a muscle working in his jaw. "We left because of that man."

Becky Lynn lifted her chin a fraction more, resisting the urge to look away, to drop the subject and hide. "Who was he?"

"Giovanni." Jack spit the word out. "The great and powerful."

The fashion photographer. She drew her eyebrows together. "But why did you—"

"Why did I leave like that?" Jack met her eyes, and she caught her breath at the coldness in his. "Because I hate the son of a bitch, that's why. Could you get in the car now. Please?"

She made a move to do just that, then stopped and looked him square in the eye. "Don't ever grab me like that again. I won't be manhandled by you or anybody else." *Never again. Not as long as she had a breath in her body.* "Do you understand?"

He met her eyes, and in them she saw something she had never seen before. Something like respect. "Yeah," he said softly, "I do understand. It won't happen again."

She nodded and climbed into the car, sitting as close to the door as possible without hugging it. He went around to the driver's side and slipped behind the wheel. He didn't make a move toward starting the car, and for long moments stared straight ahead, his expression tight. Finally, he turned and met her eyes. "I am sorry, Becky Lynn. I shouldn't have taken out my anger on you."

She curved her arms protectively around herself. "It's okay."

He started the car, and silence fell between them. As Jack drove, Becky Lynn felt his anger and tension evaporate. She glanced at him from the corners of her eyes. She saw that the line of his jaw had softened, that his grip on the wheel had relaxed, and she felt her own tension begin to dissipate.

They stopped at a red light, and he turned toward her. "Where do you live?"

"You can drop me at The Shop." He had picked her up there.

The light changed, and he started through it. "I'll take you home."

"That's not—"

"I'll take you home," he repeated. "Where do you live?"

"On Sunset. In Hollywood."

She gave him the address, and they didn't speak again until he pulled up in front of the motel. He turned to her, eyebrows arched in disbelief. "You live here? At the Sunset Motel? I thought the only people who stayed here booked rooms by the hour."

She grabbed the door handle. "I haven't found another place yet."

"Are you looking?"

"Saving," she retorted. "Not all of us were born with silver spoons in our mouths."

Jack stared at her a moment, then burst out laughing. "The only thing in my baby mouth was a latex nipple, like the majority of other kids out there. I suppose pablum and formula would have tasted better out of sterling."

Her lips curved into an involuntary smile. "Yeah, I guess."

"Look—" He rubbed the side of his nose with his index finger. "I'm not trying to be critical of your choice here, but this is a real iffy neighborhood, especially at night."

"I'm careful."

He pursed his lips. "I'm sure you are, but this is a big city, Becky Lynn. And stuff happens here. Bad stuff."

"Stuff happens in small towns, too," she said softly, re-membering. "I can take care of myself."

He looked at her. She saw the questions in his eyes and shifted her gaze. "Well, thanks for today. I really—"

"Are you hungry?" he asked suddenly, interrupting her. "I'm starved." As she opened her mouth to answer, her stomach growled loudly. He laughed and shifted back into drive. "I know a great pizza place just down the street from here. We can talk about the shoot."

Fifteen minutes later, Becky Lynn faced Jack across a

red-and-white-checked tablecloth. After the waiter had taken their order, Jack eased back in his chair and grinned at her. "So, what did you think of the shoot? Did you like it?"

"I loved it." She leaned toward him, bubbling over with excitement. "But it was different than I thought it would be."

"In what way?"

"I don't know, it was crazier. More spontaneous. I guess I imagined that the models would pose, the photographer would take a picture, then they would pose another way and the photographer would take another. I didn't expect the models to move so much, or for Avedon to take so many shots."

"He probably took four hundred today, only six or seven will be chosen for the spread." Jack leaned forward and rested his elbows on the table. "Did you see what he was trying to do, what look he was going for?"

She thought of the clothes, the location, of how Avedon had asked the models to move. She smiled. "He wants the spread to be fun, right? Jubilant, like spring."

"Exactly." Jack nodded. "Most of the country has been in a *deep* freeze, and people are sick to death of cold, gray days. So *Vogue*'s giving them color, and fun, and heat."

The waiter brought their drinks, beer for Jack and a Coke for her. Jack took a swallow of his, then continued. "The aim of a retail shot is to sell a dress, or a suit, or a pair of shoes. But that's not what a fashion shot's about, not really. A fashion shot's about look. About image and attitude, no matter whether it's for a designer, a perfume, or an editorial spread for a magazine. This industry sells fantasy. The fantasy of being beautiful, of being desired, sexy. That's what women want, it's what they dream about.

"The female consumer looks at a shot of let's say, Isabella Rossellini. They want to look like her, they want to be like her. So they buy the dress she's wearing."

"But that's not what they're really buying," Becky Lynn murmured as the waiter set the steaming pizza in front of them.

"Bingo."

She drew her eyebrows together. "But aren't they disappointed? I mean, the dress isn't going to change the way they look. They're never going to look like Isabella Rossellini."

Jack helped himself to a piece of the pie. "But for a time, they do believe the dress changes them. They believe the fantasy. And by the time they don't anymore, there's another shot, another dress, more fantasy."

"It seems kind of silly to me." Becky Lynn frowned and transferred a piece of pizza to her plate. "I mean, it doesn't matter what I'm wearing, when I look in the mirror, I know what's there."

He met her eyes. "And what's that, Becky Lynn? What do you see?"

Tears stung the back of her eyes, and, horrified, she shifted her gaze. "Come on, Jack. I think it's obvious."

"Maybe to you. Not necessarily to anyone else."

"Right." She pushed at the piece of pizza, her hunger gone.

"You want to know what I see when I look at you? I see a bright, talented girl whose talent is wasted at The Image Shop." She lifted her gaze to his, and he smiled. "What I'm getting at is, I need an assistant. I think you could do the job."

She stared at him a moment, stunned silent. Then she shook her head. "Pardon me?"

"I need a photo assistant. I'm offering you the job, Red. But you have to really want it." He reached across the table and caught her hand. Her heart leapt to her throat.

"You can't be afraid of me, Becky Lynn. Not if we're going to work together. Sometimes the hours will be long, sometimes we'll have to print all night. I can be a son of a bitch. I like getting my way. You're going to have to stand up for yourself. You're going to have to be able to tell me to go to hell." He tightened his fingers over hers. "Do you think you can do that?"

She didn't know. She sucked in a quick breath, the pulse hammering in her head. She lowered her gaze to their joined hands. *Could she do it?*

"I'm not going to lie, you'd have a lot of responsibilities. As you did the other day, you would assist me during shoots. You'd also help me in the darkroom, scout locations, screen and book models, find props.

"It's a big job, and I can't pay you a lot. I'll match what Sallie's paying you. As I get more work, as my studio grows, you'll grow with me. There are perks, too. Like going on location, seeing the world, meeting interesting people." He squeezed her hand. "What do you think?"

What did she think? she wondered, struggling for calm. She thought it sounded like the most exciting thing in the world. And the most frightening.

"Look, Becky Lynn, I don't know what happened in your past with some guy, but this offer is simple and straightforward. I need an assistant. You love the work, I can see that. You're good at it. We worked well together the other day." He met her eyes. "Do you want the job, or not?"

Photography. Creating the beautiful images she had

always admired. She wanted to do it, more than she had ever wanted to do anything in her life.

Could she work with Jack?

He wouldn't hurt her, she realized suddenly. He wasn't like her father. He wasn't like Tommy or Ricky.

If she wanted to go forward, she had to leave the past behind. Going forward was why she had come to California.

She had to leave her past behind, she thought again. She would leave it behind, once and for all.

She drew a deep breath, excitement and trepidation creating an uneasy mixture inside her. She wanted to laugh, she wanted to hide. But most of all, she wanted to be Jack's photo assistant.

She looked him straight in the eye. "I can do it, Jack. I want the job."

22

The next day, Becky Lynn gave her notice to Sallie. The other woman took her resignation quietly. She told her she had done a fine job and that there would always be a place for her at The Image Shop, or a good letter of recommendation if she ever needed one.

Becky Lynn gazed at the woman, a lump in her throat. Without Sallie Gallagher's kindness, she didn't know what would have happened to her or where she would be now. She wanted Sallie to be happy for her, she wanted her to be enthusiastic about her new opportunity, but she sensed that she wasn't. She sensed that Sallie didn't believe the job with Jack would last.

She wished she could change Sallie's mind, she wished she could say something to convince her.

She knew she couldn't.

Becky Lynn clasped her hands in front of her. "I'll stay as long as it takes for you to find someone to replace me. No matter how long."

Sallie smiled. "I appreciate that, Becky Lynn, but if you'll just finish out the week, that will be satisfactory." She shook her head, her expression bemused. "Although I already know the artists are going to be griping and complaining before the day's even over. You've spoiled us, Becky Lynn. We'll miss you."

Sallie's words stayed with her for the rest of the day,

warming her. She had made a difference here; she had done a good job. She would make a difference in Jack's life, too.

She wanted to share her news, her excitement, with Marty, but the hairdresser had back-to-back appointments. Every time she saw the stylist, she wanted to blurt it out. Several times she almost did, but she didn't want to tell her friend in front of everyone else. She wanted Marty to know first.

When the end of the day finally came and she had the opportunity to tell Marty about her new job, it poured out of her in an excited rush. But instead of the happiness and approval she had expected, Marty frowned and shook her head.

"Don't do this, Becky Lynn. It's a mistake."

Becky Lynn stared at her friend, surprised and hurt. "What do you mean?"

"I mean, you're making a mistake." Marty lit a cigarette, drew on it and blew out a long stream of smoke. "He's using you."

"Why do you say that?" Becky Lynn frowned. "He's giving me a job, he's paying me." She crossed her arms over her chest. "How does that constitute getting used?"

"You don't know him the way I do. You're not…wise to the ways of men like him."

Becky Lynn drew in a ragged, hurt breath. "This is an opportunity to do something I love. This could turn into a career for me." She took a step toward the other woman, her hand out. "We're friends. Please be happy for me."

Marty ignored Becky Lynn's hand and turned away from her, crossing to an ashtray. "You'll fall in love with him, Becky Lynn. And he'll break your heart." She glanced over her shoulder. "He's a real shit."

Becky Lynn shook her head. "No, I won't. It's not like that. It's only about the work."

Marty laughed. The sound was hard. "You don't understand. Everyone falls in love with him. They can't help it, it's his way."

Not me. I could never trust that much. Never.

Becky Lynn took another step toward her friend, searching her expression. "Did you fall in love with him, Marty? Is that what this is all about?"

"Of course not." Marty swung to face her, her cheeks bright with anger. "I'm not naive like you, Becky Lynn. I've been around."

"I see." Becky Lynn cleared her throat, realizing that Marty was asking her to choose. "Thanks for the warning, but I'm still taking the job."

Marty crushed out her cigarette in the ashtray. "Well, good for you. Just don't come running to me when he breaks your heart."

23

Within two weeks, Jack knew, without a doubt, that hiring Becky Lynn had been the absolute right decision. Now, after having worked with her for eight months, he wondered how he had ever managed without her.

Her knowledge of photography had grown by leaps and bounds, her technical skills with it. She was like a sponge, soaking up all the information she could, always hungry for more. Every day she amazed him with some new fact she had learned, another skill she had mastered.

Jack smiled to himself and circled the empty studio, jiggling the shiny new keys in his hand. His business had grown more in the last few months than in the last two years. Tyler Creative had entrusted him with several more juicy accounts, those jobs had led to other jobs, until suddenly the word was out about Jack Gallagher—he was a comer. He had been able to quit his night job, and now supported himself, his studio and paid Becky Lynn's salary all with money earned from his photography.

Jack smiled and swept his gaze over the cavernous room. *His new studio.* Eighteen hundred square feet of photography and storage space, with several hundred more in the sleeping loft. He had more than tripled his space; he had been able to move out of Van Nuys and into Los Angeles.

Jack Gallagher was preparing to play with the big boys.

He crossed to the row of windows that faced downtown L.A., his footsteps echoing in the empty room. He wasn't sure what Becky Lynn had had to do with his growing success, but he couldn't help thinking she'd played a part in it. In the past months, she had done everything she could to help him succeed, working tirelessly and enthusiastically.

And she fed his ego, to a degree no one ever had before. She wholeheartedly believed in him and his talent, she believed without a doubt that he would make it to the top.

He squinted out at the day, the bright blue sky muddied by smog. At first, it had been awkward between them. She had jumped every time he had accidentally touched her; she had kept a safe distance between them whenever possible; she had avoided being alone with him.

But little by little, she had relaxed and opened up. He had discovered a woman who was warm, funny and loyal.

And passionate. About her beliefs, about her dreams. She hadn't shared those dreams with him, but he had sensed that they were there and that they ran deep.

What had happened to her? he wondered for what seemed like the millionth time since the first. What awful thing had caused her to run away from home? Who had hurt her so deeply that she feared men, feared being touched?

He turned away from the window. She wouldn't talk about it. The few times he had tried to get her to open up about her past, she had withdrawn from him. Each time, he had let the subject drop, but his desire to know had grown until he had become almost consumed by it.

He checked his watch, suddenly edgy. Where was she? Becky Lynn was so punctual he could set his watch by her.

Just as he could tell what she was thinking by the turn of her mouth, what she was feeling by the expression in her eyes.

He swore and swung back to the window. He had been noticing entirely too much about Becky Lynn lately. Things like the way she tipped her head when she laughed, the scent of her hair, the cadence of her voice first thing in the morning.

He scowled and shook his head. He had become almost obsessed with wondering what making love with her would be like. Not that he wanted to. It was simply curiosity, a matter of biology. She was a woman, and they had a relationship. In the past, those two things added together had always equaled sex.

Not this time. Sex with Becky Lynn would be a big mistake; making love with her was out of the question. She was his assistant and they had a terrific working relationship. He didn't want to damage that relationship, and having sex with her would. Because to Becky Lynn, sex would mean a lot more than it would to him. To her, it would be more than an act of biology or a way of satisfying curiosity.

Jack shook his head again and muttered an oath. He didn't want to have sex with Becky Lynn. He was only thinking about it so much because he didn't want to. Which didn't make a hell of a lot of sense, even to him.

"Jack!" Becky Lynn burst into the studio, out of breath, waving a copy of *Los Angeles* magazine. "You've got to see this!"

Jack smiled and started toward her, pleasure at seeing her moving through him. "Hey, kiddo, where's the fire?"

She skidded to a stop in front of him. "Right here." She

handed him the magazine, struggling to even her breathing. "You're hot, Jack."

He eyed her flushed cheeks. "How far did you run? You sound like you're about to have a heart attack."

She sucked in a deep breath. "Six blocks, but never mind that. Look." She snatched the magazine from him and flipped through the pages, ripping a couple in her haste. "Here." She shoved the magazine back into his hands.

He lowered his eyes. The article's headline read: The West Coast's Twenty Up-And-Coming Photographers To Watch For.

His heart began to hammer, his palms to sweat. "What number?" he asked, not wanting to look. If he wasn't in the top ten, it didn't mean a hell of a lot. If he wasn't in the top ten, he might as well pack it up and call it a day.

"You're six, Jack."

"Six?" he repeated, meeting her eyes.

She drew in another deep breath and nodded. "Uh-huh. You beat both Hampton Smith and Jay Patrick. They're eating your dust."

It took a moment for her words to sink in. When they did, he dropped the magazine, gave a shout of satisfaction and swept her into his arms. He swung her around. "I did it! Hot damn, I made the top ten!"

She tipped her head back and laughed giddily. "I knew you would! I knew it."

He set her on her feet, cupped her face in his palms and kissed her, full on the mouth and hard. When he let her go, she stumbled backward, her hand to her mouth, her expression stunned.

He laughed again. "Sorry, doll, but some things demand a kiss. And this is one of them. Number six!"

He sat on the floor and picked up the magazine, anxious now to read the entire article, to see who else had made the list and how they were ranked.

He looked up at Becky Lynn, she hadn't moved since he had kissed her. He grinned. "Remind me not to do that again, it's not good for productivity."

She looked confused, and he patted the floor beside him. "Come on, let's check out the competition."

"Go ahead," she said, then cleared her throat. "I've already read the article."

He gazed at her a moment, narrowing his eyes. "Did you know about this?"

She nodded, her cheeks bright with color. "They called the studio some time ago asking permission to run a couple of your prints." She slipped her hands into her jeans' pockets. "They wouldn't tell me where on the list they'd placed you, only that you'd placed. I didn't tell you because of that and because I didn't want to ruin the surprise."

"I can't believe you kept this from me." He arched his eyebrows in mock outrage. "What else have you been keeping from me?"

Her flush deepened, and she looked away. "Nothing, of course. Read the article."

While he read, she wandered around the studio. Jack was aware of her, of her uneasiness and of the fact that he had crossed a line between them when he'd kissed her.

She hadn't resisted his kiss, but he had caught her—and himself—totally off guard. He had liked the taste of her mouth, he realized. Had liked the feel of her full, soft lips, had liked the feel of her pencil-slim body pressed against his. It had been a nice fit.

He shook his head and dragged his attention back to the article. They had included two of his shots for Jon Noble, both shots that he had been particularly happy with. They called his work moody and intense. They said it was full of passion and a sense of rebellion.

Passion and rebellion, he thought. He liked that. His clients would like that. "This is good," he said half to himself and half to Becky Lynn. "It'll be good for my career. Designers take note of this stuff. So do magazines. Everybody wants someone new and hot."

She didn't reply, though he didn't expect her to. He flipped the page. Carlo's image stared back at him. Jack sucked in a quick, stunned breath, feeling as if he had been struck. The magazine had devoted two entire pages to Carlo Triani, number one from last year's list and a phenomenal success.

Pleasure at his own achievement dimmed, then soured. Last year, Carlo had been number one; this year, he was being lauded as a success story. Son of the great Giovanni, the article expounded, makes a name on his own, with extraordinary talent all his own.

Jack swore and sent the magazine sailing. It skidded over the wooden floor, crashing into the opposite wall, falling open to the spread on Carlo. Jack jumped to his feet and strode across the room, the urge to hit someone or something surging through him until he felt he might burst with it.

"Jack?" Becky Lynn made a sound of dismay and crossed to pick up the magazine. "What is it?" she asked, stooping for it. "What did the article…say…that—"

"Leave it." He whirled to face her, anger and frustration clawing at him. "I don't want to see it."

At his expression, she straightened and took a step backward, fear racing into her eyes. "I don't understand," she said, her voice high and tight.

He flexed his fingers and breathed deeply through his nose, struggling to get a handle on his emotions. "Just go, Becky Lynn. Just leave me alone."

She took another step backward as if preparing to do just that, then stopped. She shook her head and clasped her hands together. "No. I'm not leaving until you tell me what's wrong."

He glared at her, and she glared back, undaunted. Mere months ago, she would have left, he realized. She would have turned on her heel and run. No more.

She scooped the magazine up and for long moments gazed at Carlo's image in confusion, then she looked at Jack. "Is this what upset you?"

He nodded, and Becky Lynn drew her eyebrows together. "But why? Who is this?"

Jack met her gaze. "He's my brother."

24

Jack told her everything. About being Giovanni's bastard, about the day he had confronted his father only to be rejected, about the first time he and Carlo met; he told her how his brother had called him an embarrassment. He shared his anger and his determination that one day he would prove to Giovanni that he had chosen the wrong son.

She had understood his anger at the injustice served him, she understood his pain. Only too well. She burned with her own anger, her own pain.

But most of all, she understood his all-consuming need to prove to those who had hurt him that they had made a mistake, and to somehow, someday, show them that they were wrong.

That same determination burned inside her, sometimes eating away every other thing in her life.

Oh, yes, she understood Jack. So well that it sometimes frightened her.

She hadn't been surprised when it had taken him a couple weeks to rebound, to rediscover his self-satisfaction at making the *Los Angeles* magazine list. The calls from well-wishers had helped, the flowers a couple of models had sent, the small surprise party Sallie had thrown.

And as he had returned to himself, he had catapulted himself into his work with an almost frenetic intensity. They had moved into the new studio and every spare moment had been spent either drumming up new business or fine-tuning the new space.

She hadn't had a day off in months. Until today. Sunday, January sixth. Her eighteenth birthday.

Tears filled her eyes and she sat up in bed, careful to avoid her reflection in the mirror directly across from her, wishing she hadn't awakened so early. At only seven-thirty, she had the whole long, lonely day ahead of her.

She drew her knees to her chest and rested her face against them.

She missed her mother. She wanted to see her, to spend this day, her eighteenth birthday with her. Last year, Becky Lynn hadn't even thought about her birthday until days after. Everything had still been so new and frightening— L.A., her job at The Shop, her living situation. She had still suffered from constant nightmares about the rape. She had been hanging on by an emotional thread.

This year was different. This year she felt her mother's absence keenly. She felt as alone as she was. She longed for her mother's soft smile and even softer "Happy birthday."

She missed her so much she hurt.

Even as her tears spilled over, she called herself a ninny. Her birthdays at home had never been particularly happy. There had rarely been a cake, and almost never a gift. She remembered the birthday when her father had blackened her eye. But even those memories couldn't ease her desire to hear her mother's voice, couldn't lessen the need to see her face.

Her phone rang; it was Jack. He needed her, after all, he said. He would pick her up at noon.

She set the receiver back into its cradle, relieved because she hadn't wanted to spend her eighteenth birthday alone, but more melancholy because when she heard his voice, she had hoped—down deep in some silly place inside her—that Jack would have known it was her birthday and wished her a happy day.

Instead, he hadn't even asked her how she was.

At noon, she went outside to wait for him. He arrived moments later, grinning like the Cheshire cat, whistling a bright tune.

She climbed into the car, and unable to shake her melancholy, turned her gaze to the side window.

"Pretty day, isn't it?" he said, easing into traffic. "Topnotch."

She glanced at him, then away. "Where are we going?"

"There's something I want to show you. Some place."

She leaned her head against the seat back. "You're the boss."

He turned to her, arching his eyebrows in question. "You're quiet today. Anything wrong?"

"No." She laced her fingers in her lap, her chest so tight it hurt. "Just quiet."

"Okay."

He drove to Glendale, a city located just north of Los Angeles. After a time, he pulled up in front of a small, pretty multiplex painted a delicate shrimp color. Every window except one had a window box filled with bright, blooming flowers.

He shut off the engine. "Come on, we're going in."

She opened her door. "Who are we visiting?"

"You'll see."

She scowled. "I'm not in the mood for surprises, Jack."

"I see that." He grinned at her and dug some keys out of his pocket. "Too bad."

The urge to tell him he could go alone barreled through her, she bit the words back and followed him. They went in the central doorway, then took the stairs up to the third floor. But instead of knocking on the door of the apartment they stopped in front of—3C—he unlocked it and ushered her inside.

"The guy who owns this place is an old friend." Jack went to the windows and opened the blinds. Sunshine spilled through. "He's agreed to waive all deposits for the apartment. As a favor to me."

Becky Lynn looked at him, confused. "But you already have an apartment. At the studio."

"Not for me, goose. For you."

"An apartment?" she said, not believing she could have heard him correctly. "You found an apartment for me?"

"I know it's not much. And the neighborhood isn't great." He lifted his shoulders. "But it beats the hell out of the Sunset Motel."

She didn't reply, and he continued. "He agreed to give it to you for three-fifty a month. That's great by L.A. standards."

She already knew that. A day hadn't gone by that she hadn't checked the real estate section of the *L.A. Times* in search of an affordable apartment; each day she had been disappointed.

Becky Lynn moved her gaze over the room, her heart beginning to pound. Her own place. No more hookers and paper-thin walls. No more wail of police sirens. No more leers from the desk clerk.

She wandered through the apartment, ending up in the

kitchen. The apartment was small—one bedroom, a tiny kitchen and bathroom and an all-purpose living area, but it was pretty, with an abundance of windows and nice wooden floors.

She ran her hand along the turquoise and silver-speckled counter. Her own kitchen. A stove. A refrigerator. She opened the oven door and peered inside, then closed it. No more peanut butter sandwiches. No more cans of tuna or greasy fast food. She could make a real meal in this kitchen. She could make meat loaf and mashed potatoes; she could fry chicken and make butter beans; she could bake an apple pie. It seemed like a lifetime since she'd had a home-baked apple pie.

Jack watched her from the doorway. "Do you like it?"

She lifted her gaze to his, tears blurring her vision. "I love it," she whispered, her words thick, choked with emotion.

"Check the refrigerator." At her expression, he grinned and started toward her. "Yeah, the refrigerator."

She crossed to it and opened the door. On the top shelf sat a big chocolate cake.

"Happy birthday, Red," he said softly from behind her.

She looked over her shoulder at him, struggling to keep from bursting into tears. "I didn't…think you knew."

"You're not the only one who can keep secrets." He touched her cheek lightly, then reached around her and slid the cake out. The top was decorated with shocking pink roses, *Happy Birthday* was written in fluorescent green frosting.

She drew in a ragged breath. "It's beautiful."

"Tasty, too, I'll bet."

From his jacket pocket he produced a box of candles,

some matches and two plastic forks. They sat on the floor with the cake between them, and Jack insisted on putting in all eighteen candles.

"What are you going to wish for?" he asked as he lit each candle.

"I don't know. Today I feel like I have everything."

He met her gaze over the dancing flames. "I'm glad."

She looked away a moment, her heart in her throat, then met his eyes again. "Why are you being so nice to me?"

He paused as if nonplussed by her question. Then he shook his head. "Why shouldn't I be nice to you, Becky Lynn? I like you. And I want you to be okay."

Tears stung her eyes again. He liked her. Nobody had ever said that to her before. Nobody had ever cared enough to want her to be okay. Her heart opened up, like a flower to the sun. She felt bathed in warmth, and for the first time in her life, as if she belonged. When she blew out her eighteen candles, instead of making a wish, she said a thank-you.

Laughing, they each grabbed a fork and dug into the cake, putting a sizable dent in the double layers, eating until they could eat no more. Afterward, they lay on the floor, facing each other but not touching. Sharing wishes of birthdays past. Sharing their dreams.

Much later, after Jack brought her back to the motel, Becky Lynn realized with a sense of horror that Marty had been right.

She was falling in love with him.

25

She had lost her.

Becky Lynn angled past two young mothers with baby strollers, searching over the tops of shoppers' heads for the tall blonde she had been following for the past half hour.

She caught a glimpse of the girl up ahead, and scooted around another group of window-shoppers. As noon had grown closer, the mall had become crowded, making her task more difficult. She needed to find the blonde, get a good look at her face and if she thought the girl had promise, give her the pitch.

Becky saw her up ahead and picked up her pace. Her quarry had paused outside a dress shop to study something in the front window. As Becky Lynn approached the girl, she strained to get a clear look at her face, but was unsuccessful once again.

Just as Becky Lynn came within a couple yards of her, the blonde turned away from the window, walking in the opposite direction. Becky Lynn followed, studying her. She looked to be about her own age, maybe a year younger, maybe one year older. She had hair the color of honey; it fell in a riot of curly waves to the middle of her back. She tossed it jauntily over her shoulder as she walked, her equally jaunty gait quick because of the extraordinary length of her legs.

She would make a perfect model.

If her face was right.

One of the ways a photographer made a name for himself was by finding and launching new talent. She and Jack were forever scouting for new girls, introducing themselves and handing out cards. As Becky Lynn had discovered, it took more than a beautiful face and body to be a successful model. A woman had to have a certain look, a chameleon-like ability to become whatever a photographer needed her to be.

Some of what she needed could be learned; the photographer groomed the novice model, teaching her how to move in front of the camera, how to emote, teaching her the simple tricks of the trade.

But the most important part couldn't be learned. The camera had to love the face. And so far, she and Jack hadn't found anyone the camera loved. They hadn't found that special face.

She had a feeling about this girl.

The blonde ducked into the rest room. A moment later, Becky Lynn followed her. The sinks and mirrors faced the row of stalls, and Becky Lynn stood in front of them, waiting. She dug her comb out of her purse and pretended interest in fixing her hair.

Several minutes later, the blonde stepped out of one of the stalls. Her eyes, huge and heavy-lidded, met Becky Lynn's in the mirror. She smiled.

Becky Lynn returned her smile, her nerves jumping. The girl had a beautiful mouth, full, soft, too big for her face. Her cheekbones were high, her nose small and straight.

She would make a perfect model.

The blonde stepped up to the sink. She washed and dried her hands, then fished in her purse and pulled out lip gloss. She applied the shiny pink, her eyes on herself in the mirror.

"Why have you been following me?" she asked bluntly, not looking at Becky Lynn. She smoothed her lips together, evening the gloss. "You queer, or something?"

Becky Lynn made a choked sound of surprise. "Hardly." She cleared her throat. "I'm a photographer's assistant, and I followed you because you caught my eye. I thought you might make a good fashion model."

"Right." The girl capped the tube, dropped it back into her purse, then turned to walk away. "Stop following me, okay? It's giving me the creeps."

"This isn't a joke, I think you'd make a terrific model. Here—" Becky Lynn dug one of Jack's business cards out of her pants pocket. She handed it to the girl.

The blonde took it and studied it for a moment, suspiciously. She brought her gaze to Becky Lynn's once more. And once more, Becky Lynn was struck by both the size of the girl's eyes and their sexy, sleepy quality.

Men would fantasize about those eyes, Becky Lynn thought. Women would aspire to make theirs look the same way.

"This isn't a gag?"

"No gag." Becky Lynn tucked her hands into her pockets. "I'm Becky Lynn, Jack Gallagher's photo assistant."

"Cool."

"So, are you interested in coming in for a sitting?"

"How much?"

"No cost at all. If Jack thinks you have the right look, if he works with you and finds you're photogenic and have talent, you sign with him. He teaches you the things you need to know to be picked up by a big agency. When you do, he gets a finder's fee from the agency. The standard fee is three years, five percent. Interested?"

"Maybe."

"Maybe?" Becky Lynn repeated, surprised. Usually, the girls she approached were not just interested, they were ecstatic.

"Yeah." The blonde tucked the card into the back pocket of her tight, white jeans. "Maybe I'll call."

She started out of the rest room, and, frustrated, Becky Lynn watched her walk away. She couldn't lose this one, she thought. This girl had the face she and Jack had been searching for.

"Wait," she called as the blonde pushed open the door. "What's your name?"

"Zoe," she said, looking over her shoulder at Becky Lynn. "Zoe Marie Tucker."

26

Done in pink and white and ruffles, the bedroom was as frilly as the top of a birthday cake. A little girl's dream room, complete with a canopy bed and white furniture decorated with tiny painted flowers, but too childish for a seventeen-year-old, especially one as worldly as Zoe Marie Tucker.

Her father had seen the room in a magazine, proclaimed it fit for a princess and had it re-created for her. That had been the year she turned six; by the time she turned eight, he was gone. Her life had changed dramatically with his leaving, but the bedroom had remained the same.

Zoe sat cross-legged on the gingham spread, naked but for her bra and panties, the photographer's business card in her hands. She studied it, eyebrows drawn together in thought.

Jack Gallagher. Fashion Photographer.

It was probably a gag. Probably a marketing ploy, a way to get a no-talent photographer a few clients. Or maybe it was a slick cover for a porno ring. At the thought of the girl from the mall, with her soft drawl and hesitant smile, being part of a porno ring, Zoe giggled. That would be like suspecting Mickey Mouse of child abuse.

Her gaze strayed to her nightstand and the picture of her and her father. She stared at their smiling images a moment, then dragged her gaze back to the business card. If Becky Lynn and this Jack Gallagher were for real…

Zoe's heart began to pound. The magazines were always printing stories about how some celebrity or other had gotten discovered in an elevator or drugstore or disco. Someday it could be her they were writing about. Hadn't she always thought so? Hadn't her daddy always told her she was the most beautiful, the most special girl in the world?

She stood and crossed to her dresser mirror. She gazed at her reflection, seeing herself at seven, her daddy crouched behind her, his arms around her middle. "Princess," he would say, "you're so beautiful, you should be on the cover of a magazine. You're the prettiest girl in the whole world."

Nobody had ever made her feel so loved, so pretty and special, the way her daddy had. He had petted and loved her, he had bought her bows for her hair, lacy dresses and shiny black shoes with pearl buttons.

She had loved him so much. Why had he left her? Zoe grasped the edge of the dresser, gripping so hard her knuckles turned white, thinking of the last time she had seen him. That morning had been like every other. He had helped her bathe and dress; she hadn't fought him the way she sometimes did. She hadn't cried or made him cry. Tears stung her eyes, and she battled them back. She had been a good girl.

She tightened her grip on the dresser's edge, her fingertips starting to tingle. His leaving was her mother's fault. Her mother had been jealous of the attention he had given his daughter; she had been jealous of how beautiful he thought his little princess was. Her mother had been jealous because he had loved her more. She had heard them fight about her, about his feelings for her. Her daddy had gone away because her mother was mean, spiteful and jealous.

But why hadn't he taken her with him?

Suddenly light-headed and queasy, Zoe pressed a hand to her stomach and struggled for an even breath. From the room next door she heard the sound of throaty laughter. Her mother's laughter. One of her *uncles* was visiting. One of her many uncles. A moment later, she heard strains of the bluesy music her mother liked so much, the music that always meant the same thing.

Zoe covered her ears, knowing what would come next. It did—the rhythmic thump of the bed hitting the wall.

Zoe threw herself across her own bed, and dragged a pillow over her head, hoping to muffle the sounds from the other room. If her mother hadn't been so cold when her daddy was around, he would have stayed. If she hadn't been so jealous, he would have loved them more.

Furious, she rolled over and tossed the pillow across the room. It landed on her vanity, sending her bottles of perfume and lotions clattering. She thought of the parade of uncles her mother had brought home over the past nine years, thought of the one in the other room now. She smiled to herself. She had fucked him. And a few others who had stayed around long enough, the ones her mother had liked best.

She had taken pleasure in knowing they liked her better than her mother, that they thought she was prettier than her mother. Just like her daddy had. The one in the other room with her mother right now, the one moaning and grunting like a pig, he thought she was prettier. He had told her so. She would bet he was thinking about her now.

The sounds from the next room stopped, and Zoe

crossed her arms behind her head and gazed up at the ceiling, smiling at the quiet, grateful that they were done.

A fashion model, she thought. She would like doing that. She would like knowing that people were looking at her, admiring her. She liked men thinking she was beautiful. It made her feel important, special. It made her feel powerful. She sat up and reached for the business card. Lying down again, she traced her fingers over the raised lettering.

Jack Gallagher. Fashion Photographer.

She smiled. Maybe this was what she had been waiting for since the afternoon she had come home from school to learn that her daddy was gone. Maybe this was what had been missing from her life, what she had yearned for so desperately that she hurt way down deep inside. She hadn't understood the ache, she had only known that it kept her from ever feeling satisfied.

She clutched the card to her chest, hope a living thing inside her. Maybe, at long last, this was it, the thing that would make her happy.

Zoe waited three days before she called the number on the business card. She figured it wouldn't look good to appear too eager. On the third ring, a woman answered, and Zoe recognized the voice as belonging to Becky Lynn, the girl from the mall bathroom.

Zoe identified herself, and Becky Lynn told her she was glad Zoe had decided to call. She made her an appointment to see Jack the following morning, gave her directions to the studio, told her to wear whatever she wanted to, then had hung up.

Zoe had been suspicious. Becky Lynn had acted as if

Zoe's calling had been no big deal, as if she talked to a dozen girls a day about modeling. Considering the rush Becky Lynn had given her at the mall, Zoe had also been more than a little annoyed by her attitude.

But now, standing in Jack Gallagher's studio, she knew she had no reason to be suspicious or annoyed. Besides noticing the unmistakable equipment and overhearing the phone conversation Becky Lynn was having, she could see that one wall of the studio was covered with fashion shots, many of which she recognized.

This Jack Gallagher was the real thing; he probably did talk to a dozen girls a day. Zoe crossed to the wall of photographs. She studied the girls in the ads, noting their hair and eyes and mouths, noting the length of their legs and the size of their breasts.

She was as beautiful as any of them. Her figure looked as good, better even. She glanced down at herself. She had chosen her clothes carefully, picking ones she thought best showed her assets: skintight, pencil-slim blue jeans, sandals, a soft clingy shirt with no bra underneath.

"Zoe?"

She turned. A man strode toward her, smiling. He stopped before her and held out his hand.

"I'm Jack."

Her breath caught in surprise. She didn't know what she had expected from Jack Gallagher, maybe some sensitive, artsy type, but certainly not this sexy, macho-looking man.

She hid her surprise and took his hand, lifting her lips into her sultriest smile. "Hi."

He held her hand in his, his gaze intently on hers, studying, assessing. Just as her heart began to thunder, he dropped her hand.

"Ever done any modeling before?" he asked, gaze still fixed on hers.

"Nope."

"Ever had aspirations to model?"

She slipped her fingers into the back pockets of her jeans, knowing that the movement forced her breasts against the light knit of her shirt. "Nope."

He swept his gaze over her, pausing on her chest, and she experienced a little thrill at knowing her ploy had worked. "But you're here today."

She lifted a shoulder. "I was curious. And it's not that I'm averse to the idea of modeling. What girl would be?"

"True."

He pursed his lips, and she had to admit he had a beautiful mouth. Strong and chiseled. Sexy. She caught herself staring at it and dragged her gaze back to his.

"Becky Lynn here thinks the camera's going to love you. But I'll tell you right now, although there's no denying you're beautiful, I have my doubts." He motioned her toward the center of the room, walking with her. "You see, Zoe, the camera likes to surprise me. Sometimes it loves the face you expect it to, but sometimes it doesn't. Even more surprising, sometimes it loves a face you would never have given a second glance. So, we'll just have to wait and see."

She drew her eyebrows together, not liking what he'd just said, not liking the possibility that she wouldn't photograph well. She rejected the possibility. "Are you going to take pictures of me today?"

"That's the plan. You up for it?"

He glanced at her from the corner of his eyes, and she realized he was measuring her every response, her every facial expression. She wouldn't forget that.

"Sure."

"Great." He stopped at an equipment table and picked up one of several cameras. He popped open a back and dropped in a roll of film, all business. "We're not going to do makeup or hair or anything like that today. That comes later. Today I'm just going to shoot you. I'll get an idea of how comfortable or how stiff you are in front of the camera. I'll get a good idea if the camera's going to like your face."

While he talked, Zoe was aware of Becky Lynn moving around the studio, setting the lights, fixing the backdrop into place and arranging equipment on a trolley.

"Models aren't born," Jack was saying, and she returned her full attention to him, "and the work is far from glamorous. Models are trained, it's hard work. Photographers aren't always nice guys. In fact, if things aren't going their way during a shoot, they're usually sons of bitches."

"He should know," Becky Lynn called from a corner of the room.

Far from being annoyed, Jack laughed and sent her a smile. Zoe watched the exchange, curious suddenly about the relationship between the photographer and assistant. She sensed a warmth between them, an understanding that went beyond that of business associates or even friends. But it didn't feel like sex, she decided. Not at all.

Zoe returned her attention to Jack as he started talking again.

"If a photographer has to give a model direction twice, he's not happy. Three times and he's downright foul-tempered."

He guided her to the tall stool Becky Lynn had set up

in the middle of the room, and had her sit on it, facing forward. "I'll be straight with you, Zoe. I won't have time to coddle you, even while you're learning. If you want to move forward with this, understand that you're entering into a professional association with me. I'll be critical, and bluntly so. Curse me, hate me, just give me what I want. Forget everything you've ever believed about modeling. It's a cold, cutthroat business."

He looked her in the eye. "You might as well find out if you can hack it now, before you've wasted too much of either of our time."

Zoe returned his gaze evenly. If he was trying to scare her, it would take a whole lot more than that. "I can hack it," she said, her softly spoken words edged with steel. "You just worry about making me look good."

Jack stared at her a moment, his expression one of grudging respect and mild surprise. Then he tipped his head back and laughed. "I'll keep that in mind, Zoe."

He turned to Becky Lynn who had come up to stand beside him. "Ready, Red?"

"Ready." She held out a piece of equipment Zoe didn't recognize. "You want to double-check the light reading?"

"Are you kidding?" He grinned. "You haven't been wrong yet. Let's go."

Jack started to shoot before Zoe had a chance to ask him what she was supposed to do. So she did nothing. He moved around her, never stopping, taking shots of her from all angles. While he did, he talked.

"The best models," he said, "the girls who make it to the top, are special, Zoe. Besides their relationship with the camera, they're able to divorce themselves from who they are and become who the photographer needs them to be. The first step is losing your self-consciousness, your fear of looking bad or foolish. Now smile for me," he directed. "That's right, tip your head a bit to the right. Good."

He stopped shooting and handed his camera to Becky Lynn. She handed him another, freshly loaded. He turned back to her, but didn't bring up his camera. Instead, he looked her in the eye. "You have to trust me, Zoe. I'm not going to let you look bad. But don't worry, in time you'll be able to feel comfortable in front of the camera. In time, it'll come naturally."

She returned his forthright gaze. "I can do it now."

He arched his eyebrows. "You think so?"

"I know so."

Jack exchanged a quick, meaningful glance with Becky Lynn. Zoe narrowed her eyes, annoyed. She didn't like them sharing a little secret at her expense; she didn't like the way their silent communication made her feel—excluded and foolish.

She tossed her head back in challenge. "Try me, Jack Gallagher."

She intended the double entendre. She saw by the sudden heat that raced into his eyes and by the way he slid his gaze appraisingly over her, that he'd caught it.

An answering challenge lit his eyes, and for a split second she wondered if she hadn't made a mistake—Jack Gallagher didn't like to lose, and she would bet money he rarely did.

"Okay, Zoe." He inclined his head slightly. "I'll take you at your word. Let's go."

Twenty minutes later, Zoe decided Jack Gallagher was a monster. He fired direction after direction at her, without pause, without giving her a moment to think or evaluate.

When she failed to respond to his demands either quickly enough or to his satisfaction, his criticism bordered on cruel. "That's not sexy," he told her, his tone scathing. "Unpucker your mouth, you look like a Kewpie doll."

Furious, Zoe decided that somehow, some way, she would bring Jack Gallagher to his knees.

By the end of the forty-minute session, she was exhausted. His "Not bad for a first try" as he wrapped the shoot infuriated her. She wanted to castrate him with a butter knife, then hang him by his toes and let the sea gulls feed on his rotting carcass.

She glared at him, not hiding her feelings, and he laughed and crossed to stand before her. "I told you it was going to be tough, babe. I told you you'd hate me. If you want to quit now, I'll understand."

She stiffened her spine. "I'd rather die."

He laughed again, then kissed her. Just a light brush of his mouth to hers, but it sent a shock of surprise—and awareness—coursing through her.

"Good girl," he said. "We'll process these, and Becky Lynn will call you. If the shots are good enough, she'll arrange another sitting. I've got a call to make, so I'll see you around."

Zoe watched him walk away, a dozen different emotions racing through her: awareness, respect, dislike.

And, more than anything else, determination. The shots would be good. So good, in fact, that Becky Lynn wouldn't just call for another appointment, she would fall all over herself to get Zoe to agree to it.

27

Becky Lynn couldn't stop thinking about her mother. Ever since her birthday six weeks before, she had been plagued by thoughts of her. She wanted, needed, to tell her mother how her life had changed, she wanted to hear her voice. The need to talk to her grew every day, until she couldn't sleep for dreaming of her.

Becky Lynn had decided that she wouldn't feel right until she talked to her mother and assured her that she was okay.

She couldn't call her directly. She was afraid her daddy or Randy would answer, afraid that even if neither did, her daddy might overhear her mother talking to her. She had decided her only recourse was to call Miss Opal at the Cut 'n Curl.

She would have to call early, before Fayrene or Dixie came in. If anyone besides Miss Opal answered, she would hang up. Eventually, she would reach Miss Opal, and when she did, she would beg her to get a message to her mama and to arrange a time and way for them to connect. Miss Opal would help her, she was certain of that.

Becky Lynn let herself into the silent studio, disengaging the alarm system as she did. She had decided today would be the day—she didn't think she could bear putting it off another. So here she was at the studio at six-thirty in the morning, wishing she'd had the funds to have a phone installed at her apartment.

Jack slept in the loft, and she moved carefully, quietly through the studio, not wanting to awaken him. He didn't know about her past. She hadn't told him or anybody else—the truth anyway. When someone asked, as Marty had, she told *The Story*. The tragic-farm-accident-and-loving-but-impoverished family tale had gone a long way, and no one had ever questioned the story.

Jack she had told nothing. The idea of lying to him felt wrong. So she had simply avoided his questions.

She reached the phone and stared at it, scared to death. She breathed deeply through her nose and told herself being so frightened was silly. Her father couldn't touch her here. Ricky and Tommy couldn't touch her. They couldn't hurt her.

But she could become the girl she had been back then.

And she couldn't bear that.

She wouldn't, she told herself. She had come too far; she had left Bend, Mississippi, and that Becky Lynn Lee behind forever. She picked up the receiver, hand shaking. She dialed Information, learned the beauty shop's number, hung up and redialed.

Miss Opal answered. The blood rushed to Becky Lynn's head and for a moment she couldn't form a thought, let alone a word.

"Cut 'n Curl," Miss Opal said again. "Is anyone there?"

"Yes, ma'am, Miss Opal…it's me."

"Becky Lynn?" The older woman drew a shaky breath. "My God, child, is it really you?"

"Yes, ma'am." Becky Lynn twisted the phone cord around the fingers of her left hand, heart thundering. "It is."

For a moment, the other woman said nothing, then she

cleared her throat. "It's a relief to hear your voice, child. Where are you? Are you all right?"

"Yes, ma'am," Becky Lynn assured her. "I'm fine."

"Your daddy spread all kinds of terrible stories about you. He said you stole his pay and ran off. He'd said you'd up and gotten yourself pregnant."

She thought of what she had been through, of the horror and pain Ricky and Tommy had inflicted on her, and then of her own daddy telling stories like that. Her heart hurt so bad, it felt as though it were busting in half.

She cleared her throat. "None of it's true. You've got to believe me, Miss Opal." She hated the tremor in her voice, hated the way the plea made her feel—as if she had to beg for her innocence, like the girl everyone had always believed her to be. "I left because…because Ricky and Tommy…"

"Dear Lord, did those boys, did they—"

"Yes." To Becky Lynn's horror, her mind careened back to that night, the dark road, the sound of her voice floating eerily on the breeze.

Her eyes filled with tears, and she blinked against them, drowning in the memory.

"I never believed those stories your Daddy spread. When you didn't come in to work the next afternoon, I feared the worst. I told myself that nothing could have happened to you because of the pep rally, then my grand-daughter mentioned that…that Tommy's face was all scratched up. I knew then…I knew." Miss Opal sighed heavily. "It's all my fault. I should have made sure you got home, I should have insisted you—"

"It wasn't your fault, Miss Opal. You did all you could."

"I just wish—"

"Miss Opal," she interrupted, not wanting to talk about that terrible night any longer, "I called about Mama."

The woman said nothing, and chill bumps raced up Becky Lynn's arms. She took a gulp of air. "I really need to talk to her. I was hoping you would set it up. It would mean everything to me."

Becky Lynn rushed nervously on, afraid to give the woman a chance to refuse, unsettled by her silence. "I wouldn't even ask, but I can't call the house because of Daddy. I know it's a big favor, but it would mean so much to me."

"Becky Lynn…honey…I don't know how to tell you this, so I'll just tell you plain. Your mama's…dead. She took real sick a couple weeks ago and just…up and died. I don't really know what she caught, only that she collapsed down at the market. They…they buried her last week."

Her mother dead? Becky Lynn shook her head, Miss Opal's words resounding in her head, her own denial with them. *It wasn't true. It couldn't be.*

"I'm so sorry, child. If I had known how to reach you, I would have. I promise you I would have."

"No." Becky Lynn's legs crumpled beneath her, and she sank to the floor, the receiver still clutched in her hand. The phone came off the counter with her, toppling a tray of slides. The slides hit the floor and scattered. "No," she repeated. "It's not true."

"I know it's little comfort now, but when I took her the money you sent, she cried. She told me she had always known you were special, she said she had never doubted that you were alive and doing well."

Despair welled up in Becky Lynn's chest, strangling

her. *Her mother had believed in her. She had been the only person who had ever believed in her.*

And now she was gone.

The receiver slipped from her fingers. *Gone. Her mother was gone.*

She drew her knees to her chest and pressed her face to them, keening with grief. *She hadn't been there. Her mama had needed her, and she hadn't been there.* Becky Lynn curled her arms around herself, hugging tightly, shock and grief creating a kind of hysteria inside her. *She had no one. No one to love, no one who believed in her.*

What was she going to do? she wondered. How was she going to go on?

A crash awakened Jack. He sat bolt upright in bed and looked around in confusion. Soft morning light peeked around the edges of the blinds and from below he heard the faint blare of a horn followed by the squeal of tires skidding to a halt.

Jack rubbed his eyes and glanced at his bedside clock. Six fifty-six. He drew his eyebrows together. The alarm hadn't gone off and it was too early for Becky Lynn. He must have been awakened by traffic noises or a neighbor arriving early for work. Or maybe he had dreamed the noise, he decided, plumping up the pillows and leaning against them.

He closed his eyes, then reopened them as he heard another sound, this one hollow and full of despair. A chill ran up his spine, and he sat back up. It was the kind of sound made by someone who had lost everything. He shook his head at his own thoughts, threw back the covers and climbed out of bed.

He pulled on a pair of jogging shorts, deciding that if anything was amiss he didn't want to face it stark naked. With that in mind, he armed himself with the baseball bat he kept under the bed and started quietly for the stairs.

The sounds of grief became louder and more wrenching as he descended the stairs. When he reached the first floor, he saw Becky Lynn. She sat on the floor, knees to her chest, face pressed to them as she rocked and cried. The phone lay on the floor beside her, a tray of slides with it.

"Becky Lynn?" he said softly, crossing to her. "Baby... what's wrong?"

She didn't look up or respond, and he wasn't certain that in her distress she had even heard him. He squatted beside her and laid a hand gently on her hair. "Sweetheart...it's Jack."

She tilted her head and met his eyes. The despair in hers took his breath. "Oh, baby...what's happened? Come here. Let me help you."

He put his arms around her. He felt her stiffen a moment as if she might reject his offer of comfort, then she sagged against him, sobbing softly, her face buried against his naked chest.

A fierce protectiveness moved through him, stirring a place deep inside. He wedged his arms around and under her, and scooped her up. He carried her up the stairs to his loft, to the unmade bed. He sat on its edge, her body cradled on his lap, and let her cry, rocking and stroking her, murmuring sounds and words of comfort.

Finally, her sobs abated, becoming soft, helpless mewls of despair. He didn't know what to do or say. He had never found himself in a situation like this one before. He had never allowed himself to get caught in one. But here he was. And he found himself torn between wanting to comfort her and wanting to run.

Such an abundance of emotion unsettled him; it frightened him. He feared if he allowed it to, it would eat him alive.

Jack swallowed past the lump in his throat, fighting the desire to escape. He couldn't leave her; she was his friend. She had no one else. He didn't know why that should matter so much to him, but it did.

She mattered to him.

"Can you tell me, baby, can you tell me what's wrong?"

She burrowed closer into his arms and murmured something he couldn't make out. Her breath stirred against his naked chest, warm and soft.

"Sweet...you'll have to speak up. I'm sorry, but I couldn't hear you."

She tilted her face up to his and again emotion clutched at him. He forced the emotion back, forced himself to breathe deeply and evenly. He smoothed his fingers ever so gently across her wet cheek. "Take your time, love. I've nowhere to go."

Her tears welled up again but didn't spill over, her lips trembled. She fought crying; he saw her battle. She was the bravest person he had ever met, he realized. What had she endured that had made her so strong? Had she ever had anyone to lean on, anyone she had trusted to catch her if she fell?

"My...mother, she's...she's—"

The words brought a fresh wave of tears. They spilled silently over, and she pressed her face to his chest once more. He stroked her hair; he ran the flat of his hand soothingly down her spine. Little by little he felt the tension ease from her, the tension and the fight, leaving her limp and spent in his arms.

She didn't look at him, but she turned her face so that her cheek rested against his left shoulder. "My mother's dead," she said so quietly he had to strain to hear. He tightened his arms around her. "I called this morning. I wanted to talk to her, I needed to tell her...I was—"

Tears choked her words and he could feel her struggle to clear them. "Miss Opal told me Mama had...that she was...dead."

"Oh, God, Becky Lynn." He held her closer, hurting for her. "I'm sorry."

"They didn't know...where I...was." She drew in a shuddering breath. "Now she's gone and I...I didn't even get to say goodbye. It hurts so bad."

The last ended on a sob, and he threaded his fingers through her fiery hair. "I know, baby. I know."

Becky Lynn met his eyes. "She needed me, Jack. I wasn't there for her. If only I'd stayed...maybe I could have done something, maybe I could have helped."

"Shh." He moved his fingers tenderly over her face. "Don't. Don't beat yourself up that way."

"Miss Opal said she'd taken sick. Maybe if I'd been there, I would have seen that she needed a doctor, maybe I could have insisted she go."

She flexed her fingers against his chest, a note of hysteria in her voice. "Instead, I...I left her alone and—"

Jack cupped her face in his palms. "You couldn't have done anything. It wasn't your fault."

She shook her head, and struggled free of his arms. "I heard her crying, the night I ran away. I almost went back, but I didn't. I didn't. I saved myself instead."

She stood, breathing hard, as if she had just run a long distance. "I would have died if I'd stayed there, Jack. They said they would do it again. They would have. I couldn't have faced them...I couldn't have faced that again. No one believed me...I was all alone. All alone."

Jack frowned, the blood pounding in his head. "What didn't they believe?" he asked quietly, forcing calm. He caught her hand, moved his thumb softly and rhythmically across her knuckles, hoping to gentle her. "What couldn't you have faced?"

She shook her head, her eyes wide and panic-stricken. "Their jeers, their amusement... I couldn't have taken it again. If they had done it again—"

She bit the words back and tugged against his grasp. "She wasn't strong enough to help me. She couldn't help me. So I left. I had to. Don't you see? I had to."

Instead of releasing her one hand, he caught the other. He shook her gently. "What, Becky Lynn? What happened? Who are you talking about?"

She pulled against his grip, moving her gaze wildly around the room. "I should go. I have to go."

"Becky Lynn." He laced their fingers together. "Look at me. Where should you go?"

"I don't know." She blinked in confusion. "Home, I guess... I need to go home."

"I'm here for you, babe. You don't want to be alone right now. I know you don't."

She stopped struggling and met his eyes. "What am I going to do," she whispered. "I'm all alone now. What if I...close my eyes and never open them again? What if I just...disappear?"

"It's not going to happen, babe," he said fiercely. "I won't let it happen."

"I'm so afraid."

"I know, sweetheart." He drew her back down to him, then to the bed. For a long time, he held her trembling body against his, stroking, running his hand from her shoulder to the curve of her hip. "It's okay, sweetheart. I'm here. I'm not going to let you go, and I'm not going to leave you alone. You don't have to be afraid when I'm with you."

She made a sound, soft like a sigh. His heart turned over; his body stirred. A flame of arousal ignited somewhere inside him, small but hot. He told himself to fight it, but when he looked down at her, her eyes on his were limpid pools of longing.

He suspected she had no idea what her eyes said to him, what they told him she wanted. Becky Lynn was inexperienced. He knew that without asking, without having to touch her.

He knew, too, that he could hurt her.

He lowered his eyes to her mouth, parted in invitation, her lips damp. The flame became a bonfire and with a groan, he brought his mouth to hers. She gasped, a tiny broken sound that he caught with his mouth. Her arms, her hands came to his shoulders, but she didn't push him away. She clutched frantically at him, opening and closing her hands, her fingers digging into his shoulders.

Stop now, Gallagher. Get out of this before it's too late.

Instead, he fitted his mouth more firmly to hers, easing hers farther open, slipping his tongue inside. He found hers and stroked, and after a moment's hesitation, she returned the caress.

He kissed her for a long time, knowing instinctively that

she was as frightened as she was aroused and that he needed to go slow, that he needed to gentle her.

As the moments ticked past, her fear lessened, her body warmed. She made sounds deep in her throat, ones that had nothing to do with fear; she moved her body, her pelvis, beneath his.

His mouth still on hers, he slid his hands under her shirt. She was very slim, so slim he could count her ribs as he moved a hand toward her breast. When he found it, he closed his hand gently over it. Surprisingly full, it fit into his palm, and he caressed and kneaded her smooth, warm flesh.

She gasped and arched against his hand. His erection grew painful, his breathing ragged. "I want to make love," he murmured against her mouth, his voice thick. "Do you want that, too, Becky Lynn? If you don't...baby, please tell me now."

He drew away from her so he could look into her eyes. Hers were heavy-lidded with arousal, and unbearably soft. The softness unnerved him, and for a split second he considered ending this himself. He could gently disentangle himself; he could beg her forgiveness and call himself a cad.

Then she shuddered and curved her fingers around his shoulders. "I'm scared," she whispered. "I want...you, but I'm afraid you'll...hurt me."

He searched her expression, a thought occurring to him that hadn't before. "Honey, are you...are you a virgin?"

She shook her head and lowered her eyes, her cheeks blooming with color.

He cupped her face in his palms. She lifted her gaze to his. "I won't hurt you, Becky Lynn. I promise I won't."

For the space of a heartbeat, she stared at him as if frozen. Then her lips curved into a tremulous smile, and he brought her head to his.

Mistake, Gallagher. Big mistake.

Jack gazed at Becky Lynn's face, soft and vulnerable with sleep, eyes bruised from crying. He swore silently. What had he been thinking of? How could he have done…this?

She was his assistant and although it seemed odd to him, she was his friend. She had needed him, had needed comfort. She hadn't needed sex. She hadn't needed him to complicate her life.

He muttered another oath. Holding her had seemed so natural, kissing her more natural still. Both had led to arousal—undeniable, all-consuming arousal. He had lost his head; he had forgotten everything but the excitement of holding her and the need to relieve the ache between his legs.

So what the hell did he do now?

Disgusted with himself, he slipped out of bed, careful not to wake her. He didn't think he could face her now, not yet. Not when her grief was still so fresh, not when the way she had looked at him, the way she had murmured his name still resounded in his head.

He crossed to the loft's one window and gazed out at the dawning day. She had been so hesitant, so unsure of herself. Her responses had alternated between panicked and passionate, and when passion had won the battle, it had been almost unbearably sweet. The kind of sweetness that could choke a man.

He dragged his hands through his hair. This had meant something to her. Something? He compressed his lips in self-derision. It had meant everything to her. He should have expected this with a girl like Becky Lynn.

She cared for him.

She might even fancy herself in love with him.

Love? He breathed deeply through his nose, panic clutching at him. Dammit, he was so deep into it now, he didn't see a win-win way out of this situation. If he broke it off and told her—no matter how gently—that their making love had been a mistake, he would lose her.

He didn't want to lose her. He needed her.

He fisted his fingers on the cool, smooth glass. And if he kept his mouth shut, they would make love again. They couldn't go back to the way they were before. *She* couldn't anyway. He would give anything right now if he could turn the clock back.

She moaned, and he turned to look at her. His throat constricted. She looked so young and vulnerable lying there, her bright hair fanned out across the pillow, her soft mouth slightly parted. Kissable, he thought, drawing his eyebrows together. She had a mouth made for kissing. Why hadn't he seen that before?

He muttered an oath. Sex with Becky Lynn had been…good. She had clung to him in a way that had made him feel almost godlike. He would enjoy being with her again save for the emotional complications. They got in the way. They ruined the sex. And with Becky Lynn, the sex had been about as emotional as it could get.

He couldn't turn the clock back. Their relationship had become physical, neither of them could deny that. Nothing else had changed between them, certainly not his feelings. He wouldn't pretend they had. He wouldn't make her any promises, he wouldn't make her any assurances.

He wouldn't lose her.

She opened her eyes and looked at him, her expression strangely calm, her gaze as clear as a summer sky. He forced a smile, hoping she couldn't see his thoughts in his eyes. "You okay?"

She nodded. "Jack?"

"Yeah?"

"They raped me. That's why I ran."

28

Becky Lynn had been right about Zoe. The camera loved her. And she loved the camera right back. Zoe strutted and postured for Jack; she had no modesty, was unembarrassable; she never hesitated or balked at anything Jack asked her to do.

She had proved to be a quick study, as well. Becky Lynn cocked her head, studying Zoe as she played in the surf. From the first, she'd had the ability to give Jack any expression he wanted for a shot. Becky Lynn had to admit to herself that she envied Zoe's ability to tune into her body and shut everything else out. She envied the complete comfort and confidence the other girl felt with her physical self.

"That's right, Zoe," Jack called. "You feel good. The warm breeze caresses your skin, the scent of the ocean and flowers fills your head…"

Jack had been hard on Zoe. Harder than Becky Lynn had ever seen him be on anybody. She had asked him about it after the girl's second session, and he had explained that he had to be that way with Zoe because she was so cocky, and because she was such a natural. Cocky girls sometimes got into trouble, they shot their careers down by being too self-confident, by not having enough respect for the job because it came so easily.

Becky Lynn had to admit that his approach had worked with Zoe. The more difficult he made it for her, the harder she seemed to work at it. The harder she worked, the better she got. In a little over four months, she had advanced from complete novice to model ready for her first professional assignment.

Becky Lynn narrowed her eyes, watching Zoe move, appraising each shot Jack took. Today's shots would be good enough to put in Zoe's book. Jack must have been thinking the same thing because he laughed out loud and shouted encouragement, something he almost never did.

She hadn't thought she would like the other woman. In fact, at first, she had disliked her—intensely. But little by little, Becky Lynn had begun to see beyond Zoe's bravado, beyond her oftentimes shocking comments. Zoe needed reassurance, constant reassurance about her looks, her abilities, her future as a model. About everything, really.

Becky Lynn sensed a hunger in the girl, for affection and approval, for someone who really cared about her. That's why she acted the way she did, why she said the things she did.

Becky Lynn couldn't dislike Zoe for that. After all, she needed and hungered for the same things herself. Over the past weeks, those similarities had drawn them together and allowed them to become friends.

"Now, you're thinking of your lover," Jack said, lowering his voice. "Look at me, smile just a bit. That's right, perfect. Flex your foot, Zoe. Arch up just a little for a better line…"

The whir of the camera's motor drive blended with the sound of the waves rushing onto the beach. It was a beautiful day, warm and blue and scented of the ocean and flowers. She was living in one of the glossy images she had once upon a time poured over at Miss Opal's.

Becky Lynn tilted her face toward the brilliant blue sky and thought of her mother. A lump of tears formed in her throat, and she fought them back. She wouldn't cry for her mother, not anymore. Her mother was happier now, Becky Lynn knew. Away from her husband's brutality and Bend's prejudices. She was with her daddy again; she was with the angels.

Even though the thought brought her a sense of peace, the tears pressed at her. She wished her mother could have seen her now, wished she could have told her how well she was doing, how happy she was. Her mother would have been happy for her. She would have been proud.

Becky Lynn drew deeply through her nose, her chest aching, knowing her thoughts were true but wishing she had been able to be with Glenna, wishing that she'd had a chance to say goodbye.

"Becky Lynn? Camera."

She jerked her gaze to Jack, startled. He looked annoyed, and she realized she didn't have a clue how long he had been trying to get her attention. "Sorry." She took the camera he held out to her and handed him the freshly loaded one.

"I pushed that roll a stop and a half. Be sure to mark it."

She nodded and crossed to Jack's camera bag. She squatted beside it, rewound the film, popped it out and marked it. After reloading, she returned to stand beside Jack.

"No, Zoe," Jack called, lowering his camera. "That's not it at all."

He handed her the camera and strode across the sand to Zoe. Becky Lynn watched him, awareness stealing over her. She ached to touch him. Not in a way that was overtly sexual or overly possessive. She simply longed to physically connect with him—to lay her hand on his arm or curl her fingers around his.

But then, she always ached to touch him.

Becky Lynn sucked in a steadying breath. Jack had set up the ground rules of their relationship. At shoots, they behaved toward each other in a strictly professional manner—no touching, kissing or discussing their relationship. Few people even knew they were lovers. Not even Zoe knew, although Becky Lynn speculated that the other girl suspected the truth.

Every once in a while, the demon of doubt would sit on her shoulder and whisper in her ear that Jack was embarrassed by her. It had taken considerable effort on her part, but each time she had shooed the demon away.

But each demon's visit put another chink in her armor. How could it not have? She loved Jack so much it scared her.

Becky Lynn thought back to the day she would always remember as the day she had lost her mother and found her love. She had told Jack everything about her past. The words had spilled out of her with the fury of water breaking a levee. She had relived the horror, the pain and humiliation of the night she had been raped, but afterward it had been better. Afterward, she had felt a sense of calm and peace, as if finally she had let a modicum of her past go.

Jack had held her quietly while she cried, he had murmured words of comfort and understanding. The words had soothed, but his believing her, his being angry and outraged for her, had healed.

She had felt that finally she had someone who not only

believed in her, but someone she could lean on. Someone strong who would catch her if she fell.

Jack was that, she thought, smiling at him as he turned and started back toward her. Strong and self-confident. So strong, he didn't need anyone.

He didn't need her.

Her smile faltered, and she pushed away the disturbing thought. It didn't mean anything, she told herself. They were together; he treated her as if she was special, like she was important to him. No one had ever been so good to her before. He didn't have to need her; he was too strong to need her. That was okay.

"We're going to finish this roll, then wrap it," Jack said when he reached her.

She handed him the camera. "I think you've gotten some really good shots today."

"Yeah." He nodded, pleased. "I think so, too."

Jack directed Zoe into the incoming waves, just far enough out so the water rushed and swirled around her. Minutes later, Jack finished the roll and as promised, wrapped the shoot. Zoe stood and raced toward them, dripping wet and laughing, her hair flowing behind her. "What did you think, Becky Lynn? Was I wonderful?"

Becky Lynn laughed and handed her a towel. "You were, Zoe. Absolutely."

Zoe patted her face, and looped the towel around her shoulders. She turned toward Jack. "Well, oh great and powerful Oz? What did you think? Go ahead, tell me all the things I did wrong."

Becky Lynn shifted her gaze to Jack, holding her breath. Zoe tried so hard to please him; she had worked so hard over the past months. If he didn't give her an unequivocal thumbs-up this time, Zoe might just kill him. And as far as Becky Lynn was concerned, it would be justifiable homicide.

Jack looked at Zoe, unsmiling, his eyebrows drawn together into a scowl. "You want to know what I think?"

The model folded her arms defensively over her chest and hiked up her chin. "That is what I asked."

"Okay." He leaned toward her, his expression ominous. "I think you're going to be big. Really big."

For a second, Zoe said nothing. The beach was silent sound save for the cry of the gulls and the crash of the surf. Then Zoe let loose with a whoop of joy and flung herself into Jack's arms. "I knew it! I knew I was good!"

Jack laughed and met Becky Lynn's eyes over Zoe's head. "You'll be big," he amended, "unless your Godzilla-size ego gets in the way."

"Silly. I don't have any ego." She kissed him hard on the mouth, then swung to Becky Lynn. "Did you hear him, Becky Lynn? He thinks I'm going to be big. The ever-unpleasant Jack Gallagher said I was going to be big."

Becky Lynn laughed and hugged her friend. "I always knew it, Zoe. From the minute I set eyes on you."

"I'll have to tell reporters I was discovered in a john." Zoe made a face. "I think we'd better come up with another story. How about you discovered me at a—"

"Hold it, girls." Jack shook his head and made a sound of disgust. "We still have a lot of work to do. We haven't even begun to work on shots for your book, Zoe. You still need training. You need to work with a few other photographers, and you haven't even had your first gig. I think it's a little too soon to think about *Vogue* and cosmetics contracts."

Zoe rolled her eyes. "Yes, master."

Becky Lynn laughed. "Come on, you two. Let's get this stuff back to the studio so we can have lunch. I, for one, am starving."

"Count me out for lunch," Jack said, fitting one of his cameras into its case. "I'm meeting the guys from Tyler."

"Oh." Becky Lynn worked to hide her disappointment. She looked forward to her lunches with Jack, during which he usually let down his professional demeanor and became just Jack—her lover and friend. When she had reviewed his calendar this morning, she had seen nothing scheduled during lunch and had planned on their being together. "Did this meeting just come up?"

He glanced at her sharply. "You mean like right now? Like I made it up?"

"No." Becky Lynn folded her arms across her chest, hurt. "I mean, it wasn't in your appointment book."

"I guess I forgot to write it in." He yanked at the bag's zipper. "Back off, okay?"

"No problem." Becky Lynn swung away from him, tears stinging her eyes. She started gathering together their equipment, her face averted. She would die before she let him know how much his sarcasm had hurt.

"We can go," Zoe said softly, coming up behind her. She took the garment bag from Becky Lynn's hands. "Just you and me. It'll be fun."

"I don't know, I—"

"Come on." Zoe squeezed her arm. "It'll be a lot better than sitting around being pissed off and feeling sorry for yourself."

She had a point. Becky Lynn met the other girl's eyes and forced a smile. "Where did you have in mind?"

Zoe picked an open-air restaurant at the Farmer's

Market, and an hour and a half later they faced each other over California chicken salads. They had talked little, and Becky Lynn pushed a slice of avocado around her plate as Zoe ordered a second glass of wine.

The waiter walked away and Zoe reached across the table and touched her hand. "Don't be bummed. Jack probably did have a meeting. Like he explained, he just forgot to tell you about it."

"It's not that. It's—" Becky Lynn shook her head. "Let's drop it, it's no big deal."

"Sure, it's not." Zoe speared a piece of grilled chicken with her fork. "So, what's the deal between you and Jack?"

Becky Lynn met her eyes. "What do you mean?"

"I'm not blind, Becky Lynn. You guys are…involved. Am I right?"

Becky Lynn nodded. "Yeah, I guess you could call it that. Involved."

"You're…lovers."

Heat stung her cheeks, and she looked away. "Yes."

The waiter delivered Zoe's wine. She flashed him a brilliant smile in thanks, and he almost swooned.

She picked up the glass and sipped. "If you're lovers, what's the problem?"

"No problem. I'm just disappointed about lunch, that's all." Zoe made a face, and Becky Lynn smiled. "But I'm very happy to be here with you. I appreciate the invitation. You were right. I'd be sulking right now."

"That's better." Zoe pushed away her salad, even though she had only picked at it. "Why are you guys keeping your relationship a secret?"

"It's not a secret. It's just…" Becky Lynn searched her memory for when and why she and Jack had decided to keep their personal life private. They hadn't decided, she remembered. He had. "Jack thought it best we keep our relationship to ourselves. He thought it would make the clients uncomfortable, and that it might get in the way of our work."

"I see."

She drew the word out in a strange way, and Becky Lynn frowned. "Why did you say it like that?"

"No reason."

Becky Lynn searched her expression, insecurity and doubt eating at her. She bit her lip. "You're sure?"

"Why wouldn't I be?" Zoe drew her eyebrows together. "Becky Lynn, are you certain there's nothing wrong? You're acting a little…strange."

"I'm fine." Becky Lynn forced a smile and changed the subject. "Tell me, what does your mother think about you becoming a model? Is she excited?"

Zoe fished a cigarette out of her purse. "She doesn't know."

"She doesn't know?" Becky Lynn repeated, surprised. "But where does she think you are when you're with us? What does she think you're doing?"

Zoe lit the cigarette and shrugged. "She doesn't care. She probably thinks I'm at the mall." She drew deeply, then exhaled a cloud of smoke. "My mother and I talk to each other as little as possible."

"Don't you live with her? Surely you must talk… sometimes."

"Almost never. I can't wait to move out." Zoe shifted her gaze to a point beyond Becky Lynn's right shoulder, her expression grim. "It's terrible living with her. It always has been."

Becky Lynn swallowed. Something in the other girl's tone tugged at her heartstrings. "I'm sorry."

"Nothing for you to be sorry about." She finished her cigarette in silence, continuing to stare out at nothing. Suddenly she stubbed out the cigarette and swung her gaze to Becky Lynn's. "Have you ever watched other people doing it? Not in a movie, but in real life?"

Startled, Becky Lynn shook her head. "Have you?"

"Lots of times." Zoe looked away once more. "I was five the first time. I got up in the middle of the night 'cause I'd had a bad dream. I went to my parents' room, and they were, you know, having sex. I just stood there…watching. It's not pretty, you know. It's kind of gross…like animals mating. And the sounds, they scared me."

"Oh, Zoe, that's…awful."

Zoe fumbled in her purse for another cigarette. When she lit it, Becky Lynn saw that her hands shook. "Actually, I think my dad saw me. I dream about it. In the dream, he turns his head and looks right at me. And he smiles. But he doesn't say anything, he doesn't…stop." Zoe sucked in smoke. "Do you think he got a charge out of that? Out of doing it in front of his little girl?"

Becky Lynn swallowed, sick at the image. "That dream is probably just your memory playing tricks on you. It was an upsetting experience and you wished your father had seen you and stopped. From everything you've told me about the kind of father your dad was, I don't think he would do something like that."

"Then why did he leave?" she murmured, half to herself, her eyes filling. "Why did he…go?"

Becky Lynn's heart turned over at the other girl's obvious pain. She reached across the table and covered

Zoe's hand with her own. "Maybe he didn't have a choice, Zoe. Maybe it had nothing to do with you."

Zoe met her gaze; Becky Lynn saw gratitude in Zoe's eyes. "You're a nice person, Becky Lynn, you know that? I think you're the nicest person I've ever met."

After that day, she and Zoe spent a lot of time together. Not just at the studio and during test shoots, but after hours and on weekends, as well. It was fun having another girl to talk to, having someone besides Jack to go places with.

She and Jack worked together and were lovers, but not in the way she had always thought lovers would be. They didn't spend every minute they could together; other than catching a movie or going out for a pizza or Chinese, they didn't go on dates. Becky Lynn secretly longed for Jack to take her out for a romantic dinner, she longed for him to send her flowers or a love note.

But Becky Lynn had learned that Jack needed his independence. He didn't like to be tied down, he didn't like to have his schedule dictated to him, not ever. He had apologized about his attitude that day at the beach. He had been tired, he'd said, and on edge. She had accepted his apology, but that day had taught her not to ask for more than he was willing to give. She had learned not to be possessive and not to be hurt when he needed space.

Becky Lynn told Zoe about her feelings, told her the things she longed for with Jack. She sometimes thought her feelings for Jack amused Zoe. Sometimes she wondered if the other woman was jealous of her and Jack's relationship.

And sometimes she didn't like the way Zoe looked at Jack, as though she wanted to eat him up. She hated her feelings of jealousy, hated when she caught herself watching the two of them, hated the way she wanted to claw Zoe's eyes out when the other woman touched or kissed him.

She called herself overimaginative and insecure, she called herself disloyal—because most of the time, Zoe just acted like her friend. A friend who was there for her a lot more of the time than Jack was.

They had so much in common, she and Zoe, even though in most ways they couldn't be more different. Zoe liked to party. She liked men and flirting; she talked dirty and had a dark side that sometimes worried Becky Lynn.

But still, it seemed natural that when Becky Lynn mentioned a larger apartment had opened up in her building, Zoe suggested they move in together.

Becky Lynn said yes and within two weeks, she had a roommate. That first night, they stayed up until the wee hours, giggling together, sharing their dreams and their secrets.

When they finally agreed they had to get some sleep and said good-night, Becky Lynn lay on her bed and stared at the ceiling for a long time. For the first time in her life, she felt really lucky. She had a love, a friend to share secrets with, a job that she enjoyed and could be proud of.

She had everything, she decided, thinking of her mother, feeling that somehow, some way, her mother was with her.

Nothing could hurt her ever again.

29

Jack began to sweat. He breathed deeply through his nose and told himself to stop thinking about what getting the Garnet McCall account would mean to his career. He told himself to concentrate instead on what he was going to say to the designer about her latest line, her photographic history, about her future and how she saw Jack Gallagher photography fitting into that future.

But how could he stop thinking about what getting this account would mean to his career when it would mean everything? He would cease to be *"Jack Gallagher, who?"* and would become *"Jack Gallagher, the guy who shoots Garnet McCall."*

He flexed his fingers as he prowled the lushly appointed waiting room. Finally, he would seriously challenge Carlo. Finally, Carlo would be forced to look over his shoulder because the *embarrassing bastard* was gaining on him.

"You're sure I can't get you a cup of coffee while you wait, Mr. Gallagher? I just brewed a fresh pot."

Jack looked at the receptionist. A pretty blonde, she smiled at him. He returned her smile and shook his head. "No, thanks. I'm fine."

He turned and crossed to a row of framed shots of garments from the various McCall collections. He cocked his head, studying both the designs and the photographs, impressed with the first but not the latter. He had heard

Garnet might be looking for a new shooter, and now he saw why—this guy's style was neither tough enough nor bold enough for her creations.

He narrowed his eyes, thinking of his chance encounter with the designer the day before. He had gone to the fashion mart in the hopes of garnering some interest in his book, enough to score an interview. Designers themselves rarely made an appearance at the mart; he usually talked to an underling—the designer's manager or assistant, the head of the sales force, even a press agent once.

Garnet McCall herself had been in the showroom. He had smiled at her, and she'd given him two minutes to show her his book.

She had been interested, very interested. She'd told him to call at her design studio the next day...so here he was, waiting and sweating.

Jack turned and found the receptionist gazing at him. Instead of being embarrassed or flustered at having been caught gaping, she sent him a slow, bold smile.

He returned the receptionist's interested smile and Becky Lynn's image filled his head. He swore silently, nodded at the receptionist and turned back to the wall and the substandard photos.

Jack scowled. He hated feeling guilty when he looked at another woman, he hated feeling as if he was cheating. He liked Becky Lynn; he liked being with her, but what he felt for her wasn't love. Even though they had been lovers for nearly a year, their relationship wasn't exclusive.

Then why did a receptionist's come-hither smile make him feel like a cheat?

Because Becky Lynn didn't understand those things about their relationship. She didn't have to say so; her feelings were clear to read in her eyes, in the way she made him the focus of her life, in the things she expected from him.

He drew his eyebrows together, thinking of their relationship, searching his memory for the things he had said to her, promises he had hinted at without realizing it.

He had promised her nothing. He had worked at keeping their relationship loose and breezy. If she thought what they had was more, he wasn't to blame. Surely she had been in California long enough, in the business long enough, to understand how the relationship game was played.

She hadn't.

He thought back to the day he and Becky Lynn had become lovers—the day she had learned her mother was dead, the day she had told him about her past. His chest tightened thinking about it, a feeling of rage, of impotence taking his breath. He hadn't led a sheltered life; he'd seen his share of ugliness and dirt, but the thought of his Becky Lynn being brutalized that way sickened him. He had wanted to hit someone or something, he had wanted to find those boys and kill them.

They had gotten away with it. They had tried to destroy her, and they had gotten off scot-free. It wasn't right that they hadn't had to pay for their crime; for him, it made the crime that much worse.

He flexed his fingers. He should never have let sex happen between them. He had known that going in, he remembered thinking it at the time. But he had made love with her, anyway.

He had wondered countless times since, if he would have called it off had he known beforehand just how vulnerable she was. Sometimes he thought yes, sometimes no. Most times, all he knew for certain was that he had gotten himself into a damn difficult situation.

He cared for her; he knew how much she had been hurt. She was a big part of his life. He hadn't a clue how to extricate himself from this situation. Not without losing her. Not without hurting her badly.

He didn't want to do either.

He thought of her excitement when he'd told her about this meeting, this chance at Garnet McCall. She had been completely confident. He smiled to himself. As far as Becky Lynn was concerned, he had the account, hands down.

"I like a man who can smile even after having been kept waiting a half an hour."

Jack turned to face Garnet McCall. She stood in the doorway to the reception area, outfitted in one of her own creations—a form-fitting purple leather dress. A wide silver zipper ran from high neck to hem and held the two pieces of stressed fabric together.

He smiled his appreciation. "A man has to consider what lies at the end of the wait," he said, crossing to her. "And in this case, what waited was quite wonderful."

She smiled and swept her gaze over him. "I do like the way you go on, Jack Gallagher."

"I do my best."

She gazed at him a moment more, her expression thoughtful. "I'll just bet you do."

She turned to the receptionist. While she gave the woman directions, Jack studied the designer. Garnet McCall was young, not forty yet and attractive in a lush, aggressive sort of way. A woman who had come from out of nowhere to occupy a tier below the likes of Calvin Klein, Garnet McCall hadn't gotten there by being passive or weak.

Jack liked Garnet's aggressiveness, her straightforward way of approaching the business. With her, he would know where he stood. And he liked her clothes. They were tough and spirited. His work was well-suited to hers. Much better suited than the guy who had taken the stuff on the wall.

"I'll be in my office, Vicki. Hold all but the most important calls. Come, Jack—" She slid her hand through the crook of his arm. "Let me show you around my shop."

Garnet took him through the facility, and he admitted being impressed. She had a large staff, all young, energetic and working at breakneck pace. The place reeked of success and of forward momentum. Everyone in Garnet's shop knew they were attached to a rising star, that they teetered on the edge of greatness. They felt it, just as he did.

He and Garnet ended up at her office, a large, spacious room complete with desk, drafting table and entertaining area. She led him to the couch and once seated, began flipping through his book, but slowly this time, studying, assessing.

Finally, she met his eyes, hers lit with challenge. She wasn't going to make this easy, he knew. But then, if she did, he wouldn't appreciate it half as much.

"I like you, Jack. I like you a lot."

"Glad to hear it."

She tapped his open book. "You have a fresh, bold style. A kind of lawlessness that fits my work."

He inclined his head. "I think so, too."

"You've had a few moments to look at my designs, a

few moments to get to know me. What do you think about my clothes, Jack Gallagher? What kind of statement do you think I'm making and where do you think I should go with my visuals?"

He met her gaze evenly, meeting her challenge, making one of his own. "Your clothes are sexy. You're sexy. And tough. Your designs aren't for the corporate woman, except when she wants to let her hair down and howl with the wolves. Your clothes are smart and stylish, they're for the woman who enjoys her body, the woman who enjoys being a woman."

He laid his arms along the back of the couch, completely at ease now. "Your designs aren't for the weak, the mousy or the romantic. Your visuals should reflect that. They haven't so far."

"In your opinion."

"Yes, in my opinion."

She stood and crossed to the desk. She leaned against it, braced on her palms. The posture accentuated the curves of her body, brought attention to the thrust of her breasts and the vee of her sex.

"You've never handled anyone of my caliber before. That concerns me."

This was the point at which he always heard, *"Come back when you have more experience."* Not today, he decided, determination burning in the pit of his gut. He didn't care what it took, but today he would not be turned away by that line.

He stood and crossed to stand before her, his gaze unflinchingly on hers. "I can handle your account, better than anyone else out there. Better than you can even imagine. I've heard that you've had your problems with photographers, with your ad agency. You won't have any problems with me. You'll be unbelievably happy with Jack Gallagher." He lowered his voice. "And with my images, the entire industry will be talking about Garnet McCall."

She smiled and slid her gaze over him, obviously pleased. He had chosen the right approach, no doubt about it. A woman like her needed someone as tough, as confident and straightforward as himself. "They're already talking."

"They'll talk more. A lot more."

She cocked her head, studying him. "You've got balls, Jack Gallagher."

"I like to think so."

She leaned toward him, and he caught a whiff of her perfume, something earthy and potent. Arousal kicked him in the gut, and he sucked in a quick breath. The interview had just shifted from professional to personal.

"Before I make my final decision," she murmured, curving her fingers suggestively around his forearm, "I'd like to get to know you better." She wet her lips. "I'd like that a lot."

His body stirred. He lowered his gaze to her mouth. He wondered how she would taste, how she would feel under his hands. Was she wet now? he wondered. He thought so. He saw the arousal in her eyes, saw her eagerness; he saw that her nipples strained against the thin, supple leather.

Nothing in this business came without a cost.

He closed the scant distance between them and lowered his voice to a husky murmur. "I'd like that, too, Garnet McCall. Very much."

"I'm glad." She caught his hand and brought it to her neck, to the star-shaped zipper pull. "Can you imagine what I have on under this dress, Jack?"

He eased a finger through the pull's wide opening. "Provocative question, Garnet." He tugged and the zipper inched downward. "One I would love an answer to."

The dress parted; he had his answer.

She had nothing on underneath.

30

A group of high-school-age boys stood outside the police barriers, ogling the models, whistling and making lewd comments. The models didn't seem to be bothered, but the boys' presence set Becky Lynn's nerves on edge. They reminded her of boys from back home, and she found herself putting as much space as possible between herself and them. It interfered with her job, stealing both her concentration and her ability to think clearly, and she found herself cursing her own fears and Jack's choice of Venice Beach for his first Garnet McCall shoot.

In her opinion, he should have picked a less public—and more controllable—location. She had argued with him about it, but Jack hadn't wanted safe for this first, all-important shoot. He had wanted bold. He had wanted excitement and movement; he had wanted, and needed, to make a statement.

He was determined to give Garnet McCall the best damn shoot she had ever had. And as much as his choice annoyed Becky Lynn right now, she would have done the same thing had she been in charge.

One of the boys made a grab for her as she passed, and she almost jumped out of her skin. She fought off the urge to slug the little creep, and instead warned him that if he dared pull another stunt like that, she would call one of the cops they'd hired as security.

The kid backed off immediately. She realized she had probably overreacted, and blamed exhaustion. The phone hadn't stopped ringing since the news about Jack's test shoot for Garnet had hit the street. Between fielding the calls, preparing for this shoot and taking care of the day-to-day running of the studio, she hadn't had more than four hours of sleep a night for a week.

Even Cliff from Tyler Creative had called. In the fashion industry, everybody knew everybody else's business, coast to coast and beyond. Being picked up and possibly signed by a comer like Garnet McCall had caused a stir. Even if the designer didn't sign him, Jack's stock had soared.

They were happy for Jack, Cliff had said, although they worried that before long they wouldn't be able to afford him. She had assured him that they had nothing to worry about, then he had said something that had struck her as odd. They were surprised by Garnet's interest, not because Jack lacked the ability but by the enormity of the step. He had wondered if there had been extenuating circumstances.

She had laughed and assured him that the only extenuating circumstances had been the enormity of Jack's talent. It hadn't been until after she'd hung up that the man's comments began to bother her.

A day or two later, she had mentioned the conversation to Jack, but he had blown the comment off as nothing. But still it annoyed her that people would think such a thing. As if there always had to be *another* reason someone got a job, a reason other than talent and hard work.

It was one of the things she had grown to despise about this business.

Becky Lynn worked her way around the perimeter of the set. She didn't like Garnet McCall, and she didn't care

for her designs. She found both abrasive and too overtly sexy. Not that her opinion mattered;
not that she wouldn't give her best for the woman.

Becky Lynn stopped and held her hands up, using them as a viewfinder. Just down the boardwalk, a half-clad young man was eating fire. Down the other way, she had seen a muscle-bound hunk juggling chain saws. She smiled to herself. Perfect images for a McCall ad.

"Jack," she called. He was a dozen feet away, talking with one of the models. When he looked up, she motioned for him to come over. "When you have a chance, I've got an idea I want to pass by you."

He nodded and returned to his conversation, and Becky Lynn swung around and bumped into Garnet McCall.

"Excuse me." Becky Lynn took a step back. "I didn't see you."

"Apparently." Garnet smiled and looked over her shoulder at Jack. "Our boy is something special, isn't he?"

Our boy. The woman had practically purred the words. Becky Lynn bristled. She wanted to tell the woman he wasn't "our boy," he was hers, property of Becky Lynn Lee.

Instead, she smiled stiffly. "Yes, he is."

The designer arched her eyebrows ever so slightly at her tone. "I overheard you call Jack. You had an idea for the shoot? I'd love to hear it."

Becky Lynn hesitated, surprised. Clients rarely asked her opinion on the creative aspect of a shoot. That was always Jack's territory, and rightly so. Feeling as if she was over-stepping her bounds, she cleared her throat. "I thought it might be interesting to work in some of the local acts, especially the fire-eater and the guy juggling chain saws. I thought their juxtaposition with your clothes would be exciting."

The designer narrowed her eyes in thought, then nodded. "I like it, Becky Lynn. It's a good idea. Tell Jack I said so."

The woman walked off and Becky Lynn watched her go, her heart thundering. Garnet McCall liked her idea. *Her idea.* She smiled, elated.

"What was that all about?" Jack came up beside her, and followed the direction of her gaze.

She turned to him and laughed. "I had a good idea." At his questioning glance, she told him about her conversation with Garnet McCall.

Jack looked over his shoulder, down the boardwalk at the street performer. He studied the scene a moment, then nodded. "It is a good idea. The only problem with using nonprofessionals is getting them to relax in front of the camera."

"We try it, and if it doesn't work, we move on."

Jack checked his watch, thinking Becky Lynn knew about time, and cost and the light. "The models are almost ready—"

"I'll go see if they're interested."

"Make it quick."

She nodded and started down the boardwalk.

The street performers worked out even better than she had hoped. Accustomed to crowds and attention, they did their thing, interacting with the models without mugging at the camera or stiffening up. In fact, they worked out so well that Jack snagged a couple of bare-chested surf bums. The muscle-bound hunks were only too happy to strut their stuff with the models.

The chromes were going to be fantastic.

"Great," Jack called, handing her the camera. "Let's do the fuchsia leather next. And, Willy—" The makeup artist looked up. "I want to see eyes and mouths from a mile away."

Willy nodded and went for his box. Jack turned to her. "Let's switch to the medium-format. Polaroid back first."

"I'll take care of it."

While she switched cameras, Jack conferred with Garnet. Becky Lynn watched them from the corner of her eye, wanting to be in place and ready when Jack needed her.

"That Hasselblad's a fine piece of equipment. It would have been my choice from the start."

Becky Lynn turned. She recognized the man who had come up behind her from the photographs she had seen of him, and because he looked so much like his father.

Carlo.

She narrowed her eyes. *He had come to try to throw Jack. She knew of no other reason for him to be here.*

"Nice touch, though, using the street performers."

"Can I help you with something?" she asked coolly, pretending she didn't know who he was.

He swept his gaze assessingly over her, pausing on her face for a long moment. "Who are you?"

She could imagine what he thought of her looks. Annoyed, she lifted her chin and narrowed her eyes. "Who are you?" she countered, deciding that she disliked this man almost as much as she had ever disliked any.

"You don't know who I am?" He arched his eyebrows in disbelief. "I'm Carlo Triani. Jack's brother. We're very close."

At her expression, he grinned and swept his gaze over her again. "You're wasted as Jack's assistant. You know that, don't you?"

"Excuse me?"

Carlo laughed, the sound deep and heartily amused. Several people glanced their way. "I guess I'll have to add being blind to Jack's many other shortcomings."

She didn't dislike him, she amended silently, she despised him. "You don't have any business here, so I'm afraid I have to ask you to leave."

"Hopelessly devoted to him, aren't you?" He shook his head. "Just like all the other women in his life. And just like all the others, he'll let you down." He lowered his voice. "Don't you see that, *bella?*"

She flexed her fingers, angry with him—and with herself—for letting his lies get to her. "Mr. Triani, if you don't—"

"Carlo," he corrected, taking a step closer to her. She forced herself not to back away from him, although she loathed his being so near her. He lowered his voice. "Besides, I've just discovered I do have business here. I've come to steal you away from Jack."

"Oh, please." She made a sweeping motion with her right hand. "Don't force me to call security. Don't embarrass yourself that way."

"You should be in front of the camera, not behind it. You're wasted as Jack's assistant."

Angry now, she folded her arms across her chest. Carlo Triani was a small, cruel man. Jack was right to hate him so much. For him to make fun of her that way, only to hurt Jack, was beyond ugly. "You're not welcome here. I don't know how to be more plain than that. Please leave."

"Turn your head, *bella*. Let me see your profile."

He reached out a hand to her chin, and she caught her breath and slapped his hand away. "Leave, now. I'm calling security."

"Becky Lynn, what's going on? We're ready—"

Carlo turned. Jack stopped in his tracks, his expression freezing.

"Hello, baby brother."

Jack released a sharp breath. "What are you doing here?"

"I came to wish you well." He smiled. "You're moving up in the world."

Jack fisted his fingers at his sides, readying for a fight. Becky Lynn put her hand on his arm. "Let it go," she whispered. "Jack, please. He's not worth it."

He ignored her. She felt his muscles quiver at the ready. "That's right," he said softly. "I am moving up in the world. And you'd better watch your back, brother." He took a step toward Carlo, murder in his eyes. "Now get off my set."

Carlo grinned, unruffled, the picture of self-confidence. "Sure, bro. Whatever you say." He walked several steps, then stopped and looked over his shoulder at her. "Think about what I said, Becky Lynn. You're wasted with him. Besides, he'll just break your heart." He shifted his amused gaze to Jack. "Ciao, brother."

31

Mission accomplished.

Carlo smiled to himself and leaned his head against the edge of the Jacuzzi. The hot water swirled and bubbled around him, bringing him to the point of liquid relaxation. The sky was a cloudless blue, the models on either side of him lush and willing, the champagne fine, cold and dry. Life was good.

The drive over to Venice had been one of the best investments of time he had ever made. It had been worth every minute of fighting traffic just to see the look on Jack's face, to see his concentration slip, even if only for those few moments, and to see the concerned glance Garnet McCall had shot his brother's way.

But meeting Becky Lynn had been the Big Bonus.

Carlo reached behind the companion on his right for his champagne.

He brought the crystal flute to his lips and sipped, his mouth twitching with amusement. His brother was blind. He had a jewel right under his nose, a diamond in the rough. Becky Lynn had the face every photographer searched for. Every photographer worth his salt, that was.

Not Jack. Carlo sipped again, then returned the glass to the spa's tile ledge. He wasn't surprised that his horny, macho brother couldn't see Becky Lynn's true worth. Her face wasn't obvious enough for him, it wasn't easy enough.

"I'm going to cool off in the pool," companion number one—Susi—said, curving her hand over his thigh. "Interested in joining me?"

Carlo cracked open his eyes. Susi wore a bright red thong bikini and her cosmetically enhanced breasts spilled out every side of the skimpy top. He lifted his gaze to her perfect face and shook his head. "You go on."

"How do you take the heat so long?" June, on his other side and also in a daring red bikini, pulled herself out of the spa. "I'm about to boil alive."

"My hot Italian blood." He grinned and arched his eyebrows. "I never get enough of it."

"Promises, promises." Susi dragged her hands over her slicked-back hair, bringing her breasts into stunning relief. "Join us later?"

Unmoved, Carlo leaned his head back. "Sure," he murmured. "Maybe later."

The girls climbed out of the Jacuzzi, and he shut his eyes, his thoughts returning to Jack and Becky Lynn. The camera would love Becky Lynn. If it didn't, well…he had nothing to lose. But if he was right, if she could be as big as he hoped—and he was hardly ever wrong—Becky Lynn would help him become a star. But even better, she would help him make Jack a laughingstock.

Carlo smiled, imagining it, imagining the entire industry laughing about how Jack had had *"this wonderful girl"* right under his nose, and had used her as an *"assistant."*

It was too wonderful, too perfect.

And maybe too late. Jack had snagged Garnet McCall.

Carlo's smile faded, hatred burning in the pit of his gut, festering. The son of a bitch had everything—looks and talent, ambition, growing success. And worse, more insufferable, Jack knew he had it all. He believed in himself with a damn-the-world arrogance that the world couldn't help admiring.

At least Carlo had always been able to compare his career to Jack's with a self-satisfied confidence. He had gotten a jump on Jack, a big jump. He had never thought his bastard half brother would be able to close the gap.

Until today.

Carlo swore and opened his eyes. The brilliant sunlight stung, and he blinked against it. But Jack didn't have Giovanni, he didn't have the Triani name, he wasn't part of the legend. And no matter how much he wanted both, he would never have them.

"Look what he's accomplished on his own." Giovanni's voice filled his head, damning Carlo. *"Look what he's done without my name to open all his doors. What would you have done without me, Carlo? What could you have done?"*

What would he have done? he wondered. Would he be another nobody photographer? Would he have given up?

Carlo muttered another oath, furious at his own thoughts, furious at the way self-doubt ate at him. He had talent. Giovanni didn't take Carlo's pictures; his images were his alone, property of Carlo Triani, fashion photographer. If there was any similarity between his and Giovanni's style, it was a matter of influence not imitation.

He curled his hands into fists, his relaxation and pleasure of minutes ago gone, replaced by resentment and tension. He hated Jack Gallagher, he had hated him from the moment he heard Jack's name on his own mother's lips.

His mother. His beautiful mother.

He had worshiped her. He had adored her—as all who had come into contact with her had. All but her own husband, all but Giovanni.

How had Giovanni been immune to her beauty? How had he been immune to her cries for attention, her pleas that he stop shaming her with his many public affairs? Carlo had often thought his father a sort of forbidding God, a figure from the Old Testament, judgmental and all-powerful.

"Hey…Car…lo. Carlo…"

He opened his eyes and saw red. His head filled with the image of his mother, naked in a pool of red, her once-beautiful face grotesquely white with death.

His stomach heaved; he couldn't breathe. He gripped the sides of the Jacuzzi, fourteen again, his world shattered.

"Car…lo… Come out and play."

He blinked and the image in his head evaporated; his vision cleared. Two red bikini tops churned in the water in front of him. He lifted his gaze. The two models stood beside the spa, hands on their hips and giggling.

Anger took his breath, white-hot and stunning. He snatched the bathing suit tops and flung them out of the spa, forcing June to duck. "I hate the color red, do you hear me? I never want to see these suits again."

The girls' faces registered shock and surprise; for a moment, the silence deafened. Then June marched across the patio and snatched up the suit tops. She tied her own on, then brought the other to Susi. She glared at him. "You bastard. Where do you think you get off?"

"Mi dispiace, bella," he murmured in Italian, sliding across the Jacuzzi. He tipped his face up to June's. "Forgive me. I'm sorry."

"Right." June bent and collected her sunglasses and keys. "I'm out of here."

He reached out and caught her ankle. *"Per favore?* I'll make it worth your while."

"Take your hand off me, you prick." Furious, June shook his hand off her ankle. "I'd sooner party with a snake."

Carlo shrugged and turned his gaze to Susi, the bit of red fabric clutched in her hands, her magnificent, manufactured breasts bared to God, the sun and his gaze.

"What about you, Susi?" He grinned disarmingly up at her. "Want to stay and play?"

Susi shot an apologetic look at the other model, tossed aside the bikini top and climbed into the spa.

With a smile, she straddled his lap.

Much later, after Susi had gone, Carlo prowled the house, on edge and antsy. He liked noise and people. He liked working. But this quiet, this emptiness meant being alone with his own thoughts, with his memories. His demons.

Red water.

Carlo shuddered and crossed to the bar. He poured a shot of vodka, the Russian brand he preferred, but he didn't drink. He stared at the clear liquid, thinking back, remembering his mother.

She had been so beautiful. Thick dark hair and velvety eyes, features that had taken the breath. Her soft, smoky voice had moved over him like a caress. He remembered it so clearly, he could still hear it in his head.

She had been famous, a fashion model, still considered by many to be Italy's most celebrated beauty—sexier than Sophia Loren, more beautiful than Isabella Rossellini.

Carlo picked up the glass and gently turned it, watching as the light caught and reflected on the clear alcohol. Sometimes he used to gaze at his mother in secret, hide and watch while she brushed her hair or bathed, when she thought she was alone. He would see her sorrow. Her unhappiness had clutched at his heart, choking him, and he had wished with everything he had that he could make her happy.

He had loved her so much. But there had always been a part of her he couldn't touch, no matter how he had wanted to, no matter how hard he had tried.

He tossed back the drink, grimacing at its burn, then poured himself another.

The industry gossip mill had had a field day with her suicide. He had heard many things, things a young man, a son, should not have heard. Many speculated that the car accident that had taken her face had not been an accident at all, but a first suicide attempt. Most said despondency over Giovanni's humiliating public affairs had moved her to take her own life.

All Carlo had known for certain was that his mother hadn't loved him enough to want to live. She had only loved Giovanni.

The phone rang, and Carlo jumped to answer it, anxious for a distraction. He thought perhaps it was June, calling to apologize, or Susi wanting to get together again.

"Have you heard?" his father demanded without greeting.

Carlo's gut tightened. His father had called about Jack's latest success. "Hello to you, too, Father."

"Have you heard?" his father asked again, impatiently. "Jack landed Garnet McCall."

"Yes," Carlo said with forced disinterest. "I've heard."

For a moment, Giovanni said nothing, then he laughed softly. "He has done much, all on his own, no? But then, with or without my name, it is my blood that runs in his veins."

Carlo drew a sharp breath, angry at the way his father's words made him feel—like a boy who couldn't please his great father, like a boy who kept trying, anyway. He made a sound of disgust. "He's still practically an amateur. Besides, I hear he doesn't even have the account yet." Propping the phone between his shoulder and ear, Carlo reached for the vodka and poured another shot. "I'm not going to hold my breath that McCall gives it to him."

"Interesting." Giovanni paused as if for effect. "Then why did you pay your brother a visit?"

Carlo set the glass down, face burning. "How did you...who told you that?"

Giovanni chuckled. "One of the models who was part of the shoot, the young one with the black hair."

The muscles at the back of Carlo's neck tightened. He brought a hand up to massage them. "You still like the young ones, don't you, Father? Funny how you keep getting older and they...don't."

His father laughed again, unaffected by the barb. "You only wish you could be as potent. The women, they love me. They can't get enough of Giovanni." He paused once more. "I hear the women, they love Jack, too."

Carlo fisted his fingers, frustration churning inside him. Meaning that women didn't talk about him, about his abilities in bed. He thought of that afternoon, of Susi and the way she had rocked and bucked on top of him. She had been satisfied. He had seen to it.

But that wasn't what his father referred to, Carlo knew. Jack had the same macho charisma Giovanni did, the same way of drawing people, of awing them. Especially women, always women.

Becky Lynn.

"I do all right," he said lightly, buoyed by the thought of the jewel he had discovered today. "In fact, I have company now. Company I'm neglecting."

The sound of his father's laughter ringing in his ears, he hung up the phone. He tossed back the vodka and went in search of the Yellow Pages. He would show his father which son deserved his praise; he would show him which deserved the Triani name.

He found the book, pulled it out and flipped it open. He would woo Becky Lynn away from Jack; he would make her a star.

And in the process, publicly discredit Jack.

He dialed the number of the first Beverly Hills florist he came to.

32

The McCall shots were fabulous, so fabulous, in fact, that Garnet McCall signed Jack to a two-year all-inclusive contract. The account was huge: seasonal catalogs, advertising, collection promotion. And as the Garnet McCall name grew to include product endorsement, the account prospects only increased. On signing the contract, Jack had immediately hired a second assistant, had begun looking for a studio manager and had given Becky Lynn a fat raise.

Becky Lynn shifted the bottle of champagne and sack of groceries from her right arm to her left, no small feat considering the balloon bouquet she had tied around her right wrist. She fumbled in her pocket for her studio keys, the balloons bobbing crazily around her head. Jack had given her the afternoon off, claiming exhaustion and the need to crash. Before she'd left, he had given her an envelope with three hundred dollars in it. Her raise, he'd told her. Retroactive.

She hadn't known what to say, so she had kissed him instead, long and deeply. When she'd ended the kiss, he had looked so surprised and pleased that she'd kissed him again. And again.

One thing had led to another and they'd ended up on the floor, making love. Their lovemaking had been slow and sweet and more tender than it had ever been before.

She had been choked with tears afterward, choked with the need to tell him she loved him.

But even as she had opened her mouth to do just that, something had held her back—maybe something she saw in his eyes, as if he knew what she was contemplating and was begging her not to do it, or maybe some innate sense told her that she would regret it if she did. So, instead, she had snuggled up against him, telling him without words everything he meant to her.

That had been hours ago. She had used the time to put together a private celebration for just the two of them. She had all his favorite gourmet food items—Brie, pâté and imported crackers, marinated mushrooms, chocolate-covered strawberries, the brut champagne he favored and the balloons just because.

Becky Lynn smiled and batted at several, then let herself into the studio. The scent of flowers was almost overpowering, and she shook her head, amused. Carlo had sent them to her, a different arrangement every day since the McCall shoot. Each accompanying card had said the same thing: *Come to me, Becky Lynn. I'll make you a star.*

At first, she had been annoyed. She thought his attempt to get at Jack through her cruel, beneath contempt. But after about the third day, her annoyance had shifted to amusement. If he wanted to throw away his money, it was fine with her. She liked the flowers.

She saw that a new arrangement had come while she was out, this one a shocking pink azalea plant. She set down the groceries and wine, and crossed to the plant. She touched one of the blossoms lightly, the blossom's feathery texture calling up memories of home, of spring. She had forgotten how beautiful spring had been in Bend: a riot of vivid blossoms everywhere—the fuchsia azaleas, fiery red zinnias—together so brilliant they had almost burned the eye.

There had been something beautiful in Bend.

The realization eased its way through her consciousness, surprising her. She stared at the flower, a warmth blooming inside her, a sense of peace. Something beautiful in Bend, she thought once more, smiling. She snapped off a blossom and tucked it behind her ear.

Collecting the groceries and wine, she started for the loft. Halfway up, she heard the sound of hushed voices, soft laughter. *Jack had the television on.* She shook her head. He hated television, although on occasion he used it as a kind of pacifier to relieve total boredom.

She laughed to herself. It looked as if she had timed their celebration perfectly.

Two steps from the top of the stairs, she heard Jack's name, spoken softly on the end of a throaty laugh. Becky Lynn stopped, her heart beginning to pound. *That wasn't the television. It was Jack's voice. And a woman's.*

With her free hand, she gripped the banister, her world tipping crazily on its axis. *Jack wasn't alone.*

Oh, God. She drew in a deep breath, her chest so tight it hurt. *What was she going to do? How could she face seeing Jack with another woman?*

There was an explanation for this, she reassured herself. A simple explanation, an innocent one. She would laugh about her suspicions later. Sure she would.

Becky Lynn looked behind her, looked back the way she had come. She could leave now; Jack would never know she had been here, she could pretend this had never happened.

She squeezed her eyes shut, feeling as if her heart were splintering in two. If she was so sure nothing was going on in his bedroom, why was she so afraid to go up? Why was she so eager to run?

She couldn't pretend. She had to know.

She climbed the last stairs, legs shaking so badly she feared she wouldn't make it. The sounds from his bedroom became louder, more discernible. The door stood ajar. With the tips of her trembling fingers, she nudged it open.

Her heart stopped, and in that first moment, she thought she was going to die. She wanted to die.

Jack was in bed with another woman. He was making love to another woman.

The sack of groceries slipped from her hands, the bottle of wine with it, hitting the floor hard but not breaking. Jack and the woman sprang apart, and Becky Lynn got her first look at Jack's partner.

Garnet McCall. Becky Lynn made a sound of surprise and pain, and took a step backward. *Jack was in bed with Garnet McCall.*

"Jesus, Becky Lynn!" Jack jumped out of bed, grabbing the blanket as he did, wrapping it around himself. "Why didn't you call? I told you to call."

She took another step backward, tears choking her. "I brought some…I thought we…" She moved her gaze from Jack to Garnet and back, her vision blurring. "Is this how you got the account?"

"Don't be hurt, honey," Garnet murmured, sitting up and pushing a hand through her wildly disheveled hair. She met Becky Lynn's eyes, looking genuinely sorry. "Believe me, it doesn't mean anything." She patted the mattress. "Join the party, you're more than welcome."

The bile of disgust rose in her throat, and Becky Lynn made a strangled sound of pain. She shook her head, turning her gaze to Jack. "I can't believe you did this. I can't believe only a few hours ago you…and I, we—" Her words ended on a sob.

"Red…please. Let's talk about this."

She shook her head again and took a step backward, the pain almost too much to bear. "Don't call me that. Not now."

Jack started toward her, hand out. "Come on, babe. We'll go downstairs and—"

"Stay away from me! Don't touch me!"

"Becky Lynn, please—"

She turned and ran. She hit the stairs, almost falling. She grabbed the railing, and a pain shot through her hip as she slammed against it. She kept going.

Jack started after, calling her name. "Becky Lynn, wait! Please, let me explain."

Sobbing, she reached the bottom of the stairs and flew through the studio. She knocked into an equipment trolley and sent it sailing across the floor. It crashed into a light stand, toppling it.

"Becky Lynn! Don't go like this!"

She heard him on the stairs behind her; he called her yet again. She didn't stop, didn't look back. She couldn't bear to see him wrapped in that damning blanket, his expression full of pity.

But not regret. He didn't even care that he had hurt her.

She burst through the front door and outside. It had begun to rain. For long moments, she stood frozen to the spot, heart racing, rain mingling with her tears. She realized the balloons were still attached to her wrist, mocking her. She clawed at the ribbons, tearing them free. As the balloons drifted to the sky, she began to run.

Her feet pounded against the wet sidewalk, the sound mimicking the thunder of her heart. Jack had never said he loved her, but she had thought, had allowed herself to believe, that they had something special. Something important. She had believed in him. She had trusted him. She had thought he felt the same about her. It hurt almost more than she could bear.

Her head filled with bits and snatches from her past— her father forcing her to look at her reflection and demanding what man would ever want to touch her; Ricky and Tommy laughing as they dragged a paper bag over her head; the boys at school barking as she passed in the hall. The memories taunted her, calling her a fool, reminding her who and what she was.

How could she have allowed herself to forget?

She reached the bus stop, and curved her arms around her middle, doubling over in pain. Everyone had known about Jack, she thought.

Sallie and Marty. The guys at Tyler. Probably the whole industry. She thought of what she'd told Cliff that day he'd called about Jack's shot at McCall— *"The only extenuating circumstances were Jack's talent."*

Yeah, she thought, hysterical laughter bubbling to her lips, his talent in bed. How Cliff must have laughed at her. How they all must have laughed at her.

The bus pulled up to the stop, and she climbed aboard. The driver looked at her with concern. She ignored him and found a seat, folding herself into a tight ball of misery. Sallie had known this would happen. So had Marty. Even Carlo.

She had been such a fool. A naive idiot. Becky Lynn pressed her face to her knees and moaned. Everyone had seen the truth but her.

Zoe wouldn't laugh. Becky Lynn lifted her face and wiped her eyes. Zoe would understand; she would comfort her.

Becky Lynn endured the rest of the bus ride, hanging on by thinking of Zoe, by focusing on the fact that soon she would have her friend to hold on to, her friend's shoulder to cry on. Every time her head filled with the image of Jack in bed with the other woman, she would force it from her mind and imagine instead, Zoe's arms around her, Zoe's murmurs of comfort and support.

The bus finally reached her stop; she walked the block to her apartment building, too drained to run. As she walked, she prayed that Zoe would be home, the silent prayer running through her head like a mantra.

Becky Lynn made it to her floor, then to her apartment door. Her fingers shook so badly it took several tries to get the door unlocked and open; when she did, she stumbled inside.

"Zoe!" she called, starting to fall apart. "Zoe, where are you?"

"Here, Becky Lynn." Zoe's head appeared over the top of the couch. She looked at Becky Lynn and her eyes widened. "What's wrong?"

"It's Jack…he…he…" She dropped her face into her hands. "Oh, Zoe, it was so awful."

Zoe sprang up and came around the couch. She crossed to Becky Lynn. "Has something happened to Jack?" Her face pinched with alarm, she grabbed Becky Lynn's upper arms. "Has he been hurt? Is he ill?"

Becky Lynn shook her head, the tears she had managed

to hold through the bus ride beginning to fall. "He...I...I caught him...in bed with...someone else."

Zoe dropped her hands. "Who?"

"Garnet McCall." Becky Lynn curved her arms around her middle, her head filling with the image of the two in bed together, filling with the sound of their enjoyment. "It was so awful. He didn't even apologize. He just—"

"Why should he?"

Becky Lynn's breath caught in surprise. "What?"

"Why should he apologize? You don't own him."

Becky Lynn stared at her friend, feeling as if the blood were draining from her body. Her fingers and toes started to tingle, and she felt cold, all over and to the bone.

"Did you really think he was being faithful to you?" Zoe laughed, the sound thin and angry. "A man like Jack? Get real, Becky Lynn."

Becky Lynn brought a hand to her mouth. She couldn't believe what Zoe was saying to her. She couldn't believe the venom in her words, the...hatred.

Why did Zoe hate her so much? Becky Lynn wondered, light-headed. What had she done to cause the other woman to treat her this way?

"Did you think he loved you?" Zoe demanded, moving her gaze contemptuously over her. "Did you really think your relationship was an exclusive one?"

Becky Lynn backed away from Zoe, shaking her head. "Why are you doing this to me? Leave me alone."

Zoe followed her, the expression in her eyes twisted and ugly. "You can't imagine what it's been like to be me, having to watch you two together. You can't imagine what it's been like to have to listen to you talk about him, like what you had was really special."

"I thought you were my friend," Becky Lynn whispered, realizing even as she murmured the words that Zoe had never been her friend.

"You make me sick. You're such a goody-goody little fool." Zoe took a step toward her, her lovely face distorted with contempt. "Don't you know how the game is played? Don't you have any idea how this industry operates?"

Becky Lynn stared at the woman she had thought her friend, sick with betrayal and a dawning horror. Zoe had known about Jack's infidelities all along.

Infidelities? All along?

There had been others. She squeezed her fingers into fists. Lord only knew how many and with whom. She thought of how he had wanted to keep their relationship a secret, thought of all the beautiful models he had shot since they'd become lovers, thought of the times he had disappeared for a few hours. Despair choked her. Maybe he had slept with everybody, every model who had walked through the studio door.

Every model. Zoe.

She looked Zoe in the eye, thinking of the way the other girl sometimes gazed at Jack, as if she wanted to eat him up, thinking of the way she sometimes touched him, the way she sometimes hung on him.

Becky Lynn swallowed hard, already knowing the answer to the question she was about to ask. She asked, anyway, because she had to hear it from Zoe's own mouth. "Did you and Jack…were you…lovers?"

Zoe met Becky Lynn's gaze. She smiled. "Of course we were."

33

The light rain had become a downpour. Becky Lynn stood at Carlo Triani's front door, soaked to the skin, her stuffed duffel bag slung over her shoulder, one of Carlo's cards clutched in her hand.

Come to me. I'll make you a star.

She stared at the card, her chest heavy and aching—with the tears she had already poured out, with the ones she held back. She wouldn't cry anymore; neither Jack nor Zoe were worthy of her grief.

Then why did it hurt so much?

She pushed the thought away and dropped the duffel to the stoop. She would sooner sleep on the street than stay one night under the same roof as Zoe.

She just might have to. Becky Lynn pushed her wet hair away from her face. She had no job, no friends, no place to live. She was alone, the way she had been the day she'd arrived in California.

She lowered her gaze to the card once more. *Come to me. I'll make you a star.*

She had no place else to go, no one else to go to. She drew a deep, ragged breath. But she wasn't afraid. If Carlo turned her away, if he laughed in her face, she would be okay. She would survive.

But this way, if Carlo meant what he'd said, she could have revenge.

Drawing another deep, steadying breath, she rang the bell. Several moments ticked past. Just as she began to fear he wasn't home, the door swung open.

Carlo stood before her, sleepy-eyed and half-dressed. Even as fear rippled over her, she hiked up her chin and met his gaze evenly, in challenge. "Did you mean what you said?"

He swept his gaze slowly over her, then brought it back to her face. His expression revealed nothing of his thoughts, nothing of his feelings. He nodded. "Yes."

"I need a place to stay."

"For how long?"

"I don't know."

He moved his gaze over her again. This time when he returned his eyes to hers, she saw a measure of satisfaction in them. Not so much, she thought, at her pain, but rather that he had been right about his half brother.

In that moment she understood the depth of his hatred for Jack—a hatred equal to Jack's for him. She shivered and rubbed her wet arms.

"He broke your heart, didn't he?"

Tears stung her eyes. She fought them back, feeling like a fool, determined she would not humble herself in front of him or any other man. Never again. "Yes. Just like you said he would."

"Are you sure you want to do this?" He narrowed his eyes. "It won't be easy. I'll expect perfection, and I'll be brutal in my criticism."

"I know how it works," she said, bringing her chin up another notch. "I know about photographers. I worked for Jack, remember?"

"I'll make Jack look like a Boy Scout."

"I don't care what it takes." She fisted her fingers. "I

don't care what I have to do. I want to hurt him, Carlo. I want to make a fool of him. The way he hurt me, the way he made a fool of me. And I don't know how else to do it."

Wordlessly, Carlo swung the door wider. She stepped across his threshold, leaving Jack and her life with him behind forever.

Book Four

Illusions

34

Becky Lynn stepped out of Carlo's Beverly Hills bungalow and into the still morning air. She locked the door behind her, then started across the veranda toward the car Carlo had left for her to drive to his studio.

Another day. Her twenty-eighth since leaving Jack.

She reached the car, and looked over her shoulder at the house. Its windows sparkled in the sun, welcoming and warm. The house was small—two bedrooms only—and rather plain, but the back, with its terraced decks, Jacuzzi, pool and abundance of flowers, she likened to paradise. Once upon a time she had dreamed of living in a place like this, an elegant and luxuriously appointed home.

She would give it all up to be living back at her apartment, she missed it almost desperately. As she missed the life she had thought she had—the love, the friendship.

Becky Lynn called herself a fool and fisted her fingers. Jack had discovered she was with Carlo and had called several times. She had refused to take his calls, so he had sent a note. In it he had expressed sorrow but not apology. He wanted her back, he had said—*as his assistant.*

Her chest hurt, and she drew a deep breath, willing away the ache. After what they had shared—what she had thought they'd shared—how could she go back to being just his assistant?

She drew another deep breath and lifted her chin. Her life with Jack and Zoe had been nothing but a cruel illusion. A hoax perpetrated by two people who had cared nothing for her, not even enough to regret having broken her heart. The more she reminded herself of that fact the better off she would be.

Becky Lynn reached the car, a late-model BMW in perfect condition, and unlocked it. She slipped inside, her hands beginning to shake. She hated driving in southern California. The traffic scared her, as did the size of the interstates and the complexity of the routes she had to take. The first week, she had ignored Carlo's offer of his second car, taking the bus instead. But the bus trip to Carlo's studio had taken nearly two hours, so finally she had given in and driven herself.

She had discovered over the past month that, unlike Jack who had hated mornings and liked nothing better than to sleep until noon, Carlo hated sleep. He needed very little of it, and left for his studio at six every morning, no matter how late he had been up the night before. On his way to the studio, he always stopped at his gym for a workout, then for breakfast. With Jack, she had always arrived at the studio first, she'd made coffee, made a first round of calls, then awakened him.

Sometimes he had coaxed her into bed with him and they had made love, him still sleepy-eyed and deliciously warm.

Emotion choked her, and furious with herself, she fought it back.

She wouldn't think about Jack, she wouldn't long for

him, she wouldn't waste one more daydream fantasizing about how he would come for her, beg her forgiveness and promise his undying love. Not anymore she wouldn't. She despised him. She never wanted to see him again.

Becky Lynn reached the studio, took one of the spots in the small parking lot adjacent to the building and climbed out of the car. Even though the air was warm and the sun bright, she shivered, a feeling of dread coming over her.

Modeling was the most frightening, the most humiliating thing she had ever tried to do. She felt like a fool and a fraud. As Carlo gave her direction, she pictured the reactions of the people of Bend, she imagined their jeers, their howls of amusement. And she pictured herself, ugly Becky Lynn Lee—too ugly to even look at while being raped—standing in front of the camera, trying to pretend to be something she wasn't.

Poor, ugly Becky Lynn Lee. She couldn't even try convincingly.

Becky Lynn took a deep breath and started for the building, battling the almost overpowering urge to turn and run in the opposite direction. Carlo did make Jack look like a Boy Scout. He didn't mince words; he didn't worry about how his criticism might make her feel. Time and again over the past month, he had brought her to the point of tears.

Each time, she had fought them off. She had promised herself she wouldn't humiliate herself in front of him; she wouldn't give him a reason to dump her.

That was coming, anyway; of course it was. Carlo had grown more impatient and short-tempered with each day, and she had grown more despondent.

She squeezed her fingers into fists. She wanted to hurt Jack; she wanted to make a fool of him. One day he would regret how he had treated her, he would regret having thrown her away.

If not for the hatred that drove her, she wondered if she would have anything at all to live for. It forced her eyes open in the morning; it propelled her out of bed and into the shower.

She would face Carlo, she would face the cold eye of his camera, today and every day if in doing so she could hurt Jack.

She rang the studio's buzzer and Jon, one of Carlo's assistants, let her in. "Hey, Becky Lynn. How're you this morning?"

"Okay, Jon. You doing okay?"

"Doing great." He locked the door behind her, and they moved farther inside. "You're right on time. Carlo and I just finished printing."

Longing swept through her, so strong she ached. She had loved processing film, had loved printing. Some days, being around the equipment was torture—she wanted to touch it, use it. She missed her old job.

She shoved her hands into her pockets. "Anything outstanding?"

Jon shifted his gaze, and Becky Lynn knew they had been processing some shots of her, and that they had been less than stellar. Several different emotions swept through her—embarrassment and anger, impotence and frustration, defiance.

Why was she doing this? Why was she putting herself through this agony? She would never be a model.

"We got some...interesting things," he answered vaguely. "I need to clean up. See you later, Becky Lynn."

She watched him hurry off, then followed him, dragging her feet, not yet ready to face the day ahead.

Carlo stood at the other end of the studio, his back toward her as he talked on the phone. At first, she had been afraid of Carlo, afraid of him because he was a man and could physically overpower her. She had locked herself in her room at night, going so far as to jam a chair under the doorknob for extra security. She had kept her guard up at all times, prepared to scream or fight if she had to. Though he rarely touched her, she had frozen whenever he had.

Gradually, she had begun to feel comfortable with him. Her guard had begun to slip, her fear with it.

Carlo was different than Jack. He didn't possess Jack's overwhelming and potent sexuality, the quality that at first had made her feel small and vulnerable, and later had kept her every nerve ending tingling with awareness. And he treated her differently than Jack had, too. Other than his desire to use her to hurt Jack, he seemed totally uninterested in her. She found living with someone so impassive, someone who kept himself so aloof, at once strange and reassuring.

He hung up the phone and turned to face her, meeting her gaze. He arched his eyebrows, and she sensed he knew what she was thinking.

"Good morning, *bella*. Are you ready to make beautiful pictures today?"

She inched up her chin. "Very funny."

"I don't joke about my photographs, Becky Lynn. Not ever. You should learn that."

She pictured herself in front of the camera and hiked up her chin another notch. "Considering the subject, perhaps you should learn to lighten up."

He narrowed his eyes. "You'll never make beautiful pictures with that attitude."

She flexed her fingers, spoiling for a fight. "Maybe I'll never make beautiful pictures, no matter what."

He swore and crossed to her, stopping so close she could touch him. He looked her square in the eye. "Then quit, *bella*. Quit now, I don't need this aggravation."

She sucked in a sharp breath, working to calm herself. Why had she started this? She had learned that Carlo used his wits and tongue to wound; she had learned that he never backed down from a verbal challenge, never tried to soothe or placate.

"I'm sorry," she said. "I'm frustrated, that's all."

For a moment, he said nothing, then he nodded. "Maybe today will be better. Juliette is in back waiting to do your hair and makeup. Go on. I've already instructed her about what I want."

Today wasn't better. It was worse.

"No!" Carlo shouted at her, handing one of his assistants his camera. "Terrible! You look like I'm trying to kill you."

"How do you expect me to look?" she shouted back, fisting her fingers in impotence and rage. "I feel like you *are* killing me. I hate this."

Carlo's assistants scurried in all directions, anxious to get out of the line of fire.

"Then go." He strode across the set, face mottled with rage. "Run to Jack. Beg him to take you back, it's what you want."

"Never!" She jumped to her feet. "I'll never go back."

"You lie. You're always thinking about him. Wishing for him to come for you."

Her cheeks burned at the truth in his words, and she wheeled away from him. "When I think about him, I think about how I hate him. About how I want to hurt him."

Carlo crossed to her, stopping so close she could feel the heat from his body, but he didn't touch her. "Then help me," he said softly. "This is how we can hurt him. But I can't do it alone."

She turned and met his eyes, pleading. "I'll be your assistant. I'm good. Really good. I worked with Jack for—"

"I have an assistant. I have several."

She caught his hands. "He would hate our working together, he would. It would hurt him."

"Nice try, *bella*." Carlo disentangled his hands from hers. "But no." He touched her cheek. "You model or you go."

Tears stung her eyes, and she spun away from him. She crossed to a small chair in the corner and sank onto it. She lowered her eyes to her feet. "Being in front of the camera is so awful. It hurts so much sometimes that I can't breathe. It's humiliating, Carlo."

"Why do you let it be so?" He shook his head. "Enjoy yourself in front of the camera. Let yourself have fun."

She worked to clear her throat, choked with tears. Finally, when she thought she could meet his eyes without embarrassing herself, she lifted her head. "How can I have fun?" she whispered. "I'm ugly, Carlo."

He shook his head. "You're not—"

"I am. I can see. All my life—"

"Forget the past." He crossed to her and squatted in front of her. "To the camera you are beautiful."

"No."

"Yes." He cupped her face in his palms, forcing her to look at him. "You must believe. You must trust."

"I can't trust. I won't. Never again."

"Trust the camera. Believe in it." He moved his thumbs across her cheekbones. "It won't hurt you, it can't."

She gazed into Carlo's dark eyes, wishing she could do as he said. Wanting to believe so much, it hurt.

"I have something to show you." He drew her to her feet. "Come."

He led her to the darkroom. The door was open, the light on. The photographs Carlo had printed that morning were clipped to the drying line. Her heart dropped. She had requested that he not show her any photographs of herself, and he had agreed. He had said he preferred it that way, anyway, as beginning models had the tendency to obsess with the product when they should be more concerned with the process.

"Carlo, no." Becky Lynn tugged against his hand. "Not my pictures. Please, I don't want to see them."

"You must." His tightened his grip, hurting her, trapping her, and panic took her breath. She struggled against him.

With a sound of disgust, he let her go, and she stumbled backward. "You look or you leave, Becky Lynn. And if you go, I won't take you back." He swept his gaze contemptuously over her. "What will it be, Becky Lynn? Will you go or stay?"

She rubbed her wrist, her fear ebbing now that she was free. She tipped up her chin. As far as she was concerned, she had only one choice. "I'm not quitting."

He pulled out a half-dozen contact sheets and threw them down on the table, one after another in a line. She stared at the photographs, not believing her eyes.

The woman in them was beautiful.

It couldn't be her. She leaned closer. *But it was. It was her.*

She stared at the proof sheets. They had taken these a week before, the first time Carlo had arranged to have her hair and makeup professionally done.

"Yes, *bella*. It's you." He touched her hair lightly. "You see what I have known all along?"

Becky Lynn shook her head, still not believing her own eyes. With trembling fingers, she picked up one of the contact sheets. She gazed at it, her mouth dry, her heart fast. The woman in the photos was beautiful. The camera had taken her strong, ill-fitting features and blended them together, reshaping the whole that was her face, creating something exotic and extraordinary.

Carlo handed her a loupe, and she looked through it, her vision blurring with tears.

She recognized the woman as herself, but not as she was, but as the beautiful woman she had always longed to be. Carlo had made magic. He had given her a miracle, had given her the most perfect gift, the one she had thought she would never have.

She lowered the loupe, and lifted her eyes to his. "Thank you," she whispered. "I never thought that I… could look…like this. Thank you so much."

For a moment, Carlo said nothing, but his expression spoke volumes. She caught her breath. For the first time, when he looked at her, she saw emotion in his eyes. It was as if, in the space of that moment, she had become a person to him.

"You see," he said softly, "I did not lie. The camera loves you." He brushed one of her tears away, catching it with his thumb. "But I had to work too hard to get these. We can't go on this way. You see how stiff and uncomfortable you look?"

She did see. For although Carlo and his camera had given her the miracle of beauty, only she could give the images of herself life.

"Can you let go and trust the camera? Can you believe?" Carlo searched her gaze. "If not, even though the camera loves your face, you cannot be a model. You must decide. Can you trust enough to give yourself over to me?"

35

In the end, as Carlo had known she would, Becky Lynn gave herself over to him. She learned; she grew. Before his eyes and in three short months, she transformed from awkward and uncomfortable in front of the camera to a bold, confident and self-assured model.

Carlo leafed through some of his shots of her, studying them as critically as he could but finding them nearly flawless, anyway. The difference between the first and the most recent shots of her was nothing short of amazing. Once she had conquered her fear and self-doubt, there had been nothing she couldn't do. From working with Jack, she had already known the tricks of the trade; she understood photography and what made a great shot. It had only been a matter of applying what she knew to herself and the art of modeling.

Carlo smiled to himself, gazing with pleasure at the photographs. He had begun, already and unbelievably, to choose shots for her portfolio. He hadn't a doubt that she would be signed by one of the top agencies; he had in mind either Ford, Elite or Davis.

He stopped on the first proofs of herself Becky Lynn had seen. He swallowed hard, remembering her expression, the way she had looked at him—as if he had given her the most wonderful gift in the world. He had never made anyone so happy before. He created beautiful photographs, images and illusions only. Never anything so real, never anything so honest as the happiness that had shown from her eyes that day.

He had made a difference in her life. He had affected her, deeply, on a level he had never affected another person.

In that moment, and for the first time since finding his mother in a pool of blood, he had felt whole and hopeful. In that moment, the world had seemed like an all-right place, and life a series of opportunities.

That moment, too, marked the beginning of Becky Lynn's transformation. Seeing the photographs of herself, seeing how beautiful she could be, had given her the strength to face her fears—she had finally begun to believe.

He flipped through several more photos, stopping on a particularly fetching shot. In it, Becky Lynn looked both little girl and woman. The look had nothing to do with what she wore or the setting; neither were outstanding. He tipped his head and narrowed his gaze. Her photographs all had something special, a quality not many other models had, even the top girls.

It was in the eyes, he realized. A vulnerability. A softness that had nothing to do with physical beauty or photographer's illusion, but everything to do with the core of the person being photographed. He flipped through several more shots, comparing them. The vulnerable quality shone from her eyes in all of them, no matter how sexy, alluring or tough the shot. Becky Lynn couldn't hide it, and no viewer would be able to resist responding to it.

Carlo gazed at the photos, a catch in his chest. Becky Lynn was special. She was going to be a special model, one of the most special faces. As his mother had been.

He glanced toward the back of the studio, toward the makeup, hair and changing rooms where Becky Lynn was getting prepared for what he felt certain would be her last training session. She was ready for her first professional assignment.

He smiled to himself. When he told her, she would be terrified. But as always, she would conquer her fear. She was one of the strongest, most courageous people he had ever met. He had seen her strength in the way she had stood up to him, day in and day out, in the way she had battled her tears even when he had dished out his worst, in the way she had kept on fighting.

Jack had been a fool for letting her slip away.

With thoughts of Jack, Carlo's smile faded. Rumor through the industry held that Jack and Garnet McCall were immersed in a torrid affair. He wondered if Becky Lynn had left Jack because she'd found out about it. She'd never spoken of why she had left Jack, but that would explain her hurt and her fury.

Carlo drew his eyebrows together. Becky Lynn never talked about her past, where she came from or her family, and when he had asked her point-blank, she had lied.

Maybe others bought her story about a farm accident and a loving but poor family, but he didn't. He had seen the evasions, the untruths in her eyes. And when he had questioned her more, when he had pushed, she'd clammed up.

He heard her laugh and looked over his shoulder once more, frowning. What was so terrible that she felt she had to lie to him? He lowered his gaze to her photographs. No doubt she had told Jack everything about her. She and his brother had been lovers, yet she wouldn't let him touch her.

Anytime he even came close to her, she froze. Frustration balled in his chest. Why? What did Jack have that he didn't?

"I'm sorry, Carlo!" Jon burst into the room, his normally mild expression agitated. "I tried to stop him, but he—"

"Where is she?" Jack angled past the assistant and strode onto the set as if he owned it. "I know she's here."

Carlo waved his assistant off and faced Jack, smiling, ready for this confrontation. He had known Jack would come for Becky Lynn, it had only been a matter of when.

"Well, well…if it isn't my little bastard brother." Carlo arched his eyebrows in cool disinterest. "What brings you to the lion's den?"

"Cut the crap, Carlo. You know why I'm here." Jack flexed his fingers. "Where is she?"

Carlo cocked his head. "Can you possibly mean *my* sweet southern flower? Can you possibly mean *my* beautiful Becky Lynn?"

Jack gritted his teeth. "I want to see her. Where is she?"

"You're presuming she wants to see you. She doesn't." Carlo laughed softly. "But you should know that. She won't take your calls. She returned that pathetic little note."

Jack's features tightened, and Carlo laughed again, delighted. "She's happy with me, Jack. I make her happy. Leave her be."

Jack took a step toward him, jaw tight with fury, hands clenched at his sides. "If you don't let me see her, right now, I'll—"

"What?" Carlo arched his eyebrows. "Punch me? Offer to meet me outside? I see you haven't changed in all these years. Still a cowboy."

"You son of a bitch."

Jack advanced on him, and Carlo took a quick step backward. "Actually, she's not here. But I have something you might be interested in seeing."

"I'm not interested in anything you have to show me."

"Except Becky Lynn?" At Jack's expression, Carlo laughed. "Here, take a look." He picked up the fetching shot of Becky Lynn, then dropped it to the table again. Jack's eyes shifted to it. His face went slack with surprise, then whitened with realization.

"She's quite something, isn't she, Jack? She has it all. Face, body, brains. She's going all the way to the top. Take a closer look if you need to." Carlo picked up the shot again and held it out to his brother. "You never saw her this way, did you, Jack? She was right under your nose all along. Imagine that."

Jack's throat worked as if he wanted to say something but couldn't. He looked as if he had taken a knife to the gut.

"She's mine now," Carlo said softly, twisting the blade. "Anything familiar about this scene?" He laughed softly. "You lose again, baby brother. Old habits can be a real bitch to break."

Jack reached for the photo just as Carlo drew it away. It ripped in half.

"You bastard," Jack said tightly. "You don't care about her. You're just using her to get to me."

"What were you using her for, Jack? At least I'm giving her something in return. Something she only dreamed of before. I treat her like she's special. How did you treat her? What did you give her? Did you ever see her as a beautiful, sexy woman?" Carlo took a step toward Jack. "You were too blind, weren't you? You were too damn selfish."

Jack narrowed his eyes. His face mottled with rage; a muscle jumped in his jaw.

Carlo could see the effect his words were having on Jack. But tormented wasn't good enough; he went in for the kill. "As beautiful and exciting as she is on film, she's ever more so in bed."

Jack drew his fist and before Carlo could move, the fist connected with his jaw. Light and pain speared through his head, and Carlo reeled backward, knocking into a light stand, sending it and him crashing to the floor.

Carlo brought his hand to his jaw and shook his head to clear it. He looked at his brother, standing above him like a bull incited by a red flag, fists still clenched and ready. His brother would like nothing better right now than to kill him.

Jack was in love with Becky Lynn.

Carlo stared at his brother, stunned. He had never even suspected his brother's feelings for her ran so deep; he doubted the Neanderthal even realized it himself. This was too perfect, too good to be true.

He rubbed his jaw, again. "Feel better now, cowboy? Unfortunately for you, hitting me doesn't change the fact that she's mine now. And I warn you, hit me again and you'll hear from my lawyer."

"Tell her I stopped by. Tell her I'm sorry and that I want her back." Jack bent and scooped up the two pieces of torn photograph, then met Carlo's gaze again, eyes narrowed. "That is, if you have the guts."

Carlo watched him stalk off, his smile fading, his brother's words resounding in his head.

"Tell her I'm sorry. If you have the guts."

"What's going on?" Becky Lynn rushed out of the

changing room, wearing a pair of partially fastened jeans and clasping a hand towel to her bare chest. She saw the toppled lights, him on the floor, and stopped. "My, God, Carlo. Are you all right?"

"I'm fine." He pulled himself up, then bent and righted the light stand. He rubbed his jaw once more.

"You've been hurt!" She raced over to him. "Someone hit you."

"It's nothing."

"It's something."

She tried to inspect his jaw, and he jerked his head away. "Forget it, Becky Lynn. We've got work to do."

She scowled. "Who did this to you?"

"Tell her I was here and that I want her back. If you have the guts."

Carlo opened his mouth to do just that, then shut it again. If he told her, she would go after Jack. For all her protestations to the contrary, he doubted she could resist.

He swore silently, despising his own cowardice. "An old girlfriend stopped by to say hello. She packs a hell of a good punch, doesn't she?" He caught his assistant's eye and sent him a warning glance. "She heard that we're living together. She's pretty pissed."

Becky Lynn shifted her gaze to the empty doorway. "An old girlfriend did this?"

"You think I'm lying?" He scowled. "What? Maybe you think it was Jack, come to beg your forgiveness and take you away from all this?" She flushed, and he took a step toward her, eyes narrowed. "You probably lie in bed at night and fantasize about how he's going to come for you, whisk you into his arms and promise his undying love. Don't you, Becky Lynn? You secretly hope he's going to realize he loves you and can't live without you."

"You bastard. I've proved I don't want to talk to him, that I despise him." Tears sparkled in her eyes, and she blinked against them. "And I'm sorry I even worried that you were hurt."

She spun around and stalked to the changing room. He watched her go, regret taking his breath. She was right, he was a bastard. A mean, sorry son of a bitch. He fisted his fingers. But she still loved Jack, despite what she said, despite the way Jack had treated her. If she had seen him, she would have gone with him. He, Carlo Triani, had given her beauty, he would give her fame, but she wouldn't have looked back even once in her hurry to get Jack.

The truth of that chewed and clawed at his gut until he couldn't see or feel anything but jealousy and hate.

He took a deep breath and followed her into the changing room, slamming the door shut behind him.

She whirled, the towel clutched to her chest. "Do you mind?"

She'd been crying; the tears had made tracks through her makeup, ruining it. Carlo leaned against the door and folded his arms across his chest. "No, I don't mind. In fact, the view from here is rather nice."

"Get out." She glared at him. "Now."

"I think we should become lovers."

She took a step backward, eyes widening. "What?"

"I want us to sleep together."

Her expression froze. He thought of a small, vulnerable animal trapped by a hungry wolf. He didn't particularly care for the image or the association. "It's the natural next step for us."

She stiffened her spine and brought her chin up. "You want us to sleep together because it's the next step?"

"What's wrong with that?"

She lowered her eyes for a moment, then brought them back to his. "I don't know why you're doing this, Carlo. You don't have to, I don't expect it. And I don't want it."

He narrowed his eyes. "And just what's that supposed to mean?"

"You're not attracted to me, Carlo. I know you're not."

"You're wrong about that." He took a step toward her, sending her a slow, seductive smile.

"No, I'm not wrong." She dropped the small towel, and reached for the silky chemise she was supposed to wear for the shoot. He lowered his eyes involuntarily to her naked breasts, then lifted them to her face once more, frustrated because he felt nothing.

And because she knew it.

He swore and swung away from her. He heard the rustle of silk as she slipped on the chemise. He fisted his fingers and fought to get a grip on his emotions.

She crossed to him and laid a hand on his arm. "It's okay, don't you see? I like the way it is between us."

He met her eyes. "But that's not the way you wanted it with Jack, is it?"

She didn't flinch at the blow, but she felt it. He saw the hurt in her eyes, saw the regret. "It's not you, Carlo. I'm not interested in having sex with anyone, ever again."

"In this business, sex is an everyday—"

"Then I'll get out of this business." She slid her hand to his and cupped it. "We're doing good together. Let's not mess it up now."

She had a point, a damn good one. For the moment.

He brought their joined hands to his mouth and kissed hers. "You're some gutsy woman, Becky Lynn Lee."

She laughed, her cheeks coloring with pleasure. "Gutsy? Me?"

"*Sí, bella.*" He kissed her hand again, then let it go. "And I think you're ready."

Her smile faltered, and she searched his gaze. "Ready for what?"

"Your first professional job. I need another model for a *Will-o-Wisp Jeans* ad."

She shook her head, her eyes wide. "No, I don't think so. I haven't even begun to learn, I—"

"Trust me, *bella.*" He caught her chin and looked her straight in the eye. "Trust the camera. You are ready for this."

36

Becky Lynn stood and carried her plate to the sink, though she had hardly touched her supper. She scraped the plate, then rinsed it and her glass and put them into the dishwasher. From outside, she heard the sound of laughter, the sound of people enjoying one another's company.

Alone again.

Sighing, she gazed out the open window above the sink. She was lonely. She had met people through Carlo and work, but she didn't know anybody well enough to call and suggest getting together. She had met some models who had been outwardly friendly, but after her experience with Zoe, she was afraid of letting anyone too close.

She missed Marty. And Sallie. She hadn't been able to bring herself to call either of them. Because of Jack, because they had both been right. And because, after all this time, she still hurt.

Maybe some people were meant to be alone.

She pushed that thought away because she didn't like it. And because she feared it was true. She turned from the window and crossed to the kitchen table. The latest *Vogue* had come today. It lay open on the table, open to an ad for Garnet McCall's spring line.

Jack's first Vogue *ad. No doubt he and Garnet were celebrating appropriately.*

Muttering an oath, she snapped the magazine shut and

returned to the window. Dusk had become dark, and the neighbors' windows glowed warmly. She would have liked some company tonight, would have liked some conversation. She lowered her eyes to her hands, realizing she gripped the edge of the sink so tightly her knuckles stood out white in relief.

Carlo hadn't called or come home, not that she had expected him to do either, not that he owed her that courtesy. Their arrangement was strictly professional. Besides, it was February fourteenth, and judging by the number of women who traipsed in and out of here, today would be a busy day for him.

Her cheeks heated as she thought of the number of women he took to his bed. It embarrassed her, and her being here embarrassed some of the women. She turned away from the window once more, but this time she prowled the kitchen. She should move out. She was earning a little money modeling, not a lot, but enough to get her into an efficiency in a marginal neighborhood. Carlo seemed to believe that before long, she would be making so much money she would be able to afford to live anywhere she wanted to.

She twisted her fingers together. But she was reluctant to go. She remembered what it had been like at first, before The Image Shop and Marty, before Jack and Zoe, and she didn't think she could face that kind of loneliness again.

If she moved out, she would be even more alone than she was now.

She had the feeling, too, that as reluctant as she was to go, Carlo was as reluctant to have her leave. For even though he had a great many business acquaintances and led a hectic professional and personal life, she sensed he was as lonely as she. She sensed he had no one who he felt close to.

Not even his father. Especially not his father.

She frowned, thinking again of the women he paraded through here—mostly models, mostly one-or two-night stands. There was something frenetic, almost desperate, about the way he pursued women. And for all his supposed prowess, he didn't seem to enjoy the women all that much, he didn't seem to enjoy the sex that much.

In a funny way, she saw something of herself in him. He seemed as uncomfortable with the opposite sex as she was, almost afraid of them. She drew her eyebrows closer together, and shook her head. That thought bordered on ridiculous—the man entertained a different woman almost every night of the week.

"So serious, *bella*. And on such a pretty night."

Startled, she whirled, a hand to her throat. "Carlo! I didn't hear you."

He grinned. "I planned it that way. I tiptoed so I would surprise you."

"But why?" She moved her gaze over him. He hid both his hands behind his back, and he looked as guilty—and as pleased—with himself as a kid who had not gotten caught while his hand was in the cookie jar. She narrowed her eyes suspiciously. "What are you up to?"

He whipped a bouquet of spring flowers out from behind his back. "Happy Valentine Day."

She stared at him, shocked speechless. He laughed and took another step toward her, flowers extended. "Take them, they're for you."

She did and held the bouquet to her face. She breathed

in their subtle perfume, overwhelmed by the sweetness of the gesture. "I don't know what to say."

"Thank you is always appropriate."

She smiled. "Thank you."

"This is also for you." With his other hand, he held out a large red envelope.

She laid the bouquet on the counter and took the card, her fingers trembling. She tore open the envelope. Inside was a big, old-fashioned valentine, complete with hearts, Cupids and fancy, flowery script.

Her heart lodged in her throat. She had always dreamed of getting a valentine like this one. *Jack. She had dreamed of getting a card like this from Jack.*

His image filled her mind, and she turned her back to Carlo, cheeks burning, feeling like a traitor. "It's…beautiful." Tears stung her eyes, and she looked over her shoulder at him. "I've never been anyone's valentine before."

He threaded his fingers through her hair, lifting it away from her neck. "Before long," he murmured, "you're going to be the whole world's valentine. Just wait and see, *bella*."

She lowered her eyes to the card once more, trailing her fingers over the delicately embossed paper. "It's so pretty, I—"

Suddenly, his arms were around her, pulling her against him. He buried his face in the side of her neck. First, she felt his breath against her skin, then his lips and tongue. His hands seemed to be everywhere at once—her breasts and waist and abdomen.

Fear took her breath, and for one split second her head emptied of everything but terror. She was seventeen again and powerless, being forced to the ground, her legs dragged apart.

"Ah, *bella*…I know another way for you to thank me. A better way."

His voice brought her back to the present, replacing her fear with a measure of fury. She wasn't seventeen, and she wasn't powerless. She never would be again.

She struggled in his arms, breaking free of his grip by elbowing him hard in the ribs. Breathing hard, her legs trembling so badly she feared she would fall, she whirled to face him. "Don't do that again. Don't…ever grab me like that again. Do you understand? Never touch me that way again." Her teeth began to chatter, and she rubbed her arms. Still, she couldn't seem to warm herself.

"Becky Lynn?" He held a hand out to her, and she backed away. "My God, *bella,* I frightened you."

She turned away from him, and crossed to the window. She reached across the sink and closed it.

"I'm sorry." He cleared his throat. "I didn't mean to scare you."

"How did you expect me to react when you…when you…" She drew a deep, calming breath, then glanced over her shoulder at him. He looked so surprised, and so chagrined, it would have been funny had she not been so upset. "Why did you…do that? I thought we'd been through this before. I'd thought we'd settled it."

"Am I so repugnant to you?" He swore in Italian and dragged a hand through his hair. "What did Jack have that I don't?"

Becky Lynn gazed at him, thinking of Jack, comparing the two brothers. Carlo was handsome, extremely handsome. He had been good to her; they had learned to get along well together.

But Jack had taken her breath away. Everything about

him, from the way he smiled, to the way he ate a sandwich, to the way he had touched her. She couldn't tell Carlo that. He wouldn't understand, and it would hurt him.

"Nothing," she lied. "I was a fool, and I'm not going to make a mistake like that again." She crossed to him and laid a hand on his arm. "I don't want to be some trophy to you, Carlo. I don't want you to sleep with me as a way to get back at Jack."

"It isn't just that." He looked at her, then away. She saw his frustration. "I care for you. You've become important to me."

Her heart filled to near breaking. That was more than Jack had ever said to her. She curled her fingers around his arm. "I care for you, too. But you don't need to prove you're better than Jack or anybody else. I like you the way you are. I feel safe with you, Carlo. But just now, what you did… I can't, I just can't."

A strange expression crossed his face, at once relieved and bittersweet. He covered her hand with one of his own. "I'm sorry, *bella,* for frightening you. Let me make it up to you. Come."

"But you don't—"

"Come."

He led her out to the foyer. On the entryway table lay a small leather portfolio, just big enough to comfortably fit eight-by-ten photos, the kind of book models brought with them on go-sees.

She looked at Carlo in question, and he nodded. "Go on, it's for you."

She picked it up. The leather was fine, soft and supple in her hands, its color a deep, rich brown. Stamped in gold on the front was the word *Valentine.*

"You can open it if you like, but you've seen all the photos before. They're all of you."

"Of me?" She traced her index finger over the lettering. "I don't understand, what does Valentine mean?"

"I went to see Tremayne Davis today."

She met his eyes. "Of The Davis Agency?"

He nodded, and her heart began to thunder. Ford, Elite and Davis were the three top modeling agencies in the world. They continually jockeyed for the top spot, stealing models and clients from one another, each outdoing the other in terms of promotion, parties and bonuses. Currently, Davis was on top—he represented the biggest names in the business and boasted the greatest annual bookings. Tremayne Davis had snagged the top of the fashion hill from Eileen Ford by anticipating the next trend in models—girls who looked less all-American and more exotic.

"I took him your book."

Becky Lynn's gaze flew to Carlo's, her heart beating so heavily now she thought she might swoon.

Carlo laughed at her expression. "He was interested. Very interested. He wants to meet you."

"To meet me?" she squeaked, terrified. "Tremayne Davis wants to meet me?"

"Actually, he wants to sign you. Meeting you first is just a formality. Don't worry, I'll be there with you." Carlo laughed again. "He was so excited by your pictures, he all but took out a calculator and started tallying booking fees."

"But what if he takes a look at me and—"

"He won't." Carlo cupped her face in his palms. "This is it, *bella.* This is the beginning." He moved his thumbs across her cheekbones. "What do you think?"

"I'm too stunned to think." She laughed and shook her head. "I may never think clearly again."

She lowered her gaze to the book—her book—again. She drew her eyebrows together. "But what about this?" She ran her fingers over the gold lettering. "Valentine. What does this mean?"

"Tremayne asked your name. It just came out of my mouth, and it felt…right."

"I don't understand."

"Remember I said that soon you'd be the whole world's valentine?" He smiled. "It's you, Becky Lynn. You're Valentine."

37

Jack remembered a time when he had enjoyed these monthly parties, parties the big modeling agencies threw both to introduce their new talent and to keep their old faces in front of the people in the industry who made the decision of who worked and who didn't—photographers, designers, art directors and editors, top support personnel. Hell, he remembered a time when he was so hungry to get into one that he had masqueraded as a waiter and slipped in through a service entrance.

Tonight he had an invitation, but these days he always did. He was a full-blown, card-carrying member of the fashionistas, as those in the beauty industry referred to themselves.

He pulled his 911 Targa to a stop in front of Tremayne Davis's Bel Air mansion. He gazed up at the neoclassical villa, lit up tonight like the top of an octogenarian's birthday cake. In addition to the West Coast fashionistas, tonight's guest list would also include a number of top plastic surgeons and dentists, a smattering of pro-ball players and rock stars. The champagne and caviar would flow and sometime during the evening, mysteriously, it would begin to snow, cards would be exchanged as would tongues, false promises and provocative innuendos. Many a deal for a nose or breast job had been negotiated at one of these parties, more than one liaison between rock star and model had begun at such an occasion.

Once upon a time, he had thought being here, having reached this pinnacle, would feel like a bigger deal. He had thought he would feel important, powerful, even a bit invincible. Now he saw how ridiculous it was to take himself, his position, too seriously. Photography was his life, his chosen work, and he loved it. But it was still a job, and he was still Jack Gallagher, the same person he had been at eight and fifteen and twenty.

He swung out of the car, tossed his keys to the valet and started toward the villa's front entrance. The elaborate, pillared portico had been swathed in billowy, white fabric, then laced in white lights. Like a beautiful woman draped in diamonds and sheer silk sheets, the effect was at once ethereal and sensual.

Jack tipped his head in appreciation. Tremayne Davis knew how to throw a party. He'd been to them all—Elite's and Ford's and a multitude of other smaller agencies, and in his estimation, Davis's were the best.

He stepped inside and was immediately approached by several up-and-coming models who recognized him, one after another. He was polite; he turned down each of their invitations—subtle and blatant—to get to know them better, and as quickly as possible disentangled himself from them. The hungry always worked the hardest; each of the models hoped to earn his favor and a booking.

He understood how the game was played; he simply had no interest in playing.

He scanned the crowd, looking for a particular face, a special face, looking for the vibrant red hair that had become her trademark. Valentine, the girl everyone was talking about. The girl, the person, Becky Lynn had become.

He frowned, annoyed with himself and frustrated when he couldn't spot her. She would be here. As one of the models of the moment and The Davis Agency's face of the day, she wouldn't dare miss the party unless she was on location. Valentine was everybody's darling; everyone wanted her face and body to promote their product or look.

And no doubt she would be with Carlo—she always was. Jack gritted his teeth, recalling his half brother's smug expression that day at his studio, remembering his comment about Becky Lynn in bed. He could understand Becky Lynn's leaving him, wanting to hurt him, he supposed he deserved it. He could even understand her taking Carlo up on his offer to make her a star. But now…why did she stay with the snake? Why Carlo?

Jack didn't particularly like the answer and took a sharp right toward the bar, deciding to forgo champagne in favor of something stronger. He ordered a shot of tequila and a beer.

"Jack. How's it going?"

Jack turned to the man who had come up behind him, and he smiled. "Cliff, doing all right, man." They shook hands. Six months ago, he'd had to give up shooting for the Tyler guys—he hadn't had the time anymore and they'd no longer been able to afford his day rate. He had regretted having to do it; he appreciated that they had given him his first real break. "How are things at the shop?"

"Great. We've got more work than we can handle." The man downed his drink and motioned the bartender to bring him another. "We haven't been able to find another shooter who can please Jon Noble. You spoiled him, Jack."

"Sorry to hear that." He grinned, obviously not sorry at all.

"Yeah, right." Cliff stirred his drink, then dropped the swizzle stick onto his cocktail napkin. "That's really something about your Becky Lynn. Took us all by surprise."

Your Becky Lynn. Jack swallowed hard. "Yeah, me, too."

"You never mentioned she was interested in modeling."

And you were too blind to see her potential. She was right under your nose all the time, asshole. Jack tossed back the tequila, then took a long swallow of the beer. "Yeah, well…it was kind of sudden."

"When you see her, tell her the guys down at Tyler are real happy for her."

"I'll do that." Jack forced an easy smile. "I need to mingle. See you around, Cliff."

Jack walked away from the bar, aware of Cliff's speculative gaze on his back. He muttered an oath. He couldn't get away from it. Everywhere he went, everybody was talking about Becky Lynn or Valentine or both. The fashionistas had all had a good chuckle over how Carlo Triani had stolen Valentine right out from under Jack Gallagher's nose. And those who hadn't heard the story, those who hadn't known Valentine had been his *photo assistant,* had quickly been told. And he had a good idea by whom.

That son-of-a-bitch Carlo. He was enjoying the hell out of this.

Jack took another swallow of his beer and started for the back terrace. He saw her. Although surrounded by a group of admirers and hangers-on, with that wonderful red hair of hers, she stood out in the crowd. He swept his gaze over her, a lump in his throat. He had always loved her hair, its color and texture, the way it had felt against his skin.

Jack searched his memory. Had he ever told her that? Or how much he liked her laugh? Or how the way she looked at him made him feel special, like the only and most important man in the world?

He didn't think so. He drew his eyebrows together. What had he said to her? What had they talked about in those dizzying minutes after making love?

She looked up then and their gazes met. In that moment, she was Becky Lynn again, and she was his. He felt the connection like a punch to his gut.

Then she smiled, a practiced, alluring camera-smile he recognized from countless ads and countless other models. Oh, yes, gone was the Becky Lynn of old. The girl who had worn threadbare jeans and tattered sneakers, the girl who had pulled her hair into a ponytail and forgone all cosmetics, even lip gloss. Gone was the girl who had been insecure and shy and scared of her own shadow.

Left in her place, smiling at him with practiced ease, was a woman he didn't recognize, wonderful-looking but about as genuine as a paper doll.

Anger and frustration took his breath. He had been a blind fool. He deserved to be laughed at. But he didn't like it, and he wouldn't take the bullshit from her.

He worked his way through the crowd, being forced to stop along the way and make small talk. By the time he reached the place where she had been standing, she had moved out onto one of the covered porches. He followed her out.

She stood with her back to him, gazing down at the pool

and partiers below. On the night air, the music from the poolside band sounded hollow and a bit sad. "Hello, Red."

She stiffened, then turned slowly to face him. She met his eyes in cool challenge. "The name's Valentine."

"Oh, that's right. I forgot." He crossed to her, stopping so close she had to tip her head back slightly to meet his gaze. "Carlo's turned you into a glamazon."

She arched an eyebrow. "Jealous because you didn't think of it first?"

He tipped his head in acknowledgment of the shot, then delivered one of his own. "Maybe I was too busy thinking of you as a photographer."

"As your gofer, you mean. Your girl Friday." She angled up her chin. "You never thought of me as a photographer."

"I admired your talent, your eye, your sensibilities. I valued your opinion. And I never thought you would be an assistant forever. You were too good."

She sucked in a quick breath. "You never told me that before."

He wanted to touch her, he realized, tightening his fingers on his beer glass, desire clawing at his gut. What would she do if he did? How would she respond if he pulled her to him and caught her mouth in the kind of all-consuming kiss they had once shared?

"I should have," he said softly, lowering his eyes to her mouth. "I should have told you a lot of things."

She cleared her throat, struggling, he saw, to compose herself. "That's nice to know, Jack. But it's too late."

As she made a move to walk away, he caught her hand. "Is it, Becky Lynn? Is it too late?"

She met his eyes, then looked quickly away. Hers sparkled as with unshed tears, with hurt. He curved his fingers closer around hers, a sense of urgency pressing at him. "Why are you with Carlo? I can understand your going to him because you wanted to hurt me, but why are you still with him? What can you possibly see in him?"

Her expression froze, then tightened with anger. She jerked her hand free of his. "Now I understand what this is all about. Your vendetta. Your stupid little competition with Carlo."

He shook his head and took a step toward her. "You've got it all wrong, Becky Lynn. It's not like that."

"Oh, I'm sure it is." She swung away from him and crossed to the edge of the terrace. She gazed out for a moment, then turned to face him once more. "Why do you think I'm with him? Have you considered that maybe it's the way he treats me? Like I'm of value? Do you think that maybe he has something you don't?"

"You can't be in love with him." Jack drew his eyebrows together, his heart thundering. "I know you can't be."

She laughed, the sound cold on the warm night air. "Why? Do you think I'm in love with you?"

"Because the girl I knew couldn't be in love with Carlo Triani."

"You don't know me, Jack. Not anymore." She shook her head. "I'm not sure you ever did. But then, how could you? You never really looked at me."

He thought of their time together, thought of the girl she had been when he'd found her, and the woman she had been when he'd lost her. "I looked at you. Maybe I was the first person who ever did."

For a moment, she said nothing, but the expression in her eyes—vulnerable and full of bittersweet wishes—had him longing to take her into his arms and hold her, just hold her for a long time.

She angled her chin up. "Let me ask you, Jack, have you ever paused to think about someone other than yourself?"

Brushing by him, she walked away.

38

Becky Lynn picked her way through the throng of partiers, aware of the increased distance every step put between her and Jack, grateful for every inch. If she'd had to face him a moment longer, she would have totally humiliated herself.

Her vision blurred with tears she vowed would not fall, and she made her way upstairs to the bedrooms. She found an empty one and ducked inside, locking the door behind her.

She crossed to the bed and sank onto an edge, beginning to tremble. She brought her hands to her face, breathing deeply, working to compose herself. Seeing him had hurt—hurt so bad it had felt as if her insides were being ripped to shreds. She had known once and for all and for certain, that nothing had changed, that Jack hadn't changed.

With Jack, it had always been about him. Everything. What he felt and what he needed. His career, his hopes and dreams. Back then, she had been so grateful for every scrap of attention and kindness he had tossed her way, she hadn't cared. She'd been willing to give him everything and get nothing in return.

Jack hadn't congratulated her. He hadn't wished her well or even asked if she was happy. Everything about her had changed—her looks, her career, her entire life—and he hadn't commented.

He hadn't apologized for how he had hurt her. He had never apologized.

She stood, crossed to the mirror above the dresser and gazed at her reflection. Did she look different to him? Did he think she was beautiful now, did he think she was special? Or was he disappointed in the way she had changed? Was he jealous of her sudden success? Was he even surprised?

All he cared about was his vendetta with Carlo. It was all he had ever cared about.

She swung away from the mirror. That line he had started to feed her, about all the things he hadn't said to her but should have, what a bunch of self-serving, manipulative garbage.

And she had fallen for it hook, line and sinker. She made a sound of self-derision. He'd said a few apologetic things to her and she had been ready to fall into his arms. What a fool she was. What a hopeless romantic.

Jack wanted to steal her away from Carlo. He wanted to make a fool of Carlo, the way Carlo had made of him. She was just a pawn to Jack, a way to get to his half brother. Unlike Carlo, Jack couldn't even be honest about it.

She swallowed hard, past the knot of tears that formed in her throat. She lifted her chin. She wouldn't settle for scraps anymore. She was Valentine now; she deserved more.

She gazed into the mirror once again. She brought a hand to her cheek and trailed her fingers across it. Funny, she didn't look any different to herself. She looked into the mirror and saw the person she had always been. It was the camera that molded her into a beauty. Oh, the makeup helped, the professional hairstyling, the beautiful clothes. But to her she was still the ugly girl from Bend, Mississippi, the one the boys had barked at.

She lifted her chin. But to everyone else, she was Valentine. So she played along, pretended; she acted the part, became the illusion. She didn't believe in it, but she had learned that if everyone else did, she didn't have to.

She straightened her shoulders and turned away from the mirror. She had been hiding up here long enough. Carlo would be looking for her, and she didn't want Jack to think he had reduced her to tears.

He almost had. But not quite.

Never again.

She unlocked the door, opened it a crack and peeked out. As she did, another door opened and a couple, a man and a woman, stumbled out. They'd been making love, obviously; the woman's hair was a tangled mess, her dress twisted and rumpled. And they were also, obviously, high.

Valentine started to ease the door shut, when the woman turned and she realized it was Zoe. Her stomach dropped. In the year and a half since Zoe had told her about her and Jack sleeping together, she had seen the other model a great number of times. She, too, had signed with The Davis Agency; she had become a busy and successful model. But they had never spoken to each other, even the one time when they had been booked for the same shoot. But Becky Lynn had caught the other model looking at her, regret and need in her eyes.

Becky Lynn couldn't forgive Zoe her betrayal, it still burned hot and bright inside her. As did her anger and hurt.

But over time, she had come to realize it hadn't been Zoe's fault. It had been Jack's. Zoe had been so vulnerable to him, she'd had such a need for love and approval, she had so longed to impress Jack. Becky Lynn understood why the other woman had done it, she understood how it could have happened.

None of those things excused Zoe's behavior, but understanding them allowed Becky Lynn the ability to worry about the other woman. And according to the industry grapevine, she had reason to worry about Zoe. Word had it that she was getting heavily into drugs, that she had missed some go-sees, that she had started showing up late for shoots.

And that she slept around—a lot. That, coming from people who worked in an industry like this one, one that traded on sex and beauty on a day-to-day basis, meant something. It meant that Zoe's behavior had gone beyond abnormal. She was out of control.

The man kissed Zoe, then released her and ran a hand over his hair, making sure it was smooth. He swept his gaze over Zoe. "Better straighten yourself up, babe. You look like shit."

He turned on his heel and walked away, and Valentine's heart went out to Zoe. In that moment, Zoe looked as if the man had taken out a gun and shot her.

Zoe ducked back into the bedroom, and making a snap decision, Valentine glanced down the hallway to ensure no one was looking, then followed Zoe into the other room.

She found the other woman in the adjoining bathroom, standing before the vanity mirror, fumbling in her purse with hands that shook.

She lifted her gaze to Becky Lynn's, her beautiful blue eyes dulled by drugs. "You following me into a bathroom? I think we played this scene before."

Becky Lynn ignored her sarcasm. "We need to talk."

"Do we?" Zoe found what she had been seeking and pulled out a small cosmetics bag. "I thought we'd said all we had to say to each other a long time ago. But back then you were just plain Becky Lynn. Now you're *Valentine*."

Becky Lynn winced at the memory. As she recalled, the last time they had spoken, Zoe had done all the talking because she'd been too busy being ripped to pieces.

She took a deep breath and pushed the hateful memory away. "We need to talk about you this time. We need to talk about what you're doing."

"Yeah? And what am I doing?"

"Screwing up your life, your career. People are talking."

Zoe laughed and opened the bag, but instead of taking out lipstick and a comb, she retrieved a small mirror and a vial, a razor blade and a straw. She set them on the counter, then looked defiantly at Becky Lynn. "Do you think I give a fuck if people are talking? Do you think I care what they're saying?"

"You should."

"Well, I don't."

Becky Lynn stared at the other woman, horrified as Zoe laid out a line of fine, white powder on the mirror, cut it, then bent and snorted it through the straw.

Becky Lynn folded her arms across her middle, repulsed. "Don't you think you've had enough? Zoe, for God's sake, don't you see what you're doing to yourself? You're out of control, you need to get a handle on your life before it's too—"

"Oh, Lord. Here comes a lecture from Miss Goody-Goody."

Becky Lynn turned her head, sickened as Zoe snorted another line of cocaine. It hurt to watch Zoe do this to herself. And she felt responsible. She shouldn't, Becky Lynn told herself. Zoe had problems long before she had ever spotted her in that mall.

But if she hadn't discovered Zoe, if she hadn't brought her into this business, maybe her life would have taken a better, healthier turn. She wanted to help her.

"Why are you doing this?" she asked softly.

"You want to know why?" Zoe swayed on her feet as she stuffed all her drug paraphernalia back into the bag. "Because it makes me feel good. Real good."

"Do the men make you feel good, too?" Becky Lynn took a step toward her. "Did that man make you feel good? But for how long? Ten minutes? Twenty? What about finding something that will make you feel good for twenty years? Or a lifetime?"

She reached a hand out to the other woman. "There are places you can go, Zoe, places you can check yourself into where you'll learn to feel good without drugs and sex—"

"Knock off the sanctimonious bullshit! I can handle the drugs. And the sex, well…the sex is part of the business."

"It doesn't have to be." She laid a hand on Zoe's arm, imploringly. "Look at me—"

"Yes, let's look at you, *Valentine.*" Zoe shook her hand off. "Carlo gets you jobs. Carlo makes sure you're seen, makes sure you're noticed. Where would you be without him? Fighting and clawing for each booking, just like the rest of us."

She leaned toward Valentine, eyes bright with anger.

With resentment. "Tell me this, what's the difference between balling one man for jobs and balling twenty? No difference, I think. So don't stand there thinking you're so much better than me."

Becky Lynn forced back her hurt, forced back the urge to turn, walk away and leave Zoe to destroy herself. She owed this woman nothing. But she couldn't just walk away. "I don't think I'm better than you. I'm worried about you, that's all. I hate to see you throwing your life away. I'll help you. Just ask and I'll do anything."

"Ask you for help? Beg, maybe?" Zoe took a comb out of her purse and began working it through her hair. "You'd like that, wouldn't you? You'd like to get back at me for Jack."

Becky Lynn shook her head. "Maybe that's the way you think, but I don't. I want to help you."

"I don't need, or want, your help." Zoe dropped her comb into her purse, straightened her minidress, and started out of the bathroom. "So if the sermon's over, please excuse me."

Becky Lynn watched her go, heartsick at what had become of the woman she had thought she'd known. "Why do you hate me so much?" she asked softly. "What have I ever done to you besides try to be your friend?"

At her words, Zoe's steps faltered. She turned and met Becky Lynn's eyes. In hers, Becky Lynn saw regret, so bitter and sad she caught her breath. Then, without a word, Zoe walked away.

For a long time, Becky Lynn didn't leave the powder room. She sat on the vanity stool and gazed blindly into the mirror. She hurt for Zoe, for her confusion and pain, ached at her own inability to help her.

And she reeled from what Zoe had said to her. Zoe thought she and Carlo were lovers. If Zoe thought it, so did everybody else. Why hadn't she realized that before? It made sense; after all, she and Carlo had lived together for some time, he had discovered and groomed her, he used her for so many of his jobs, many called her his muse.

Her cheeks burned with embarrassment and indignation. Of course, no one would ever consider that they were simply friends, or just business partners. Oh, no, they had to think they were sexual partners.

Industry standard, she thought cynically. I'll give you something, if you give me something in return. That kind of sexual bartering went on all the time.

Jack and Garnet.

She fisted her fingers. And now she and Carlo were being lumped into that same category. It made her sick.

Her indignation faded as an idea occurred to her. She could use her relationship with Carlo to discourage that kind of sexual bartering. To a certain extent, she already had been.

She hated the blatant come-ons as much as the sly innuendos, she hated being forced to constantly dodge invitations for sex. The world already believed that she and Carlo were lovers, let them believe it more. Let them believe she was completely devoted and ever-faithful to her lover. She would let everyone know that Carlo was the only man for her.

Two models strolled into the bathroom, chatting with each other and laughing. Becky Lynn recognized them but couldn't recall their names. They stopped when they saw her.

"Sorry," one of them said. "We didn't know you were in here. All the johns downstairs are occupied."

"It's that time of night," the other one said and giggled.

"Go ahead." Becky Lynn stood and ran a hand over her sheath. "I was just leaving."

She left the bedroom and stepped into the hallway, realizing as she did that she had left her evening bag on the vanity. She turned and walked back into the bedroom, stopping just inside as she heard the two models talking about her.

"Isn't she the one who came out of nowhere to become everybody's favorite face."

"No kidding. And what about that name. *Valentine.* Really, she couldn't use Nancy or Cheryl or something ordinary like the rest of us?"

"What is her real name, anyway."

"It's probably something like Mildred." The model made a gagging sound. "It must have been too awful to use."

Becky Lynn's cheeks burned and she decided she could do without her purse. She turned to leave, but their next words stopped her.

"It sure doesn't hurt to have a photographer like Carlo Triani mad about you. Talk about getting a leg up on everybody else. It's just not fair."

"I don't know. I think I'd rather do without. I've heard things about him."

"Really? What?"

The first girl lowered her voice to an exaggerated whisper. "I heard he likes men."

"No!"

"Yes."

"Carlo Triani?" The momentary silence was pregnant with thought. "No way. He's like a man possessed in the way he pursues women. He's screwed almost everybody. Just like his old man."

"I know. But my source was awfully reliable." She giggled. "Maybe he swings both ways. It's not unheard of, especially in this town."

The commode was flushed, and Becky Lynn darted out of the bedroom, heart hammering.

Carlo liked men? She brought a hand to her mouth. *Carlo? It couldn't be true.*

She hurried down the hallway, not wanting the models to discover her still upstairs and figure out she had been eavesdropping on their conversation.

He pursued women like a man possessed. She drew her eyebrows together. Hadn't she sensed that herself? Hadn't she thought there was a desperation about the way he chased women? A desperation but also a discomfort?

This was nonsense. She started down the wide, curved staircase. It was just ugly gossip that had no basis in reality. The two models were admittedly jealous, and had tried to make themselves less so by spreading ugly untruths.

She caught sight of Carlo across the room, in an animated discussion with another photographer. He pursued women like a man possessed, she thought again, reaching the bottom of the stairs. But possessed by what. Love of women? Sexual desire? Or something else?

Just like his father.

"Valentine. You look simply fabulous. *Fantastico.*"

As if her thoughts had conjured him, she turned and faced Giovanni. They had met several times before and although he had never been anything but charming toward her, she didn't like him. No matter how he treated her, she couldn't forget how he had treated an eight-year-old boy who had needed a father's love.

"Hello, Giovanni."

He caught her hand and brought it to his mouth, lingering over it a moment too long for comfort. "The most beautiful woman in the room. Why haven't I worked with you yet, *bella?*"

Bella. That was what Carlo called her. She found something distasteful about that and about the way he was looking at her—as if she were a tasty prize to be won and sampled.

She suppressed a shudder and eased her hand from his. "I can't imagine."

He took a step closer, sliding his gaze assessingly over her. "I think we would work very well together. Like a hand and a glove, if you know what I mean?"

She did and it made her sick. She fought the urge to tell him exactly what she thought of him. She smiled sweetly instead. "Actually, I enjoy working with Carlo. I enjoy it very much. You've heard that, I suppose?"

"Ah, yes, Carlo. I have heard that." He leaned toward her, his dark eyes alight with challenge. "But why settle for youth when you could have experience?"

Giovanni, she decided, was a pig. He didn't care about Carlo; he saw his son as competition. And he wanted to beat him, no matter what it took, even if it meant sleeping with the woman many believed to be his son's lover.

Did he feel the same way about Jack? she wondered suddenly. Did he want to beat him, too? Had he played the two sons against each other?

She smiled again, but this time dreamily, as if thinking

of Carlo's arms. "But I don't feel like I'm settling. In fact, I think I must be the most…satisfied woman in the world."

Color stained the old photographer's cheeks and Valentine realized he was angry. Apparently, the great Giovanni wasn't used to rejection. Poor baby. She almost laughed out loud, it felt so good.

She caught sight of Carlo across the room. "And look, there's my man now. If you'll excuse me?"

"Of course," Giovanni said tightly, stepping aside so she could pass.

As she walked away, she couldn't help but chuckle.

39

Jack tapped his portfolio against his leg, his muscles jumping with nerves and the need for activity. He had caught the red-eye from Los Angeles to New York's La Guardia Airport to arrive in time for the start of the business day. He felt as if he had been sitting forever. The flight had taken just over five hours; the cab ride from the airport to Manhattan's garment district had taken twice the normal time because of rush-hour traffic, and Hugh Preston of H. P. Macro-Wear had kept him waiting forty minutes—so far.

Jack stood and crossed to the reception area's single window. Rain threatened; the heavy sky met the steel, glass and concrete world of Manhattan, closing the city into a stifling box of gray.

Two days ago, his rep had called to say that the designer had requested Jack's book, and was so impressed with his images, he wanted to meet him.

Hugh Preston and his Macro-Wear line made Garnet McCall's operation look small-time. At forty, Hugh Preston was surprisingly young to have achieved all he had. He had come out of nowhere to jet directly to the top. The marketplace had needed what he'd had to offer: a line of men's high-end casual wear, cool, hip and sometimes funky, always comfortable, designed for the yuppie with both cash and style.

The designer was preparing to launch Macro-Wear for women. He needed a photographer to launch with him.

Jack wanted to be that photographer. He wanted it badly. He had spent the two days since his rep's call studying Hugh Preston and his line of clothing. Many in the industry called him Fashion's Boy Wonder because of his meteoric rise to the top; others had dubbed him The Golden Child because of his unerring ability to turn his ideas into solid gold.

Jack worked to suppress his excitement. He didn't have the account yet, not by any stretch of the imagination, but he knew he was right for the job. He knew his work was right for this line of clothing. The most right of any of the top shooters working today.

He slipped his hands into the pockets of his loose-fitting Macro-Wear trousers. He had some ideas for direction already. And he'd already chosen the model he thought should be the first Macro-Wear woman—Valentine.

She had the right face and body, had the look Preston's clothes called out for. She was red-hot right now, she embodied the forward-look he envisioned for Macro-Wear.

Bullshit, Jack. You just want to work with her.

Jack breathed deeply through his nose, annoyed with himself. So what if he did, he thought. That didn't mean she wasn't right for the job; that didn't mean seeing her the other night had turned him inside out and backward.

"Hugh will see you now." The receptionist stood and smiled. "I'll take you back."

Jack followed the woman down a long corridor to Hugh Preston's office. The designer stood and came around the desk when they entered. "Jack, glad you could make it."

They shook hands, and Jack smiled. "I'm glad to be here."

"Let's sit down and talk." The designer motioned a

grouping of chairs near the picture window that looked out over Manhattan.

"Great view," Jack murmured, taking one of the leather and chrome chairs.

"I like it." Hugh Preston smiled. "And I like your work. I've followed what you've done for McCall. I particularly liked the series of shots for her spring collection. Impressive."

"Thank you. I was pleased with those, too."

"Good, you brought your book." Jack handed it to the other man. He opened it and leafed through a moment, as if refamiliarizing himself with the images. He met Jack's gaze once more. "Let's talk about what Jack Gallagher could do for me."

Jack began. He talked about who he perceived would be the market for the new line, what he had conceived for the images "look," told him about his choice of Valentine for Macro-Wear's first spokesmodel. His enthusiasm came through, and before long, he and the designer were animatedly discussing the possibilities.

After a time, the conversation shifted to more personal topics. They swapped stories, talked about mutual acquaintances in the business and laughed.

Finally, Hugh checked his watch. "I hate to cut this short, but I have someplace I need to be."

Jack smiled and followed the man to his feet. "I appreciate your taking so much time with me. I know how busy you are."

Hugh looked down at Jack's book, then met his eyes once more. "How long are you in town for, Jack?"

"Just the day. I fly out this afternoon."

"Why don't you stay overnight? We could do the town. I'd like to get to know you better."

Jack opened his mouth to accept, then hesitated, something plucking at the back of his memory.

"I'd like to get to know you better," Garnet had said. "Before I make my final decision."

Déjà vu. With a twist.

Jack cleared his throat, and told himself he was wrong, that he was overreacting. He'd been in this business a lot of years and he had never been propositioned by another man.

But in this industry, anything was possible.

"Sounds great, Hugh. I know some ladies here in town, can I bring a date?"

"I was thinking just the two of us." The designer smiled. "It would give us a chance to see how we get along. Creatively."

A lump formed in Jack's throat. He swallowed hard, but kept his expression casual. "Creatively," Jack murmured. "Interesting choice of words, but I'm not sure what you mean."

"You know. I'd like to see how our minds meld." The designer swept his gaze appraisingly over Jack. "We could find out how attractive we are to each other."

Shit. Damn. Son of a bitch. He hadn't overreacted, Hugh Preston was coming on to him. Jack stiffened. "I'd love to do the town, Hugh, but I really do need to get back to L.A. tonight."

"I'm sorry to hear that." The designer handed Jack his book. "I like your stuff, Jack. I'll call."

He wouldn't call, Jack acknowledged four hours later as he boarded a plane back to Los Angeles. He'd lost the account.

He swore silently. Macro-Wear would have made him *it*. Sleeping with Hugh Preston hadn't even been an option.

He swore again, this time under his breath. He handed the stewardess his ticket, then slipped into his seat. The first-class section was nearly empty, its only other occupant a pro-football player he recognized. He nodded at the man, then returned to his thoughts and the frustration roiling inside him.

He had been the best choice for the job; he had wanted it badly, he still did. The want burned, unrelieved, in the pit of his gut. The stewardess offered him champagne; he turned it down in favor of orange juice. With any luck, getting back to California would eradicate the bad taste the Preston interview had left in his mouth.

His deal making with Garnet hadn't made him feel sick at heart; that negotiation hadn't made him feel used. Because she had been a lush, sexy woman, and the thought of sleeping with her had been pleasurable.

In retrospect, it did. In retrospect, it made him feel like shit.

The plane reached its thirty-two thousand feet cruising altitude, and Jack put his seat back and closed his eyes. What if he hadn't wanted to sleep with Garnet? Would he have been turned away as he had been today, despite his talent? Would he have still been in the trenches, fighting for his first big break?

The sour taste in his mouth turned bitter. He sipped his orange juice. The system sucked. He hadn't realized that before. He'd grown up in the industry, he had been weaned on the way it operated, but until this moment, he hadn't seen the harm in the system.

But then, the system had never bitten him in the ass before.

It had today, big time.

The Macro-Wear account would have propelled him to the top of the fashion heap. He wouldn't have had to play the game anymore; he could have made his own rules, called his own shots.

All he would have had to do was adjust his line and lower his pants.

His line didn't adjust that far.

He thought of Becky Lynn, of Valentine, again. Was the system why she stayed with Carlo? Was it a way of playing the game? Carlo ensured her a place in the industry. He used her so much that her star had risen to the level of his. She didn't have to fight for jobs, she hadn't had to endure the worst of what beginning models went through—the cattle calls, the foreign circuit, the casting couch.

She'd had to endure only one casting couch. Carlo's.

He tightened his fingers on his glass. No matter her reasons, the thought of her and Carlo being lovers made him crazy. It affected him in a way he wouldn't have expected, deeply and in the pit of his gut. He found himself wanting to take out his anger and frustration in an irrational, physical way, found himself wanting to beat the hell out of someone or something.

Preferably Carlo.

Jack narrowed his eyes. He despised his half brother, he hated the thought of him touching Becky Lynn. He hated the thought of her being with the son of a bitch. She had asked him the other night if he ever stopped to think of someone besides himself. That comment had gnawed at him, not because he thought she was entirely wrong, not because he'd been insulted or shocked or ashamed.

But because most days, he thought of little else besides her.

If she only knew.

40

Becky Lynn couldn't put the gossip she had overheard about Carlo out of her mind. She despised that kind of talk, that kind of ugliness, so rife in the fashion industry, yet she hadn't felt outraged, she hadn't wanted to march into that bathroom and boldly defend Carlo.

She had felt as if what they were saying was true. She had felt a sense of *ah-ha,* a sense that everything she had felt about Carlo, all the conflicting vibrations she had picked up about his relationships with the opposite sex, suddenly made sense.

She frowned and turned onto Carlo's palm tree-lined street. But if the gossip was true, why hadn't he told her? If it was true, why did he pursue women so relentlessly? Why did he pretend to be something he was not? After all, in the fashion industry, being gay was neither unusual nor a detriment. Why the charade?

Becky Lynn pulled up in front of Carlo's bungalow, surprised to see both his cars parked in the driveway. She checked her watch. *Nearly eight.* On a normal day, he was usually long gone by now, never mind the fact that he had an important trip to New York to prepare for.

She swung out of her car. He must have had a big night last night, she thought, smiling. He had told her he was going clubbing on Sunset with friends. Her smile faded.

Or maybe he was ill. In all the time she'd known him, he had never slept in on a workday.

She crossed to his front door and fished his house key out of her purse. She had forgotten her book when she'd stopped by two evenings ago, and needed it for a go-see this morning. She had planned to slip in and out, but maybe she would check on Carlo first, just to make sure he was okay.

The house was completely quiet, unnaturally still. Her book lay on the entryway table, right where she had left it. She collected it, then started for the back of the house.

Carlo's bedroom door stood ajar. A shudder of déjà vu moved over her, a memory of the last time she had been in the same position, the last time she had eased open a bedroom door.

That time, she had discovered the man she loved in bed with another woman.

Only Carlo wasn't the man she loved—he was her friend, her mentor. And she wanted to make sure he was okay. She drew a deep breath and pushed the door the rest of the way open.

A woman, tangled in the sheets but obviously naked, lay across Carlo's bed. Carlo stood beside the bed, gazing down at the woman, his face a mask of misery.

Becky Lynn caught her breath. He lifted his gaze. The emptiness in his eyes, the hopelessness, tore at her.

She no longer suspected the gossip had been true. She knew it was.

Carlo was gay.

She took a step backward, then another, a feeling of betrayal spiraling through her. Why hadn't he told her? Why hadn't he trusted her? She thought of the times he had tried to get her into his bed, all the while knowing it was a lie. That hurt. It made her feel used, it made her feel valueless.

He opened his mouth to speak, and she turned and started down the hall, uncertain what she wanted to say to him, what she needed to say.

As she had known he would, Carlo followed her. She waited for him in the foyer, her heart thundering, her palms damp. She felt as if she had been tricked, duped. Jack had betrayed her; now, in a different way, she felt that Carlo had, too. She didn't even know him, she thought, light-headed. He had been hiding himself from her all this time.

As she had been hiding herself from him.

She clasped her hands in front of her. How could she be angry with him when she had been just as secretive, just as dishonest?

"Becky Lynn?"

She turned and met his gaze. He looked so unhappy, she thought, searching his expression. He looked desperate. Her anger and disillusionment dimmed, then disappeared.

She crossed to him and caught his hands. "Why didn't you tell me, Carlo? Didn't you feel you could trust me?"

"Tell you what, *bella?* I don't know what you mean."

She took a deep breath and tightened her fingers on his. "I know you're gay." His expression froze, and her heart turned over for him. "Please don't hide from me. We're friends. I would never hurt you."

He cleared his throat, battling visibly to look unaffected. "Valentine, *bella,* I don't understand. Why do you say this? How could you think that I—"

"I know, Carlo." She looked him straight in the eye.

"You don't have to pretend with me. I don't care about your…sexuality. I only care about you."

His throat worked; she could see how her words upset him, how much he wanted to deny them. But he couldn't.

"I love you, Carlo," she whispered, her voice choked with tears. "You don't have to prove anything to me, you don't have to pretend to be someone you're not. I love you for who you are and how you've treated me."

He eased his hands from hers, and turned away, shutting her out. Tears flooded her eyes. She couldn't imagine her life without him. She wouldn't have one real friend in this business without Carlo. And above all, she wanted him to be happy.

She crossed to him and laid a hand on his shoulder. He jerked away from her touch. The rejection hurt, and she stiffened her spine against it. "You can't go on this way," she said softly. "I see…how it hurts you. It's like…every time you're with a woman, a little piece of you is ripped away. You're bleeding to death, Carlo. Let me—"

"Just go."

"*Bello*…please. Let me help you."

He faced her, fists clenched, expression devastated. "I want you to go."

She recalled something the models had said and suddenly she understood. "It's your father, isn't it? You're trying to prove something to him. You're trying to live up to some stupid legend that has nothing to do with the person you are inside."

Carlo swung away from her. He crossed to the French doors that looked out over the pool and gardens. For a long time, he said nothing, and Becky Lynn sensed his struggle to compose himself.

"What do you know of my father's legend?" he said finally, tightly. "What do you know of what I want or feel? How dare you come here, into my home, and say these things to me. What have you shared of yourself to give you the freedom to do this?"

"You're right." Becky Lynn drew a deep breath. "I haven't been open with you. I wanted to bury the past. I thought that if no one knew about it, about me, that it didn't exist. That the girl I was back then didn't exist."

She crossed to stand beside him, but didn't look at him. Outside, the sun glittered off the smooth blue of the swimming pool. "I was gang raped when I was seventeen," she began softly. "Actually, there were three boys, but only one had time to…do me. They shoved a paper bag over my head because they didn't want to look at me while they did it. You see, I was too…ugly to even look at while…"

Emotion choked her, and she cleared her throat. "Those boys did that to me because they knew they could get away with it, and because they thought I was…nothing." Carlo turned slowly; she felt his gaze but couldn't bring herself to meet it. "And in a way, they were right. I was poor white trash, my daddy was a no-good alcoholic who hated me about as much as they did."

Her eyes swam, and she blinked, determined not to cry. "My whole life, it was my dreams that kept me alive. If I hadn't had them…I would have died."

She met his gaze then. In his, she read sympathy, compassion, but most of all, understanding. "You made my dreams come true, Carlo. You've given me…everything. How could I not love you? And how can I stand back and watch you killing yourself?"

"Becky Lynn, I—"

His throat closed over the words, and she caught his hand and brought it to her mouth. "I'll go now. Think about what I said, please. Call me when you get back from New York."

She crossed to the door, stopping when she reached it, looking over her shoulder at him. His anguish tore at her. "He's not worth it, Carlo. You know in your heart he's not."

41

He had gotten the account. Carlo Triani was now the photographer of record for H. P. Macro-Wear.

Carlo gazed out at the crimson flowers in his back garden, vibrant and bursting with life. He smiled to himself, liking the image, for once feeling as full of life himself.

Hugh Preston. Carlo's smile widened. He had made a friend, had found a kindred spirit. Their minds worked synchronously, their ideas, their thoughts meshed—on the industry and fashion, on photography, on life. They had so much in common, it was almost scary.

Carlo's smile faded. Hugh was braver than he. He was stronger, bolder. Hugh wouldn't hide who he was, he refused to pretend to be something he wasn't. He said he never had.

Hugh had understood Carlo's predicament, however. He had been sensitive to his feelings. And Hugh had told him, in no uncertain terms, that he wanted to be with him again.

Carlo threw open the French doors and stepped out onto his terrace. The smell of the day, the flowers and fresh-cut grass, the sun and water, assailed him. He shut his eyes and breathed it in, letting the life fill him.

He recalled the feel of the other man's hands on him, recalled every moment of their too-short time together. It had been incredibly exciting, fulfilling; it had been like magic.

He was falling in love.

Carlo grinned, feeling like a ridiculous, smitten adolescent for even thinking such a thing. But he couldn't deny the way he felt. And he couldn't deny that he wanted to see Hugh again.

What if Giovanni found out?

His heart began to pump wildly; his chest tightened until he had to fight to breathe. He could imagine his father's disgust, his revulsion. Every scrap of respect Giovanni had ever shown him, respect Carlo had fought for—respect he had, in a sense, died for—would have been lost. He would never measure up to the legend.

Giovanni would turn to Jack. Macho Jack. Jack whose way with women matched his own; Jack who seemed to be able to do everything and anything he put his mind to.

Oh, yes. Giovanni would choose Jack, once and for all.

Carlo flexed his fingers, a feeling of impotence and rage racing over him. He cursed his mother, Giovanni, himself. He hated being weak, being afraid. He hated the fact that he didn't have the guts to be the man he wanted to be. He swung around, and his gaze landed on the Jacuzzi.

Red water.

He shuddered and his head filled with the image of his mother, the last of her life leaking from her.

He had thrown himself at her still body and had clung to her, begging her not to leave him. They'd had to drag him off of her. Her one arm had draped over the side of the tub, and he had slipped in the puddle of blood. When he'd fought them, it had gone everywhere, staining his skin and clothes, staining his life.

Even now he could hear that lost boy cry out, *"Why didn't you love me, Madre? Why didn't you love me enough to want to live?"*

Then there had been only Giovanni. Unforgiving and critical. Impatient and cold. Giovanni whose great legend preceded him like an impenetrable field of bright ice.

Carlo blinked and turned away from the pool, yet away from the garden, too. Becky Lynn had been right. He couldn't go on the way he had been, he couldn't keep pretending by sleeping with women.

But he couldn't face Giovanni's learning the truth. That would be worse than the slow death he was already living.

He brought a hand to the back of his neck and massaged the knot of muscles there. He thought of the things Becky Lynn had told him that morning two days ago. He understood her so well now. Before that morning, he had known what kind of person she was, he had liked and respected her. But he hadn't understood her. Now he did.

No wonder she feared men, no wonder she disliked being touched. He understood now how much courage it had taken her to give herself over to him and his camera. Now, he did understand the enormity of what he had given her when he had transformed her into Valentine, even if his reasons for doing so had been less than altruistic.

And he saw what shams both of their lives were, how ridiculous and sad.

Carlo drew his eyebrows together. He didn't understand her feelings for Jack, though. His half brother was the only piece of the puzzle of Valentine's life that didn't fit. What had Jack given her that had earned her respect and trust? What had she seen in Jack to love?

Maybe he, Carlo, couldn't see, only because he didn't

want to. Maybe his fear and jealousy had blinded him to something of the man Jack really was.

Carlo shook his head, annoyed with himself. He had missed nothing; Jack was as little and as narrow as he had always thought him to be. Becky Lynn had simply fallen under the spell of Jack's macho charisma.

Besides, Jack was a part of Becky Lynn's past. Carlo narrowed his eyes in thought. He was her future. They could help each other, protect each other. And he loved her, in a way he had never loved another woman besides his mother.

His blood began to thrum. Carlo Triani and Valentine, together they would be invincible. They would be safe. Together, there would be nothing they couldn't do.

All he had to do was convince her.

42

Where was she? Zoe looked around her in confusion, searching her memory, wishing she could think clearly. She had gone to a bar. On Sunset. But which one?

They all looked alike, murky and crowded, with weird, frenetic lighting. They were all loud, too loud. She drew a shaky breath, dizzy, slightly queasy. The music thundered in her head, and with a sense of horror she realized that what she heard wasn't music—it was the sound of her own blood pumping through her veins.

A man on her right pressed closer to her. He smelled too sweet, like cheap cologne and bourbon. "Hey, baby." He slurred the words in her ear. "What'say we get outta here?"

Zoe looked at the man, her breathing quick and shallow. Did she know him? Had she spoken to him? She didn't think so. He had black hair and a beard; his eyes were light, so light they seemed to burn into her. Demon eyes, she thought, a shudder racing up her spine.

She opened her mouth to speak, but nothing came out. She reached for the glass in front of her, her mouth dry like death's ashes. What if she just dried up and blew away? What if she were dying right now and nobody knew, nobody could tell?

Heart pounding, she curved her hand around the damp glass, then brought it slowly to her mouth, her hand shaking so badly, some of the liquid sloshed over the side of the glass and spilled onto her hand.

"So, babe? You want to take off?"

Her gaze flew to the demon beside her. He leaned toward her; she recognized the sickly sweetness of his breath as the scent of death. Fear choked her. "I have to go to the bathroom," she whispered, slipping off the bar stool, stumbling a little when she reached her feet.

The man caught her arm, steadying her. "Come back, babe. I'll be waiting."

His touch stung, and she jerked her arm away and started blindly through the packed room, the strobe lights alternately illuminating and shadowing the faces around her.

Frightened, she searched the sometimes incandescent faces for one she recognized. The crowd pressed closer; her heart beat faster, harder. She couldn't breathe; it felt as if her heart was going to pop right out of her chest.

She lowered her eyes to the dance floor and squeaked in terror. Her heart lay at her feet, bloody and still beating.

"Hello, princess."

Princess. The voice reverberated through her head, and she swung in its direction. *Daddy. Her daddy had come for her.*

"Whoa, beautiful." Strong hands steadied her. "I don't know what you've been into tonight, but I think you've had enough."

"Daddy," she whispered, tears flooding her eyes. She moved into his arms. He began to sway to the music. Zoe pressed her face to his chest, to the reassuring beat of his heart, and squeezed her eyes shut. Her daddy had come for her; she was safe at last.

"I guess tonight's my lucky night." He laughed and pulled her closer. "I found me a beautiful princess."

Her heart filled to near bursting. She tilted her face back and smiled up at him. Her daddy smiled back. Zoe knew she would never be frightened again.

Zoe awakened slowly. She hurt. Her head, her chest and neck, her eyes. Her entire body ached, everywhere and in a way she couldn't remember hurting before. She moaned and stirred, then cracked open her eyes. The light burned them, and she snapped them shut once more. She shifted and encountered something warm and hard.

She cracked open her eyes again. A man lay beside her, a man she didn't recognize. She frowned, working to remember who he was, where she had found him.

She drew a blank.

Careful not to awaken him, she slid out of the bed. As her feet hit the floor, the world tilted. A hand to her head, she stumbled to the bathroom.

She relieved herself, then dragged herself to the sink. She felt bad. Worse than she had ever felt. She passed a hand over her mouth, it was dry and crusted at the corners.

She turned on the cold water and rinsed her mouth, then splashed her face. Why couldn't she remember anything? Every morning, she was a little fuzzy, but after a few minutes, her memory always returned. But as hard as she tried, she couldn't recall how she had gotten here.

She must have gotten really wasted. She remembered the coke and the pills. What kind of pills? She drew her eyebrows together. She couldn't remember. She had gotten them from a guy in a parking lot.

She leaned toward the mirror and peered in. She looked

awful. She blinked and leaned closer, frowning at a mark she saw on her left breast. She brought her hand to it and winced.

What was that? She squinted into the mirror, then recoiled in horror. Teeth marks. Not a hickey or love bite—a bite. Whoever had done this had drawn blood. She saw the imprint of a mouth, of teeth, so clearly etched on her skin she could count them.

Horrified, she pushed the hair away from her face, off her shoulders. Then she saw them—bruises circling her neck. Imprints of fingers. She caught her breath. Vague, distorted images played through her head. Ugly images. Frightening ones. She remembered struggling to breathe, remembered him, the man in the bed, turning her to her stomach, remembered screaming as he shoved himself into her.

He had hurt her. He could have killed her.

She had to get out of here. She had to get out before he woke up.

Breathing hard, fighting hysteria, she tiptoed out to the bedroom, more afraid than she had ever been in her life. She didn't look at the man, afraid if she did, she would remember more of what had happened, more of what he had done to her.

She searched for her things, settling for what she could find, yanking each article of clothing on as she uncovered it. He muttered and stirred; her heart leapt to her throat, and her gaze flew to the bed.

He stirred again. His eyes opened, meeting hers. His eyes were cold and flat, like a shark's. Or a devil's. Terror choked her.

Turning, she raced for the front door and ripped it open.

She stumbled through, and sunshine spilled over her. Zoe cried out with relief.

Never again, she promised herself. Never again.

43

Becky Lynn stared at Carlo in shock. When he had called and asked if he could stop by to talk, she had thought he wanted to discuss Macro-Wear. She shook her head. "You didn't just ask me—"

"I did." He reached across her little kitchen table and gathered her hands in his. "Marry me, Becky Lynn."

"But Carlo—" She sucked in a quick, steadying breath. "We both know that you and I…that we're not, that you're…" Her words trailed off, and she searched his gaze. *He couldn't be serious, he couldn't be…but he was.* "I don't know what to say."

He squeezed her hands, then released them. "Then just listen."

She nodded and he stood and crossed to the breakfast-room window. "You were right the other day," he began. "About everything, me, Giovanni, about what I needed. And you were right about what pretending has been doing to me." He swung to face her. "I've felt trapped for so long. Now I see a way out. For both of us."

When she opened her mouth to comment, he held up a hand to stop her. "Yes, you, too. Look at yourself. Here you are, you're supposed to be this beautiful, sexual creature, working in an industry that takes sex as a day-to-day part of business, yet you can't stand to be touched.

If you were married to me, you would have a cover, an easy out of any situation that made you uncomfortable."

He crossed to where she sat and knelt in front of her. He caught her hands in his. "Imagine, *bella,* not having to put up with the come-ons, the sexual innuendos, the body-bartering. After all, we would be the most deliriously happy couple. And everyone would know it."

He drew a deep breath. "It would be a cover for me, too. I wouldn't have to prove myself by bedding everything that moves. And even if an occasional rumor circulated, how much could people say when they saw how happy and satisfied the beautiful Valentine was?"

She lowered her eyes to their joined hands, her heart hammering. Once upon a time, she had dreamed of a romantic moment like this one, had dreamed of a handsome man, a diamond ring and a promise of undying love. Once she had dreamed about hearing those words from Jack. Tears stung her eyes. Would she never be totally free of him?

"You've thought this all out, haven't you?" she whispered, voice trembling.

"Is that so wrong? Look at me, sweet." She met his eyes once more. "You believe in me. Do you know how rare that is in this business? In this world? Do you know how special?" He feathered his fingers across her cheek. "And I believe in you, too."

Becky Lynn thought of her own parents, thought about Carlo's, thought of others she had known. Perhaps they would have been better off if they had married for reasons other than passion and love.

"It's a way out of the trap for both of us," he murmured. "It's a way to be free. Marry me, *bella.* I love you."

She swallowed hard, feeling panicky and uncertain. "Carlo, I'm...stunned. I don't know...what to say."

"You're not surprised." He moved his fingers over hers, stroking, reassuring. "*Bella,* be honest, you already use me as a cover. You already pretend we're lovers."

She flushed and looked away. He caught her chin, and turned her face to his. "I do love you, Becky Lynn. Not as a lover. But as a friend. I care about you, I want to take care of you." He cradled her face in his palms. "We could take care of each other. Neither of us would ever have to be alone again."

The image of Jack filled her head, and tears flooded her eyes. She blinked against them, cursing him, cursing herself for being unable to let him go. She had never wanted anybody but Jack; she never would.

But she would never have him. He was an impossible dream, the man she had thought she loved had never even existed—not completely.

With Carlo, she would never have to be alone again. She would never have to face a cold dawn without someone to hold on to, would never have to face the night and the fear of disappearing, of dying, and no one even knowing she'd gone. With Carlo, she would forever have someone to share her dreams and fears, joys and sorrows.

Becky Lynn drew a shaky breath. She cared for Carlo. She loved and trusted him. He made her feel safe; when she needed support, he would be there for her. He had seen beauty in her no one else ever had.

Becky Lynn looked away, struggling to sort out her thoughts and feelings. She swallowed hard and returned her gaze to his. "Are you sure, Carlo? Loving someone and not being with them is harder than you can imagine. If you ever…fell in love with someone else, and if I knew you were with that person, I would feel so alone and so…left out."

He brought their joined hands to his mouth. "I can't promise I'll always be faithful, but I promise I'll never forsake you for another. I'd never do that to you. So, will you?" he asked softly, his voice thick. "Will you marry me, Valentine?"

Becky Lynn lifted her gaze to Carlo's. She never wanted to be alone again.

Her heart in her throat, she said yes.

44

Jack stared at the party invitation that had just come, stunned, disbelieving. He reread the invitation for a third time, hoping that he had somehow misunderstood the first two times. He hadn't. Tremayne Davis requested the honor of his presence at a prenuptial bash for Valentine and Carlo Triani, the lucky couple.

Becky Lynn was marrying Carlo. Jack sucked in a sharp breath. *How could this have happened? How could she be marrying Carlo?*

Did Becky Lynn know he had been invited? he wondered. He could almost hear Tremayne telling her that everyone must be invited. Even Jack Gallagher, the man who had known the great Valentine when she had been just plain Becky Lynn, the idiot who had been too blind to see the jewel he'd had right under his nose.

Oh, yes. Jack narrowed his eyes. This was southern California, all would be invited. Even the bride-to-be's former lover and the groom's bastard half brother. And the party would be a one-hundred-percent deductible PR event and everybody would be happy. Especially the lucky couple themselves.

Disgusted, Jack tossed the invitation down. *How could this have happened? How could he have let it happen?*

Muttering an oath, he crossed to his photo wall. He'd never shot Valentine, although he had tried to book her many times. She had always, conveniently, been unavailable. But he had several candid shots of her before she had become Valentine, when she'd been Becky Lynn—his assistant, his friend, his lover.

Two of them were still tacked to his wall. He'd left them up as a punishment of sorts, and as a bittersweet reminder of what he had had and lost. Jack studied the photographs, an uncomfortable catch in his chest. In one, she was crouched down, fiddling with lighting equipment; she had looked up at him and laughed just as he snapped the shot. In the other, she was simply gazing at him, at the camera, her expression at once vulnerable, adoring and sweetly sensual. That expression had made her a famous and wealthy woman.

He reached out to touch the photograph, then realizing what he was doing, dropped his hand. How could he have spent so much time with her, and never really seen her? He looked at these photos and saw Valentine, saw what Carlo had recognized immediately. Why hadn't he been able to see back then?

He stuffed his hands into his pockets, feeling like a fool—and like a loser. He recognized the feeling; it was an ache, deep in his gut, an ache he'd experienced for the first time at age eight, when his great father had looked at him as if he were nothing, then turned and walked away.

He gazed at the images of Becky Lynn, his chest tight, thinking of the way she had once looked at him. Did she look at Carlo that way? Did she love him?

Jack drew his eyebrows together in a scowl. She was making a mistake. A big mistake. Why couldn't she see that?

"Hey, Jack. Have you heard?"

Jack looked over his shoulder at his photo assistant Pete. The other man stood in the doorway to the studio, two bags of take-out nestled in his arms. "Yeah," he said tightly, "I heard."

"Sorry, man. I know how much you wanted that account." Pete shifted the bags. "I thought you just might get it. I really did."

Jack shook his head, still thinking of Becky Lynn and Carlo. "What account?"

"H. P. Macro-Wear." Pete made a sound of disgust. "That Triani's one lucky bastard. First discovering Valentine. Now this."

Jack stared at his assistant, not comprehending. "Are you saying…Carlo got Macro-Wear?"

Pete looked at him as if he had lost his mind. "I thought you said you'd heard."

"No." Jack shook his head. "I thought you were talking about…something else."

"Nope, Macro-Wear. Triani got it."

"Son of a bitch," Jack murmured, the ramifications of the news rocketing through him. He looked at Pete. "You're sure?"

"Contracts are signed." Pete juggled the bags. "Look, I'll be in the kitchen if you need me."

"Fine." His heart thundering, Jack turned back to the wall of images, to the photographs of Becky Lynn. *Carlo had gotten Macro-Wear. Carlo had slept with Hugh Preston.*

He couldn't believe it. Over the years, he had heard gossip about Carlo. He had ignored it, partly because his half brother had bedded a great number of women, and partly because this town, this industry, thrived on nasty gossip.

But now he wondered if the talk had been true. Was

Carlo gay? At the very least, he was bisexual. At the very least, he had cheated on Becky Lynn.

Jack shook his head, thinking of the twisted irony of it—Becky Lynn had left him for the very same thing, betraying her with someone else, sleeping with someone to get an account.

He crossed back to his worktable, to the invitation he had tossed down in disgust. He retrieved it and tapped it against his palm. Becky Lynn didn't know, she couldn't. If she did, she wouldn't marry Carlo. He still knew Becky Lynn well enough to be certain of that.

She was making the worst mistake of her life.

He had to save her.

Jack narrowed his eyes, determination and dislike churning inside him. That son of a bitch. Duping Becky Lynn this way, tricking her into believing he was not only faithful but heterosexual, was beyond contempt.

Was Carlo doing it to hurt him? Jack wondered, fisting his fingers. Or simply to permanently attach himself to Valentine's blazing star.

Would Becky Lynn believe him?

Becky Lynn was loyal. If she had heard gossip, she would never believe it. She would never think ill of Carlo, unless she had proof. He searched his memory, trying to recall the times he had heard rumors about Carlo, trying to recall who he had heard the rumors from.

Jack squared his shoulders. He would get her proof; he had to save her.

45

Becky Lynn and Carlo decided to forgo a church wedding in favor of a quick exchange of vows at the courthouse. Considering the circumstances, it didn't seem right to get married in God's house.

Instead of throwing themselves a party after, as they were both scheduled to go on location, they decided to have one the night before. Tremayne had insisted on giving it to them as his wedding gift, and when Becky Lynn had balked at the enormity of the cost, he had reminded her that it would be good publicity and that he could write off the entire thing. So she had agreed.

Everybody in the industry had been invited, even Eileen Ford and John Casablancas, Tremayne's main competition. Becky Lynn had wondered if Jack would attend, then had cursed herself for wondering. She was marrying Carlo, and when she did, Jack would be completely and truly a part of her past. No matter what her and Carlo's arrangement, no matter that their reasons for marrying were far from traditional, she intended to be a good and faithful wife. She intended to take her wedding vows seriously.

Even if Carlo didn't.

Becky Lynn caught her bottom lip between her teeth, fighting indecision and doubt. Was she doing the right thing? In the weeks since agreeing to marry Carlo, she had been plagued by doubt, she worried that she had rushed into her decision, that she hadn't thoroughly contemplated the emotional toll of a marriage to a man who wasn't in love with her. A man who would prefer to be with another man.

Would he ever want a family? She wanted children someday; she couldn't imagine growing old without them. Yet, how would her and Carlo's unusual arrangement affect a child?

She drew a deep, calming breath. Carlo loved and respected her. He believed in her, as she believed in him. They already had so much more than many other couples just starting out. Who needed passion when she had respect? Who needed sex when she had affection, real and true?

She had made the right decision, she told herself. She and Carlo were going to be stronger together than apart; together, they would face and conquer each problem, every trial, as it arose.

Taking another deep breath, she turned her gaze to the dressing-table mirror. She had chosen a suit for the party, in a deep, vibrant pink. The pink of spring back home, she thought, smoothing a hand down the front of the jacket. The pink of the azalea plant Carlo had sent her so long ago.

The day Jack had broken her heart.

She shook her head. She didn't want to think of Jack; she hated that no matter how hard she tried, she couldn't keep the thoughts of him, the comparisons between him and Carlo, at bay.

Becky Lynn scowled at her reflection. There was no comparison between the two, she told herself firmly. Carlo was giving and loyal; Carlo needed her. He believed in her.

Jack had never needed or believed in her. He never would.

"You look wonderful."

She lifted her gaze and met Carlo's in the mirror. He stood in the bedroom doorway, the picture of self-confidence and sophistication, almost breathtakingly handsome in his natural-colored linen jacket and slacks.

"Pink and black is awfully bold together," she murmured, referring to his black raw-silk shirt. "You don't think we're going to clash, do you?"

"Are you kidding? In this industry, there's no such thing as being too bold." He smiled and crossed to her. "Besides, tonight all I can think about is how lucky I am."

He laid his hands on her shoulders and squeezed—the reassuring touch of a big brother, of a good friend. Emotion welled up in her chest—even as she told herself it was happiness, she acknowledged despair.

"I heard the phone," she said quickly, hoping to keep him from seeing her fears. "Who called?"

Carlo hesitated, then cleared his throat. "Hugh Preston. He called to... He's sorry he couldn't be here."

"Are you sure?" She drew her eyebrows together. "That's all?"

"Of course."

Carlo's smile looked forced, his voice sounded hollow. The knot in her stomach tightened. "If you want to back out, I'll understan—"

"No way." He squeezed her shoulders again, then dropped his hands. "It's time. You almost ready?"

She nodded, swallowing hard. "I just need my shoes."

She retrieved them from the closet and slipped them on. In them, she stood several inches taller than Carlo. But no

one would look askance at that; in this business, many a
bride towered over her groom.

*She wouldn't have towered over Jack, no matter how
high her heels.*

"What's wrong?"

Her gaze flew to Carlo's; guilty heat stung her cheeks.
"Nothing. Why?"

"For a moment, you looked…sad."

"I'm just nervous, that's all." That wasn't a lie, she was
more nervous than she had been in a long time. She hadn't
a clue how she was going to get through the next five or
so hours, no clue how she was going to keep up her
besotted blushing-bride facade.

In the end, Becky Lynn kept up her facade by doing the
same thing she did every time she stepped in front of the
camera—she became Valentine, playing the part that had
been created just for her, the part that kept the world from
touching her.

After a couple hours of people wishing her and Carlo
well, of them telling her how lucky she was and what a
striking couple the two of them made, Becky Lynn realized
she wasn't having to work at her role anymore. She was
happy, perhaps not in the same way as she had once
dreamed of being, but happy nonetheless.

Alone for the first time all night, Becky Lynn took a
deep breath, grateful for the opportunity to clear her head.
Carlo had gone off with Giovanni and Dick Avedon, and
for the moment, the partiers seemed to have forgotten that
they had come tonight to wish her well. Which suited her
just fine—even when playing the part of Valentine, she
preferred to be Becky Lynn the wallflower.

She wandered farther from the tightest throng of party

guests, moving toward the formal fountain. The three mermaids at its center had been fashioned in the images of the first three of Tremayne's clients to achieve supermodel status. She took a sip of her mineral water, then lifted her hair off the back of her neck. She pressed the cold, damp glass to her warm skin, making a sound of relief as she did. The night was warmer than she had expected when she'd chosen the suit.

"Hello, Red."

Jack. She let her hair drop and turned slowly to face him. Even when she had wondered if he would come tonight, she had known he would. She should have been prepared, she told herself. She should have a well-rehearsed word or two on the tip of tongue, something she could spit out, then walk away, head held high.

But she didn't, damn it. She was on her own.

"Hello, Gallagher."

"You look beautiful," he murmured, moving closer. "You'll make a radiant bride."

Pleasure at his comment moved through her, and annoyed with herself, she kept her gaze trained on his. "What are you doing here?"

"I got an invitation, just like everybody else. And I must say, how *fashion* of you to celebrate an event before it's even happened." He lifted his beer in a mocking salute. "And of course, I came to wish the bride and groom well."

"How nice of you," she said coolly, her heart a hammer in her chest. "Wishes accepted. Goodbye."

She started to brush by him, he caught her wrist, stopping her. She met his gaze again, and realized he was angry. Surprised, she searched his expression. What did he have to be angry about?

"Why are you marrying him?" he asked softly, an edge of steel in his voice.

"Why do you think?" She tugged against his grasp. "Why does any woman marry?"

"I'm not asking about any woman, Becky Lynn. I'm asking about you." He tightened his fingers. "Do you love him?"

She sucked in a sharp breath. "Of course I do. I adore him."

For a moment, Jack said nothing, then he leaned close. "Does he make you happy?" he asked, lowering his voice to a seductive murmur. "Does he make you ache the way I did? When he takes his hands from your body, do you beg to have them back?"

Memories swamped her. Pain and longing with them. It had been that way between them, hot and explosive. The more they had made love, the hungrier she had become, the more insatiable.

It had been so long. So long.

"Remember how it was? Remember, Becky Lynn?" His grip on her wrist eased, and he moved his fingers in slow, drugging circles. She wondered if he could feel the thunder of her pulse, and if he did what he thought of it.

He leaned closer yet, and his breath stirred erotically against her ear. "Carlo doesn't do that for you, does he? He doesn't make you weak and strong at the same time. He doesn't make you sing. I know he doesn't. He can't."

It took a moment for his words to fully penetrate, when they did she freed herself from his grasp, and swung to face him. His being here had nothing to do with his feelings for her, he didn't love or want her. He was here because he hated Carlo. And because he wanted to beat him.

"Your ego is eclipsed only by your gall." She drew a deep, shuddering breath. "I'm going to marry Carlo. It's too late, Jack, you lose. There's nothing you can do or say to change my mind. There's no possible way you're going to make Carlo look the fool by stealing me the night before our wedding, because I won't let it happen."

"Carlo's gay."

Her stomach dropped, and she took an involuntary step back from him. "What did you say?"

"Carlo's a homosexual."

Fear took her breath, her ability to think clearly. She swung away from Jack and brought her hands to her cheeks. Jack knew about Carlo. If Jack knew, he would tell Giovanni. She couldn't let that happen. It would destroy Carlo.

"I'm sorry, Becky Lynn." He crossed to her and touched her shoulder lightly. "I know what a blow this must be."

"How did you…when did you—"

"When Carlo got the Macro-Wear account, I knew. You see, I lost the account because I wouldn't sleep with Preston."

"That doesn't mean—"

"Yes, it does." He lowered his voice. "I did some checking around, asked a few questions."

She turned slowly to face him. She shook her head. "No, Jack, please… You didn't ask questions? Please tell me you didn't."

"I'm sorry," he murmured, his eyes soft with regret. "I thought you should know. I couldn't let…I couldn't let him do this to you."

She caught his hands. "Jack, I beg you…please, don't tell anyone. Don't ask any more questions."

For a moment, Jack gazed at her, shocked. "Are you saying…you already knew?" Her expression told him everything, because he shook his head, dumbfounded. "But then…why? He's gay, Becky Lynn. How can you… Why are you marrying him?"

She owed him nothing, and certainly not an explanation. He had thrown her away, not the other way around. She lifted her chin. "Figure it out, Jack. Take a long look in the mirror and figure it out."

He narrowed his eyes, a muscle jumping in his jaw. "So you're determined to do this stupid thing? There's nothing I can say to change your mind?"

Tell me you need me. Tell me you believe in me. Becky Lynn stiffened her spine, angry with herself for her thoughts. He cared for his vendetta with Carlo, not for her. He had come here tonight not to try to win her, but to hurt Carlo.

"Tomorrow at four-thirty, I'm marrying Carlo Triani. And if you tell anyone what you know, if you tell Giovanni, I'll fight you, Jack. I don't know how, but I'll find a way to hurt you."

She pushed past him, and for the second time, he stopped her by catching her hand. "Just tell me one thing. Are you in love with him, Becky Lynn? Is that why you're doing this?"

She gazed into his eyes and for the space of a heartbeat she thought her answer might actually matter to him, that she might matter to him. She called herself a fool.

"You lose again, Gallagher. And it's your own damn fault." She shook her hand free of his grasp. "Next time you see me, I'll be Mrs. Carlo Triani."

The nightgown had been a wedding gift. Made of white satin and lace, it was the most beautiful piece of lingerie

Becky Lynn had ever seen. So beautiful, she had almost cried when she opened it. She curled her fingers into the slippery-soft fabric and brought it to her cheek. She had more than she had ever hoped for, the kind of life she hadn't known enough to even dream of, and yet she wanted more. She wanted the impossible.

After a moment, she slipped the gown over her head, and the sensuous fabric whispered against her skin as it fell softly to her ankles. She crossed to her vanity, picked up her brush and ran it through her hair. She looked at her funny face in the vanity mirror and thought of the absurdity of it all—the same face that had been reviled as too ugly to look at, had earned her nearly two hundred thousand dollars last year, and even though she had more money than she knew what do do with, she missed her five-dollar-an-hour job as a photo assistant.

She shook her head at her own thoughts and dragged the brush rhythmically through her hair. Carlo had rented them a luxurious two-bedroom suite at the Bel Air Hotel. After the ceremony, they'd had dinner in the hotel dining room, then taken a stroll around the hotel grounds, admiring the elegant swans in the stream that wound its way through the property.

Now Carlo waited for her in their sitting room. She laid the brush carefully on the dressing table and went in search of her husband.

Room service had brought champagne and strawberries. Carlo had dimmed the lights and turned on soft music. He wore dark-colored pajama bottoms, they looked to be made out of some soft, slippery fabric. His naked chest, smooth and muscled, gleamed in the soft light, and she had to admit he was beautiful.

"Hi." She clasped her hands together, nervous, not knowing exactly what to expect.

He looked up and smiled. "You look…exquisite."

Her vision blurred. "Thank you."

"Come here." He held out a hand.

She crossed to him, the thick carpeting softly cushioning her bare feet. She fitted her hand to his, and he folded her into his arms, holding her lightly. "I love you, *bella.* I'll take good care of you."

"I know." She tipped her head back and met his eyes. "I love you, too."

He smiled tenderly, and brushed away a tear that rolled down her cheek. "Don't cry for him, he's not worth it."

Emotion choked her. When had Carlo learned to read her mind? "I know."

He kissed her forehead, then released her. "Have some champagne. It's a very good Dom."

"All right." She swallowed hard and watched him pour. The situation felt strange and wrong—too intimate for the friends they were, but not intimate enough for husband and wife. It would take some time to adjust, she decided, taking the glass from him. But once she did, it would be…fine. It would be good.

"To us."

She smiled and tapped her glass against his. "To us."

They sat on the small couch for a long time, sipping their champagne, making small talk. After a while, their conversation dwindled, then ceased altogether.

He met her eyes. "I suppose it's time to turn in."

"I suppose." She set her glass on the table and stood. "Thank you for…everything. It was a very…nice day."

He followed her to her feet. "You're welcome."

They stared at each other a moment, awkwardly. She cleared her throat. "Well...good night."

She started for her room, stopping when he called her name. She met his gaze over her shoulder.

"Would you like to share my bed tonight?"

She understood his offer and it had nothing to do with sex. Tears stung her eyes. "I don't want to be alone."

"Me, neither, *bella*. Come." He drew her toward his bedroom and the big four-poster bed. The maid had turned it down while they were at dinner, and it beckoned.

They climbed in, and Carlo eased her against his side, holding her carefully. His skin was warm against her, strong and male, and suddenly she felt more lonely than she ever had. This was the wedding night she had always dreamed of—the gown and bed, the tenderness and warmth. But not the love. Not the passion.

She drew in a tiny, broken breath. She bit her lip, not wanting him to know she was crying, not wanting to hurt him. He had given her so much.

Carlo propped himself up on an elbow and gazed down at her. She felt his gaze, though she didn't look up. "Don't be sorry, *bella*." He stroked her arm, her hair, her back. "Don't be sad."

"I'm not," she whispered. "You made me very happy today."

He turned her to face him and brushed her hair away from her face. Strands stuck to her wet cheeks and he smoothed them away, too. He searched her expression. "Then why are you crying?"

Her eyes brimmed again, and she cursed her tears. "Because I'm silly. Because I...I have so much. More than I ever thought I would."

"I know what's wrong, and I understand. You don't have to try to hide it from me." He caught a tear with his thumb and brushed it away. "I do want you to be happy."

He bent and kissed her softly and deeply, but without passion. She stiffened and tried to move away.

He stopped her, catching her hands and folding them in his. "Let me make you happy, Becky Lynn."

"You do, Carlo. You—"

"No, *bella*." He tightened his fingers over hers. "That's not what I mean. I want to please you tonight. On your wedding night."

She flattened her hands against his chest and looked helplessly up at him. Suddenly, she ached to be touched. Suddenly, she needed to be held and stroked and loved, she needed that so much, she hurt.

She swallowed her needs and shook her head. "You don't have to do this. Don't you see? It's not necessary."

"It is." He trailed his fingers over her face, then bent his head to hers once more. "Close your eyes," he whispered, his breath stirring against her cheek. "Let me make you happy."

She did as he asked, letting her head fall back against his chest. At first, his hands on her felt strange, wrong. At first she felt uncomfortable and like a fraud. But as he stroked her, softly, patiently—too patiently for a lover, too selflessly for passion, yet still sweetly and warmly—she began to relax.

With her eyes shut, she could close out her uncertainty and self-doubt, she could close herself off from everything but the gentle stroke of his flesh against hers. A flame, small but bright, ignited deep inside her, and she stirred, needing, and wanting, more.

He responded to her needs, sliding his hands under her gown, moving them up her thighs until her found her center. He sank into her; she whimpered and arched against his hand. He moved his fingers, caressing her deeply, rhythmically.

He bent and caught her mouth, her tongue, murmuring sounds of encouragement, still stroking, exciting her more. She curled her hands around his neck, her nails into his skin, her heart thundering. It had been so long…and she was hungry, so hungry.

Jack's image filled her head, and she remembered—everything. She arched up against Carlo's hand, clamping her thighs around him, holding him hard against her.

As she exploded with orgasm, she cried out Jack's name.

46

The bar resembled any number of others on Sunset, places where the young, rich and beautiful of Hollywood came to let down their hair and have some fun without being recognized or hassled.

Jack had come for neither. He had come to celebrate Becky Lynn and Carlo's nuptials by getting stinking, fall-down drunk. He intended to find company for the night, and to wake up tomorrow with a hangover the size of which he would never forget. He wasn't certain who this behavior would punish, but at the moment, he wanted to punish Becky Lynn.

Mrs. Carlo Triani.

The bartender poured him another shot of tequila, and Jack lifted it in a mocking, drunken salute. She had done it. Becky Lynn had married his snake-in-the-grass, faggot half brother.

Jack pulled his mouth into a tight, grim line. He hoped they would be as unhappy as hell together.

He tossed the shot back, then sucked on one of the stack of fresh lime wedges on the bar in front of him. He dropped the lime onto a cocktail napkin, turned over the shot glass, snapping it sharply onto the bar in front of him. He motioned the bartender to bring him another.

She had known about Carlo, and it hadn't mattered to her. Jack dragged a hand through his hair, dumbfounded.

It hadn't mattered to her. He couldn't figure it. Becky Lynn was devoted to the son of a bitch. She loved him.

Why? She had told him if he wanted an answer, to take a long look in the mirror. Right. She was marrying a guy who would never be a real husband to her, and she told him to look in the mirror? He couldn't figure it.

"Hey there."

Jack moved his gaze to the woman who had taken the bar stool next to his. He skimmed his gaze over her. She was beautiful, with thick dark hair and a full, slightly parted mouth that begged for the pressure of a man's against it. He lowered his gaze. Her silk blouse was partially unbuttoned, the gaping fabric revealed the curves of her lush, full breasts.

He lifted his shot glass in acknowledgment of her greeting, then tossed the drink back. He snapped the glass down on the bar, and wished she were a redhead, a natural carrot top with a slim, curveless body and a face with features that…a guy couldn't forget.

He swore under his breath and forced his attention to the woman beside him. "What's your name?"

"Meredith."

Shit. Strike two.

She motioned the bartender. After giving the man her order, she turned back to Jack, leaning provocatively forward. "What's yours?"

"Jack." He sounded surly even to his own ears.

She arched an eyebrow. "Why so glum, Jack?"

"Long, boring story," he muttered, gazing into his drink.

"I have all night."

He slid his gaze to hers once more. "Yeah?"

"Uh-huh." That sexy mouth curved into a suggestive half smile. "Maybe some company would cheer you up?"

She wet her lips. His body stirred. She was beautiful and willing. She was just the kind of company he had hoped to find when he'd walked into the bar at four-thirty this afternoon, hours ago now. No strings, no emotional involvement. They could pass a couple of hours, maybe the entire night, in the best possible way. And for those few hours, he could forget that this was Becky Lynn and Carlo's wedding night.

Mrs. Carlo Triani.

You lose again, Gallagher. And it's your own damn fault.

He tossed back the remainder of his drink and stood. "Thanks, Meredith. And I have to say the offer's tempting. But I'm afraid I wouldn't be good company tonight."

Book Five

Red

47

Becky Lynn and Carlo celebrated their fourth wedding anniversary on the island of St. John. They were on location together, doing a resort-wear spread for *Vogue.* That morning in private, they congratulated themselves on the success of their union. It had worked out just as they had hoped and planned. Occasionally, the rumor mill buzzed about Carlo's having male lovers, but the buzzing always died down. The industry accepted them as a couple, and although the marriage seemed incongruous with the customary standards of behavior, they accepted Valentine as a true and faithful wife.

That evening, their fellow fashionistas threw them a surprise party, and in testimony of how well she and Carlo had fooled the world, one of the other models got sloppy drunk and wept on Becky Lynn's shoulder about how jealous she was of her and Carlo's wonderful marriage.

Later that night while Carlo slept, Becky Lynn walked the floors of their elegant suite. She couldn't sleep, couldn't settle down enough to even try. Sleeplessness had become a recurring problem for her. It had gotten bad enough that she'd seen her doctor about it. He had suggested a mild sleep aid, but she had refused it. She had seen the devastation drugs wrought, and she was not about to exchange one prison for another.

Prison? She stopped on the description. Was that what she thought of her life? Was that what she thought of her marriage?

She shook her head. Of course not. She was happy. She and Carlo were happy together. It was just that she was... lonely.

The realization, one she had been unwilling to acknowledge to herself until now, echoed through her. She drew a deep breath. Even with her husband sleeping only a few feet away, she felt alone.

Longing for fresh air, Becky Lynn stepped out onto the small balcony off their sitting room. The sweet island breeze cleared her head, but didn't chase away the truth. Carlo was her friend, and during the course of their marriage, he had always been there for her. She had never had to face a decision or problem alone, she had never worried that she had no one she could trust or turn to if she needed a shoulder or an ear; she had known, without a shadow of a doubt, that she had someone in her corner.

But having a friend wasn't the same as having a love. And she couldn't deny the deep, hollow place inside her, the place that ached for something to fill it up, something that had nothing to do with beauty or professional and financial success.

Love. Intimacy and passion. She needed them to ease the ache. She needed the love of a man for a woman, the tie of passion and intimacy that bound two people together.

Jack.

Becky Lynn crossed to the balcony railing and curved her fingers around it. She leaned into the breeze, enjoying its tug against her hair, finding the way it molded her thin cotton gown to her body sensuous. She closed her eyes and allowed herself a moment to remember, to relive the exquisite pleasure of making love with Jack.

She sucked in a sharp breath and opened her eyes, forcing the memories away. Jack had forever become a part of her past when she had promised herself to his brother. She didn't miss his ego or his selfishness, didn't miss the way he had never looked at her as anything beyond his devoted little assistant.

But she did long to be held and stroked, to be excited and aroused, to be fulfilled. She longed for a man's hands—Jack's hands—longed for the way she had felt when he made love to her.

She doubted Carlo felt the same longings she did. He took the occasional lover; she had known up front that he would, he had been honest with her. And although she knew she shouldn't feel betrayed, she did, anyway.

She turned her back to the sultry tropical night, returning to the suite, shutting the balcony doors behind her. Her gaze lit on Carlo's photography gear, stacked by the sofa. It beckoned her, and she crossed to it, at once eager and hesitant.

She took one of his cameras, the 35mm, out of its case. She weighed it in her palm, then ran her fingers lightly over its sleek metal body. The camera brought back memories, holding it called to her in a way nothing else ever had except, perhaps, the glossies all those years ago.

She shook her head. Now she was one of the glossy illusions she had once pored over. Out there somewhere, was there a young girl, as lost and alone as she had been, poring over images of her and wishing for another life? Was she, in some way, making a difference in a confused and lonely existence?

She thought of her career, of her phenomenal success. Although not elevated to the status of supermodel, she wasn't far from it. Carlo predicted she would be offered a cosmetics contract—the crown jewel in any model's career—this year.

She should be excited. She should yearn for the success, the adulation. Instead, she worried over how visible she was becoming; she feared that somehow, some way, her past would find her. Becky Lynn shuddered. She couldn't imagine anything more horrible than having to face her past, and her father, again.

Because of her fear, she guarded her privacy, dodged interviews and the limelight, dodged the kinds of celebrity publicity events that most models craved.

It was holding her back; both Tremayne and Carlo said so. As was her refusal to shoot with Jack, who in the last two years had become one of fashion's premier photographers. When Tremayne groused about it, she simply told him that if he wouldn't put up with her decision, John Casablancas would.

The truth was, she didn't like modeling all that much. She had become adept at playing for the camera, at pretending, but it had never gotten any less painful. She still felt like a fraud, she still heard the jeers of the good people of Bend in her head.

She fitted a lens on to the camera body, and held the camera to her eye. Even though the camera was empty, she aimed and shot, then did it again. A modicum of tension eased from her; she smiled to herself and framed another shot.

"Having trouble sleeping again?"

She lowered the camera and looked over her shoulder. Carlo watched her from the bedroom doorway, his eyes heavy with sleep. Her cheeks heated at having been caught playing with his gear. "Yeah, I am."

"Is there anything I can do to help?"

She shifted her gaze to the camera in her lap and battled the ridiculous urge to cry. "I don't think so."

"Tomorrow night we'll be home. You'll be in your own bed. That should help."

Your bed—not ours. Never ours. She detached the lens, then slipped it and the camera into their respective cases, her vision blurring. "You're probably right."

For a moment, he said nothing, then he sighed. "Are you…unhappy, Becky Lynn?"

She hesitated, then shook her head. But she wasn't happy, either, and she couldn't tell him that. "I'm just…" She lifted her gaze to his. "I don't know what I am, Carlo. I guess I'm just tired."

"Come to my bed, *bella.*" He held out a hand. "I'll rub your back. You'll be asleep in no time."

She nodded, stood and crossed to him. Taking his hand, she let him lead her to their passionless bed.

Tremayne had outdone himself this time. He had managed to book Piquant, L.A.'s hottest new club, for an agency party. Consequently, nearly everyone who had received an invitation had decided to attend, and the club was filled to near bursting.

Becky Lynn sipped a mineral water, and moved through the crowd. She had arrived home from St. John less than twenty-four hours ago and would have skipped out tonight if Tremayne himself hadn't called to make sure she would be in attendance. Carlo had gone directly from St. John to a shoot in New York for a Macro-Wear menswear ad. Tonight she was on her own.

Someone was staring at her.

A shiver raced up her spine, and she glanced over her shoulder and scanned the crowd. No one seemed to be paying her any undo attention, but she shifted uncomfortably, anyway. All evening she'd had the feeling that someone watched her. She couldn't seem to shake the sensation, no matter how many times she looked over her shoulder and assured herself she was wrong.

"Valentine, love, welcome back."

She jumped, spilling some of her drink. "Tremayne! You startled me!"

"I see that." He gestured toward the dark stain on her silk skirt. "I hope it's not ruined."

She dabbed at it. "Not to worry. It's just mineral water."

"Mineral water," he repeated. "I wish all my girls had your self-control."

She followed his gaze to Zoe. The other model stood— if the way she had draped herself on a rock star could be called standing—across the room from them, obviously high out of her mind. Tremayne, Becky Lynn could tell, was not pleased.

Sympathy for Zoe curled through her, and Becky Lynn steered his attention away from the other model, hoping she would disappear before Tremayne called her aside and gave her a dressing-down. "Thank you so much for the beautiful flowers," she said brightly, touching his sleeve. "Carlo and I were touched that you remembered our special day."

Tremayne smiled affectionately. "Glad you liked them. How was St. John?"

"Glorious." From the corner of her eye she saw Zoe head out of the club, and she breathed a sigh of relief. "I see now why their beaches are called some of the most beautiful in the world."

Tremayne murmured something about the beaches of Monaco, then launched into a description of his last vacation there. Becky Lynn only half listened to him, her attention focused instead on the disturbing sensation that she was again being watched.

Tremayne leaned toward her conspiratorially. "I had a call from Martin Sebastian yesterday. He was asking about you."

She jerked her attention back to the agency owner, wondering what she had missed. "Should I know him?"

"You should." Tremayne arched his eyebrows every so slightly in reproach. "Sebastian Cosmetics. *The Sebastian Girl.* Moira Louise's contract is up this year."

"Is it? I—" Gooseflesh raced up her arms, and she looked quickly over her left shoulder, expecting to find someone right there, his—or her—gaze boring into her. Instead, of course, there was no one.

"Are you all right, Valentine?" Tremayne laid a hand on her arm in concern. "You're as nervous as a cat tonight."

She forced a smile. "I'm tired. In fact, I'm exhausted. I think I'd better beg off tonight, go home and get a good night's sleep."

He nodded solemnly. "You do that. Come in to the agency tomorrow and we'll talk."

Eager to escape the suffocating crowd and the creepy feeling of being watched, Becky Lynn said good-night to

Tremayne and started purposefully toward the door. She kept her gaze straight ahead, determined not to be stopped and drawn into conversation.

She shivered as she stepped outside. The night had grown cool, and she longed for the shawl she had decided to leave in her car. Hugging herself, she started for the parking lot across the street. When she'd arrived earlier, the valet line had been so long, she had decided to park the car herself.

"Miss Valentine, wait!"

She stopped and turned. The valet—one of the nice young men Tremayne hired for every one of his parties—jogged toward her. When he reached her, he looked a little embarrassed, and she smiled reassuringly. "What's up, Kenny?"

"I know you didn't valet tonight, but I don't think it's a good idea for you to walk clear over there by yourself. I'll get your car."

"Thanks, Kenny." She smiled again and handed him her keys. "That's real sweet of you."

He blushed and started off, and she wondered if he wasn't the tiniest bit smitten with her. She shook her head at the thought. Sometimes she—

"Becky Lynn?" a man said from behind her. "Is that you?"

She froze. The voice was one she recognized from her past, deepened with age and maturity, but still recognizable from the darkest days of her life.

Her brother. Randy.

She turned slowly, pulling her armor around her, calling forth every scrap of her in-front-of-camera experience to hide her feelings. But even with all that, she couldn't quite prepare herself for the shock of seeing him, of seeing the changes in him, or for the way memories spewed forth inside her.

A catch in her chest, she studied him. He had grown up, gotten even bigger, filled out. The lines that etched his eyes and mouth spoke of a hard life, of experience won through pain. *Randall Lee's brutal legacy.*

"It is you!" Her brother moved his gaze almost frantically over her. "Thank God…you're alive…you're well."

He hugged her to him. Caught off guard, she found herself pressed against his massive chest. She struggled to breathe evenly, struggled to keep from drowning in her own turbulent emotions. She stiffened, and held herself rigid in his embrace.

Randy dropped his arms and drew away from her. She saw the regrets in his eyes, the ghosts of their tragic past.

"Look at you," he said, going on as if he hadn't noticed that she had yet to speak, that she hadn't smiled. "So successful. So beautiful. You've just…blossomed."

How had he found her? she wondered, a bubble of hysteria rising inside her. What was he doing here?

He must have seen the questions in her eyes, because he answered them without her asking. "I'm a rookie with the L.A. Rams. A defensive tackle. When one of the other guys gave me an invitation to this party, I never thought…I mean, Becky Lynn, it's really you."

And it was really him—Madman Lee. The best football player Bend High School had ever had.

"We made it out, Becky Lynn." He grasped her upper arms and smiled. "We did it, kid. We did it."

Anger hit her with the force of a freight train at full speed. Now he wanted to be her brother. Now he wanted to smile and share self-congratulations, but when she had needed him desperately, he had betrayed her.

She began to shake, to tremble so badly, she knew he

could feel it. In her mind's eye, she could see him sitting beside their father on that battered, filthy couch, could see the moment he had looked up at her in shame and guilt.

He had known what Ricky and Tommy intended to do to her.

"Don't you lump us together," she said, her voice quivering with fury, with outrage. "Don't you stand there and act like we have anything to say to each other." She looked him straight in the eye. "And don't you dare try to act like you're my brother. A brother would never have done what you did."

She pushed past him, crossing to the valet station to await her car. He followed.

"Becky Lynn, please." He stopped beside her and touched her arm lightly. "Talk to me."

She swung to face him, not caring now if he saw everything she felt. "We have nothing to say to each other. Ten years ago, you made your choice. Live with it."

He caught her hands, his expression twisted with despair. "I have lived with it. Every day, every minute of these last years. Not one moment has passed that I haven't loathed myself for my cowardice, that I haven't wished, prayed, that I could turn the clock back. I let you down, I know that—"

"You let me down?" she repeated, incredulous, tugging her hands from his, unable to bear his touch. "Letting someone down is forgetting their birthday. Letting them down is breaking some small promise." She lowered her voice. "You tried to destroy me. You allowed three boys to knock me down and drag me behind some bushes. You allowed them to shove a paper bag over my head, you allowed them to force my legs apart and shove their penises into me. I thought I was going to die, it hurt so much."

His face contorted with misery. "I didn't know they were going to…do it. They'd talked, but I didn't—"

"You did nothing." She curved her arms tightly around herself.

"And when I came home, when you saw me…you lied for them. You covered for them."

"I'm sorry. So sorry, Becky Lynn. I know this doesn't excuse me, but I was scared. And so…alone. At the time, it seemed like those boys were all I had. I was so afraid that if I stood up to them—"

"So you sacrificed me?" Tears flooded her eyes. "You weren't alone, none of us were. We had each other, you had me." Her throat closed over the words and she struggled to clear it. "I was your sister. Your own flesh and blood. To betray me that way…to allow Ricky and Tommy—"

Her throat closed over the words once more, and she turned away from him. Ahead, she saw her car swing out of the parking lot across the street. *Kenny. Thank God.*

"Please, Becky Lynn. Forgive me. I have paid, you can't imagine how I've paid."

She lowered her gaze to her feet, then glanced over her shoulder at him. "Talk is cheap, Randy. Your actions all those years ago told me everything I need to know forever."

"Mama forgave me," he said quietly. "She understood. She—"

"Don't you say her name!" Becky Lynn whirled to face him, his words twisting inside her like a dull blade, sawing and tearing. "Don't you mention her to me."

"She died. Did you know that? Before she did, she talked about you. She said you were better off. She said—"

"Leave me alone!" Becky Lynn covered her ears. "You're dead to me. The past is dead to me."

Kenny roared up and hopped out of the car, his expression murderous. "Miss Valentine, are you okay?"

"This man's bothering me," she said, her voice shaking. She hurried toward the valet, and Kenny put himself between her and Randy, even though he was a third her brother's size.

"Get lost," Kenny said, sounding nervous but determined. "Before I call the cops."

Becky Lynn swung into her 450 SLC, shaking so badly, she wondered how she was going to be able to drive. She could hardly hold on to the steering wheel.

"Ricky and Tommy went to jail," Randy called as she started to close the door. "For raping Sue Anne Parker."

She stopped, her heart thundering. *Sue Anne Parker. Oh, God... Poor Sue Anne....* She squeezed her eyes shut, Randy's words echoing through her, touching every part of her. *Ricky and Tommy had gone to jail. They'd gone to jail.*

Dear Lord, it was the answer to a prayer.

"I testified, Becky Lynn. So did Buddy. They bragged about it and...and I couldn't let them get away with it again. I did it for you."

She sucked in a deep breath, and met his gaze through the open car door. From the corner of her eye, she saw Kenny's confusion and concern. "You should have done it because it was the right thing to do." She shook her head. "It's too late for us."

"Becky Lynn!"

The pain in his voice tore at her, but she hardened her heart against it. Randy had betrayed her—first by allowing Ricky and Tommy to hurt her, then later for lying about it, for letting them get away with it.

Her brother was dead to her. She would never forgive him. Never.

48

Becky Lynn sat bolt upright in bed, breathing hard, wet with the sweat of fear. She looked wildly around her, confused, expecting to see the shanties of Sunset, waiting for the smell of fecund earth and poverty to fill her head. Instead, she caught a whiff of the sandalwood potpourri she kept in a crystal bowl on her nightstand, and her gaze lighted on one after another of her things—the Chagall print above her dresser, the Victorian rocking chair draped with a cashmere shawl, the bottle of Chloe on her vanity, the silver music box Carlo had picked up for her in Spain.

She was home, in her own bed. She was far away from Bend, Mississippi; she was safe.

She breathed deeply through her nose and worked to dispel the lingering effects of her dream. In it, they had all been there—Ricky and Tommy, Randy and her father, all the good people of Bend, Mississippi. They had formed a circle around her, trapping her, pointing and laughing.

At first, their teasing had been good-natured, even if cruel and humiliating. But as she had tried to escape their circle, they had closed it on her, tighter and tighter. The closer they got to her, the uglier their taunting had become.

Becky Lynn brought her trembling hands to her face. They had begun to rip at her, tearing at her clothes and hair and skin, clawing off the illusion of beauty Carlo had created for her. She had cried for them to stop; she had tried to act like Valentine but when she had, they had heckled and jeered at her.

She wasn't Valentine, they had chanted. She was ugly Becky Lynn Lee, poor white trash.

Breathing deeply once more, Becky Lynn dragged her hands through her hair. What was she going to do? Tonight hadn't been the first time she'd had the dream. It had plagued her ever since she'd run into Randy at the agency party.

It had gotten so bad, she feared going to sleep at night. Hysterical laughter bubbled to her lips. Now she had two things to worry about—not being able to sleep, and when she could sleep, having nightmares.

She threw off the covers and crawled out of bed, going to the bathroom for a drink of water. She filled a glass and drank, then sank to the tile floor. Her thin gown served as no protection from the cold floor and her teeth began to chatter. She drew her knees to her chest and rested her forehead on them. She blamed Randy for the nightmares. He hadn't taken no for an answer, had ferreted out her address through the agency and had begun sending her letters. In the two weeks since that night, he had sent a dozen letters and cards. On the envelope of the last one, he had scrawled a plea to please talk to him. She had added her own to it—if he cared for her, please leave her be.

Other than that brief message, she had refused to communicate with him. And although she had sent back each letter unopened, each had served as a reminder of her past, each had torn a small hole in her veil of security.

She feared one day she would open the door and find him camped on her doorstep, or come home and find her answering machine filled with his voice.

Or worse, that she would find her father on her doorstep, his gravelly, evil voice on her machine.

Becky Lynn shivered, suddenly icy cold. She rubbed her arms in an attempt to ward off the chill. If only Carlo were home. Since St. John, he had been from New York to London, now back to New York. He had spent a total of four days in Los Angeles, and those he had spent in his studio, processing film. She hadn't told him about Randy; she had thought she could handle it.

She couldn't, she realized, standing. She needed him to comfort her, to assure her everything would be all right. He would probably be able to tell her how she could end this situation, quickly and efficiently. He was her husband, after all. He should know what was happening to her.

She was falling apart.

Pushing that thought away, Becky Lynn flipped on her bedside light, checked the clock. *Just after midnight.* Three hours later in New York, it was the middle of the night there. She hesitated a moment, then dug the number of Carlo's hotel out of her nightstand drawer.

A man answered the phone, a man whose voice she didn't recognize, although she had obviously awakened him from a deep sleep. At first, she thought the hotel operator had rung the wrong room, then realized she had not.

Carlo had company for the night.

Hugh Preston.

She felt the realization like a blow to her chest. Tears

flooded her eyes, and a small sound slipped past her lips, a whimper of pain and betrayal.

She hung up the phone without speaking.

49

The entire studio waited for Zoe. Restless energy crackled in the air, a combination of tension and boredom, anger and expectation. And nerves, stretched to the snapping point.

As each minute ticked past, with an entire shoot crew left twiddling their thumbs, money simply whirled down the drain.

Jack checked his watch and swore silently. He had booked Zoe despite the things he'd been hearing about her performance. She had never failed to perform for him; and when she was on in front of the camera, she made magic. He had decided to give her the benefit of the doubt. Now his ass was on the line.

The advertising agency's art director strode toward him, his expression thunderous. "Where the hell is she, Jack? This is costing us money. A lot of money."

Jack worked to keep his expression and stance relaxed, his voice calm and confident. "She'll be here, Bill. She's probably run into traffic. Pete's talking to the agency now." He placed a hand reassuringly on the other man's shoulder. "Don't worry, I can make up for this lost time. We will absolutely wrap today."

"You're certain?" The man looked relieved, if only a bit. "We can't afford overtime."

"I'm positive." Jack motioned the spread of pastries and

breakfast breads. "Have another cup of coffee, and I'll get an update."

Jack crossed to his assistant, furious now. He had just made a promise he had to keep, but if too much more time passed, it would be near impossible to do so. "Dammit, Pete, what did the agency say?"

"They're trying to find her. Gail sent someone over to Zoe's place, she wasn't there."

Jack swore under his breath. Zoe was already an hour and a half late; he had better face the fact that she might not show at all. "Call Gail back. Have her get somebody else over here."

"Who do you want?"

"I want fast, and I want now. And I need somebody with experience, we have time to make up for." Jack made a sound of disgust. "Ask for somebody who looks like Zoe. Bill wants long blond hair and tits."

Pete nodded and started for the office. Jack stopped him. "Make sure Gail understands how unhappy I am about this."

Pete nodded again and hurried off. Minutes later, he rushed back, out of breath. "Call made, but…she's here."

"Zoe's here?"

"Yeah."

"Great. Get her into makeup then cancel that ca—" Jack bit the words back at his assistant's expression. "What now?"

"You'd better take a look at her, Jack. She's in the office."

Jack nodded and followed Pete, dread forming a knot in the pit of his stomach. When he caught sight of Zoe, he stopped, shocked and sickened. She looked wasted—as if she'd been out all night, many nights running. Her face was gaunt, her eyes dark and hollowed; she looked as though she hadn't bathed. And her head kept bobbing—like one of those tacky dogs he sometimes saw in the back of cars in east Los Angeles. She could hardly keep her eyes open.

He turned to his assistant. "Bring me a sweet roll, the gooier the better, a Coke and a cup of strong, black coffee. Then tell makeup and hair to get ready to do the work of their lives."

"Should I cancel that call—"

"Hell no. We'll get started, but I'm not confident Zoe's going to be able to pull this off." As Pete started to walk away, Jack stopped him. "And keep Bill the hell away from her, or our asses will all be in the fire."

Jack stepped into the office, snapping the door shut behind him. Zoe's head sprang up, and again he thought of one of those ridiculous dogs. "What were you thinking of?" he demanded. "Coming here an hour and a half late, and looking like…like this?"

Her eyes flooded with tears and her chin trembled. "I'm sorry, Jack. I really am. I—"

He cut her off, and advanced on her. "This isn't just your reputation you're fucking with. It's mine. It's the ad agency's." He stopped directly in front of her and he saw how difficult it was for her to stay focused on him. "Today you put the client's budget at risk. In the process, you put all of us at risk."

"I'm sorry, Jack." She twisted her fingers in her lap. "I just forgot, I didn't set my alarm and—"

"Don't give me any shit." He rested a hand on each of her chair arms and leaned toward her. "You're in trouble,

Zoe. You're trashing your career, your life. Already most of the shooters in town won't work with you. And what do you expect me to do? Do you expect me to book you again after you pull a stunt like this?"

"Please don't fire me." She grabbed his shirt and clutched at it. "Don't call Tremayne. Please, Jack."

Compassion pulled at him. And concern. He remembered the sassy, bright girl she had been when he first met her, and the memory hurt.

He shouldn't let personal feelings get in the way of his professional duty. He hadn't miscommunicated to her the seriousness of her actions—she had put them all at risk. But he couldn't just…abandon her.

He made a sound of self-disgust and straightened, forcing her to drop her hands. "If it were anybody but you, I'd kick you off my set right now, then I'd call Tremayne and raise hell. One chance, Zoe. Do you understand me? I'm giving you only this one chance."

"Thank you, Jack. Thank you." She stood, swaying a little when she made it to her feet. "I'll do better, you'll see. I will."

Pete eased into the office with the food and drink. Jack glanced over his shoulder at his assistant, then turned back to her, narrowing his eyes. Zoe had always been tough, if he was going to reach her, he had to be just as tough, and as blunt as he could be.

"It's sickening to see you this way, Zoe. You could have had it all, but instead, you're throwing it away on drugs. Your career, your health, your looks." Pete brought her the sweet roll, and she stared at it as if it turned her stomach. Jack shook his head. "Get some help, girl. You really need it. If you don't, I'm afraid I'm going to be attending a funeral. Yours."

Two hours later, Jack called a break. This shoot, the last two hours, represented a professional low. Pulling shots out of Zoe had been like pulling nails out of concrete. She could hardly keep her eyes open, let alone focused. He had worked with first-timers who had been better able to follow his direction.

Hiding her needle tracks had been almost impossible. The makeup artist, a seasoned veteran who had dealt with almost everything, had been near tears with frustration.

Jack marked several rolls of film and dropped them into his bag. Until he had seen the tracks, he hadn't realized Zoe was using. He hadn't realized she had graduated to needles or just how deeply in trouble she was.

He had seen this sort of thing happen to models before—suddenly they had money and attention; they became addicted to the life-style, to the men and parties and substances. Then, just as suddenly, they were missing jobs, losing bookings. Once a model started that deadly downward spiral, it was almost impossible to pull themselves out. A few made it, a very few.

"Jack! Christ, you're not going to believe this."

Jack looked at his assistant's face, so pale his freckles stood out in shocking relief. His stomach sank, and he knew without asking that what his assistant had to say he wouldn't like—and that it was about Zoe. He asked, anyway. "What?"

"She's gone. Zoe's…gone."

"Gone?" he repeated, his heart beginning to thunder.

"She climbed out the bathroom window."

She hadn't heard one thing he'd said. Jack dragged a hand through his hair, angry and frustrated, disappointed.

"There's more, Jack. She…she left wearing the dress."

Jack searched Pete's expression waiting—praying—for a punch line, a *gotcha!* he knew wouldn't come.

Zoe's career was over, Jack acknowledged. Now it was a matter of finding a way to save her life.

Jack figured if anybody could get through to Zoe, it would be Becky Lynn. The two had been close at one time, when they'd all been young and struggling, before everything had changed.

Before he had screwed everything up.

He frowned and pulled his car to a stop in front of her and Carlo's bungalow. He should have tried calling, but he had decided that giving her an opportunity to refuse to speak with him wouldn't be the wisest strategy. Besides, a face-to-face discussion would be more effective.

He had wanted to see her.

He frowned again, not liking the direction of his thoughts. He had come here out of concern for Zoe, not for other, more personal reasons, not because the need to see Becky Lynn clawed at his gut. And certainly not because he couldn't put her out of his mind.

He crossed to the front door and rang the bell. She answered within moments, and he could see she wasn't happy to see him. Of course, he hadn't expected her to be.

"What do you want, Gallagher?"

He flashed her a cocky smile, knowing it would send her blood pressure skyrocketing. "Hello to you, too, Red."

As expected, fire flew into her eyes. "I don't have time for this."

She swung the door shut; he caught it with his palm. "I came to talk to you about Zoe."

Becky Lynn hesitated, then frowned. "What about Zoe?"

"May I come in?"

She glanced over her shoulder, and he saw her uncertainty. She still felt something for him, he realized, self-satisfaction curling through him. Otherwise, she wouldn't hesitate to let him in; otherwise, she wouldn't think twice about being alone with him.

"What's the matter?" he asked, purposely pushing her buttons. "Don't you trust yourself with me?"

Just as he had known it would, his comment got her back up. She made a sound of disgust. "You have three minutes."

She threw the door open and stalked inside, expecting him to follow. He did, glancing around in curiosity as he crossed the threshold. "Nice place."

Fists on her hips, she glared at him. "Clock's ticking."

He slipped out of his jacket and tossed it over one of the rattan and suede chairs. She narrowed her eyes, obviously annoyed at the way he was making himself at home. He lifted his eyebrows in exaggerated innocence. "You don't mind, do you?"

"Not at all. Put your jacket back on and your time's up." She folded her arms across her chest. "You came about Zoe?"

"Yeah." He frowned. "I'm worried about her. She's in trouble. Big trouble." His frown deepened. "She came to a shoot yesterday, and she was pretty messed up." He filled Becky Lynn in on the details, and as he did, her expression became concerned.

"Needle tracks?" she repeated, surprised and distressed. "You're sure?"

"Oh, yeah, I'm sure. The makeup artist couldn't even conceal them. And by the looks of her arms, she's been using for some time." He drew his eyebrows together. "You didn't know she'd graduated to needles?"

Becky Lynn shook her head. "Did you?"

"Hell no. I wouldn't have booked her if I had."

Her mouth tightened. "Of course you wouldn't have."

"What's that supposed to mean?"

"As if you didn't know." Becky Lynn tipped her head back and met his eyes. "Jack Gallagher would never let anything get in the way of his career, his ambition. And certainly never a friend."

He narrowed his eyes. "Zoe's not my friend. She never has been. Besides, business is business."

"'Business is business,'" she mimicked, taking a step toward him, her expression furious. "So what was that thing with Garnet McCall all about? Where do you draw the line between business and personal?"

"That's ancient history."

"Is it? Well, Zoe's not. You don't call her a friend, but you slept with her. God, you make me sick!"

She spun away from him, and he followed, pulse pounding. He caught her elbow. "Wait a minute! What do you mean, I slept with Zoe?"

"Which part don't you understand?" she asked scathingly, jerking her arm from his grasp. "You didn't think I knew. You didn't think I had found out. Now you're concerned about her, but back then, instead of helping her, you fed into her sickness."

"Hold on." Jack looked Becky Lynn dead in the eyes, not believing what he was being accused of. "I didn't sleep with Zoe. Not ever."

"Oh, please." She placed her fists on her hips. "Don't lie about it now, Zoe told me ages ago. Surely you're man enough to stand up for your own actions, despicable though they may be. After all, now you have nothing to lose."

He took a step toward her, jaw and fists clenched. "I did not, repeat did not, sleep with Zoe."

"Oh, come on, Jack—"

He cupped her face in his hands. "I didn't sleep with her because of just what you said. And because I was with you then."

Tears flooded her eyes, and she broke free of his grasp. She crossed to the doors that led to the terrace and gazed out. "Because you were with me," she repeated, her voice thick. "That didn't stop you from screwing Garnet McCall, did it?"

Jack felt her words like a punch to the gut. What could he say? To claim youth, bad judgment, or whatever now, from this point in his life, after having made it to the top, seemed both weak and pitiable. Besides, looking back, there had been many reasons he'd done what he had— business, immaturity, maybe even fear.

He stopped on the thought. He had been afraid— because he'd gotten so close to Becky Lynn, because he had grown to care too much for her, because caring, and exclusivity, had never been a part of his plans. Wouldn't she laugh at that now?

After a moment of his silence, she glanced over her shoulder at him. "Why did you come here today? Why did you think I could help Zoe?"

Those were two unrelated questions, he realized. His coming here, in truth, had had little to do with Zoe. "I thought you were friends."

"We haven't been friends in a...long time. Actually, I discovered we never really were."

She tried to mask the hurt in her voice but couldn't, and he longed to touch her, to comfort her. He jammed his hands into his pockets. "What about us, Becky Lynn?"

"There is no us." She turned back to the window and the brilliant garden beyond. "There hasn't been in a long time."

He crossed to stand beside her, his proximity forcing her to look at him. "I think you're wrong. I think there still is an us, even if we both want to deny it."

"I'm a married woman."

He laughed, the sound tight and angry even to his own ears. "Your marriage is a sham. And you know it." He took a step closer to her; she took a step back. "I think you still feel something for me, Becky Lynn. I think you still want me."

Color stained her cheeks. "Get out."

"If not, why won't you shoot with me? Why, for five years, have you refused to work with one of the top fashion photographers in the world? If you feel nothing for me, what's the problem?"

"I've been booked." She narrowed her eyes and tipped her chin up. "If you haven't noticed, I'm in demand these days. I hardly have time to be at your beck and call."

He leaned toward her, a smile tugging at his mouth. "You're running scared."

"Go to hell."

She moved away from him, he followed her. "Prove you don't want me… Shoot with me, Becky Lynn."

"I don't have to prove anything to you." She faced him, shaking with anger. "Don't you get it? You mean nothing to me. Nothing."

"Then prove it to yourself."

Her breath caught and he knew he had touched a nerve. "For the second time, go to hell, Jack Gallagher."

He laughed. "You're so scared, you're practically wetting your pants. You're afraid if you shoot with me, you'll end up in my bed."

"You bastard, you egotistical jerk." She fisted her fingers. "You offer me a booking I'm available for, and if you can afford my day rate, I'll shoot with you."

"You're on, Red." He collected his jacket, then crossed to the door, stopping and looking over his shoulder at her when he reached it. "I look forward to working with you. I'll be in touch."

Grinning, Jack crossed the driveway to his car, slid inside and picked up his cellular. He started the car and simultaneously punched in the number for The Davis Agency. No way was he going to give her the opportunity to change her mind. And if he gave Becky Lynn time to cool down, she would.

He asked for Valentine's booker, and had the woman check Valentine's schedule. He knew just the shoot he wanted her for—Garnet's fall catalog. The designer had done her entire line in shades of red—from fire engine to rose, from cinnabar to melon. They were shooting in sultry New Orleans, and he wanted all redheads for the shoot. His first choice had always been Becky Lynn, but he hadn't thought he had a chance of booking her.

Now he did. He smiled again. Now, even if he had to completely reschedule the dates of the shoot, he would have Valentine.

As he hung up the phone, he acknowledged that wanting Valentine for a job had little to do with why he wanted Becky Lynn in New Orleans with him.

50

Becky Lynn couldn't sleep. Her French Quarter hotel room was hot, stifling. The ceiling fan turned slowly, stirring up the moist, warm air, creaking with each revolution. She rolled onto her side, then switched to her back. The damp sheets tangled around her legs, anchoring them together like some sort of bizarre chastity belt.

From outside drifted in the raucous sounds of Bourbon Street, the haunting strains of a saxophone on some nearby corner, the faint click of high heels on the courtyard floor below.

Damn this city, she thought, viciously plumping her pillow. It had gotten to her. Sex was everywhere here—in the strip clubs on Bourbon Street, to couples groping in doorways, to the way the women moved, slowly and with a distinct sway, to the moist heat that permeated everything, even air-conditioned rooms.

She slammed her fist into the pillow again. And damn Jack Gallagher, for maneuvering her into this untenable position, for booking them in adjoining rooms and for being in that room with another woman.

She flipped onto her back and swore. Teri, one of the other models on location, had been all over Jack for the entire shoot—touching him, teasing him, coming on to him. And Becky Lynn knew Jack-the-ever-ready-wonder, wouldn't miss the opportunity to bed a beautiful babe. By the end of today, the last day of the shoot, she had been ready to scratch the other woman's eyes out. And ready to do worse to Jack. Much worse.

She thought of Jack and Teri, together in his bed. Twined together, panting, making love. Swearing, Becky Lynn sat up. She lifted her hair away from her neck and drew in a deep, agitated breath.

She shifted her gaze to the French doors that led to her balcony, and glared at the gentle moonlight that streamed through, making soft squares of light on her bedroom floor.

The balcony that connected her room to Jack's.

She pictured Jack, naked, thrusting into a woman—into her. She imagined his hands on her, imagined arching into those magic hands, crying out his name with her release.

A shudder of awareness rippled through her; she cursed it, cursed this wanton, red town. The atmosphere had gotten to her, the shoot had gotten to her. Not Jack. Not the husky way he had murmured her name while giving her direction, not the way he had gazed deeply into her eyes, not the way his smoky voice had moved over her like a caress.

She fisted her fingers into the damp, tangled sheets. Tomorrow she left for home; once there, in her own safe bed, she would be fine, she would have her sanity back.

Her own safe bed. Her lonely bed.

She didn't want her own bed, she wanted Jack's.

With a cry, she ripped back the sheet and jumped out of bed. She crossed to the French doors and gazed out at the night, at the cool, shadowed courtyard two floors below. She pressed her fingers to the glass, longing to go out, longing to escape her suffocating room and her own desperate thoughts.

She threw open the doors. Silence greeted her, as did the crisp night air, deliciously cool against her damp, fevered flesh. She sucked in a quick breath of pleasure and moved farther out on the balcony to its edge, to the wrought-iron railing that circled it. The scent of a flower, its perfume heavy and fragrant, assailed her. The tinkling splash from the courtyard fountain melded with the sound of her own breathing, her own heartbeat.

She wasn't alone.

Gooseflesh raced up her arms, and she turned her head. Jack stood on his half of the balcony, his doors, as hers, thrown wide to the night. The moonlight fell across his naked chest, creating sensual shapes of light and dark on his skin. Although shadowed, she felt his gaze as strongly as if he touched her.

He wore nothing but a pair of brief running shorts, and she moved her gaze slowly, hungrily over him. She thought of the first time they had been together, when they had come together in her grief. So much time had passed since then, she thought, her heart heavy and fast, so much time and space and life stood between them.

One moment became many. Still he gazed at her, until the air crackled with something electric, undeniable and red-hot. Her nipples hardened and pressed against her light cotton gown, aching for a rougher, more intimate touch. Lower, much lower, she grew hot and wet. She heard the thunder of her own heart, the quick hiss of his sharply indrawn breath.

Without a word, he strode across the balcony. His hard hands found her face and cupped it; his mouth crashed down to hers. Her head bent backward under the force of his kiss, and she brought her hands to his hair, twining her fingers in the crisp strands, anchoring him to her, meeting his force with her own.

They stumbled into her room; he kicked the doors shut behind them, then spun her around and flattened her against one. "Damn you, Becky Lynn," he muttered against her mouth, bringing his hands to her breasts, cupping them. "Damn you to hell."

She broke free of his mouth, panting. "What's the matter, Teri turn you down?"

"I didn't want Teri," he said tightly, grabbing the neck of her gown, ripping it away from her, revealing her breasts. "I want you. Only you." He brought his head to her chest, and she arched against his mouth, raking her nails over his shoulders and down his back, as desperate for him as he was for her.

He bit; she clawed. They pushed at each other, ripped at each other like animals. He tore away the last of her gown; together they struggled with his shorts, yanking them frantically over his hips, coming together again, completely naked.

Jack lifted her onto him and thrust into her, forcing her so hard against the French door that the panes of glass rattled. She curved her legs around him, anchoring him to her, meeting each of his thrusts with one of her own. Their mating wasn't pretty, it wasn't soft or affectionate. It was angry and desperate and all-consuming.

Jack caught her mouth deeply and passionately. Possessively. He caressed the inside of her, exploring every inch of her mouth—and every inch of her sex. She cried out, curling her fingers into his hair, tightening them until she knew she hurt him but unable to ease her grip.

They climaxed together.

Without drawing out of her, he carried her to the bed. They fell onto it, him taking their weight. When she tried to extricate herself from him, he tightened his arms around her and shifted so they lay on their sides facing each other. He kissed her, slowly and softly, moving his hands and his hips, growing hard again inside her.

The second time was tender, exquisitely so. Jack roamed her with his hands and mouth, exploring and enjoying, arousing and relearning, but most of all adoring. He worshiped her body, treating her to a tenderness he had never shown her before.

She quaked and shuddered and held him to her, crying out his name, her hips bucking up off the bed, anxious, so anxious to join with him again. But he held her off, making her wait, bringing her to the brink time and again, until finally, with his own groan of need, he drew her on top of him.

The ride was swift and tumultuous. She collapsed against him at the same moment he shuddered with his own release. For long moments, they lay like that, neither speaking. As the seconds ticked past, their hearts slowed, and their flesh cooled. Still, they didn't speak.

She loved him. Becky Lynn squeezed her eyes shut. *She had never stopped.*

Becky Lynn bit down on her lower lip to keep from crying out. She'd let herself down, she'd let Carlo down. She had promised herself she would be faithful to her husband; they had promised to forsake all others. Yet, even after everything, she had never stopped loving Jack.

She eased off him and onto her side. She felt his questioning glance but didn't meet it.

What was wrong with her? She wanted him so badly, she was willing to lay herself bare for him, yet he would never do the same for her. He had never believed in her, had never seen her as anything but an addendum to him and his needs, be they professional or sexual.

"What's wrong?" he murmured, mimicking her thought of a moment before but with different intent. He moved his hand gently over her hair.

She squeezed her eyes shut against the tears that rushed to her eyes. When she spoke, her voice was clear and without waver. "I want you to go now."

"Becky Lynn?" He turned her face to his; she met his gaze evenly. "Is something wrong?"

"I just… I want you to go back to your room."

For a moment, she thought she saw hurt in his eyes, then she called herself a fool. Jack had a much thicker skin than that—to be able to hurt him, he would have to care for her.

"Fine," he muttered and swung out of bed. She curled into a ball of misery. He found his shorts, then pulled them on; she felt his gaze on her. She didn't look at him, she couldn't. If she did, she might beg him to come back to bed, she might totally humiliate herself and beg him to love her.

He released a pent-up breath. "What do you want me to say, Becky Lynn? What do you want me to do?"

"Nothing," she whispered. "There's nothing to say or do." She drew a ragged breath. "Just go. Please."

For a long time after he left, she lay unmoving on the bed. She had let herself down, she had let Carlo down. She was a fraud; she felt like a cheat.

And neither changed the fact that she still loved Jack.

Becky Lynn turned onto her back and gazed up at the slowly spinning ceiling fan. Tangled in the sheets that smelled like their sex, she wondered what she was going to do now.

51

Jack awakened to find Becky Lynn had gone. Sometime during the night, sometime in the few hours between when he had left her room and when the group assembled at the airport for their return flights, she had returned to Los Angeles. She had left a message at the front desk for one of the other models. She missed her husband, she'd written. She had gone home early.

She had run back to Carlo's safe arms, Jack thought, his mouth twisting cynically, back to her husband's passionless arms.

That had been a month ago; he hadn't seen or talked to her since.

Frustration tightened in his gut, and he muttered an oath. What they'd shared had been special, cataclysmic and stunning. It had changed the way he would look at women, and at sex, forever.

And she had simply walked away. She had kicked him out of her bed, then left without a word.

He hadn't a clue how she could have done that—he had been unable to sleep, eat or concentrate for wanting her. The want burned hot and bright inside him, stealing his sense of balance, his focus.

All he could think of, even all these weeks later, was of making love with her again.

Jack stepped into one of the Plaza Hotel's elevators

and punched the appropriate floor for the grand ballroom. He would see Becky Lynn tonight, finally. As Carlo's *adoring* wife, she would be required to be in attendance at this glittering tribute to Giovanni.

The fashionistas were throwing the old photographer a gala sixty-fifth birthday party, using the occasion as a tribute to his contribution to the art of fashion photography and his lifelong impact on the fashion industry—the man who had created the Fashion Scenario and had forever changed the face of fashion photography. Being held in conjunction with the New York showings of the designers' fall collections, fashionistas from coast-to-coast—and beyond—would be in attendance. Jack doubted many RSVPs had been returned in the negative.

He narrowed his gaze in determination. Tonight, he and Becky Lynn would talk.

Jack alighted from the elevator, nodding to various people he recognized on his way to the ballroom, but intending to stop and speak to only one.

Becky Lynn.

The ballroom had been lavishly decorated with the usual fare—balloons and streamers, elaborate flower arrangements and ice sculptures—but also with wall-size enlargements of some of Giovanni's most memorable, and influential, images.

Jack moved his gaze over them, their power stirring him deeply. No matter what he thought of Giovanni as a man, Jack couldn't deny either his gigantic talent or his awesome contribution to the medium.

The crowd parted and Jack caught sight of Becky Lynn, her bright hair a beacon in a room full of ordinary blondes and brunettes. He gazed at her, his heart in his throat, his pulse buzzing in his head.

As if she sensed his gaze, she turned her head. Their eyes met. He felt the connection as an almost physical thing, as a shock to his system. He started for her, picking his way through the throng, never taking his gaze from hers.

When he got close enough to see the awareness in her eyes, she turned and walked away. For the entire evening, in a kind of sexual thrust and parry, a kind of frustrating and erotic mating dance, they circled each other. He caught speculative gazes on them, he didn't care if anyone knew what he was thinking and feeling; he hoped they did. He wanted to stake his claim on Becky Lynn Lee, and he intended to do just that.

She wouldn't stay with Carlo. After what they had shared, she couldn't.

"Hello, son."

Jack drew his eyebrows together and turned to face Giovanni.

Several times during the evening, he had been aware of the old man's gaze on him and had wondered about it. Giovanni had never paid him any attention before, why tonight?

Jack lifted his eyebrows in cool question. "Hello, Giovanni."

The older man smiled. "I see I've surprised you."

Jack inclined his head. "We haven't spoken to each other in a long time. But then, we've had no reason to."

"No?" Giovanni swept his gaze speculatively over Jack. "I've watched what you've done, what you've accomplished over the years."

"Have you?"

The man nodded. "I've been proud."

"Really? Proud?" Jack slipped his hands into his trouser pockets and arched his eyebrows again. "But what do you have to be proud of? You have had nothing to do with my success."

"No? My blood runs in your veins. It has been obvious all along."

Jack narrowed his eyes. This was the moment he had worked for, yet he felt nothing but a vague dislike for the man standing across from him, a mild revulsion. "How do you figure that? I seem to remember something about you already having a son. I seem to remember something about an arrangement with my mother."

Giovanni lifted his shoulders, as if tossing the comments off as insignificant. "Neither changes the fact that you have Triani blood. That I am a part of you." He made a sound of disgust. "Carlo, he is dead to me. He is weak, like his mother was. And he is not a man."

Jack frowned. "What do you mean?"

"Even the woman Carlo calls his own, she is besotted with you." Giovanni shook his head. "I had heard rumors about Carlo, but I had not known for sure. Until tonight."

At Jack's look, Giovanni laughed. "You don't think I see? The sex, it smolders between you two. I can smell it. It has never been that way between her and Carlo, Carlo and any woman." His gaze traveled over Jack's head, and his mouth twisted with disgust. "But with Carlo I have smelled it with other men. *Malato.* It makes me sick."

Jack glanced over his shoulder. Carlo and Hugh Preston were together, talking quietly. They had been inseparable all evening. And although they stood respectable distances from each other, even though their body language remained businesslike, Jack saw an unmistakable intimacy in the way they reacted to each other.

Jack had figured he'd picked up on it because he knew the truth about the two men, he hadn't thought anyone else would. He'd been wrong, obviously. He felt a moment of sympathy for his half brother, an urge to deny Giovanni's assertions, to hotly defend his brother.

He called himself a fool. Carlo would never defend him. He had done everything he could to keep him down and hurt him, including stealing Becky Lynn.

He returned his gaze to Giovanni's. "What are you getting at?"

Giovanni looked at Carlo once more. A small, self-satisfied smile tugged at his mouth. "They have asked me to say a few words to the gathering. Stay. They will be interesting words."

Jack watched the photographer, his father, walk away, struggling to sort through the storm of emotion raging inside him. He thought of the eight-year-old boy who had conquered his fear and taken his heart to that man, only to have it crushed, only to be cruelly rejected. He thought of his vow, his promise to himself, that one day his father would want him, and realized that victory was almost his.

Giovanni was proud of Jack's accomplishments. He had called him son; he had acknowledged their shared blood.

Where was his elation? he wondered, frowning. Where was his sense of accomplishment? His pleasure?

Giovanni's choosing him over Carlo had nothing to do with him or his accomplishments. He had become the favorite son by default—simply because he was sexually aroused by women instead of men.

Jack swore, swung away from the dais and started for one of the ballroom's side exits. He had no intention of listening to anything else Giovanni had to say, he had no want to hear him. Just their brief exchange had left him with a sour taste in his mouth.

As he stepped out of the ballroom, he saw Becky Lynn up ahead, disappearing down the hallway that led to the rest rooms. He darted a glance over his shoulder, then followed her.

The hallway was empty. Smiling to himself, he followed her into the ladies' room.

Becky Lynn stood at the mirror, straightening the bodice of her low-cut gown. "Alone at last," he murmured, his lips lifting, arousal kicking him squarely in the gut. "And not a moment too soon."

She turned and met his eyes, her mouth forming a small, surprised *oh.* She harnessed her surprise and shook her head, managing to look indignant. "You can't be in here, Jack."

He cocked an eyebrow and started toward her. "No? But I am. What does that mean?"

She took a step backward, a lovely shade of rose climbing up her chest and neck, over her cheekbones, going all the way to her hairline. "That you're a pervert?" she suggested, her cool tone belied by her wild flush.

"A desperate pervert." He took another step and so did she. Her backside encountered the sink. "Desperate for this." He took yet another step forward; his hips met hers.

She sucked in a sharp breath. "Jack...please."

He leaned his head close to hers. "Please?"

"Don't." Even as she murmured the words, she arched ever so slightly into him, pressing her pelvis closer to his.

"Don't what?" He laid his hand on her chest, on the creamy skin and curve of her breast exposed by the gown's daring neckline. "This?" The breath hissed past her lips, and beneath his palm, her heart beat wildly. Her nipples hardened, and gooseflesh raced over her skin.

With a soft laugh, he trailed his fingers over the delicate bumps. He leaned his head to hers, his mouth to her ear. "I want you, Red. Since New Orleans, I haven't been able to think of anything but you…and me…together." He punctuated each word with a nip to the fragrant flesh of her throat.

She flattened her hands against his chest, her own chest rising and falling with her agitated breathing. "Anyone could come in."

"Let them."

He slid his hands into the vee of her dress and cupped her breasts. She shuddered and curled her fingers into his tuxedo lapels. "This is a mistake. New Orleans was a mistake."

"Mmm." He moved his palms back and forth across her erect nipples. "Is that why you left?"

"You know why I left." Her head fell back as he lowered his mouth to her breast. "I missed Carlo—"

"Liar." He bit her gently, and she moaned. "You left because what happened between us frightened you."

From outside the door, came the sound of women's voices. Jack spun Becky Lynn into the last stall, snapping the door shut just as the women walked into the bathroom.

Becky Lynn looked horrified. He smiled and laid a finger against his lips, then pointed to the floor. With her standing between him and the door, her evening gown blocked any view of his feet from outside.

He bent his head to her and pressed his mouth to her ear. "Now I have you just where I want you."

Her eyes widened, then she shook her head and glared at him.

He pressed his mouth to her ear once more. "Yes," he whispered, only for her. "I'm going to make love to you, Becky Lynn."

She glared at him again. He ignored her wordless warning and brought his mouth to hers in a deep kiss. She refused him her tongue. Undaunted, he lowered his lips to her throat and shoulders; he trailed his fingers across her collarbone and down the sides of her breasts.

Becky Lynn began to tremble. Her breath came faster, and she bit down on her bottom lip to keep from verbalizing her arousal, her pleasure. She flexed her fingers, fighting the sensations, fighting him, then finally brought her hands to his hair and twined her fingers in it, clutching him to her.

And as the women chatted and smoked just beyond the stall door, she offered him her mouth and her tongue.

Her dress zipped on the side. Ever so slowly, careful not to make a sound, he eased the zipper down, then slid a hand inside. Her abdomen was smooth and soft and slightly damp. He skimmed his hand lower; her panties were soaked.

She began to quiver. He nudged the bit of lace and nylon aside and buried his fingers inside her. She widened her stance, bucking and arching against his fingers, pressing the flat of her hands against the stall walls, bracing herself.

Her head fell back, and a soft, sweet moan passed her lips, a moan that couldn't be mistaken for anything but what it was. The women outside went silent, then figuring out what was going on in the end stall, vacated the bathroom in a shocked rush.

Becky Lynn stiffened and tried to move away from him. He refused to release her, but instead began his debilitating attack again. One moment became several; her hands came to his shoulders. She cried out again, this time with orgasm, then sagged against his chest.

He held her to him, stroking her hair, his heart thundering, his erection painful. He pressed his mouth to her hair, and squeezed his eyes shut, breathing in the scent of her, letting it fill him like the sweetness of spring.

She drew away from him, tears sparkling in her eyes. "I hate you."

"I can tell." He smiled softly and smoothed the dampened tendrils of hair away from her face. "Remind me to have you hate me more often."

"I love Carlo."

Her words hit him like an unexpected right hook. Jack stiffened, not believing he could have heard her correctly. "What did you say?"

She angled up her chin. "I love Carlo. I'm not going to leave him."

Jack dropped his hands, furious. "Your marriage is a sham. It's a prison."

"I won't leave him."

"You will." He cupped her face in his hands and looked her in the eyes, his heart thundering. "You will leave him."

She shook her head. "I won't, not ever. He needs me."

"I need you." Angry, he caught her to him and rotated his pelvis against hers. "You need this."

She wrenched free of his grasp. "This is just sex, Jack.

Don't you get it? I made a vow to always be there for him, I won't break it."

He met her eyes, realization dawning inside him. She meant it. She had no intention of leaving Carlo.

"What are you saying?" he asked softly, hearing the furious edge in his own voice. "That you'll fuck me every once in a while, just for kicks? So you don't atrophy and because your husband has other inclinations in the bedroom?" He jerked away from her and straightened his clothes. "No thanks, babe."

She sucked in a sharp, hurt breath. "That was good enough for you before, wasn't it? Wasn't a 'fuck' just for kicks the only thing you ever wanted?"

He glared at her. She was right, dammit. Used to be, as far as he was concerned, an easy, uncomplicated lay was the only lay. Not anymore. For the first time in his life, it wasn't only sex he wanted. For the first time in his life, sex wasn't enough for him. He wanted more with Becky Lynn, he wanted something deeper. He wanted, he needed what he'd had with her before.

He swore, furious with her, with himself. He yanked open the stall door. "Well, it's not enough now, Becky Lynn. I'm not going to play stud for you or anybody else."

52

Becky Lynn went to Carlo's side. It took every scrap of her control to make it to the ballroom and across to her husband without falling apart. Her encounter with Jack had left her shaken, raw. It had left her feeling cheap and weak-willed. She caught her bottom lip between her teeth. Why was she surprised? With Jack, it was always the same: he touched her and she melted, he crooked a finger her way and everything else—her vows about not wanting him, about refusing him—flew out of her head, and she ended up panting in his arms.

Her cheeks burned as she remembered her behavior. Those women had heard her and had known what she and Jack were doing. Would they recognize her by her gown? Had they already? Becky Lynn glanced quickly around her, relieved to find no one staring at her, no one looking at her and whispering behind their hands.

Trembling, she slipped her hand through Carlo's arm, hoping to steady herself. Carlo looked at her in question and concern, and covered her hand with his own. She tried to smile reassuringly, but her lips trembled so badly, she suspected the line of her mouth resembled a grimace more than a smile.

He tightened his fingers over hers and leaned close to her ear. "Are you all right?" he whispered.

"Yes. Just let me hold on to you."

He nodded. "Giovanni's been asked to say a few words. After that we can go."

Becky Lynn only half listened as Giovanni, up on the dais, began thanking all for coming tonight, as he expressed his appreciation for having been given the honor of working in the fashion industry for all these years.

Her mind drifted back to her encounter with Jack. It was over between them, finally and completely. Jack wanted more than sex from her, but she had made her promise to Carlo. She would never forsake him.

Had he meant what he said? she wondered, her chest heavy and aching. Did he want more with her? Or did he only want to steal her away from his half brother? Tears stung the back of her eyes. Could this whole thing be about his competition with Carlo? It hurt to think that; her instinct told her it wasn't true, but she had been a fool for Jack Gallagher too many times to count.

Beside her, Carlo drew a sharp breath and stiffened. Becky Lynn looked up at him, then at the dais, her focus reeling back to Giovanni and what he was saying. Her heart flew to her throat as she realized the old photographer was singing the praises of his son.

But not his son Carlo...his son Jack.

Becky Lynn listened in horror as Giovanni humiliated Carlo by listing and lauding Jack's accomplishments. Helpless to stop him, she listened as in front of the entire crowd, all who were anybody in the fashion community, he rejected Carlo by embracing Jack as his real and true son.

A buzz moved through the crowd. She heard it, as did Carlo. *What was happening?* people whispered. *Why had Giovanni pointedly excluded Carlo?* The buzz became a hushed roar. Something was happening, and everyone wanted to be in on it.

Becky Lynn shifted her gaze to Carlo. She understood his devastation; she recognized it. She likened each word Giovanni delivered to one of Ricky's raping thrusts into her. For Giovanni was raping Carlo as surely as Ricky had raped her, and just as surely, Carlo would never be the same.

Empathic pain ricocheted through her. She thought back to that night more than ten years ago, working to remember how she had managed to survive, what had kept her from curling into a ball and dying.

Her dreams had kept her alive, she realized. As had focusing on the future, focusing on the new life she would make for herself.

But what of Carlo? she wondered, a catch in her chest. Did Carlo have dreams to hold on to? Could Carlo make a new, a better life for himself? Or had all his dreams come true already, only to be ripped from him now?

Becky Lynn brought her hand to his, laced their fingers. She wanted to let him know without words that she would stand by him, always and forever.

His face a mask of pain, he disentangled his hand from hers. She tried to catch his eye, but he wouldn't look at her. "Carlo," she whispered. "Please…"

He shook his head and eased through the crowd, wanting nothing more, she knew, than to escape.

She watched him go, aching for him, fury building inside her. This was Jack's doing. He had always hated Carlo; he had always wanted to hurt him, to destroy him. Tonight, he had staged and delivered the finishing blow.

The fury became immense, taking her breath. Earlier

she had seen him talking to Giovanni. She had seen them glance over at Carlo and Hugh Preston several times. At the time, she had thought it odd, but now she understood. Jack had told Giovanni about Carlo's sexual orientation. He had waited, had bided his time, until the perfect moment presented itself, the moment when he could completely devastate his half brother.

She fisted her fingers, her heart beating almost out of control. He'd used her, lied to her. Seducing her had only been a part of his plan to destroy Carlo. Her behavior, her own gullibility, sickened her.

Giovanni called Jack up front to join him, and she turned and started pushing through the crowd to go to Carlo. He needed her. She would find him and together they would face this and go on, better and stronger than before.

She made it out of the ballroom and started for the elevator banks.

"Becky Lynn, wait!"

Jack darted out of one of the ballroom's side doors and caught her arm. She whirled to face him, shaking with rage. "You son of a bitch," she said, her voice quivering with emotion. "How could you do this? How could you hurt him like this? And then you…in the bathroom…" She made a sound of self-disgust. "How could you, Jack?"

"It isn't the way it looks." He reached out to touch her, and she slapped his hand away. "Becky Lynn, you don't understand—"

"I understand perfectly. You told Giovanni. I saw you two talking. You waited for the moment when you could damage Carlo most, for the moment you could break his heart and publicly discredit him." She balled her hands into fists. "You bastard, you are Giovanni's son. You've asked me why I stay with Carlo. Well, I'll tell you. He's a real man. He's kind and moral and caring. He isn't totally fixed on ambition and revenge.

"It's not sex with him, Jack. He cares about me. He needs me. He believes in me. You never did." She broke free and stepped away from him, "But how could you? You've never cared about anyone but yourself."

Jack followed her. "It was seeing us together tonight that tipped Giovanni off. He told me so. He said he had heard rumors about Carlo, but seeing us together—"

"Don't you try to blame this on me! Don't you try to make me feel more guilty than I already do." He tried to catch her arms, and she swung at him, her eyes filling with tears. "I'll never forgive you for this, Jack. Never."

Jack dropped his hands and stepped away from her, a mask coming over his expression, the line of his mouth hard, without remorse. She felt as if her heart were being ripped from her chest. "Go," she said. "You got what you wanted. Your father is waiting for you."

Blinded by tears, she turned and walked away.

Carlo wouldn't let her help him. He wouldn't let her comfort him; he wouldn't talk to her or anybody else. Their flight home was agony. He turned away from her and into himself, refusing to look at or speak to her. She told herself he would be better when they got home, that he would seek her support and comfort, but once there, he still refused to allow her close to him.

At first, although deeply hurt, she had assured herself his withdrawal was natural, a normal part of the healing process. She had assured herself that, in time, he would turn to her. But as the days passed, he became more withdrawn.

And she became frightened, that she had lost him, that once again she was alone. And as her fear and alienation grew, so did her anger at Jack. It grew until it burned hot and bright inside her, until it eclipsed everything in her life other than her concern for Carlo.

Carlo refused all calls, all jobs. The industry had begun to talk. All knew about Carlo's lies, about hers. Their little drama was all anybody seemed able to talk about—how Carlo Triani had pretended to be something he was not.

She had no doubt that Jack had helped spread the talk. No doubt he was enjoying Carlo's destruction. For herself she didn't care. She stood by her husband steadfastly, either ignoring or denying the gossip, always defending her husband.

Becky Lynn crossed to the terrace doors and gazed out at him. He sat staring at the spa and garden, he had been for hours—and for days now.

Jobs he had already been booked for, he either hadn't shown for or had sent his assistants in his stead. If he kept this up, he wouldn't have a career left when he pulled himself out of his depression.

She wouldn't let him blow off today's shoot, she decided. It was too important. And it was time Carlo returned to the world of the living.

Taking a deep breath, she stepped outside and crossed to where he sat. She stepped between him and his view of the spa. "We have to talk, Carlo."

"Go away."

She battled the hurt at his rejection. She had to be strong for him; whether he wanted her help or not, he needed it.

He needed her. "Let me in, Carlo. *Bello*…please." She knelt in front of him and gathered his hands in hers. "I love you, I want to help."

She curved her fingers tightly around his. "You said we would be there for each other, that we would care for each other. It's why we married. Let me do both. Let me help you."

He shifted his gaze, and her breath caught. "You're breaking my heart, Carlo. Don't turn me away, it hurts when you do."

He touched her cheek with the fingertips of his right hand. His eyes were sunken, red-rimmed and shadowed from lack of sleep. "Do you know how beautiful you are, *bella?*"

When she protested, he shook his head. "You are. Don't ever forget."

A thread of fear wound through her. She squeezed his fingers. "You'll be with me. I trust you not to let me forget."

"You deserve someone better than me. You deserve a real man. I never should have condemned you to this mock marriage. I've seen that you needed more. I know you've been unhappy."

She thought of Jack, thought of New Orleans and guilt took her breath. "You are a real man. Don't you see, you give me so much."

"I'm weak. A man stands up for who he is and what he believes in. I didn't. I was…afraid."

"You believed in me," she said, her voice thick with tears, frightened by the self-loathing in his voice. "You stood up for me."

His gaze drifted over her right shoulder, toward the

spa. "Once, Jack said to me, 'Tell her, if you have the guts.' I didn't tell you. I was so certain you would leave me. Just as I was always so certain Giovanni would leave me if he knew the truth. I was right."

She searched his gaze. In his, she saw more than a measure of the boy who had come home from school to find that his mother had rejected him through death. "It doesn't matter, Carlo. Nothing matters but that you come back to me."

"It matters…to me." He touched her face again, lightly. "Before you ever became Valentine, Jack came for you. He came to apologize. He told me to tell you he was sorry and that he wanted you back."

Carlo's words echoed through her. *Jack had come for her. He had wanted to apologize. He had wanted her back.*

It changed nothing, she told herself. She hated him now.

"Go to him, *bella*. I see it in your eyes, I see how much you want him."

A cry flew to her lips. "It's not true. I wouldn't have gone to him then, and I won't now. I won't leave you, Carlo."

His gaze shifted away, and he closed himself to her once more. She reached up and cupped his face with her hands, his unshaven cheeks rough against her palms. "What about the *Vogue* shoot today?"

"I'm not going."

She tightened her fingers, forcing his gaze to stay on hers. "Carlo, you must! You can't stand everybody up. Jon called, they've heard rumors in New York… He assured them you would be there."

"He can do it."

She shook her head. "Carlo…he can't. He doesn't have your eye, your talent."

Carlo covered her hands with his own, and took them from his face. "Go away. Leave me alone."

She stood, frustrated, near tears. "You'll ruin your reputation. There will be nothing left."

"There's nothing now," he muttered, staring at the Jacuzzi. "They're laughing…they're all laughing at me."

"Who cares? Carlo, none of them matter."

He lifted his gaze to hers, and her heart broke. To her, they didn't matter. To him, they were everything. She took a deep breath. "I'm not going to let you ruin all that you've built. I'm not going to let that happen."

"*Bella,*" he murmured, "don't you see I'm not worth it?"

Becky Lynn stiffened her spine, furious suddenly. "No, I don't see that. I don't see it at all."

Turning, she marched inside, going straight for the phone. She meant what she said, she wasn't going to allow him to ruin himself. If she had to, she would do the job herself.

Thirty minutes later, Becky Lynn hung up the phone. She drew her eyebrows together in concern. Jon couldn't do the job, a holiday wear spread, he was nearly incoherent with stress and self-doubt. The models and support staff were booked, *Vogue*'s fashion editor and art director were en route, the studio was ready.

At least she wouldn't have to deal with a location shoot.

Becky Lynn sank into a chair. So, she had decided. She would go in Carlo's place. She glanced down at her hands, expecting to see them trembling. Instead, they were rock steady. She was rock steady.

She could do it, she realized. She wanted to do it.

She drew a deep breath and squared her shoulders, determined. She and Carlo had taken a vow to protect and care for each other; he needed her now, more than he ever had.

But her doing the shoot was about more than that, Becky Lynn admitted to herself. She had never loved modeling, but had always longed to pick up the camera. If she could do this and do it well, she would help Carlo and have an entrée into the business.

Decision made, she sprang into action.

Vogue's fashion editor stared at her, aghast. Beside the woman, the art director made small, nervous clucking noises with his tongue.

"But, Valentine…dear…you're a model."

Becky Lynn met her gaze confidently. "I was a photographer first." *A small white lie.* Becky Lynn crossed her fingers. "A fashion photographer."

"Really?" The woman's forehead wrinkled with thought and Becky Lynn knew she was searching her memory. "I can't recall…who were some of your clients?"

Becky Lynn chose some of the smaller accounts she had shot with Jack, not wanting to tip the woman's memory to the fact she had been Jack Gallagher's photographic assistant. "Jon Noble Clothiers," she murmured. "*Los Angeles* magazine, P&J Unlimited."

"Oh, yes…well." The woman made a small, fluttering motion with her right hand. "That's very nice, dear, but those clients are certainly not on a par with *Vogue*."

For a split second she considered giving up, then she thought of what Jack had said to her all those years ago, when she had pretended to be his assistant—*Illusion is everything. Act like you know what you're doing, and everyone will believe you do.*

"Look, Bev—" Becky Lynn slipped her arm through the other woman's. "These shots are going to be fantastic, sensational. You'll be the one lauded as having given me my start. Quite a coup for you and *Vogue.* Besides—" She met the editor's eyes. "What do you have to lose?"

Bev narrowed her eyes on Becky Lynn. "You really think you can do this?"

"I know I can. Bev, darling…" She leaned a fraction closer to the other woman. "I'm a photographer and a top model. Who could possibly know more about what makes a great shot?"

Bev agreed to let her shoot, but not without hesitation. Jon looked as if he were either going to wet his pants or have a heart attack, and the art director couldn't stop making duck noises.

An hour later, that had all changed. Bev was smiling, the art director's mouth had stop twitching and Jon was following her every order, looking capable and completely relieved.

Becky Lynn smiled to herself, elated. The camera felt like an extension of her arm and eye, her mind. She felt totally in tune with her camera assistants, with Bev, the models.

When she had began this, she had intended to follow Carlo's plan for the spread. It hadn't worked out that way. Her own ideas, her own head, had taken over. She realized now that she couldn't have followed Carlo's plans—the shots would have been wrong, they would have rung false.

Because she was a female, the models' reactions to her

were different than they would have been to Carlo. The sex thing was gone, replaced by something friendlier, like girlfriends at a slumber party. That change in energy was being reflected in the models' body language, subtly in their expressions, their eyes. The camera would catch those changes, it would magnify them.

"Oh, Christy," Becky Lynn exclaimed, "how wonderful. Perfect." She shot and moved and shot again, all the while calling out direction and giddy praise.

"I like that." Bev circled behind her. "Let's try that again. Oh, and bring Jasmine in."

Becky Lynn did, a feeling of power and self-satisfaction sweeping through her. That worked, so she tried another variation, then another.

By the end of the session, Becky Lynn was exhausted, energized and totally sated. The way she had felt after making love with Jack, she realized. Only this time, she had been making love—making magic—with the camera.

She sat cross-legged on the floor, the camera in her lap, the studio empty now, and silent. She had sent Jon for food, informing him that they were going straight to the darkroom when he returned. If they processed until the wee hours, she could be in New York with chromes for Bev by tomorrow, late afternoon.

Becky Lynn tipped her face toward the ceiling and laughed. She had done it. She had pulled it off. And, as she had promised Bev, the shots were going to be sensational. She was as certain of that as she was that Christmas would come, she felt it deep inside her, in a place and a way she couldn't articulate but recognized.

This was what had been missing from her life, she realized. This was what she had wanted, what she had yearned for—her own studio, her own career as a fashion photographer. Her entire life had been building to this. She felt the truth of that deep in the pit of her gut.

Her smile faded. What would Carlo think of this? Would he be happy for her? Or would he see her success as his failure?

He would be happy for her. They didn't have any jealousy between them; he would know that initially, she had done this to help him.

Tremayne, on the other hand, would be most unhappy. Although she didn't intend to get out of modeling immediately. It would take time to make the transition, time to earn and save enough money to set up her own studio and keep her and Carlo financially comfortable.

But once she made the transition, she would never look back, and she would never miss being in front of the camera.

Becky Lynn closed her hands over the camera and drew in a deep, healing breath. She had found the course for the rest of her life.

53

"It's eleven a.m., southern California, and another perfect California dreamin' day."

The radio station's two deejays went on the describe the latest midmorning traffic crisis, and Carlo tuned them out, gazing at his garden, thinking of Becky Lynn. The garden reminded him of her—vibrant and strong, full to bursting with life. His lips lifted. There was nothing Becky Lynn couldn't do.

Even take his pictures for him.

Sunshine spilled over him, bright and hot. He slipped his hands into the deep pockets of his silk robe. He could imagine the industry talk now: *"Carlo's wife, a model, for heaven's sake, takes his pictures for him. And they're wonderful...simply wonderful."*

His lips lifted a fraction more. He supposed he should feel emasculated or shamed, but he didn't really care. In the months since the gala and Giovanni's rejection, he had moved beyond worrying what the industry thought of him. He had moved beyond caring about making beautiful images. It all seemed so silly now.

He was happy for Becky Lynn. She had found something she could hold on to. Knowing that made it easier for him.

He turned his back to the garden and faced the spa, its water clear crystal blue. The cleaning crew had just left;

he had called them out special—he wanted the water to be perfect.

Red water.

A catch in his chest, he thought of his beautiful mother, thought of her death and his own upon finding her. Funny how death didn't frighten him anymore, funny how running from it made less sense than facing life.

He had called Hugh this morning, had left a message for him on his apartment answering machine. He had admitted to the other man what he had been afraid to admit until today, admitted the depth of his feelings. He had asked Hugh's forgiveness in advance, for everything.

A sparrow flew across his line of vision, darting toward the fruit trees at the edge of his property. His father hadn't called; he hadn't talked to him since the night of the gala. He had wondered how his father had discovered the truth about his sexual orientation, then had decided that it, too, didn't matter.

Giovanni should have known a long time ago. He should have told his father, he wished he had had the guts.

He hated having been a coward. As he looked at his life, that was the thing he most regretted.

Jack. Carlo thought of his half brother, but didn't feel any anger toward him or blame him for this, although he suspected Becky Lynn did. He knew that he could blame no one but himself.

Carlo lifted his gaze to the blue sky. *He would have liked to have had a real brother. He would have liked it if he and Jack had been friends.*

Carlo threw off his robe and stepped nude into the spa. He had been running from death for so long.

The time had come to stop running.

The deejays announced the time again, and Carlo calculated. *Twenty minutes*. That's all the time it would take.

Still and warm, the water enfolded him like a womb. He poured a glass of champagne, then sipped, enjoying the crisp, dry wine, savoring its cold sting against his dry throat. He did love the taste of good champagne; it was one of the things he had enjoyed very much.

He set the wine down and rested his head against the side of the Jacuzzi. In the background, he heard the start of an old Jackson Browne tune. He tried to remember where he had been during the song's heyday, but couldn't and let the search go, let his mind drift, picturing endless blue skies and drifting white clouds.

He saw now; he understood and forgave. It wasn't that his mother hadn't loved him, but that she had been unable to bear the pain of not being loved. Just as he couldn't bear it.

He hoped Becky Lynn, too, would understand and forgive.

Twenty minutes.

He opened his eyes and reached for the razor blade, shiny and new. The metal was cool and smooth against his fingertips, but hot and sweet against his wrists. After a moment, the burning sensation passed, replaced by a vague, reassuring numbness.

Carlo leaned his head against the spa side and dreamed of endless blue skies and the sweet absence of pain.

54

Unable to quell the sense of urgency clawing at his gut, Jack changed lanes, roared around several cars, then cut them all off to fly down an exit. He flipped on the car radio. Jackson Browne's classic "Running on Empty" was winding down, fading into a more recent hit by Bruce Springsteen.

He had to see Carlo. He had to try to talk to him.

Jack muttered an impatient oath as a truck pulled out in front of him, forcing him to slow up. Since the night of the gala, the sense of urgency had been steadily growing inside him. The more he thought about Giovanni's actions, the more they sickened him.

And the more he understood them.

He saw everything so clearly now. He had been used as a pawn in Giovanni's game, a game that had fed Giovanni's giant, twisted ego. Just as Carlo had been used, as the entire fashion industry had been used the night of the tribute.

He drew his eyebrows together and gripped the steering wheel more tightly. He had spent his entire life trying to win the affection of a man who was worth less than nothing. He had longed for the admiration of a man who had, without hesitation, crushed the heart and hopes of an eight-year-old boy. He had fought for the admiration of a man whose values were so skewed as to equate a man's

value only with his sexuality; a man who before everyone
to whom it would matter had purposely humiliated his son.

Giovanni had never loved or respected anyone but
himself, yet both he and Carlo had spent their entire lives
trying to win his approval and affection. Giovanni wasn't
good enough to lick either of their boots. He saw that so
clearly now, why hadn't he before?

He wanted Carlo to see it, too. Carlo needed to see it.
And maybe then, they could start over. Maybe then, no
longer adversaries, they could begin being brothers.

Jack had heard talk since the gala, talk about Carlo
burying himself in his house, refusing to come out, can-
celing shoots. The gleeful edge to the talk had made him
angry, had made him defensive for his half brother and
Becky Lynn.

Becky Lynn. His heart turned over, and he swore
silently. She had called Carlo a real man, kind and giving.
She had accused him, Jack, of being totally fixed on
ambition and revenge.

She had been right.

If he had been able to see further than his need to discredit Carlo and prove himself to Giovanni, he wouldn't
have betrayed her. And he wouldn't have lost her.

The night before her marriage to Carlo, she had told
him to take a good look in the mirror if he wanted to know
why. He had finally understood what she meant. And when
he had taken that look, he had come up lacking.

Becky Lynn had married Carlo and stayed with him
because of the way he treated her—as if she was special,
important, as if they were a team. Jack had never treated
her like the treasure she was. Everything had always been
about him, his needs. He had been a fool.

Jack swung onto Carlo's street, sped up it, then wheeled into his brother's driveway at a breakneck speed.

Today he had changed that. He had let go of his anger; he had forgotten revenge. In truth, he had started letting go of them, bit by bit, a long time ago. The night before Becky Lynn married Carlo, he realized. The night he had realized how much she cared for his half brother and *the why?* had started to eat at him.

Jack swung out of the car and jogged to Carlo's door. He rang the bell, then pounded on the door. "Carlo," he shouted, "it's Jack." He pounded again. "Open up. We need to talk."

Music came from around back, Jack recognized the song was the same one he had been listening to in his car. He went to the side of the house, letting himself in through the unlocked gate.

"Carlo," he called again. "It's Jack. We have to talk."

At first, he thought Carlo was asleep, sprawled against the side of the spa, one arm dangling over the side. Then he saw the blood, the red water.

A cry of denial in his throat, Jack raced to his brother's side. He pressed his shaking fingers to Carlo's neck. Even as he found a faint pulse, Carlo's eyelids flickered open. *Alive, he was still alive.* Jack tore off his T-shirt and ripped it in strips, frantically wrapping one piece tightly around Carlo's left wrist, the other piece around his right.

"Don't," Carlo managed to say, his voice faint, almost unrecognizable. "Don't…stop me."

A cordless phone sat on the edge of the spa; Jack grabbed it and dialed 911, wondering why Carlo had placed it there and who he had hoped would call and stop him. Giovanni? Becky Lynn?

Or had he left it close in case he changed his mind?

Choked with emotion, he spoke as clearly and succinctly as he could to the 911 operator, then hung up the phone and turned to his brother. Carlo's skin had taken on an ashen cast, but his mouth formed a small, peaceful smile.

"No, damn you...don't you do this." Jack gathered Carlo in his arms as best he could, pressing frantically on the bandages, hoping to stop the steady seep of blood. "Don't die, Carlo... Becky Lynn needs you. I need you. Dammit, Carlo..."

Carlo's lids fluttered up again. He met Jack's gaze though his eyes didn't quite focus. "He...always threw you up...to me." Carlo dragged in a shuddering, weak breath. "I...wished...we were...brothers."

Carlo's eyes shut, then eased open again, but Jack saw the incredible effort it took. Frightened, he held Carlo tighter. "Tell Becky Lynn I..."

The wail of sirens ripped through the morning air, and Jack shook Carlo. "No, damn you! You can't die. I won't let you." He held Carlo's head against his shoulder, cradling it, rocking back and forth. "You're the only brother I've got, you son of a bitch. You can't die...you just...can't..."

The paramedics arrived and shoved Jack roughly out of the way. Jack cried out in frustration, not wanting to let go, not wanting to give up. He didn't have to ask to know it was too late.

"It's eleven forty-two and a perfect seventy-nine degrees, California. And for all of you beach bunnies out there, it's Time to Turn!"

With a howl of rage and pain, Jack snatched up the radio

and flung it as hard and as far as he could. It crashed onto the concrete, shattering, a splinter of plastic skittering into the pool.

Eleven forty-two. He dropped his face into his hands. *Too damn late... He had been too damn...late.*

From out front he heard the slam of a car door, then heard Becky Lynn call Carlo's name, a hysterical edge in her voice. *He couldn't let her see Carlo this way.*

She came around the side of the house. He darted toward her, trying to block her view of Carlo as the paramedics lifted him out of the spa.

He was a second too slow. She saw Carlo and screamed.

Jack caught her and hauled her against his chest. A bird burst from its hiding place in the branches of a tree above them, the frantic beat of its wings mimicking the flailing of her arms and legs as she fought him.

She wrenched herself free and threw herself at Carlo, hanging on to him, weeping, the blood staining her white linen shirt and slacks, the vivid slashes of color an obscenity on the pristine white.

Jack went to her. "Come on, baby," he coaxed, gently prying her fingers loose, then her arms. "Come on, honey, let go. That's right...you have to let go."

Sobbing, she released Carlo, and the paramedics lifted him onto the stretcher. Jack held her against his chest, grief rising inside him, threatening to swallow him whole. He pressed his face to her hair, the clean fragrance of her shampoo a breath of life in this moment of death.

"I'm sorry, baby," he whispered brokenly. "So very... sorry."

With a cry of pain, she jerked out of his arms and whirled to face him. "Don't you tell me how sorry you are!

You did this! You killed him, you son of a bitch...you killed him."

She lunged at him, striking out at him with her fists, sobbing out her hatred for him. He blocked her blows, but didn't try to stop her. Her accusations ripped at him, bruising him more than her fists ever could.

The police arrived on the scene and pulled her off him. The fight drained out of her, she sank to her knees and wept.

Jack gazed at Becky Lynn, hurting with a depth he hadn't felt since he had faced his father and offered him his eight-year-old heart. He drew a shuddering breath, longing to hold and comfort her, longing to take her grief and give her his own.

One of the officers laid a hand on his arm, but Jack didn't look at him, he couldn't take his gaze from Becky Lynn. He needed her so much, he couldn't draw a whole breath without her; yet she wouldn't let him touch her. She hated him; she blamed him for Carlo.

"We'll need to get a statement."

Jack dragged his gaze to the officer and nodded. They moved away from her, but not far enough to escape her soft, brokenhearted keening.

"Is there someone you can call for her?" the officer asked. "I don't think it would be wise for you to stay."

He had said there was, but minutes later, when he'd finished his statement, he realized he hadn't a clue who he should call. As far as he knew, Becky Lynn had no one she was close to—no family or close friends. Carlo had been her everything. The truth of that resonated through him, and suddenly he understood what Carlo had meant to her.

The understanding did not bring him peace.

In the end, he called Sallie. Stunned, she had come right over. To his great relief, Becky Lynn had turned to his mother, allowing the older woman to hold and comfort her. Jack found a prescription for Valium in Carlo's medicine cabinet and urged his mother to convince Becky Lynn to take one.

Wanting, needing to help her, he called Tremayne so she wouldn't have to, then arranged to have the spa emptied and cleaned. With nothing else to do but listen to Becky Lynn's sorrow, he left her in his mother's capable hands.

He had had a brother, now he had none.

Jack climbed into his car and drove, no destination in mind, his rage and grief churning inside him. Jack gripped the steering wheel, his jaw set so tightly it hurt. He had hated his father, yet he had tried to become him. He and Carlo had been brothers, they had needed each other, but they had both been too blinded by their ridiculous competition over Giovanni to recognize that.

He saw what was important now, who was important. He wished with all his heart that he could have seen it sooner. If he had, maybe, just maybe he would still have a brother.

He drove recklessly, his Porsche eating up the miles, and suddenly he realized his course hadn't been aimless. He had found his way to Giovanni's studio. He angled into a spot in front of the building, then slammed out of the car, his rage and grief growing to immense proportions, twisting together to form something awesome and frightening.

He burst into the studio, slammed Tank out of the way

and strode across the set, murder in his heart. A collective gasp moved through the room, then a deathly silence.

Giovanni lowered his camera, turned and saw Jack. He paled.

"You son of a bitch! You killed him!" Jack grabbed the old man's shirt in his fists. "He's dead, you bastard. Your son is dead."

For one thin, bloodless moment, as Jack stared into Giovanni's eyes, he thought about killing him, imagined pounding him senseless, then finishing him off. Then he thought of Becky Lynn, of Sallie, and of Giovanni himself.

The bastard wasn't worth it.

Jack released him. The old photographer stumbled backward, into a tripod. It and the camera fastened atop it crashed to the floor. Giovanni righted himself, barely, and Jack advanced on him, breathing hard, fists clenched.

He met his father's eyes evenly, coldly. "You have no son now, old man. It's Sallie Gallagher's blood that runs in my veins. And what there is of you, I deny. You have no one."

As Giovanni crumpled, Jack turned and walked away.

55

Even after a month, the flowers kept coming.

Becky Lynn accepted this latest arrangement with a wan smile. The deliverywoman looked a bit sheepish, as if she, too, felt enough was enough.

Becky Lynn carried the flowers inside and set them beside another grouping on the cocktail table. Tremayne sent a fresh arrangement every day; she had gotten some from The Shop and Sallie, her brother Randy and a myriad of photographers, designers and editors.

People were simply trying to be nice, attempting to show their affection and concern, but now the flowers only served as a constant reminder that Carlo was gone.

As if she needed a reminder.

She sank into an oversize stuffed chair that had been Carlo's favorite and drew her knees to her chest. At first, the flowers and cards had been for Carlo, and as an expression of sympathy for her loss. Now they were for her. People were worried; Christmas had come and gone, then the New Year, they thought it time for her to get out and begin living again.

They thought it time, but she wasn't ready. She just … wasn't.

She rested her forehead on her knees. Except to attend the funeral, she hadn't been out. She had refused all jobs, most calls. The media had jumped on the story. Carlo's drama, especially considering some of the names involved, had made for some big, juicy stories. Reporters had called repeatedly for the first few weeks, but she had refused all interviews. Her publicist had pressed her, so she had fired him.

The only person she had allowed inside was Sallie. Becky Lynn would be forever grateful for the other woman's support and understanding. And for not pushing her, for allowing her to grieve Carlo's death as she needed to.

Becky Lynn drew a ragged breath. Carlo had promised her she would never be alone again, he had promised her that he would take care of her, that they would take care of each other.

He had broken his promise.

She was alone again.

Tears stinging her eyes, she pressed her face to her knees and swore. She was sick and tired of crying. She was sick of the hollow ache in the pit of her gut, an ache that couldn't be assuaged with food or drink or flowers.

She wanted Carlo. She wanted her friend and companion, her only family.

She couldn't have him; he was gone.

She swiped at the tears that rolled down her cheeks, and leaned her head against the back of the chair. Why hadn't she seen how desperate he was? Why hadn't she suspected he might take his own life? She had known he was depressed, despondent, but she had believed he would pull through. She had never doubted it.

She hadn't gotten him help. She hadn't tried hard enough to help him.

Now he was gone.

As guilt twisted through her, she turned her thoughts to

Jack, working to replace her guilt and grief with anger. Anger hurt so much less than sorrow, placing blame on him hurt so much less than accepting blame herself.

But even her anger felt weak-willed and unfocused. Instead of burning with fury and blame as she had right after Carlo's suicide, she pictured Jack's face that terrible moment she had come around the side of the house, pictured his bare chest and hands marred by Carlo's blood, remembered the stark anguish in his eyes.

He had tried to save Carlo. He had been too late.

Why had he come here that day? To see her? Or Carlo? She had asked herself that question often over the last month. At first, she had told herself he had come to gloat over his winning Giovanni, to rub salt into Carlo's wounds. But as much as she wished she could believe it, she didn't. Jack wouldn't do that. He simply wouldn't.

Becky Lynn sighed. She may never know for sure why; she hadn't heard from Jack since. And after the hateful accusations she had hurled at him, she wouldn't be surprised if she never did again.

The phone rang and as she always did these days, Becky Lynn let it ring, counting until her machine picked up.

"Valentine...love...it's Bev, from Vogue.*"* The woman clucked her tongue. *"You naughty minx, you really must get a rep. I had to track you down through Tremayne and it was most awkward.*

"Anyway, we love your pictures. They've been quite a hit, we've gotten mail. I have another small spread for you, but you must call!" Bev laughed, the sound genuinely amused. *"Really, dear...getting your start in* Vogue *is most untoward. Call me."*

For long minutes after the woman hung up, Becky Lynn stared at the ceiling. *Vogue* wanted her to do another spread, she thought, a stirring of life inside her, a stirring of excitement. Her photos had been a hit. She straightened, her heart beginning to thrum. They had gotten mail about her photos.

Becky Lynn scooted out of the chair and went to the kitchen, to the answering machine. She rewound the tape and played back the message. She listened to it several times, then crossed to the sink and gazed out the window above it.

They loved her photographs.

The ones she had done for Carlo.

She drew a deep breath. What would Carlo want her to do? How would he feel about this?

He would be happy for her. He would want her to be happy.

Carlo had loved her. He had believed in her. Her eyes filled. He just hadn't loved or believed in himself. And no matter how hard she had wished she could change that, she hadn't been able to.

He would want her to go on. He would want her to live. She squeezed her eyes shut and remembered the way she had felt that day at the studio, when she had finished that shoot. She remembered her elation, her self-satisfaction, the sensation of being superalive.

She wanted to feel that way again, she realized. Now. Today. She wanted to call Bev and accept the job, she wanted to move forward with her life.

She wanted to live.

56

Zoe struggled to breathe. The men, their hands, were everywhere. There were three of them, holding her, muttering things she couldn't understand, muttering in a strange language of animals.

The hands clawed and squeezed at her, they worked at places and in ways that frightened her, that hurt. She caught her breath finally; the air smelled foul, overripe. She gagged.

There were other men, too. Men who didn't touch, but watched, men who spoke in words she understood but couldn't make sense of.

What was happening to her? she wondered, feeling the frantic beat of her heart like the wings of a bird trapped in a too-narrow cage. Where was she?

A fix, she remembered. They had promised her a fix. Had they given it to her yet? She searched the fog of distorted images in her head, trying to remember, wondering why she couldn't.

Pain shot through her. She screamed and fell forward.

"Great," one of the talking men said. "Hold her down, and do it again. Give her everything."

She was crying now, clawing at the sheets, desperate to escape. *Dear God...someone had to save her... Somehow...she had to find a way to escape.*

She did.

The world faded to black.

Zoe awakened slowly, coming back to consciousness with a sense of dread. She hurt, in ways and places she hadn't thought possible. Ugly, terrifying images filled her head, and tears welled up in her eyes and slid down her cheeks, so hot they burned.

She couldn't remember exactly what she had done, couldn't remember exactly how she had come to be in this place, but it had been something bad. She had been a part of something vile.

And it had hurt.

Her stomach heaving, Zoe rolled onto her side and hung her head over the side of the bed. She was so empty, she couldn't even retch. *So empty.* She drew her knees to her chest, and her teeth began to chatter. She curled herself into a tighter ball. *So cold.*

She moved her gaze over the room, until it came to rest on the bedstand. A syringe lay on its scarred surface, a bloody piece of sheet beside it.

With a whimper of relief, she reached for the syringe. Then with a cry, she let it slip from her fingers to the floor. Empty. It was as empty as she was.

Zoe pressed her fist to her mouth. She had been paid for whatever those men had done to her. She had allowed them to hurt and violate her, she had allowed them to do unspeakable things to her body.

The sound that passed her lips came from the very bowels of her being. She pressed the fist tighter. She couldn't do this anymore. She couldn't live through it again. She curled the fingers of her free hand into the stinking bedclothes, clutching them, hanging on because her life depended on it.

She didn't want to die, Zoe realized, starting to cry. She didn't want to die.

57

Becky Lynn didn't recognize the strangled whisper on the other end of the phone. Still half-asleep, she pushed the hair out of her eyes and glanced at her bedside clock. *Two-twenty, the middle of the night.*

"Please," the person whispered again, "help me."

Becky Lynn tightened her fingers on the receiver, heart pounding. "Who is this?" she asked.

The woman on the other end of the phone began weeping, the sound hopeless and lost. Gooseflesh raced up Becky Lynn's arms. "I'll help," she said quickly. "I promise, I will. Just tell me who this is. I have to know who…"

Zoe. It was Zoe on the other end of the line.

Becky Lynn took a deep breath, struggling to stay calm. If she panicked, she might lose her.

The way she had lost Carlo.

"Zoe," Becky Lynn said evenly and with as much authority as she could muster. "Tell me where you are. I'll come and get you."

The weeping increased. "I…I don't know."

Becky Lynn twisted her fingers around the phone cord. "Are you inside someplace or outside, at a pay phone?"

Zoe hesitated, as if she had to think about it. Becky Lynn's hopes sank. How was she going to find her if Zoe couldn't tell her where she was? She could be anywhere.

"Inside," she said finally. "I'm in a room."

"Are you alone?"

She began to weep again. "They might…come back. I don't know if…they're done."

They might come back. Becky Lynn took a deep breath, frightened now for a different reason. Who? Dear Lord, done with what?

Panic crept up on her, and Becky Lynn fought it off again. "Describe where you are."

Because of Zoe's confused state, it took some time, but eventually Becky Lynn was certain the other woman was in a motel room. "Okay," she murmured, "good. Now, can you get to the nightstand? Great…open the drawer… Is there something with the motel's name on it? An envelope or stationery? A Bible?"

When that search proved futile, she instructed Zoe to try the dresser drawers next. While Zoe did, Becky Lynn rummaged through her own dresser for clothes, then slipped out of her nightgown and into a T-shirt and a pair of light sweats.

The motel drawers were all empty, and frustrated, Becky Lynn told her to check the phone. "Is there a number on it?" she asked.

There was. *Room twenty-two.*

Something tugged at her memory, and she struggled to figure out what it was. Avocado green carpeting, she realized. Lord, how she had hated living with that color. Zoe had described her old room at the Sunset Motel.

"Describe the room again," she said, excitement edging into her voice. "Everything you see."

Zoe did, and although Becky Lynn had lived with the orange, avocado and bloodred bedspread, had lived with the matted avocado-colored carpet and the cardboard-patched walls for more than a year, she couldn't be certain that's where Zoe was.

How many other motels might have the same cheap and tacky interiors, she wondered, frustrated. She couldn't take the chance she was wrong.

She drew a calming breath. "Zoe, go to the window. Look out, then tell me what you see."

It took Zoe several moments to get across the room. Becky Lynn heard her stumble and whimper, heard the rattle of plastic blinds as Zoe pushed them aside. "There's buildings and a…a sign. But I don't know what it says… I can't…read… it."

Zoe's voice faded out, becoming fuzzy and indistinct. Becky Lynn's heart leapt to her throat. She couldn't lose her now. She wouldn't. "Try, Zoe," she said sharply. "It's important, read me what the sign says."

"The unset otel."

The Sunset! She'd been right. She knew where Zoe was.

"I'm coming to get you, Zoe. But first I have to hang up." Terrified, sobbing, Zoe begged her not to hang up. No matter how Becky Lynn tried to reassure her, the other woman couldn't seem to understand. Finally, as she had no other choice, she told Zoe she would be there soon, then set the receiver back onto its cradle.

Severing that fragile connection while Zoe pleaded with her not to was one of the hardest things Becky Lynn had ever had to do. She feared what would happen to Zoe if she was wrong about the motel; she worried that, confused and frightened, Zoe would run off, and she couldn't stop thinking about Carlo and how she had lost him.

Heart pounding, Becky Lynn stared at the phone. She couldn't do this alone, she realized. She was afraid. Whispering a quick prayer, she picked up the phone and dialed Jack's number. He answered on the fourth ring; his voice fogged with sleep.

"Jack, it's Becky Lynn."

"Red? What—"

"There's no time to talk. Zoe called, she needs help. She... I'm frightened for her. I didn't know who else to call, and I don't think...I can't do this alone, Jack."

"Where is she?" Jack asked, his voice instantly clear and authoritative, free of sleep.

Becky Lynn's knees went weak with relief, and she sank onto the edge of the bed. He would help her; Zoe would be all right. "She's at the Sunset Motel. Room twenty-two."

"You stay put." She heard him fumbling around while he talked. "I'll get her."

"No! I'm coming, too. She called me... I promised."

"You're not going there without me. I'll pick you up."

"Hurry, Jack," she whispered to herself as she hung up the phone. "Hurry, before it's too late."

Suddenly cold, she grabbed a sweater and went outside to wait.

Twenty minutes later, she climbed into Jack's car. He glanced at her, his mouth set in a tight, grim line. His eyes were shadowed, the lines bracketing his eyes and mouth more deeply etched than before. He looked as if he had aged years since she had last seen him.

Smeared with Carlo's blood, his expression naked with pain.

Emotion choked her, and she tore her gaze away. She

slammed the car door and fastened her safety belt. That done, she glanced at him. His hands in a death grip on the steering wheel, he stared in the direction of the side of the house and the gate the paramedics had carried Carlo through.

The urge to comfort him, to reach across the seat and lay a hand over his, came upon her suddenly, so suddenly it took her breath. He hurt, she realized. In a different way than she did, but just as deeply.

She shuddered and rubbed her arms. "We'd better go."

He nodded and shifted the car into gear.

They drove for several minutes in silence. She clasped her hands in her lap, trying to quell their trembling. She swallowed hard, then looked at him. "She sounded bad, Jack. Really bad. And she…she mentioned other people. It scared me."

Panic rose inside her, and she worked to tamp it back. "I'm so afraid… What if we get there and she's gone? What if…those people—"

"We'll find her," Jack said with grim determination. He took his eyes from the road to meet hers. "Somehow, we'll find her, Becky Lynn. I promise."

They drove the rest of the way in silence. She hadn't been wrong about the Sunset Motel. They found room twenty-two, knocked and called Zoe's name. She didn't answer, but from inside they heard her weeping.

Becky Lynn knocked again. "Zoe, it's me, Becky Lynn. Jack's with me. We've come to help you. Open up," she coaxed softly. "Come on, Zoe, open the door."

Zoe's weeping became hysterical. "Don't touch me! No…don't…I can't…"

Becky Lynn grabbed Jack's arm, her heart in her throat.

"There's someone in there with her. Oh, God…we'd better get the manager, we'd better—"

"Fuck that," Jack muttered, shaking off her hand. "Stand back." He drew back and slammed his foot against the door. The thin wood buckled with the first blow and caved with the second.

Zoe was alone, crouched naked in the corner, panting like a trapped animal. Her eyes were wild, her pathetically thin body marred by long red welts, the hair on the right side of her face matted with blood.

Becky Lynn cried out at the sight of her and brought a trembling hand to her mouth. "What did they do to you?" she whispered, taking a step toward her. "Oh, Zoe, what did they—"

Jack laid a hand on her arm, stopping her. "Let me, she might fight."

Becky Lynn nodded, her stomach rising to her throat. She tried not to watch, tried not to see. But she knew the image of Zoe this way would haunt her forever.

Jack started across the room. "Come on, baby," he crooned. "It's Jack and Becky Lynn. We're here to help you."

Wild-eyed, Zoe scrambled away on her hands and knees, trying to hide, to escape, so weak, the attempt was little more than heartbreaking.

"We're not going to hurt you," he murmured. "We're here to help you. Jack and Becky Lynn are going to take you out of here."

Finally, he caught her. She fought for a moment, scratching and kicking, trying to bite, then simply gave up and sagged against him.

Becky Lynn slipped off her cardigan. "Here."

"Thanks." He took it and folded it carefully around Zoe. "Check the bathroom, see if there's a clean towel."

Becky Lynn did as he asked, though not without trepidation. The bedroom was so filthy, she feared what state she would find the bathroom.

It was as vile as she had expected, though surprisingly, on a wire rack above the commode lay a folded towel. She reached for it, then noticed the empty film boxes and wrappers littering the floor, along with cellophane wrapping off some sort of package.

"Becky Lynn? What is it?"

She turned. Jack stood in the doorway, Zoe in his arms. "Look. Film boxes and...stuff." She drew her eyebrows together and nudged the cellophane with her foot. "What do you think—"

"Pornography," he said tightly. "Come on, let's get out of here."

Becky Lynn grabbed the towel and helped Jack tuck it tenderly around Zoe. He carried her out to his car, then folded her frail body carefully into the minuscule back seat of his 911, the whole time murmuring soft sounds of comfort.

That done, they both climbed into the car, anxious to be away from this place and the horror that had happened here. Jack started the engine and hauled out, the back of the small car fishtailing as he floored the accelerator. The speed, his recklessness, didn't scare her. Becky Lynn hadn't a doubt that after what she had seen tonight, many things would have lost the power to frighten her. She had glimpsed a small piece of hell itself.

Becky Lynn closed her eyes and said a silent prayer of thanks that Zoe had called and that they had found her in time. Thoughts of what could have happened filled her head. She pushed the terrifying thoughts away and glanced over her shoulder at the other woman. Zoe appeared to be asleep, although her mouth moved as if she were talking to someone.

"What now?" Becky Lynn asked, shifting her gaze to Jack. "What do we do next?"

He met her eyes briefly. "We get her help. I know a place we can take her."

58

As rehabilitation hospitals went, Oceanview Rehab was pretty, with a multitude of windows and plants, and pastel, patterned wallpaper instead of institutional green walls. Becky Lynn stepped off the elevator and smiled at the floor nurse. "Good morning, Anne. How is she today?"

The nurse returned her smile. "She's doing well this morning, Mrs. Triani. Very well. I think you'll be pleasantly surprised."

That would be nice, Becky Lynn thought, smiling again and moving down the hall toward Zoe's room. She paused outside her friend's door and took a deep, fortifying breath. In the month since she and Jack had brought Zoe to Oceanview in the middle of the night, the woman had made progress, although painfully slow.

Zoe was a troubled young woman, so much more troubled than Becky Lynn had realized all those years ago. But she had hope for the other woman, anyway. Zoe wanted desperately to get it together, she wanted to live.

If only Carlo had been that strong.

Becky Lynn had come to see her every day. Some days, Zoe spoke to her, and some days she didn't; some days, she was angry and accusatory, other days, depressed and self-loathing.

What would it be today? Becky Lynn wondered, tapping on Zoe's half-open door. She peeked inside. Zoe sat cross-legged on the bed, staring blankly at a magazine open in front of her. Zoe's health and appearance had been ravaged by the drugs. Even though her color had improved and she had gained a few pounds, it still hurt to look at her. Becky Lynn wasn't sure which hurt more—comparing Zoe to the way she had looked that day she discovered her in the mall, or remembering the way she had looked that night in the motel room.

Becky Lynn forced a bright smile. "Hi. Feel like some company?"

Zoe looked up but said nothing, and Becky Lynn forced another smile and walked into the room. "Look." She held up the bright pink hydrangea plant she carried. "The market was overflowing with these, each prettier than the other. I thought you might enjoy one."

Becky Lynn crossed the small room and set the plant on the dresser, aware of Zoe's gaze on her. She searched for something to say, wishing she was anywhere but here.

"There." She fluffed the leaves and checked the soil, then turned to Zoe. "Did I tell you I shot an Armani ad Monday? I was terrified. Moving from in front of the camera to behind it feels so strange. To everyone, I think. The other models don't quite know how to treat me and I—"

"Why are you being so nice to me?"

Becky Lynn looked at Zoe, startled silent.

"You're even paying for this place. I mean, I don't get it."

Becky Lynn lifted a shoulder. "There's not much to get. I care about you."

"Why?" Zoe inched her chin up, defensive. "I don't deserve for you to care about me."

"That's not true. You—"

"It is true," Zoe said flatly. "I was a real bitch. I used

our friendship, I used you. I treated you like—" She clasped her hands together, so tightly her knuckles popped out white in relief. "I did a bad thing to you, the worst thing I could think of."

She was talking about Jack, Becky Lynn knew. And although it still hurt, all these years later, she shook her head. "You were vulnerable, Zoe. You needed...so much. He shouldn't have allowed anything to happen. I don't blame you."

"You should, you..." Zoe lowered her eyes for a moment, then returned them to Becky Lynn's, the expression in them haunted. "I lied about me and Jack. I never slept with him." She twisted her fingers together. "Not that I didn't try. He wouldn't."

Zoe's words rocked her, and Becky Lynn swallowed hard. She had believed Zoe without question, even when Jack had denied it years later.

She had thought Zoe more deserving of Jack's attention and affection than she herself was, Becky Lynn realized, feeling sick. She had had that low an opinion of herself.

"Why, Zoe?" she whispered. "Why did you lie like that?"

The other woman lowered her eyes to her hands once more. "Because I hated what you and Jack had. I hated that you had each other, and that I had...no one."

"Oh, Zoe..." Becky Lynn's eyes filled. "We didn't have so much. We didn't have love."

"Yes," she whispered brokenly, "you did. Jack loved you. And I never...nobody ever loved me. It hurt."

And it still did. Becky Lynn crossed to Zoe and sat beside her on the bed. She gathered her into her arms and held her while she cried, great, racking sobs of despair and loneliness, held her until she had too little strength to cry anymore.

Becky Lynn cried with her, but quietly, for different reasons. She cried for the past, for her and Jack and what they had lost, for Carlo and Zoe, and the battered seventeen-year-old who had felt herself so unworthy of love.

"I'm so sorry," Zoe said, wiping her cheeks with the backs of her hands. "I was so awful to you, but I…needed your friendship so much. After I had driven you away, I wished we… I hated what I had done."

They talked for a long time. Becky Lynn told Zoe about her and Carlo's marriage, about his suicide and how much she missed him. She told Zoe about how she had been right about Carlo's protecting her from the worst of modeling; she told her about her photography and her plans to leave modeling for good.

They didn't talk about Jack, but he was on Becky Lynn's mind the entire time. In truth, he had been since the night he had carried Zoe out of that foul motel room.

He had been so gentle with Zoe, so kind and caring, that night and since. He had been to visit Zoe many times, Becky Lynn had seen the balloons, the teddy bear and flowers he had brought her; Zoe had mentioned his visits.

That was the Jack she had fallen in love with. The man who had treated a frightened waif from Mississippi with kindness, the man who had offered her the door to a whole new life. Carlo had seen beauty in her, but Jack had seen talent. Jack had valued her ideas and opinions, had valued her.

At times, he had been selfish, at other times, completely self-absorbed. But he hadn't been cruel. He hadn't been the monster she had made him out to be. In the pain and shock of his betrayal with Garnet McCall, she had forgotten the good things, she had forgotten about her eighteenth birthday and sharing a too-sweet chocolate cake and dreams that had been sweeter still.

Jack hadn't lied about Zoe, and he hadn't lied about how Giovanni had learned the truth about Carlo. She'd had as much a part in that as he. She had been too angry, too hurt for Carlo, to see that then.

Or maybe she had seen, she thought, but hadn't wanted to. Placing blame was so much easier than accepting it.

She thought back to the night they had checked Zoe into Oceanview. Jack had driven her home after, and she had felt a yawning, black chasm between them, a chasm filled with the terrible image of Zoe in that motel room, the image of Carlo being hauled from the hot tub, filled with the memory of hateful words and ugly actions.

She had felt responsible; Jack had, too. She had seen the sadness in Jack's eyes, the regret. She knew he had seen the same in hers. The chasm had been too great, too risky to span, so they had said nothing to each other but goodnight.

Now, she wished she had tried. Now, she longed to take the risk, longed to reach out for him. But now, she feared it was too late.

She and Zoe talked a while longer, until finally, regretfully, Becky Lynn checked her watch and saw that she had to go. She hated having to put an end to the minutes she and Zoe had shared. It felt so good to be with her like this again, to be friends again.

"You're going to make it," Becky Lynn whispered, hugging her. "I know you are."

Zoe clung to her. "I don't know if I can face the past, Becky Lynn. There are things… I don't know if I can do it. I'm so scared."

Becky Lynn tightened her arms. "You can do it, Zoe. You can face it. You're stronger than you know."

59

Zoe's whispered words about facing the past stayed with Becky Lynn for the rest of the day. They echoed through her, affecting her in strange and unexpected ways. She had been unable to shake thoughts of her own past, of her brother and father, of the girl she had been all those years ago in Bend.

Her thoughts had left her feeling fragile and edgy, but also elated. For the thoughts of her past had brought ones of Jack, of their shared past, and about the man he really was. And as she had run a myriad of errands, she had wondered whether there could be a future for them, or if it really was too late.

Becky Lynn wheeled her grocery cart to the checkout line. She had chosen the worst time to shop, the little corner market could hardly accommodate the predinner rush of shoppers, and she resigned herself to a lengthy wait in line.

She parked her basket, then crossed to the magazine rack. Even as she reached for the latest *Vogue,* the front page of one of the tabloids caught her eye. She looked closer, and her heart stopped. The image splattered across the front page was one she recognized from her darkest fears, her worst nightmares.

Becky Lynn gazed at the photo of herself at seventeen, feeling the veil of security and illusion she had erected around herself being ripped away, leaving her naked and completely exposed. Suddenly, she was that girl again, unloved, an ugly outcast; suddenly, the people of Bend were around her, taunting her and laughing.

She reached for the tabloid, her hand shaking. *Her father had found her.* She drew a ragged breath. *He had told the world who she really was.*

Only he had lied, too. She scanned the article, tears burning her eyes. He had told the world that she had been promiscuous and willful, that she had stolen his paycheck and run off, not a thought for her hungry family. He said that she owed him now.

Becky Lynn thought of the night she had run away, of how she had dragged herself home, bloody and battered, only to be battered more by her own family. She remembered her desperation, remembered her certainty that if she stayed in Bend, she would die.

She had taken twenty dollars, far less than he had taken of her Cut 'n Curl earnings, week in and week out. Far less than he spent on booze, never a thought for his hungry wife and children.

How could he have said these things about her? she wondered, the type blurring before her eyes. How could her own father lie this way? How could he think so little of her?

Choking back a sob, she slipped the magazine back into the rack and left the store. She found her car and then her way home, though she couldn't have said how.

Jack was there, waiting for her on her front steps. With a cry of relief, she swung out of the car and ran to him. He folded her into his arms, holding her tightly.

"I'm sorry, baby," he murmured. "So sorry."

She clung to him, pressing her cheek to his chest, to the

place where his heart beat, sure and steady. She drew a shuddering breath. "Why did he have to find me?" she whispered. "Why couldn't he just leave me alone?"

"I don't know, sweetheart." He stroked her hair. "The past just has a way of catching up with us."

"I was happy being Valentine." She pressed closer to him. "My life has nothing to do with him. I don't want to go back."

"You don't have to go anywhere." Jack leaned away from her so he could meet her eyes. "But you can't let him get away with this. You have to fight him."

"With what?" She drew out of his arms and fumbled in her purse for her house keys. "I have nothing to fight with."

"You have the truth, Red. That's a powerful weapon."

"You don't understand." She found the keys, but her hands shook so badly, she couldn't get the key fitted into the lock.

"Let me." He took them from her and after a moment, swung the door open.

She stumbled inside, going through the foyer to the living room, going to the couch. She sank onto it and dropped her face into her hands. "What am I going to do?" she whispered, then lifted her gaze to his. "What should I do?"

"Call a press conference." He crossed to her. "Tell your side of the story. Tell the truth."

"A press conference?" She shook her head. "I don't think so."

"You can't run from this. It's not going to go away."

Her father's image filled her head, his voice with it, and she shuddered. "I could give him money. He would disappear, that's all he wants."

"But he would come back, leeches like him always do."

Jack crouched in front of her. He touched her cheek lightly, tenderly. "Becky Lynn, Red, you have to face this."

She met his gaze, her vision swimming with tears. "Now everybody knows. I'll never be...Valentine again. I'll be Becky Lynn Lee, the girl who was too ugly to look at while being raped." Her breath caught on a sob. "I'll be nothing again."

Jack muttered an oath and tightened his fingers over hers. "You were never nothing, Becky Lynn. You were always special, always beautiful."

He brought her hands to his mouth. "You're the kindest person I've ever known. The most generous. The strongest."

She opened her mouth to protest, he stopped her. "The strongest," he repeated. "You came through hell, and you not only survived it, you conquered it. Do you know how special that is? Do you know how unusual?"

She caught her bottom lip between her teeth, eyes brimming with tears. "Then why don't I feel strong? Why am I so...scared?"

"Come here." He drew her to her feet. "I want you to see something."

She followed him to the foyer, stopping when they reached it. She looked at him in confusion. "What do you want me to—"

He turned her to face the mirror above the entryway table. Her reflection stared back at her.

"Do you remember," he murmured, standing behind her, placing his hands on her shoulders, "a long time ago, when you asked me why I called you Red? You remember that I said I didn't know, but that it just seemed to fit you?"

He tightened his hands on her shoulders. "Now, I know why. You're strong, Becky Lynn, just like the color. And

you're vibrant, full of passion and life. Look at yourself
in the mirror, babe. I see a strong, confident woman, a
woman who has faced the worst life has to offer and beaten
it. I see Becky Lynn Lee, smart and talented and kind.
Beautiful." He brought his head close to hers. "Everybody
else pales in comparison. You have to see it, too."

Becky Lynn squeezed her eyes shut. "I can't," she whispered. "I see an ugly seventeen-year-old, an outcast. I see
a girl who has nobody."

Jack turned her to face him. He cupped her face in his
hands, catching her tears with his thumbs. "You have me,
Red. You always have. Even when I was too shallow and
self-absorbed to see it, you had me."

He bent and brushed his lips softly, tenderly against
hers, then lifted his head once more. "You've got to face
your past," he murmured. "You have to let it go."

She rested her hands against his chest, then her face.
*She had Jack. The one she had always wanted, the only
one.* She curled her fingers into his pullover, wanting to
hold on to the reassuring beat of his heart, wanting to hold
on to this perfect moment.

He tipped her face up to his. "You need to take care of
this now, you need to jump on the story while it's still fresh
news. Call Tremayne, he'll get the agency's publicist to
set up a press conference."

"I don't know if I can do it. I don't know if…I…if I'm
ready." She searched his gaze, wishing desperately to find
her answers there. "I need to think. I…I just don't know."

"Well, while you're thinking," he murmured, his voice
thick, "think about this. I love you. It's not just sex, it never
has been. I need you. I believe in you. And I'm going to
be with you, whatever you decide."

He loved her? Could it be? Wonder bloomed inside her, brilliant white and warm. *Jack loved her.*

He kissed her hard, then drew away. "I'm going now. I'll be at the studio." He started toward the door. "Call me. I won't go anywhere until I hear from you."

"Don't go! Jack…" She folded her arms across her chest, cold suddenly, frightened. "I don't want to be alone."

He came back to her and cupped her face once more. He gazed deeply into her eyes. "I'm here for you, babe. But you've got to make this decision alone. I can't make it for you."

His lips lifted a fraction, curving into the cocky half smile that had always sent her blood pressure skyrocketing. "Besides, I'm selfish. If I stay, I'll want you in my arms. I'll want us in your bed. And I'll want to talk about us, about how much I love you and how much I want you by my side."

He shook his head, his expression rueful. "That'll keep, it has this long. But this thing with your father won't."

Becky Lynn knew he was right, and let him go. For a long time after he did, she stared at the closed door, her emotions a confused jumble.

Jack loved her. He needed her, he believed in her.

Her father, her past, had found her.

She brought a trembling hand to her forehead. She thought of Zoe, of her whispered words that morning, the ones about the past and her fear of it.

She was afraid, too, Becky Lynn acknowledged. But the time had come to face her fears.

Becky Lynn crossed to stand before the mirror. She gazed at her reflection. As she did, her mind tumbled to the past. She thought of the girl she had been and the woman she was now. She thought of Ricky and Tommy, of their hatred. She thought of her father and mother, of her brother Randy. With the thoughts, she hurt. She wished she had been loved and cherished, she wished her life had been different back then.

It hadn't been. But that part of her life was over. The past was only a series of memories now, she realized. Ugly memories but powerless to hurt her—unless she allowed them to. Jack was right, she'd not only survived her past, she had beaten it.

She was Red. Like the color, vibrant and strong, full of passion and life. Undeniable, unbeatable.

She had to let go of her past. She had to face it and go on. More than a decade ago she had run away from Bend, Mississippi, vowing to leave that place, her horrible life, behind forever. But instead, she had clung to her past, had clung to the image of the frightened and lonely girl she had been. She had allowed that image to color her life, dim her happiness.

She touched the mirror, her breath catching in her chest. She was Becky Lynn Lee, beautiful and strong, worthy of love. She smiled at her reflection. She hadn't pretended to be Valentine; Carlo hadn't created an illusion—he had merely seen what she already was.

Just as Jack had seen. Just as he still did.

Jack loved her. But best of all, she realized, she loved herself. A sense of freedom swept through her, sweet and dizzying. She tipped her head back and laughed, then twirled in a circle, arms out.

The journey she had begun all those years ago ended today, this moment. She'd finally found what she had been seeking.

It was called peace.

60

Becky Lynn chose a brilliant red sheath for the press conference. In her matching three-inch heels, she topped six feet, taller than most men. Smiling to herself, she crossed the Westin Bonaventure's dramatic six-story atrium lobby to the elevator banks, her stride jaunty. She drew glances, some of appreciation, some of surprise; when she could, she met them boldly, smiling and nodding.

Walking tall today, Becky Lynn Lee. Walking mighty tall.

She stepped into the glass-enclosed elevator, and breathed deeply through her nose. She wouldn't confuse the flutter of nerves in her stomach for fear. For the first time in her life, she was unafraid—of her father, or what other people thought of her, or of anything else. No one's opinion of her mattered but her own. And she was damn proud of who she was.

The elevator whisked her to the third floor, she stepped off. A group had assembled outside the meeting room at the other end of the corridor. She had eyes only for Jack. He waited for her, slightly apart from the rest of the group, fidgeting and pacing, worried, she knew, about her.

She had someone in her corner. Someone strong who loved her. Her lips lifted, happiness filling her to near bursting. She wasn't alone; she never would be again.

He looked up. Their gazes met. He smiled and the inside of her lit up like a Christmas tree. *He loved her.* Holding on to that magical thought, she started for him, he for her. They met halfway, and he caught her hands, lacing their fingers together.

"You're ready for this?" he asked softly.

"Completely."

He searched her gaze, his filled with loving concern. "They might throw you some curves, just keep focused and stay cool."

"You worry too much."

"I love you so much." He cupped her face in his palms. "I don't want there to be any surprises for you. I don't want you upset or hurt."

"It's going to be fine." She laid a finger lovingly against his mouth. "I love you, too."

His expression told her more than a million more words could, and taking his hand, she walked with him down the hallway. The group began filing into the meeting room, all except one man—her brother, Randy. Her steps faltered. He watched them approach, hands fisted at his sides, his square jaw jutted defensively.

Jack glanced at her. "What?"

She squeezed his hand. "It's my…it's my brother, Randy."

Jack followed her gaze and narrowed his eyes. "You want me to—"

"I need to do this. I can do this." Even as a knot of apprehension settled in the pit of her stomach, she closed the remaining distance between them. "Hello, Randy."

He jutted his chin a fraction more, and narrowed his eyes. "I know you don't want me here, Becky Lynn. But I'm not leaving."

"Why?" she asked, tilting up her chin. "Have you come to further his lies?"

The line of his jaw softened, as did the expression in his eyes. He cleared his throat. "No. I've come for you, Becky Lynn. Because it's the right thing to do, and because…you're my sister."

She held out her hand, happiness spiraling through her, another wound beginning to heal. "Then I'm glad you're here."

He stared at her hand a moment, his expression stunned, then grasped it. She felt him tremble and curled her fingers more tightly around his.

"Ready?" Jack asked. "They're waiting."

Becky Lynn met his gaze and nodded. Together, they entered the packed room and walked up the center aisle to the podium. She had drawn a crowd, she saw; even *Entertainment Tonight* had come. She heard the whispers, the murmured questions and smiled to herself, ready for them.

Her love on her one side, her long-lost brother on her other, she faced the reporters. Head held high, she began, "My name is Becky Lynn Lee and I was born in Bend, Mississippi…"

REQUEST YOUR FREE BOOKS!

2 FREE NOVELS
FROM THE ROMANCE/SUSPENSE
COLLECTION PLUS 2 FREE GIFTS!

YES! Please send me 2 FREE novels from the Romance/Suspense Collection and my 2 FREE gifts (gifts are worth about $10). After receiving them, if I don't wish to receive any more books, I can return the shipping statement marked "cancel." If I don't cancel, I will receive 4 brand-new novels every month and be billed just $5.49 per book in the U.S. or $5.99 per book in Canada, plus 25¢ shipping and handling per book plus applicable taxes, if any*. That's a savings of at least 20% off the cover price! I understand that accepting the 2 free books and gifts places me under no obligation to buy anything. I can always return a shipment and cancel at any time. Even if I never buy another book from the Reader Service, the two free books and gifts are mine to keep forever.

185 MDN EF5Y 385 MDN EF6C

Name _____ (PLEASE PRINT) _____

Address _____ Apt. # _____

City _____ State/Prov. _____ Zip/Postal Code _____

Signature (if under 18, a parent or guardian must sign)

Mail to **The Reader Service:**
IN U.S.A.: P.O. Box 1867, Buffalo, NY 14240-1867
IN CANADA: P.O. Box 609, Fort Erie, Ontario L2A 5X3

Not valid to current subscribers to the Romance Collection,
the Suspense Collection or the Romance/Suspense Collection.

Want to try two free books from another line?
Call 1-800-873-8635 or visit www.morefreebooks.com.

* Terms and prices subject to change without notice. N.Y. residents add applicable sales tax. Canadian residents will be charged applicable provincial taxes and GST. Offer not valid in Quebec. This offer is limited to one order per household. All orders subject to approval. Credit or debit balances in a customer's account(s) may be offset by any other outstanding balance owed by or to the customer. Please allow 4 to 6 weeks for delivery. Offer available while quantities last.

Your Privacy: Harlequin is committed to protecting your privacy. Our Privacy Policy is available online at www.eHarlequin.com or upon request from the Reader Service. From time to time we make our lists of customers available to reputable third parties who may have a product or service of interest to you. If you would prefer we not share your name and address, please check here. ☐

A new thriller from the author of *Body Count*

P.D. MARTIN

Increasingly haunted by her ability to experience the minds of killers in the throes of heinous crimes, FBI Profiler Sophie Anderson's talent is uncontrollable and unpredictable. When bodies start showing up on a university campus, she and Tucson police detective Darren Carter are pulled into the case. However, Sophie's puzzled by the fact that certain signature elements are different in each killing. The FBI database has a record of many of the signatures—but they have been used by different serial killers.

As the bodies continue to appear, Sophie must hone her terrifying skills to try and track down the killer—or killers.

THE MURDERERS' CLUB

"Enough twists and turns to keep forensics fans turning the pages."
—*Publishers Weekly* on *Body Count*

ERICA SPINDLER

32579	LAST KNOWN VICTIM	___ $7.99 U.S.	___ $7.99 CAN.
32445	COPYCAT	___ $7.99 U.S.	___ $9.50 CAN.
32376	CAUSE FOR ALARM	___ $4.99 U.S.	___ $5.99 CAN.
32305	KILLER TAKES ALL	___ $7.99 U.S.	___ $9.50 CAN.
32169	SEE JANE DIE	___ $7.50 U.S.	___ $8.99 CAN.
66751	FORBIDDEN FRUIT	___ $6.50 U.S.	___ $7.99 CAN.

(limited quantities available)

TOTAL AMOUNT	$ _____
POSTAGE & HANDLING	$ _____
($1.00 FOR 1 BOOK, 50¢ for each additional)	
APPLICABLE TAXES*	$ _____
TOTAL PAYABLE	$ _____

(check or money order—please do not send cash)

To order, complete this form and send it, along with a check or money order for the total above, payable to MIRA Books, to: **In the U.S.:** 3010 Walden Avenue, P.O. Box 9077, Buffalo, NY 14269-9077; **In Canada:** P.O. Box 636, Fort Erie, Ontario, L2A 5X3.

Name: _____
Address: _____ City: _____
State/Prov.: _____ Zip/Postal Code: _____
Account Number (if applicable): _____

075 CSAS

*New York residents remit applicable sales taxes.
*Canadian residents remit applicable GST and provincial taxes.

MIRA®

www.MIRABooks.com

MES1208BL

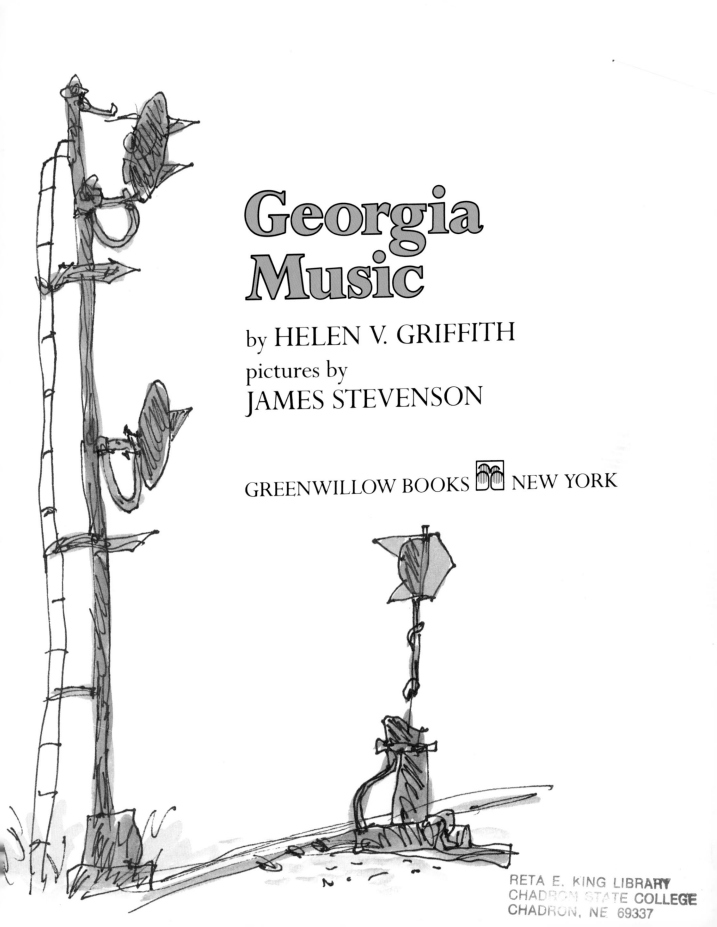

Georgia
Music

by HELEN V. GRIFFITH

pictures by
JAMES STEVENSON

GREENWILLOW BOOKS · NEW YORK

FOR SUSAN,
WHO KNOWS HER OWN MIND

The full-color art was
prepared as black line
with watercolor paints.
The typeface is Perpetua.

Printed in Hong Kong by
South China Printing Co.
First Edition
10 9 8 7 6 5 4 3 2 1

Library of Congress
Cataloging-in-Publication Data
Griffith, Helen V.
Georgia music.
Summary:
A little girl and her grandfather
share two different kinds of
music, that of his mouth organ
and that of the birds and
insects around his cabin.
[1. Grandfathers—Fiction.
2. Music—Fiction.
3. Nature—Fiction]
I. Stevenson, James, (date) ill.
II. Title.
PZ7.G8823Ge   1986
[E]   85-24918
ISBN 0-688-06071-4
ISBN 0-688-06072-2 (lib. bdg.)

An old man lived by himself in a cabin near the railroad tracks in the state of Georgia.

He spent his winters doing odd jobs and watching the trains go by and thinking about old times.

But as soon as it was spring he put on his straw hat, pulled his hoe out from under the porch, and chopped out a good-sized patch of garden beside the cabin. Then all summer long he worked in that garden, growing collards and melons and black-eyed peas.

One summer the old man's daughter took the train from Baltimore to Georgia for a visit, and she took her own daughter along with her. After a few days she had to get back to Baltimore, but she left the girl there with her grandfather for the whole long summer.

The old man never said how he felt about that, but he didn't seem to mind. The girl didn't mind either. She liked it right away. She liked the hot garden patch with its green rows of seedlings, and she liked the little cabin that shook when the trains thundered by. When she stopped being shy of her grandfather she liked him, too. She followed him around his garden while he worked, and sometimes she stepped on the little green seedlings, but if the old man noticed, he never said anything.

He found her an old straw hat and a hoe that wasn't too heavy and showed her how to chop weeds. It was hard work, and at first she was clumsy at it, but the old man said he didn't know how he'd ever done without her.

They would work all morning, their hoes going chink, chink up and down the rows, while a mockingbird flew from fence post to fence post, flapping his wings and singing noisy songs at them.

"Sassy old bird," the man would say, and the girl would say it, too, "Sassy old bird," and they would look at each other and laugh out loud.

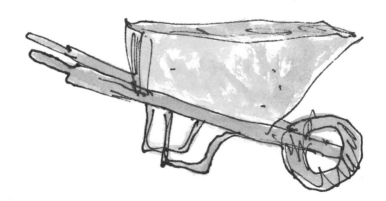

At noon they sat under a tree and ate their lunch, and then they would lie back on the grass and rest. The old man would pull his straw hat over his face, and the girl would make a pillow out of hers and lie looking up at the leaves and the sky.

It was so quiet that they could hear the leaves touching each other, and the bumblebees bumbling, and the crickets and grasshoppers whirring and scratching. And every now and then the old man would nod his head under his straw hat and say, "Now, that's music."

Then they would go to sleep under the tree while the summer sounds went on and on in their ears and in their brains.

In the evenings the two of them sat out on the rickety porch steps and the old man played tunes on his mouth organ. He knew a lot of songs and he taught the words to the girl so she could sing with the music.

The old man said he was really playing for the crickets and the grasshoppers because they made music for him in the daytime. He said they liked it, and the girl thought so, too.

At night they went to sleep hearing the katydids and the tree frogs and the chuck-will's-widows singing and singing, and some nights the mockingbird called nearly all night long. Then the girl would smile to herself and whisper, "Sassy old bird."

When September came the girl didn't want to go home and she could see that her grandfather was sorry, too. Her mother promised that she could come back next summer, and they had to be satisfied with that.

But the next summer wasn't the same.

The girl and her mother knew something was wrong as soon as they saw the cabin. Weeds were growing through the steps and a wild rosebush had almost taken over the porch. They found the old man sitting in a chair with a quilt over his lap and his eyes closed.

"I ain't sick," he told them. "Just mighty tired." But they closed up the cabin and took him back with them to Baltimore. The girl knew he was sicker than he said or he never would have gone.

There was nothing wrong with their home in Baltimore, but the old man wasn't happy there. He sat in a chair looking worried and sad, and the girl knew he was thinking of the old cabin and the garden that didn't get planted that year.

She tried to talk to him, but nothing seemed to interest him, and it just wasn't like it had been in Georgia.

One day the girl got out the old man's mouth organ and put it in his hand.

"Play me a tune, Grandaddy," she said, but he just held the mouth organ in his hand and looked at it.

The girl took it back and put her lips on it and blew, and when the old man heard the sound his eyes opened wide and he looked right at her, something he never did anymore.

So she made more sounds come out of the mouth organ, and then she began blowing in and out, finding out how it worked, and at last she was able to play a little tune on it.

"Did you like that, Grandaddy?" she asked, but she already knew he did.

From then on the girl sat with her grandfather every day and practiced playing the mouth organ until she began to be good at it. She taught herself all the old songs her grandfather had played for her, and she played them over and over.

One day, after she had played everything she knew, she found herself playing a different kind of music and making up brand new songs. Except it wasn't exactly music and they weren't real songs. They were the sounds she remembered from that Georgia summer— cricket chirps and tree frog trills and bee buzzes and bird twitters.

She shut her eyes and swayed back and forth and she could almost feel the hot sun on her back and the hoe handle in her hands, and for a while it was like being right back in Georgia.

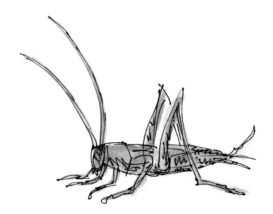

Then the old man gave a little chuckle and the girl heard him whisper to himself, "Sassy old bird." So she said it, too, "Sassy old bird."

And then the girl and her grandfather looked at each other and laughed out loud.